DON'T
Let Go

Sheryl Wright

BELLA
B O O K S

2016

Bella Books, Inc.
P.O. Box 10543
Tallahassee, FL 32302

Printed in the United States of America on acid-free paper.

First Bella Books Edition 2016

Editor: Katherine V. Forrest
Cover Designer: Judith Fellows

ISBN: 978-1-59493-509-1

About the Author

Sheryl Wright is a native of Toronto. A flying lesson at age thirteen seared in her a passion for all things aviation. Now retired from a flying career that included the Royal Canadian Air Force and Canadian Airlines, she lives with her partner near the shores of Port Whitby. *Don't Let Go* is her third novel and her first foray into lesbian fiction. To learn more about Sheryl visit her website at http://sherylwright.com or connect on Facebook: https://www.facebook.com/sherylwrightauthor

For Vicky, my baby sister

Acknowledgments

Gratitude is the first teaching of the elders.

I find it easy to say thanks and impossible to convey just how thankful I am. Please know whether your name is here or not, I am grateful for everyone who has touched my life. First let me thank Linda Hill for taking the time to listen to my pitch at the annual Golden Crown Literary Society Convention in New Orleans. And to Dawn Hogarth, who knew I was too shy to ask Linda for the pitch session, and did so for me. Linda was incredibly patient and gracious with me, immediately setting me at ease. I can't tell you how nerve-wracking it was waiting for her phone call all those months later. There is a certain joy in the creation of a story but the real thrill is in knowing you have written something other women are sure to enjoy. Thanks to Jessica Hill, the Queen of Production at Bella. I would be lost without you and your staff. And as to editorial, I was amazingly lucky and grateful to have the venerable Katherine V. Forrest as my editor. Her brilliant insights and gentle teasing made the editorial process fun and a remarkable learning experience. I will never again look at the word 'clearly' without imagining Katherine clearing her throat in a teacherly effort to break my compulsion to overuse the word. Katherine, I cannot thank you enough, especially when it comes to 'that dress' and what lesbians want. You got it!

And before anyone gets the idea that writing is a solo endeavour, let me correct you now. The love and support of friends and family are a gift, one all creatives need to function. To Dawn Hogarth for always being there. Vicky Furman, for listening to me complain. Joanne Vacanti, our longtime Buffalo friend, for always talking up the lay of the land whenever we were in town. And to the women who are always there to support me, Michelle Barrett, Sheila Collins, Olivia Collins, Kandy and Gen Kennedy, and of course, my cousin Lori Nelson and her wife Rae. And I can't forget my constant companion, my service dog Stella, all 150 pounds of drooling love and support.

One day I'll figure out a better way to show my gratitude, until then please accept my heartfelt thanks. *Niá:wen*

Want to drop me a line? Please do. I can be reached at: info@sherylwright.com

CHAPTER ONE

I've never been good with change. Honestly, who has? History is rife with all our misguided attempts to change the inevitable.

It was all she could think of, trying desperately to convince herself to keep moving. Tyler climbed out of her beat-up Chevy and retrieved her briefcase and winter coat from the backseat. She inspected the ski jacket in the shivering damp of the freshly shoveled parking lot. Unwilling to risk looking anything less than professional, she tossed it back in the car. This was her last scheduled interview. If it went well, the job would be hers. Not that this was a great job but she was desperate and already having spent more than a year unemployed, she was determined.

When HR had called to book what they described as nothing more than a rubber stamp meeting, they instructed her to give her name to the parking lot attendant, who would have a parking pass ready. He had given her the pass, directing her to a visitor's spot, along with the obligatory visitor's badge she would need to access anyplace beyond the lobby. Attached to the visitor's pass was a Post-it note. "Seventh floor, ask for Georgie." Freezing cold and shivering painfully, Tyler stopped to take a careful look around, thinking the parking lot might tell her something about the company, at least something that hadn't been written and posted by DME's public relations people. Not that it would make a difference now, but it would be nice to know her desperate attempt to secure a crappy job wasn't all bad.

While DME was no longer considered upstate New York's landmark boat builder, it had evolved into a leading-edge marine engineering firm. That had to count for something. Taking in the cars parked closest to the entry told her something else. Either the executives at DME all drove crappy winter beaters, or the reserved spots were not for them. Did they lease out their parking? After her first visit to DME, she had only researched the businesses residing in the DiNamico Building. It looked like DME occupied all the floors above the third. There were no tenants listed for eight or the penthouse, and she assumed those floors, like so many in the neighborhood, were probably converted to lofts long ago. All the lower levels were leased out to long-term tenants, except for a meeting room on the lobby level. Both of her previous interviews had been held there.

Boarding an empty elevator she pressed seven but the button didn't light up. Impatient, she pressed it several more times before trying other buttons, with the same result. Beside the elevator panel, a small placard read Visitors: Please see Security on the Lobby Level for a Visitor's Badge. Ready to do just that, Tyler stopped herself, unclasping her badge from her suit jacket. There was no key card slot or input panel, but feeling like this was some sort of test, she looked around carefully. On the opposite side of the doors, the smooth stainless-steel panel was without markings, except for a fist-size circle delineated by a dozen blue LEDs. Tyler smiled. *You can't fool a PhD*, she offered under her breath, before swiping the visitor's badge past the circle. Sure enough, the seventh-floor call button lit up and the elevator began to move. *Maybe this Personal Assistant job wouldn't completely suck?* HR had warned her that she would meet the

CIO, or Chief Innovation Officer. If they meshed, the job would be hers. "Just watch me mesh!" Tyler growled her warning, her deeply ingrained competitive streak rearing to life.

When the elevator doors opened, she charged out only to halt abruptly. Directly in front of her, marred only by a single set of glass doors, was an unobstructed view of Lake Erie. Forcing her eyes from the early December grays and blues outside, she took in her surroundings carefully. The small lobby around the elevator area was completely glassed in. Two reception counters were located on each side, their dark wood stain a stark contrast to the white and gray marble floors. Each was positioned in such a way as to enhance the view. And, while one counter was heavily laden with envelopes and packages in various liveries of overnight couriers, the other was attended by a tall and very attractive African American woman. Tyler waited patiently while the woman spoke amiably to a caller over her wireless headset, her long slender fingers skimming expertly over her keyboard. Her voice had a singsong quality to it, leading Tyler to contemplate her lineage. She wasn't good with accents, especially those tempered by the American melting pot.

When the woman turned her attention to Tyler, a warm smile melted the last of the anxiety she had been carrying. "You must be Tyler Marsh? I see you conquered the gauntlet!"

"Sorry?" The woman's smile was so bright and enthusiastic, Tyler couldn't help but acquiesce to her charm. "Yes, I'm Tyler. Oh, you mean the elevator?"

Reaching across the reception desk, the woman offered her hand. "Name's Zoe. I'm Marnie's PA, and as you can see, sometimes I fill in on reception." At the look on Tyler's face, she waved an excited hand. "No worries, love. Working for Georgie means never having to say welcome to DME!"

Tyler let that fact sink in. Bad enough that she had to lie about her education, and dumb down her CV to even get in the door. Having to do double duty as a receptionist would have felt like the final insult to her academic career. While she was immensely relieved, she didn't want to insult the first friendly face she encountered. Accepting the outstretched hand, she gave it a firm shake accompanied by a sincere smile. "Thanks, Zoe. I must admit I'm a little overwhelmed today, and I don't know who Marnie is or Georgie for that matter."

Zoe walked around the reception counter, slipping her arm through Tyler's in a colluding fashion. "Come on. I've been ordered to introduce you to Georgie. She's our Chief of Innovation, Georgina DiNamico. Once you two have a nice chat, I'll take you round to see Marnie Pulaski. She's our COO and Georgie's sister."

Tyler simply nodded, taking everything in as Zoe steered her toward the glass doors and the breathtaking view of the lake. When Zoe waved her hand over a blue light embedded in the glass door, it and its partner unlocked simultaneously and whooshed aside. "How did you do that?"

Holding out an empty hand, palm up, Zoe explained simply, "Embedded technology. Georgie came up with it, but don't ask her too much or she'll chat your ear off."

Tyler gave her a perfunctory smile, but didn't ask more. She had no idea what the woman was talking about, but decided to wait, observe and learn what she could. Eyes fixed on the spectacular view, she was surprised when Zoe pulled her back by her arm just in time to prevent her from tumbling down the stairs in front of her. She had completely missed that, the stairs, the room, and she now understood that the office had been designed so the view of the lake took precedence over everything. She thanked Zoe for preventing her fall. Following her down the stairs, they made their way to a grouping of white leather couches around a large square coffee table. While the sofas looked comfortable, the grouping was stark and functional and suited the space. She had to wonder if that was a reflection of her new boss, or should the ambience be credited to some unnamed office designer?

"How about you have a seat and relax," Zoe instructed warmly. "Listen, I know you interviewed with Susan. Did she talk much about Georgie's...challenges?"

"I...challenges, I'm not sure what you mean."

Sitting on the sofa, and patting the place beside her, Zoe was the picture of the perfect young professional in a slim-fitting dress and a cute little jacket. Her smile bordered on beguiling as she explained, "Georgie's my aunt and a veteran, a royal pain in my backside too but she's come a long way. All I can suggest is be patient when she's speaking. Try to hear her out. She may take the long way about but she gets there. Now," she said, and stood, her smile and charm irresistible, "Georgie's asked me to bring tea in. Do you have a preference, or will you drink that weak granny tea she's always after?"

Tyler considered her options for a moment, knowing that in an interview, asking for what you want as opposed to simply accepting what was offered was often a test of what you would and wouldn't do in your job. "Actually, I would prefer coffee," she said, without second-guessing herself, "please."

"Sorry, Tyler. How about some juice for now? Once you head over to Mrs. P's office, I can bring in the java but not here. No coffee in Georgie's office." As explanation, she offered, "It's just her thing!"

"Oh, okay...then I guess I'm having tea." Tyler smiled, then turned to take in the rest of the office. One wall seemed to be constructed solely of opaque glass partitions that closely matched the marble floors. The wall opposite was constructed of stone and featured not only a fireplace, but the largest flat-screen TV she had ever seen. A remote and wireless keyboard lay on the coffee table, carefully aligned and offset to suit a user who would sit at one end of the couch, directly across from the flat-screen. If she were asked to analyze the room as a characterization of its owner, she would speculate minimalist, dissociative, OCD, and...

The opaque glass panels suddenly cleared revealing a more traditional office. Moments later, several of the panels whooshed aside. The sole occupant of the adjoining office, a striking, dark-haired woman, seemed to hesitate before finally making her way to Tyler. "This used to be...Grandfather's office."

"It's breathtaking. I was so entranced coming in, I almost tripped down the stairs."

That remark made the woman smile. "Don't tell...I have too...more than once."

That comment went a long way to helping her relax, that and seeing a certain kindness in her eyes. When Zoe had said the woman was her aunt she had pictured an elderly matriarch, not the unassuming woman before her. It was hard to pinpoint her age, maybe forty, she figured. It was hard to actually catalog her physicality. She was impeccably dressed in a conservatively cut suit. She immediately noticed the woman's confidence. She walked with a military bearing but without the type of swagger she had come to think of as a guy in uniform thing.

"May I ask, when did your grandfather buy this building?" With its distinct art deco feel of the 1930s, certainly her grandfather could not have been old enough to be the original occupant.

"Grandfather bought...under construction. He...he was fourth, owner of...blueprints, permits...hole in ground. He...modified plan. This," she pointed to the stairs, the gallery and the two-story ceiling, "was two floors."

Tyler took her time to examine the features she pointed out, and to adjust to halting, almost disjointed speech which was completely at odds with the woman's appearance. For an older woman, she was very attractive, her athleticism lending an air of quiet strength to her countenance. Her short-cropped hair was thick and black, except for a bold stripe of pure white high on the right temple. And her light olive complexion held the kind of radiance that came with summers spent in the sun. She was dressed impeccably, in a charcoal suit that Tyler would bet was custom made. Still, her cheap blue cotton shirt, although starched, lacked any adornment. The pressed cuffs that jutted from her jacket sleeves were fastened with plastic buttons instead of the expected mother of pearl and the edges seemed close to frayed. The woman was a study in contrasts.

Focusing on the details being mentioned she followed the woman around the executive office. Like the stunning art deco exterior of the nine-story brownstone, the interior was flawlessly finished and maintained. It was obvious the office had been designed to impress. Stunning views abounded regardless of where you stood or looked. The building had been designed with a strange bullnose feature something similar to a flat iron, but more bow shaped and protruding from its long rectangular form. Standing in the CIO's office, Tyler saw why. The unusual bow shape provided stunning views both north and south of the Erie shoreline. It had been designed to impress, and it succeeded.

"We replaced...all glazing...twenty years ago." Pointing to the office partition walls, she added, "SmartGlass... programmable...new. Old panels, glass and oak...hard to clean. Floors. Six, seven...senior staff. All visitors...see..." She failed to complete the thought, for some reason preferring instead to simply wave her hand as evidence of her sentiment.

"Very impressive," Tyler offered noncommittally, wondering again at the woman's difficulty with speech. She thought the decor was overkill. As a business major, she had been taught that the point of any head office would be to highlight the products, not their environment. But who was she to say? DME, in one guise or another, had been a Buffalo keystone enterprise for more than seventy years. Not wanting to prejudge her host and determined to make a good impression, she offered her hand. "I'm Tyler Marsh, pleased to meet you."

The woman, who she had to assume was Georgina DiNamico, stared at her without what would appear to be simple comprehension. Finally, seeming to catch on, she accepted Tyler's outstretched hand and shook it amiably. "Georgina DiNamico...Junior. Georgie."

"Should I address you as Georgie? If it bothers you, I'm happy to address you in any appropriate form."

That seemed to confuse the woman even more. "Oh... Georgie. Everyone...Henry too...Georgie."

"Who's Henry?" Tyler asked, before she could catch yourself.

"My uncle, Dad's brother...partner...best friend," she explained, waving her guest to the sitting area.

Tyler nodded, carefully taking her place on the love seat beside the couch she assumed Georgie usually occupied. Sure enough, she sat in the place directly across from the flat-screen, where the remote and wireless keyboard were arranged.

Without preamble, or explanation, she began to type in several commands on the keyboard. She continued without comment even when Zoe returned with a tray loaded with a mismatched tea set, two bowls of freshly diced melons and heavy matching coffee mugs. Tyler examined the mugs without actually picking one up. Zoe, seeming nonplussed by Georgie's behavior, explained while pouring tea, "Henry Phipps, my granddad, and Uncle Danny served together in the Red Tails."

"I'm sorry. I don't know what that is. The Red Tails?" she asked.

"Oh sorry, it's their squadron from when they were in the air force. It started as the Tuskegee Airmen, you know, the all black flyers who started out in the Second World War. They distinguished their Mustangs, their airplanes, from all the rest by painting the entire tail section red: Hence Red Tails!

"Anyway, my granddad and Georgie's dad served together. After the air force was organized properly, and integration was in full effect, they started filling slots in their highly decorated unit with the best men for the job, regardless of color. Uncle Danny was one of the lucky sods to join Granddad's squadron. They served together up in Newfoundland and Vietnam before coming back here and taking over the company." Zoe, chatting amiably, continued as if it were the most natural thing to carry on a conversation around, but not with, Georgie DiNamico. "My granddad met my grandmom up in Newfee. The old boys used to ship us kids off there every summer. Henry said it was to run the devil out of me. Never had more fun! Have you been to Newfoundland?"

Tyler shook her head. "I've never been out of the country, other than a conference I went to in Toronto. Does that count?"

Zoe laughed with an easiness that Tyler could appreciate. "Newfee was still part of Britain back then."

"Sort of like a fourteenth colony?"

The vivacious grinning young woman laughed appreciatively at that, turning without comment and heading back up the stairs to the reception counter.

Not sure what to expect next, Tyler turned back to her noncommunicative and hopefully soon-to-be boss. "Should I pour?"

"Black...please."

Once Tyler had filled the two mugs and doctored her own cup, she turned her attention to the large porcelain mug. On it was an illustration of an aircraft with the entire tail painted red and the nose in a checkerboard pattern. Along the bottom of the illustration, the caption read, P-51 Mustang, 332 Fighter Group, United States Army Air Corps.

"You lied on your résumé."

Tyler almost choked on her tea. It was everything she could do to keep from spewing it across the coffee table and at her interviewer. "Sorry?"

The woman she had hoped would be her new boss looked at her without judgment, without any emotion at all. She then turned her attention back to the large flat-screen, entering a few more keystrokes, "You signed...NDA. Background check... Understand?"

"No, I mean, yes." She couldn't help the frustration. "I mean...yes, I know I signed the nondisclosure agreement and yes I lied on my résumé. If that means I don't get the job, then fine," she offered, upset. "Can I at least explain the situation?"

Her interviewer seemed surprised by the question as she signaled with her hand for Tyler to continue. "No judgment... Dr Marsh. I do not...why hide...accomplishments?"

Tyler pushed out an angry breath, barely able to remain calm. "That's easy for you to say. You have a job. I don't expect someone like you to understand how tough the market is out there. I took my academic achievements off my résumé after being told, time after time, that I was too qualified for the job!"

"Which job?" DiNamico asked, as if someone in her own company had given her that advice.

"It wasn't any specific job. It was just every job I was applying for." Thinking the interview was over and frustrated beyond belief, Tyler got to her feet and turned for the stairs, adding, "I don't need this—"

Georgie stood too, giving Tyler a curious look, "Dr Marsh? I do not...understand. Do not want...the job? No?" She too was clearly upset. "I...not interesting. You may...research...lots of time...work on...stuff!"

One hand already on the antique circular staircase, she said bitterly, "Stuff?"

That seemed to confuse Georgie DiNamico even more. "My sister...she told you? This...this job...I need...SIT!" she ordered in a tone both autocratic and frustrated.

Tyler turned at the command, surprised to realize the woman was as frustrated as she was. She watched as DiNamico took a long moment to order her thoughts. Rubbing at her temple before closing her eyes and announcing, "Dr Marsh, I am an engineer...A good engineer. Everything else...really..." She stopped abruptly, flopping back onto the couch. "I thought Marnie...explained my...me..."

Tyler took a deep breath, forcing herself to relax a little. Whatever Georgie DiNamico's problem was, it wasn't about her. "You don't have to call me Doctor. Yes, I have a PhD but it hardly applies here." Walking back to the sitting area, she offered more calmly, "I think we got off on the wrong foot." Then she asked boldly, "Are you usually this forthcoming?"

"I cannot help...I have...issues...social graces...no good. Not on purpose." She closed her eyes again for a moment. "Marnie wanted to hire you for..." As if sensing Tyler's movement, she waited patiently as Tyler resumed her seat. "Your job. Your job...to keep me out of trouble or...explain things," she confessed, almost under her breath, adding, "Doctor...I call you, what?"

"That depends, how do *you* want to be addressed?"

Confused, she answered, "Now just Georgie."

The now indicated something had changed, something significant, Tyler guessed.

"This," she said, waving an arm at the room and the view, "was my grandfather's...I like the shop better. The machine shop...Downstairs with Henry."

"Your father's business partner works in a machine shop?"

"Tinkers…me too."

"Do you like being Chief Innovation Officer?"

She nodded. "But…sometimes…working with family…" She finished the sentence with a two thumbs-down gesture.

Tyler simply nodded. She couldn't imagine working with her own sisters, much less a platoon of siblings and cousins. "Please call me Tyler."

"Tyler," Georgie DiNamico repeated it as if trying the name on for the first time. "You like boats?"

Tyler nodded. "I don't really know anything about them. I do know DME is still building world-class sailing yachts but it's no longer your core business."

Grabbing the keyboard, Georgie tapped in a few keystrokes before slapping Enter. A detailed company organizational chart popped up on the widescreen display. It was color-coded and provided the names, titles, and a brief description of responsibilities under each heading. "Marnie explain…about…a family company?"

"I haven't met Mrs. Pulaski. I interviewed with Ms. Chan."

That information temporarily stalled Georgie's train of thought. "Susan Chan. Director of recruiting." She clicked on the box with Susan's name in it. A pop-up window displayed a professional photograph and a high-level CV of the recruiting manager, including awards and years in service with DME. Georgie opened an unseen menu and selected the second organizational chart. This one was far more detailed and technically more complicated. "Family…company," Georgie said as explanation.

Tyler looked at the org chart again, only then realizing it was actually a family tree. Susan Chan's name was highlighted, probably because Georgie had followed the link from her corporate webpage. Susan was connected to the family tree by marriage. According to the chart her spouse was Anthony DiNamico, master boat builder.

"Susan will explain."

"I'm sorry, explain what about your family?"

She shook her head, returning her attention to the keyboard. The pop-up window and the company org chart were replaced by the job posting with title and description. It was far more detailed than the posting she'd applied for. Listed under the title Executive and Personal Assistant to the CIO were specifics that surprised her. Items like research product liability and ethics exclusive of financial responsibilities were right up her alley. Others, however, left a little to be desired. Having to maintain your boss's daily calendar was menial enough without adding duties like personal shopping to the list. Still, it didn't look as bad as she had imagined it would be. Pointing to the widescreen display, she asked point-blank, "Are you telling me I'll have the opportunity to research and formulate opinions when it comes to issues that may be involved in new products?"

Instead of answering directly, Georgie returned her attention to the keyboard. She opened the text box and began typing furiously.

It took a moment before Tyler realized she was typing a response instead of answering the question. She read the point notes word by word as they appeared on the screen. Her could-be boss was describing the opportunities that would be made available to her to continue her own academic research and writing while she examined the new issues facing their technology branch. Before she could comprehend why someone would consider paying her a salary to not do a particular job, the second pop-up window appeared. The bullet points streamed up on screen even faster. This list closely matched the job description she had been provided in her last interview. According to the note Georgie was furiously typing, these were the duties Marnie Pulaski had deemed required for any assistant or researcher she hired.

"Does that mean you're offering me the job?"

The question appeared to confuse Georgie even more. "I… you want to…babysit?"

Tyler carefully surveyed Georgie's curious self-control. From where she was sitting, the woman was the embodiment of contrast. Obviously she could afford better shirts than what she wore. Did she choose the suits and just accept the shirts or was it the other way around? Then there were her hands. Small, even petite, but strong somehow. They still showed a tan from the summer and a myriad of tiny white scars, the type gained from rough work. Still they looked soft, gentle almost with short-cropped nails that reminded her of a surgeon's hands. These were hands, she imagined, that never hesitated. Maybe she spent her summers on the lake, sailing one of her family yachts. "What is *your* job?"

Georgie clicked a few buttons, displaying the company org chart again. "CIO," she said, pointing to the organization chart. "Chief Innovation Officer."

"I didn't ask what your title was." Tyler pushed her, much as she would a presumptive student. "I asked what it is you do?"

Seemingly oblivious to her attitude, Georgie appeared more surprised by the question than anything else. "New product technologies...build or license. Improve or innovate." When Tyler didn't comment, she seemed to interpret her silence as a lack of understanding. Resting the wireless keyboard on her knees, she typed furiously, head down, her too-long bangs bobbing in her eyes and with the fixed concentration of a small child. On the flat-screen several file folders popped up, then one opened to display a portfolio of jpegs from which she selected four thumbnails to expand.

The images were of some safety device. That was an easy guess. Tyler recognized the red stripe across the white waterproof case. Of course, the stenciled "RESCUE" was a dead giveaway too. The second photo showed inside of the case which was packed like an egg carton with what looked like six flashlights and an iPad.

"Sea Rover Rescue. DynaCraft standard equipment," Georgie explained.

Moving closer to take in the images displayed, she had to ask, "What does it do?"

Georgie stood too, moving to stand beside her. "Man Overboard rescue," she said, pointing to a photo of a life jacket. An expanded illustration detailed some sort of microchip. "GPS tracker...iPad controller."

Pointing out the six flashlight-style objects, shown in the open equipment case, Tyler asked her, "What are these other things?"

The last of the open images showed a person in the water, maybe twenty, thirty yards behind the rear of a sailboat. With snow falling on a slush-churned surface, the image was more than frightening but failed to answer the question. When Georgie realized she wasn't following, she clicked on the last image and opened a video file. The title read: DME Man Overboard Tracking System. There were other details too, like the Field Test number and the date.

That caught Tyler's attention. "You test marine safety equipment in December?"

Taking a seat back on the couch, Georgie motioned for Tyler to do the same before pressing play on the video. Automatically tilting her head to match the keeled over angle of the horizon, Tyler realized the camera had to be hard mounted to the deck of a sailboat, and assumed they were using a company sailing yacht as the test vehicle. The rearview perspective painted a picture of the fiercely frigid day. The boat's wake cut like a knife through the inches of snow that had accumulated on the surface. A person, clearly the test subject, dressed in what appeared to be a heavyweight wetsuit, stepped into the camera's view before donning one of the company's patented life jackets. A second person held up the iPad in its waterproof case at an angle easily covered by the camera. With heavy gloves on and through the waterproof case, the operator easily opened the DME rescue app. Within seconds the screen displayed several overlapping icons. One was shaped like a boat while another reminded her of those international swimming symbols she saw at high school meets. The iPad app clearly showed the test subject was still on board. At that moment the person holding the iPad gave a thumbs-up and without hesitation, the person in the wetsuit leaped backward and overboard.

"Oh my God!" Tyler immediately clamped her hands over her mouth. She watched in horror as the distance between the rear of the boat and the person in the water expanded at an alarming rate. Considering the conditions, she expected the people on board to immediately make haste. Instead, one crew member remained standing with the iPad in clear view of the camera, while another held up one of the flashlight devices. With a quick twist, it emitted a flashing light...

"Boosters...Range boosters," Georgie qualified.

As they watched, the second crewman continued to casually remove boosters, one at a time from the equipment box, activating each with a quick twist before tossing them into the open water. As each one went active, another icon appeared on the iPad screen. When the last of the boosters were in the water, the crewman holding the iPad selected a single button. While it continued to show the position of the lost crewman and each of the boosters, it now added a recovery course. The camera angle then changed to show the helm and compass. The crewman at the wheel turned for the heading specified on the screen and followed the track line exactly as detailed. Within minutes the course line of the sailboat and the position of the man overboard intersected. The camera was twisted back around to follow the recovery operation. First hooking the overboard crewman, they then turned back to the original course and, with a pole net, swept up the six floating boosters. Chasing after the line of flashing beacons, Tyler was transfixed by the sight of the sailing yacht surging against the unforgiving brutality of the frigid cold gray lake.

"That's me," Georgie DiNamico said proudly.

"Holding the iPad?"

Seeming confused by the assumption, she pointed to the person who had been hauled aboard and was hunkered down while a second person covered her with a heavy blanket.

Tyler gave her a hard stare. "That water must have been freezing! The swells look to be at least six feet high!"

"Yes," she confirmed without elaboration.

"Are you crazy?" She hadn't meant to say it out loud. Though, considering how shocked she was, she was relieved to realize she hadn't been screaming at the top of her lungs. No wonder the company thought she needed a babysitter! What kind of person would throw herself overboard during a snowstorm? Even the person holding the iPad was bundled in a heavy-looking slicker and waterproof gloves. "Is that snow? Where the hell were you?"

"There," she answered, pointing out the window to Lake Erie. "Marnie...was angry. At Henry...too." At that admission, Georgie appeared seriously bothered. "He is my friend," she lamented. Without saying more, she turned and walked toward the overly large window facing the lake.

Not sure what was happening, Tyler stood and watched as her perspective employer brooded by the window. Before she could apologize or even comprehend her own reaction to the video clip, she was startled by the clicking sounds from a dog's paws pacing across the marble floor. From behind the glass partition wall that separated Georgie's office space from the meeting area, a large chocolate Lab sauntered out, leash in mouth, heading straight to Georgie's side. It nuzzled up to the suddenly pensive woman, pestering her until she finally wrapped her lower arm around the big brown dog's head and held it comfortingly against her hip.

Tyler was at a loss for words. Georgie DiNamico had withdrawn like a hurt child. A child who brought her dog to work? Before she could think of what to say, or even what to do, Zoe slipped into the office from an unseen entrance. "Georgie! Henry's waiting downstairs for you and Maggie. Why don't you head out while Tyler and I have a visit with Marnie?"

Turning and accepting the leash from her dog, Georgie looked to Zoe and Tyler as if almost surprised by their presence. "Good to go?"

"Good to go! Now off with you. Henry's waiting. No worries. Tyler and I have everything under control."

Nodding her acceptance, she turned and addressed the dog with less hesitation than Tyler had experienced in the entire meeting. "Come Maggie. Let's see...Uncle Henry found bone," she offered with childish enthusiasm, and without a second glance she and the dog were gone.

With a heartfelt apology, Zoe said, "Sorry about that. I would've given you a bit more warning that she's having a bad day but Marnie really wanted you to see what you're getting into."

"And what am I getting into? I have no idea what just happened!"

"Come on. Let's head next door and let my aunt do the explaining."

Tyler followed her through Georgie's office and into a corridor that connected the other executive suites. "Marnie's in the corner office. Just close enough to keep an eye on our girl without cramping her too much."

"What's wrong with her? I mean, she's obviously very smart…"

"Get in here and sit down. Both of you!" a strong female voice ordered. They had just reached the threshold of another large office suite. The door signage read, Marina Pulaski, Chief Operating Officer. "Is there a problem?"

"Marnie! Take a chill pill," Zoe offered with a cheeky smile.

Marina Pulaski stood up from behind her desk and walked across the office, extending a hand. There was no denying the family resemblance. She was the spitting image of her sister with only slight variations. She wore her dark hair long in kinky flowing waves that contrasted with her macho bossiness. She carried a few more pounds than Georgie, adding a feminine air to her executive demeanor. Like her sister, she was dressed impeccably but her suit was far more stylish. Tyler would characterize her appearance as lady boss chic with designer heels, expensive jewelry and what could only be a real Italian silk blouse. "I've heard very good things about you Ms. Marsh, or should I call you Dr Marsh?"

Tyler colored at the comment, more than aware that everyone knew she had omitted her academic achievements from her résumé. "I hope you're not offended. I just found it not…helpful."

"Relax," Marnie ordered. "I don't really care, but you will have to give me an updated CV for our records. That is, if you're still interested in the job?"

"That's my cue to leave," Zoe said. "Anyone for a real cup?"

"Coffee," Marnie explained. "Yeah, I guess I can handle another one. How about you, Tyler?"

"Thanks."

"Good. Okay, let's have a sit-down. I'm sure you have several questions at this point, but before I answer anything, I need to remind you that you signed a nondisclosure agreement. Anything discussed here today, including personal information involving my sister, is covered under that agreement. Is that understood?"

"It was when I signed it, although I'm curious now why it's so important that I understand that Ms. DiNamico is included in your gag order."

"Why it's so important?" Marnie asked. Her hands fisted. Her right hand was strangling a ballpoint pen, which she clicked several times before finally putting it down and laying her hands flat on the desk. "Dr Marsh, you're obviously a well-educated woman. I don't know why my sister's interested in an academic with graduate degrees in ethics and economics, but she says it works with her future plans. And if that works for her it works for me. I understand she told you a little bit about one of the new products she's developed?"

Tyler nodded, uncomfortable challenging this woman in the way she had the sister.

Marnie picked up her ballpoint pen and began clicking it again before slapping it back down, and forcing her hands to rest. "I'm going to give you the quick version. If, when I'm done, you're still interested in the job, I'll be more than happy to provide additional details.

"To begin with, my sister has an IQ of 164. I assume you know what that means. What she doesn't have is any real EQ, you know, Emotional Intelligence. Which I understand is par for the average genius. What isn't par…" she began, picking up the pen and clicking it several more times before placing it down and asking, "Do you know anything about head injuries?"

Tyler thought she was prepared for anything, but this wasn't what she had been expecting. "Just the basics. What happened to her?"

"Did you see that stripe of white hair? Where do I start?" she asked rhetorically as Zoe sailed in with three cups of coffee in hand.

"Start with Danny and Henry," Zoe suggested.

Marnie groaned at her niece, who planted herself in a chair beside Tyler. "Let's wait until Tyler says she wants the job before giving her the whole family sob story."

"It's not a sob story. We're very successful, Marnie. Why are you always such a drip?"

Marnie groaned again, this time more for effect than anything else and began sipping her coffee. Finally setting her cup down and retrieving her pen, she turned her attention back to the subject at hand. "Five years ago my sister was in Afghanistan, flying a search and rescue helicopter. They were shot down by a surface-to-air missile. Georgie was the only one to survive. Evidently the missile struck somewhere near the tail, causing the whole thing to cartwheel into the ground. The main propeller thingy came flying off the top and ripped through the cockpit. It's lucky Georgie's such a short ass! The blade glanced off her helmet, then proceeded to take the copilot's head right off. Georgie says she has no memory from the moment of impact. But the soldiers who found her said she'd managed to crawl out of the wreck and to a hiding spot several hundred yards away. Her first memory after the crash was waking up in the hospital in Germany. No one really understands how she survived after breaking just about every bone in her body. But it wasn't until we got her home and she was on the mend physically when we realized that mentally and emotionally something was very wrong."

Marnie clicked her pen several more times before forcing herself to put it down. OCD, Tyler decided.

"Don't get me wrong, Georgie was always brilliant, but in the last five years she's generated more patents than the entire company did in the last five decades. From a work perspective, she's unstoppable. It's just that outside of work, outside of her relentless need to take our engineering expertise to the edge, she's lost. My sister can barely care for herself anymore, nor can she handle herself in social situations. Plus she can't stand crowds of any type." Marnie picked up her pen, clicking out her frustration, before turning her attention to her niece. "Zoe?"

"It's as if she's a child in some regard and an adult in others. Can I get into personal matters?" she asked. At Marnie's nod, she pushed forward. "Before Afghanistan, she just did her monthly bit with her Guard unit. Don't get me wrong, she loved serving with the Air National Guard and her mates respected her but she wanted to be out. Of course, she couldn't."

"I thought serving with the National Guard was voluntary. How come she couldn't get out?" Tyler asked, wanting to understand what had happened.

Zoe smiled at her assumption. "Sorry, I meant out as in lesbian. Before her last deployment, she had finally met someone. She had never considered leaving the Guard until she met Margaret. That's how we knew it was serious. I think she meant to marry old Mags once she was home from Afghanistan, but…"

"Anyway," Marnie pushed her back on topic.

"Oh right. Well, other than serving with the National Guard, she was a competitive sailor with the local club. She had a scandalous social life before Margaret, but more than anything, Georgie was smart and fearless and fun. She's still those things, but not in the same way. She can be fearless, but not in a smart way. As for having fun and enjoying people and family, there are only three people in the world she will let close to her. My Aunt Lori, Marnie here, and my granddad, Henry."

Marnie translated this last part. "Henry Phipps was my father's business partner and his best friend. Zoe is his granddaughter. I hope Susan warned you during your last interview that working here means dealing with our family?"

"She did, and she mentioned that Georgina would need to be handled, but I assumed it was more of a public affairs issue."

"Right. Not an idiotic genius who can address a crowded auditorium full of engineers without batting an eye, but can't make it through a dinner party without having a full-blown anxiety attack."

"Okay…" Tyler conceded. "Not exactly how I would describe the situation, but I get your point. Georgie told me she thinks you're trying to hire a babysitter. Are you telling me she actually chose me from the candidates that Susan Chan selected? I'm assuming she screened and interviewed other candidates?"

"She did, and to be honest you weren't Susan's first pick. We still keep Georgie involved in all the decision-making around here. We just aren't always prepared for how she will react to a given situation."

"That's what Maggie's for," Zoe added, as explanation. "The dog! Maggie is a service dog. She senses, before the rest of us, that something's amiss. Usually all it takes is a quick walk with Maggie and Georgie immediately settles down. She's made a big difference in her sleep too. Since we got the dog, she sleeps most nights and when the nightmares come, Maggie wakes her up and gets her moving."

Tyler considered the expectant looks from both women. What the hell was she getting herself into? "Please excuse me if I'm out of line here, but it sounds like what she needs is full-time medical care."

"We have a nurse who comes in, a nutritionist, and a speech therapist. And once a week, either Zoe or I take her to group counseling at the Veterans Center. She doesn't like that one as much, but she goes," Marnie explained. "What we need is someone to be her assistant, but more than that, to be her friend. She needs to learn to trust someone else besides us. And, she needs someone to translate the world for her, to help her see things the way she used to see things."

"If I wasn't your first pick, why am I here?"

"You're Georgie's first pick."

"And you're trusting her on this?"

Fisting her pen like a warrior's mace and tapping the heel of her hand as if she were setting the pace for a parade, she promised, "There are many things I don't trust my sister to do. I don't trust that she won't throw herself overboard in the middle of Lake Erie during a raging snowstorm! I don't trust that she will remember her coat when she takes that mangy doormat of a dog for a walk, or that she'll remember to come back! I don't trust that she won't try to drive her car, or sail her boat! I don't trust her to remember board meetings, or meals, or meds, or sleep, without help. Good God, there are a million things I don't trust Georgie with but business decision-making is not one of them." She leaned forward to say in a more relaxed tone, "I don't know why she wants you on her personal staff, which currently consists of Henry, Skip, and that dog, but she does and that's all I need to know. Now, if you're not too scared, please read this. It's the complete job description." Before Marnie handed the sheet over, she clicked her pen, and wrote something on the bottom of the page. "That's my offer. I know Susan gave you a range but this number makes more sense, considering the extent of your responsibilities."

Tyler accepted the single page, quickly reading through the expectations from her perspective employer. When she reached the bottom, the number scratched there was significantly larger than she had been expecting. "I don't want to imply I'm complaining, but that seems quite generous for this job?"

"Maybe. Maybe not," Marnie offered cryptically. "My sister intends to put your advanced degrees to work. I don't know what an engineer needs with an economic ethicist, but she says she does or will, and from my perspective that means you'll be doing work at a management level. If your job description didn't include the more basic duties involved in managing Georgie, I would be making you an even higher offer. We may be a family company and small, but we are a world leader in marine technology and we reward our employees, not just for hard work, but for their education and their community involvement. Any more questions?"

"Millions, but none that I'm comfortable asking at the moment. When do you require a decision?"

"I'd like one now," Marnie said plainly, "but if you need time, take the day."

"Can I keep this?" Tyler asked, holding up the job description.

"Of course. I'll let Zoe walk you out. And just so you know, she is the family gossip. So, go ahead and get the inside scoop on anything you might not feel comfortable asking me or can't find on the Internet."

Tyler nodded, standing and offering her hand. "I do want you to know I'm very interested. I just need a little time to consider the range of responsibilities involved."

"Good." Marnie shook her hand before turning her attention back to her ballpoint pen and her computer monitor.

Zoe directed her out of the office and toward the elevators. "Just let me grab my jacket, and I'll head down to the lot with you."

Embarrassed to have someone see her beat-up old car, Tyler waved her off. "That's okay. I can see myself out."

"You could, but then we wouldn't get to chat."

"Love your accent. I know you say you grew up here, but it sounds like you've spent time in Britain?"

Zoe smiled at the compliment. "It's my half-Newfee accent. If you ever go to Newfoundland, you'll hear it. It's a wee bit Scottish and Irish, with a bit of mangled good old Yankee slang thrown in for fun."

"I thought it was pronounced New-found-land, not whatever it is you just said."

Chuckling, she pronounced it as her great-grandmother had taught her, "We say Newf-in-land. Don't know why, but that's just how it's always said."

As they stepped on the elevator, Tyler took in Zoe's cheeky grin. "You look like you're ready to bust. What's that smile for?"

"Nothing, I just think you'll be great for Georgie. I love her dearly, but that girl is a pain in my backside."

"How so?"

Leading them through the lobby and directly to the visitor parking area, Zoe explained as she walked, "I've adored Georgie since I was a tot. She taught me how to tie my shoes and my skates. She taught me how to swim and sail. But more than that, she taught me the importance of having fun. I miss that," she said, stopping in front of what she obviously had decided was Tyler's car. "I miss Georgie having fun. Since the accident, since Margaret, it's as if she doesn't understand the concept. Don't get me wrong, she's good, or at least better, but..."

"You do understand she may never be the same. Sorry, I'm not an expert on head injuries, but I do know she may not get any better."

"Of course. It's a concern for me and Marnie too. Still, we need to give her every chance we can. God knows she did it for us while we were growing up. Georgie is the oldest of all of us—second and third generation that is."

Tyler stood by the trunk of her Chevy, holding her briefcase in both hands and desperately trying not to shiver. "I'm a little confused about the family part. Sorry, was that rude of me to ask?"

"Not at all, and not around here. If you ever need to know anything, you come ask me. See, my granddad Henry Phipps, and Danny DiNamico, Marnie and Georgie's dad, married sisters. Two lovely ladies they met while serving in Newfoundland. So we're related maternally and we were all raised up like one big happy jumbled up family."

"So you work as Marnie's assistant and sometimes receptionist?"

"I see your look. You're indeed a clever one but don't read too much into it. We might all be family, but we still have to earn our place. My dad's the CFO. His background is accounting and investment. He's a CPA, with a master's. When he started with the company, he was a junior accountant. He had to work his way up and so will I but unlike my dad, I haven't finished my undergraduate degree and I haven't a clue what I want to do with my life. So, for now I'm Marnie's PA and that suits me fine." Zoe gave her a quick wink. "Besides, if it weren't for Marnie taking me on, I wouldn't even qualify for a job at DME. Except maybe out at the boatyard, but not here. Could you see that," she teased, "me, without my makeup and heels?"

Tyler smiled at her new friend. While she suspected Georgie was close to ten years older than she was, she guessed Zoe was a good ten years younger. It was easy to remember university and how she didn't get serious about her studies until her junior year. Maybe Zoe had been in the same place. Making a decision opposite to what Tyler had when the time came to buckle down. "Can I ask you an inappropriate question?"

Zoe practically squealed in delight. "Now we're talking. What terrible indiscretion can I share with you?"

Tyler bumped her briefcase against her knees, not sure if she should even ask. "Did she name that dog after her girlfriend?"

"What, Maggie? No, she came from the service academy with that name, but there was some painful overlap."

"How so?"

Zoe puffed her cheeks and let out a low, slow whistle. "When Georgie got back from the veterans hospital, Margaret was all in our face about how she wanted to care for her and so on and so forth. You know, wanting to be in charge. That probably wouldn't have been a big deal, if it wasn't for the fact that Georgie had no idea who she was."

"Oh my God!"

"Yeah, I know. Can you imagine? Anyway, Margaret didn't take it well. Actually, she was a bitch on wheels and it wasn't long until we realized she was battering Georgie over it."

"She was beating her?"

"No, sorry. I mean battering her emotionally. She was always trying to wear her down. It wasn't what Georgie needed. Not that we knew what to do for her, but the way Margaret behaved was unforgivable. About a month after Georgie was back with us, in the home she and Margaret built, Georgie asked to be moved. The minute we did, Margaret filed for separation and sued for damages from emotional abuse. The funny thing was, Georgie's memory around Margaret came flooding back in soon afterward."

"I take it Margaret wasn't pleased her memory was returning?"

"Not at all. As a matter of fact, in her witness statement, she said that Georgie's returning memories were causing her more emotional anxiety than relief. I can't say I believed it. I always thought that bitch was after more than Georgie's loving affection."

"Wow! How did Georgie handle things?"

"Oh, she was a mess. By the time things progressed to where the court date was set, Georgie remembered everything and was overwhelmed with pain over Margaret's betrayal. The thing is, she was already gutted from the loss of her crew. Then Margaret walking out, which was bound to happen, was more than she could bear. Margaret was always interested in the fastest and easiest way to get ahead. I guess having to take care of Georgie was more than she was willing to invest."

"How did the court case go? Sorry," Tyler said with regret. "I know it's none of my business."

"Not at all. Certainly not if you're going to help us with my eldest aunt. It never got to court. The whole thing was taking such a toll on Georgie, she was at a point where she never wanted to see or hear a single word from Margaret. So, she asked Marnie to make an offer. Margaret got to keep their house and all their belongings, plus a financial settlement, a rather handsome one I might add, in exchange for never coming near Georgie again. Since then, Georgie has really retreated emotionally. If it wasn't for my granddad and that bloody dog, which came with the name Maggie, I don't think we would've ever gotten her to reconnect with her life at all. I think that's why Marnie's being so generous with her offer. You're the first person she's taken an interest in since coming home. I'm not saying that to pressure you. I like you and have a feeling you'd be good for her. Who knows, in a way, she might be good for you too."

Tyler shook her head in puzzlement. "How's that?"

"Well, you're a professor. Don't all you academic types like to write gads and gads of books about some such garbley-goop?"

"Garbley-goop! Well put; and yes, I've been looking for time to do some writing. Do you really think Georgie would allow me time to do that?"

"If it fits in with what she has planned and I know she has plans. She believes your education can be put to good use. If you're truly concerned with the day-to-day demands of the job, why don't you talk to her? She's really quite accommodating, if you can be patient enough to communicate your needs."

"I guess that's the part I'm worried about. Maybe I should've paid more attention during psychology one-oh-one."

"Really? That was one of my faves. Tell you what, you take the job and I'll do all the psychology one-oh-oneing, while you help Georgie with her new project."

"You know what the new project's about?"

"Hardly," Zoe retorted, turning for the main entrance. "I don't understand the projects she's finished, much less anything she's just starting." She backtracked to where Tyler stood, retrieving the visitor's badge pinned to her jacket. "I hope you take the job, Tyler. I think we'll be great friends." With that, she moved as fast as her stilettos would take her, waving her goodbye as she slipped through the lobby door.

Tyler slid into her Chevy, tossing her briefcase on the passenger seat. She crossed her fingers, turned the ignition key and listened to the starter grind until the engine finally turned over. As much as she hated the car, she did want to thank the good people at Chevrolet for the industrial heaters they built. Once her hands began to warm again and she could feel the circulation returning, she pulled out the single sheet of paper that described the job she'd been offered.

Executive and Personal Assistant to the Chief Innovation Officer.

EA Duties: Performs administrative duties for the CIO. Responsibilities may include screening calls; managing calendars; making travel, meeting and event arrangements; preparing reports and financial data; training and supervising other support staff; customer relations. Requires strong computer and Internet research skills, experience writing technical reports, flexibility, excellent interpersonal skills, project coordination experience, and the ability to work well with all levels of internal management and staff, as well as outside clients and vendors. Sensitivity to confidential matters is required.

PA Duties: Supervise the daily activities of the assigned executive. Responsibilities may include: setting and maintaining a personal schedule; booking personal and medical appointments; shopping, including wardrobe, prescription medications, etc; driving the executive to appointments and events; accompanying the executive to conferences and on all business travel. Complete confidentiality in all matters relating to the executive is required. The PA may on occasion be called on to represent the executive at meetings, conferences, or corporate events.

The EPA position requires significant travel, irregular work hours, and advanced project leadership skills. The standard benefits in the remuneration package include medical; dental; hearing and vision care; along with a company matching retirement plan. A company vehicle will be made available when needed. Additionally, a wardrobe stipend is available for those occasions when the EPA must accompany or represent the executive at conferences or corporate events.

Tyler wasn't sure which startled her more, the fact that they were offering her use of a car and expenses just to babysit Georgie DiNamico, or the number Marnie had scrawled at the bottom: 94k.

Who the hell pays a secretary ninety-four thousand dollars a year just to babysit a crazy, hit in the head savant?

Tyler pulled out her cell phone, and happy to get a signal, she speed-dialed her most called number. When the line picked up, she smiled. "Hi Dad. Are you free for lunch?"

CHAPTER TWO

Tyler pushed her eggs around her plate, not really interested in the meal in front of her. Across from her, in their regular booth at her dad's favorite greasy spoon, her father sat studying his daughter.

"Come on Tyler. Tell the old man. What's got you so troubled?"

"I had my final interview today." She gave up the pretense of eating and dropped her fork on her plate, retrieving the folded job description from her pocket. She tossed it unceremoniously across the table to her dad. "Read that and tell me what you think?"

Carl Marsh unfolded the printout. "Executive assistant? Tyler! Is it that bad out there? Jesus girl, I would rather see you come work for me."

"What am I gonna do at a body shop, Dad?"

He shrugged. "You're damn good with spot touch-ups. Maybe we could promote custom paint work or you could find some officie stuff to do."

"Offic*ie* stuff? Thank God Mom manages the business, or you would've been out of it years ago."

"You don't think I know that? Pumpkin, there isn't a day goes by I don't thank God for your mother!" He picked up the folded page and read through it again, this time much more carefully. "I'm under the impression you want me to notice something? Maybe the 94K scribbled at the bottom?" he asked.

"That's what they're offering me, salary-wise."

Her father blew out a long, loud whistle, accidentally attracting the attention of the nearby waitress. He waved her off with his schoolboy charm, "Sorry Gale," before returning his attention to the job description. "That's a lot of money to play secretary. Let me guess. This guy's some sort of troublemaker who needs reining in?"

"Yes. No. Well…First off, he's a she. Georgina DiNamico and she's in charge of innovation over at DME."

Dressed, as always, in jeans and the heavy blue work shirt she knew her mother still ironed for him, he gazed at her, his big blue eyes dancing with interest. "DME? As in Dynamic Marine? Down at the Irvine boatyard?"

"Well it's just DME now. Evidently they concentrate on engineering, even though they still take orders for the boatyard but that's not where I'd be working. I'd be downtown in the old DiNamico building."

"And this DiNamico woman? I assume she's related to old man DiNamico?"

"Daughter," she added simply, crossing her arms and slumping down in her seat. "I met her this morning. She's very smart, but…" Tyler struggled, at a loss for words to describe her feelings. "This is the best job offer I've had in over year. Actually, it's pretty much the only real job offer I've had. Teaching college students for ten bucks an hour, part-time, is not my idea of a real job, but this…this makes me feel like I'm at a critical turning point in my life and I'm not sure if I should make the turn. God, help me out here," she begged.

"Pumpkin, you've got to stop beating yourself up. First of all, the economy tanked and for once most of the schools around here took a hard hit too. That's not your fault. The university canceling your program was a matter of funding, nothing else."

"Yes, but I should've been able to bring in my own funding or raise some grant money. That's what professors do."

"For your whole department? Come on pumpkin, give yourself a break here. Two years as a junior professor does not make you responsible for an entire department. If anything, I'd say the Dean of Economics and his buddies let you and your cohorts down."

Tyler sat up a little straighter. "I know you're right. It's still hard though."

"That's not what's bothering you about this new job offer. Are you worried how it will look on your résumé?"

"No! Yes. Maybe? Sorry."

"Tyler, your mother and I have never known you to worry about what others think. You've been telling us how much research and writing you want to do on your own. How's that going?"

She wilted slightly before picking up her fork, pushing her eggs around her plate.

"Tyler Ann, don't make me tell your mother you're behaving like a child. Tell me what's really going on," he demanded.

"Dad, I feel like I'm lost. I've never been so…without focus. I haven't been able to settle on a subject I want to dig into. Everything I start, I lose interest in. It all seems so lame." As much as she detested complainers she did feel a need to voice her frustrations and there was no better listener in her family than her dad. Oh, he wasn't short of suggestions but unlike her mom who saw every problem as an opportunity she could solve, and her twin sister who saw through everything she said, her dad was the one she could count on to just listen.

A gentle giant of a man, Carl Marsh had played pro football before starting his own auto body shop with his young wife and twin baby daughters. Now he had three daughters to fuss over and a wife he loved and adored. Tyler loved him for that, loved his gentleness with each of them but more so, she appreciated the way he adapted to their varying needs and personalities.

"Do you miss teaching, or is it really just the money?" he asked.

Contemplating his question, she was honestly surprised by her response. "No, I don't miss teaching at all. And I certainly don't miss dealing with undergrads and their crap."

"So it's the money?"

"Yes and no. The truth is, I'm hating myself for having to live with you and mom. Not because you're there, I love that part. It's just that I feel like I'm not carrying my own weight. I'll be thirty-four in three months! It's not right that I have to live off my mom and dad. Hell, I can't afford my own car anymore. If it wasn't for Mom's beat-up old Chevy, I'd be riding the bus."

"Is that what's got you down, that old beater?"

"No Dad, that's not it. I'm grateful for the loan of the Chevy, I really am. It just makes me feel like a failure to have to borrow my mom's car to go to an interview for a crappy job that pays three times what it should."

"So it's the job again. Tell me about it. About this DiNamico woman and Dynamic Marine. You know, back in the day, they made a hell of an engine. You might not remember this but your grandfather used to have one of their outboard motors on his ski boat. Remember that little bow rider you used to love so much?"

Tyler smiled for the first time since joining her father. His vibrant blue eyes sparkled at the memory, a match to the mischievous smile he always had for her and her twin. "I didn't know they made outboards. I thought they just made custom yachts."

Laughing good-heartedly, he chastised gently, "Now I know you weren't serious about this job or you would've researched them to death. So, I've never actually seen one of their yachts but I've read a couple of articles. I'll admit I've always been a fan of their engines. I hear their diesel inboard is very impressive. Hey, I bet your grandpa's still got his old DynaCraft outboard sitting in the cottage shed."

Tyler sat up a little straighter, taking an interest in her father's knowledge. "So they made different kinds of engines for different kinds of boats? You know they only make sailboats now?"

"Yeah, they started out just making the engines, at least that's the way I seem to remember it. I think they only got into boatbuilding in the sixties. I think they still build some engines, but not under their own name anymore."

"They're into marine technology now. I did learn about one product. Some sort of safety system to track someone if they fall overboard. It looked interesting, Georgie seemed pretty proud of her design."

"Georgie?"

"Georgina DiNamico."

Carl Marsh was a big man. A onetime linebacker, his intimidating size was softened by the laugh lines in his face and a caring smile. "So you interviewed with the big boss and she offered you a job?"

"I had several interviews. The last one was with Georgie," she said, trying to decide how much to share. Unlike that of his wife or daughters, Carl's hair was sandy blond which worked well to hide the gray just starting to make itself known. He wore it a bit shaggy and she often teased, accusing him of fronting some sixties' boy band.

"And?" he pushed.

"And…God, it's complicated."

"Too complicated for an auto body mechanic?" The hurt in his eyes was easy to see.

"Dad! No, it's not that. It's just…" She hesitated, unsure what to share. "Georgie's an air force vet. She suffered some serious injuries over there and she needs more than an assistant."

He studied her for a long moment, as if trying to read between the lines of what she'd said. "So, your concern is what? That she'll need more attention than you want to waste? Or being an assistant just plain sucks?"

Tyler grabbed the job description, shoving it back in her pocket. "I have two words for you!"

He laughed so hard his belly shook. That he was a big man explained where she got her height, but her lean, long form could only be attributed to her mother's slender physique. "If I didn't know better, I'd say you're actually intrigued by this job, but it's going to take you in a whole new direction you aren't prepared for. I've never known you to turn your back on a challenge."

"Okay, okay," she groaned in response. "When I was considering the private sector, I was thinking more of an economics think tank or someplace where I might spend my days writing white papers on ethics, not a babysitting job!"

"Dynamic Marine is into all this new tech stuff, and you say DiNamico herself is leading the department that creates all that technology. Wouldn't it follow that there would be ethical issues involved in some of that or at least in the direction the company might be heading?"

"Perhaps, but—" She knew he was right even if she was in the mood for an argument or at least some debate.

"You didn't do a lot of research on the company. Is it possible there's a way you could take this crappy job, help out a veteran, and put your skills to use?"

"When I was waiting for you to arrive, I went on the Internet to look over their website. I didn't realize they'd been operating without a CEO or president since Mr. DiNamico died two years ago. From the few articles I skimmed through, it looked like Georgie had been groomed to take over. After meeting her, I'm pretty sure that will never happen." At her dad's raised eyebrow, she explained, "Dad, I signed a gag order but basically between you and me, she suffered a serious head injury over there. I mean, she's still brilliant at her work but evidently that's it. I do feel like this is someone I might be able to help but I'm not sure that's any basis for a career decision."

Seeming to understand, he bobbed his head in agreement. "Tell me about this Marnie. What does she do?"

"Chief Operating Officer. My guess, she's actually running the company and judging by how concerned she was about making things better for her sister, I think she may be holding back from taking over, based on some sort of hope Georgie will get better."

"And Zoe?"

"Oh, she's Marnie's assistant. She is a real sweetie, Dad. You'd love her. She's Marnie's niece and she practically begged me to take the job." She didn't bother to share other details like how attractive she was or how flirty.

"Why do you think it was so important to her and the other woman?"

Tyler blew out a frustrating breath. "Honestly? I think it has something to do with Georgie. Evidently, she chose me from all the screened candidates, saying she would need my academic skills for a future project."

"Well, there you go. Did you ask her what the project was or what you would be doing?"

She sat silently, uncomfortable with admitting her reaction to Georgie's behavior. "We didn't actually get that far in the interview. I kind of freaked out."

"What?" He couldn't hide his shock at her confession.

"Yeah." Tyler crossed her arms, slumping down further. "I'm not proud of it, Dad."

"Okay…Can you tell your old man what happened?"

Grabbing her coffee cup and swallowing a cold mouthful, she took in his tender look, surrendering the last ounce of embarrassment. "She was showing me one of the new products they've developed. She called it a man-overboard tracking system. I got spooked when I saw the video of the test she'd done out on the lake. Dad, they went out in a snowstorm in December and she jumped in the freezing water to prove the tracking system worked. All I saw was rough stormy water, ice, wind and snow, and the thought that someone would actually voluntarily jump in freaked me out! The worst part is how hurt she was by my reaction. Maybe it was from her war experience. I don't know. Later, when I was talking to Marnie and Zoe, they mentioned that you can't trust her not to do stupid things like that. It's as if her head injury has erased all common sense. It scares the crap out of me!"

"That I understand. It's like being a dad. You can't help but freak out now and then, worrying about your three daughters."

Tyler gave him a lopsided grin, appreciating how he still worried even with them all grown. "You never freaked out. That was always Mom's job."

"You are so right, but that didn't stop me freaking out on her, every time I was worried about you girls!"

His grin was back and so was the sparkle she adored. "You never told me that."

"Hey, a guy's got a rep to maintain!"

She giggled, starting to feel better. "You know, you're right. I should just go back over there and ask her what she has in mind."

"That's my girl!"

* * *

Tyler called the contact number she had for DME, hoping to connect with Zoe but the woman who answered transferred her directly to Marnie Pulaski. She invited her to return and speak with Georgie or tour the office, anything Tyler needed to help make her decision.

The twenty-minute drive was just long enough to let her misgivings creep back in. She fought with herself until the moment she pulled into the parking lot.

Waiting, Zoe was grinning like a rock star. "I'm so glad you came back. I've got a pass and badge right here. Between you and me, I haven't seen Marnie move that fast since the twins first learned to drive!"

"She has twins?" she asked amiably.

"Boys. They're sixteen now and are just learning to drive. Can you imagine?"

"Oh I can! I'm a twin. I think the year Kira and I learned to drive almost killed my parents. You?"

Zoe was laughing. "Oh my God! I've a twin brother and he works here too. Can you imagine that?"

Tyler laughed at her banter. Zoe had a real zest for life. She had a reasonable idea that Zoe flirted with everyone. It was hard to tell whether the flirtatious banter meant she was interested in her or simply pleased that she had returned for Georgie's sake. "How is she doing? I mean, since I left?"

Linking Tyler's arm with hers, Zoe half dragged her into the waiting elevator. As the doors closed, and they began to climb, Zoe patted her arm encouragingly. "She and Henry have just finished their lunch. Now Granddad's off for his nap and she's got her head deep in a book." Her arm still linked through Tyler's, she led her directly to Georgie's office.

Tyler pulled them to a halt before they could interrupt Georgie. "Shouldn't I wait until she's done reading?"

Zoe rolled her eyes. "Come on. She reads for an hour after lunch every day and only because Marnie insists she take time to do something beyond all that geeky stuff."

Georgie reclined on the sofa, feet on the table, e-reader in hand, her attention fixed on her book. She seemed not to notice their nearness, even after Zoe unceremoniously kicked her feet off the coffee table.

"Georgie, come on, time to reenter the real world!"

Completely unfazed by Zoe's behavior, she folded the e-reader and laid it carefully beside the wireless keyboard. "Good to go."

"You feel like a cup of tea?" Zoe asked, "I thought we'd sit down and have a chat. Sound good?"

Georgie nodded. "Good. Yes…Tyler? Tea?"

Tyler quickly decided it was time for a little test of her own. "No actually, I'd prefer a coffee."

Georgie shook her head. "Smell…I vomit."

That surprised her. Not the vomiting comment, simply the fact that Georgie DiNamico explained herself without rancor or further detail.

"Is that a continuing problem? The vomiting, I mean."

Georgie nodded, taking the time to appraise Tyler directly. "Good questions. I forget…to explain…limitations. Do you understand?"

"I understand but I have concerns. I certainly don't want to invade your privacy but there may be times when I might require more information." Tyler wasn't surprised when Georgie didn't immediately answer but when the long, thoughtful moment began to stretch into an uncomfortable silence, she was unsure how to proceed.

Thankfully, Zoe intervened, jostling her cousin, giving her a playful grin. "I'll go plug in the kettle. Tyler here wants to learn about some of your new projects. Are you up for that?"

"Really?" Georgie asked, looking directly at Tyler, her expression conveying her pleasure at being asked.

Tyler took the same seat she had occupied earlier. "Ms. DiNamico, I really am interested in this job. My concern stems—"

"Marnie's offer...not acceptable?" she asked, clearly confused. "Just Georgie," she backtracked, instructing Tyler amiably about her name.

"Okay Georgie. I haven't accepted the job yet, because, well, because I want to put my skills to work. I'll be honest with you. I've been out of work for over a year. I don't want to just accept any position that comes along. After all, I've waited this long, I might as well shoot for what I really want."

"Which is?"

As much as she knew the question was coming, she hadn't realized until that very moment that she hadn't been honest with herself, much less anyone else about her real desires. "I'm not sure where to start. I did my masters in economics, which I really, really enjoyed but it wasn't until I started working in ethics that I found something to sink my teeth into. So, I guess I'm asking, do you intend to put those skills to use?"

"I read your thesis. Agree...hypothesis, most...insightful. Question...questioning my suppositions. Good!" She held a hand out flat and moved it in a straight course, much the way pilots and small children pretend their hand is an airplane zipping through the air. Then her left hand zoomed up, heading straight for the other hand. At the point where the two imaginary airplanes would collide, she stopped. Turning her right hand over, she explained, "Technology." Turning the left over, she added, "Ethics." She separated the two hands, then dove them toward each other; they missed each other by inches and headed in separate directions. If Tyler had missed the metaphor, the frown Georgie was sporting made her opinion clear. She flew the two hands at one another again but this time the action resulted in a collision. Both the hand signals and her expression said, this is not acceptable. In a third example both hands were held out straight and level and fit perfectly with what she was learning about this woman—and warned her of the challenges ahead.

Tyler had to ask, "It looks like you're suggesting they are equal but separate states."

"Balanced…or symbiotic?"

"Are you asking or telling?" Tyler demanded, and suddenly realized how that must have sounded. *Shit.* This was still an interview! She needn't have worried. Georgie was sporting a mischievous grin. For the second time Tyler found her own assumptions being challenged. Changing direction, she asked, "You read my thesis?"

Georgie pointed to her e-reader, as if that explained her interest.

"Why would you do that?"

Before she could answer, Zoe was back with her tray loaded with the old teapot, the usual makings and two mugs. These were decorated with old-style jets in camouflage paint.

"Looks like you two are getting on fine. Unless you need me to stay, I've a ton of work to finish up for Marnie."

Georgie nodded. Once they were alone again, she pulled the keyboard onto her knees, clicking away before the glass walls changed from transparent to opaque. As explanation, she said simply, "No one…yet. Your input first."

Tyler nodded reflectively. This woman was certainly full of surprises. On the flat-screen monitor above the fireplace, file folders were displayed and sorted, then one was selected. A new organization chart popped open, this one drastically different from the one she had been shown that morning. Marina Pulaski's name was in the CEO box. Below that, the company was divided into three separate divisions: DME Holdings was the first, DynaCraft Yachts second, and something called BioDynamic last. "BioDynamic?"

"Biotechnology…embedded technology, wearable tech."

"What? How do you get from building boats to biotech?"

Georgie seemed unfazed by the question and completely unaware of Tyler's skepticism.

"Good. I design…safety, marine safety." To demonstrate her point she displayed the Man Overboard photo again, then pulled up a design specification page and highlighted one of the bullet points.

Tyler read the text, understanding the detail was important. "Wait, your original design called for an RF chip to be injected into people?"

Georgie nodded. "Marnie said no…no microchips in children. True?" she asked, as if oblivious to the concerns her sister had raised.

"Of course it's true." Realizing she'd been getting riled up, she took a deep breath, choosing her words carefully. "Biotechnology is a landmine of ethical issues. I can't believe you would actually consider marketing a product that requires a medical procedure!"

Georgie held up her hand, as if a proof of her theory. "We have them. I made them. The nurse…injects…" As explanation, she offered her hand for inspection.

Tyler gently took hold, giving it the careful examination of a palm reader. Her hand, smaller than her own was warm to the touch and surprisingly soft. "Where is it?"

Using her free hand, Georgie squeezed the skin between her thumb and index finger.

Fascinated and still holding Georgie's hand, she asked, "What happens to employees who aren't willing to let you inject them with a foreign object?"

Making a circle motion, as if searching for the right word or phrase, she stopped and pointed to the visitor's badge on Tyler's jacket. Taking her hand, Georgie stood, signaling wordlessly for Tyler to follow. Walking to the glass partition wall that separated her meeting space from her work area, she waved her hand over a blue light in the glass. The white panels slid aside, opening up the two areas.

When Tyler had been taken into Marnie's office that morning, it had been by the private corridor. She hadn't had a chance to look around then, and she took her time now, appraising Georgie's work space. There was a large work desk with multiple computer monitors; several overloaded, but well organized bookshelves; and an old-fashioned partner's desk.

Heading for the desk, Georgie opened the single drawer facing her chair and pulled out a small box, dumping the contents on her blotter. Turning on a bright task light, she invited Tyler closer. "Look...RF chips."

"You designed these?"

"No...never reinvent." Retrieving her smartphone from the pocket of her suit, she opened a proprietary app and then selected the information tab before handing the phone to Tyler.

She read through the About screen then tapped on the More link, and carefully read through the operational statement. The app allowed her to control several functions, from the glass privacy settings to door locks. "This identifies the position of everyone in the building. Can everyone see this?"

"No."

Not satisfied with the answer, Tyler said point-blank, "You need to tell me who can. You may be violating the rights of your employees."

Georgie shook her head, retrieving her phone and pulling up an access list. "Company officers," she said as explanation, handing the phone back.

The list was short and included the expected names: Marnie Pulaski, Henry Phipps and Georgie DiNamico. Plus several more she had never seen. "Luigi Phipps?"

"Lou...VP finance."

"Jack Pulaski?"

"VP sales."

Tyler read the remainder of the list off, "Lori Phipps, Leslie Phipps and Stella Phipps. All family members?" she asked, not really expecting an answer, but secretly pleased when Georgie made the effort to connect the dots for her, explaining in her halting way that Lou was her cousin and Henry's only son. And then there was Jack Pulaski. Jack, it turned out, was Marnie's husband and the face of DME. They were definitely all family. She had made a funny gesture while trying to explain the working relationship of her cousin Lou and her brother-in-law. Fisting both her hands as if ready for a prizefight, she smashed them together a few times then shrugged. Her crooked grin made it clear she found the discord between the two men amusing. Before Tyler could even sort out what other questions she had, Georgie grabbed a tablet and opened the PDF for Tyler to read. It was the company's employee privacy statement, which explained the security procedures in place and stipulated the responsibilities and privileges of employees at every level within the organization. It also reassured employees regarding the use of embedded technologies.

It was right there in black and white for her to read. She, like everyone else, would have a choice of what technologies she chose to adopt and which were required for use on the job. She liked that. She liked the tone of the document and the scope of the procedures outlined, including what privacies would and would not be protected. The best part was how the document had been written. It was well organized and stated the expectations and responsibilities of both the company and the employee. It was written in everyday, easy-to-understand language and included a clause that invited input and change. "Who wrote this?"

Georgie pointed to herself in a manner that was both unassuming and shy. "Good?" she asked, waiting expectantly for Tyler's input. When she didn't immediately respond, formulating her thoughts, Georgie appeared crestfallen, shaking her head. "No?"

"No? I mean yes, it's very good. I like that it lays out the expectations from both sides and that it's written in a manner that's easy to understand."

Tyler switched to the second file which appeared to please Georgie. It was a wish list of sorts, and included items like position papers on the company's new technologies, and something identified as the company's E^3 Policy: Ethics, Economy and

Environment. It described the importance of identifying future challenges to corporate and product liability in each category including the pressures induced by a global market.

"Examining the efficacy of marine products is a long way from probing global economics," Tyler remarked. "There are several things to consider. Would I be writing from the viewpoint of your family, your employees, the actual market economy or the environment? And that's just for openers."

Georgie sat quietly without comment.

"All right, let's start with liability first. Who do you want to protect?"

"Everyone…customers, employees, family. All…Owners…Operators…Polar bears. Dynamic Marine people, old…new…We are responsible…them, they, are family."

She wasn't sure what made her smile more, the fact that her new boss had managed to string so many words together at once, or that she actually believed the company should be responsible to and for both employees and customers. To say it wasn't what she had been expecting was an understatement. "I can work with that. Tell me exactly what you mean by responsible. Responsible to what, or whom?"

"Company, employees…customers."

"I feel like we're going in circles. What exactly is the corporate position? Georgie?" Tyler prodded.

The woman simply shrugged. Her almost black hair falling in her eyes. Her hair, while pageboy short, was rich and vibrant much like the woman herself. She watched as Georgie absently brushed her bangs from her eyes; pointing to Tyler, indicating she thought defining future corporate policy was Tyler's job not hers. "Propose…strategy."

"And the goal of this strategy?"

Instead of answering, Georgie waved a hand indicating she wanted Tyler to join her.

Pulling out the matching task chair on the opposite side, she slipped into the seat, watching carefully as Georgie pulled out a large pad of graph paper and made a list. An old-fashioned, written on paper list. Considering their high-tech surroundings and all the gadgets at the woman's disposal, it was refreshing to see. She passed the pad over along with the pen. Tyler began reading the list silently, then chided herself. She didn't have a problem communicating verbally. "You want to reduce your carbon footprint. Design responsibly. I'm not sure what that means. While producing energy efficient products, you want me to figure out the best strategy to accomplish these goals?"

Georgie took the notepad back and began to make additions.

While Tyler waited for her response, she turned her attention back to the RF chips. Picking up one of the tiny capsules, she had to admit her astonishment. "This is unbelievable. How does it work?"

With her attention fixed on the notepad, Georgie halted her work just long enough to answer, "Simple dongle."

"Dongle?"

The look she gave Tyler was intensely serious. Tearing the top sheet of paper off the pad, she drew a circle, writing Dongle inside while explaining, "Think…serial number…electronic serial number," she said, pointing to the circle. She then drew a rectangle and labeled it Security/Access Points. "Interrogator," she said as explanation for its function. Finally she drew a symbol Tyler recognized as representative of a database. "Comparison." Then, using arrows, she linked the three objects and then looped the process back to the starting point.

"Oh, I think I get it," Tyler said, with some delight. "Tell me if I'm right. Whenever the RF chip gets close to any of the readers, interrogators you said, they read the serial number and compare it to the database while recording the employee's position in the building. If it's a security point, like a locked door, it must also check to see if the serial number on the chip is actually authorized entry. If it is, that information is passed back and the door unlocks. If it doesn't match the database list then the door remains closed. Very interesting. And you're right, the simplicity is quite elegant."

It was easy to see Georgie was pleased with her answer. "Nice!" was her unadorned but keen response.

Tyler rolled the soft bead of the RF chip in her palm, contemplating everything she had learned. "Do you have a corporate policy on any of the issues you're asking me to address?"

Georgie shook her head. Turning to the shelves behind her desk she retrieved a large binder marked Media Releases, and flipped through several pages before finding what she wanted, passing it across the desk.

Scanning several pages quickly, Tyler noted this particular report was a summary of the company's position on out-of-production patents. It seemed DME had made a public statement saying they would not sell, license, or allow other manufacturers anywhere in the world to produce two-stroke engines based on their legacy products. The statement went on to estimate the size of the two-stroke engine market, and why, regardless of the estimated loss of projected profits, DME had divorced itself from the product line. Two-stroke engines, while offering much more horsepower per cubic inch, were huge polluters, spewing out three times more carbon monoxide than their four stroke big brothers while adding insult by polluting the water with unburned lubricating oil. When companies from China and India had come looking for cheap two-stroke designs, DME had only offered their four-stroke engines. There were other similar releases. Some went on to describe improvements to the DiNamico building and the Dynamic Marine boatyard and included changes like adding solar panels on the roof and low-voltage lighting inside.

Tyler closed the press book and took a careful look around the office. This wouldn't be such a bad place to work. The combination of stone, glass and aged oak made the place seem organic and inviting, or maybe it was the woman herself. She had to admit that Georgie DiNamico was like no one she ever met. With nothing but simple sentences, the woman had explained herself in more detail than Tyler had ever pulled from chatty-Cathy faculty members. "I would need access to everything, business plans, financial statements, product proposals, everything!"

"Okay."

"I would need input from all the top players."

"Okay."

"That's it? That's all you're going to say?"

"Yes." She stood, waving casually as she said, "Director level access."

Tyler marveled at her open trust. "What happens if you choose not to start the new company? What will I be doing then?"

That question seemed to knock the wind from the woman's sails. "I will not...lie. This job...babysitting. The rest...up to you." She retrieved the notepad, bending over the desk to scribble. She handed the page back to Tyler. She had written the word Questions and underlined it. Below it, a point list:

Privacy.

Personal liability, long-term impact.

Fluctuating global money markets. Exchange rates.

Accounting and investment ethics.

Environmentally responsible legacy of products and technologies.

The last bullet point was underlined. In brackets, she had written and underlined, *Past – Present – Future!*

"I take it you feel very strongly about this?"

Again, Georgie looked genuinely surprised by the question. "My dad...struggled. Family or work." She was quiet again, clearly contemplative. "We...me, Dad, Henry...would talk... issues, upcoming." She slipped back into her chair. She looked good behind the large desk. There was something calming, almost soothing in seeing her there. At odds with her Mediterranean coloring, her intelligent eyes were a shade of green Tyler had never encountered.

She watched with interest while her new boss worked to organize her thoughts. Consciously forcing herself to sit up straight, she placed both hands flat on the desk determined to project an air of openness and patience, something Georgie immediately seemed to comprehend and appreciate.

She gave her a grateful nod before turning her attention back to the notepad, and scribbled furiously for two, three minutes straight. When she was finished, she surprised Tyler again. This time, instead of handing her the notepad to read, Georgie read to her from her notes. Remarkably, the woman could both read from her rushed notes and maintain eye contact. The transformation was extraordinary. If Tyler had not been witness to her previous attempts and frustrations, she would have immediately dismissed everything she'd been told.

"...Environmental impact is a big concern. One reason we only build sailboats. There is a good margin in fiberglass runabouts, if you build to the lowest standards. We will not do that. To build a power boat we would be proud to put our name on, we would price ourselves out of the market. It would not matter that our boat would last longest. Today customers ask how many years they can finance a boat. Not how many years of service they can expect. A good deal is not a good deal. It is a mistake to play the economics of volume game. Not for us. I need you to explain that to the Board. We must demonstrate how to take the high road and turn a profit."

"What if I can't find a profitable economic model that fits your high moral ground?"

Georgie scooped the RF chips into her hand and back into the small paper box, silent and brooding again. Finally, she looked back at Tyler. Instead of trying to explain, she picked up her cell phone and navigated to a webpage.

Accepting the phone, Tyler read aloud, "Miami International In-Water Boat Show. February twenty-third through the twenty-eighth. "I assume this is a big event for the company?"

"Industry," Georgie explained.

Tyler wasn't quite sure of the point—then the implication dawned on her. "Oh my God, you're planning to pitch this right after the Miami Boat Show."

"During," she corrected. "Everyone...in Miami."

"Oh my God! I can't even begin to tell you how much work is involved." She was surprised by the smile she saw across the desk. "You're liking this. This idea of putting a proposal together. Taking the company in a new direction." Tyler had to think about that for a minute, only then admitting how empowering it would be to work with this woman. "All right, let me get this sorted in my head. You've got this idea to split the company into three divisions. And you have a very strong feeling about the way you want to structure your corporate ethics policy including licensing and legacy. And, you plan to pitch this while your family's in Miami for the boat show."

Georgie nodded her confirmation, her too-long bangs falling into her gorgeous green eyes. Even in the plain gray suit and the shoddy blue shirt, there was no denying how attractive she was, especially with that beguiling smile.

"I hate to ask this but what happens if the board rejects your proposal and wants to go in a different direction?"

The smile vanished and in its place came disappointment. Then Georgie shrugged, pointing at herself and said, "Unemployed."

"You? That doesn't make sense!"

Georgie nodded, again playing the airplane game with her hands. Once again she flew the two airplanes on a collision course but narrowly missed, each continuing on in opposite directions.

Silently contemplating the woman across the desk, Tyler counted herself surprised once again. *What the hell is with her?* Remarkably forthcoming and thoughtful, she was woefully unaware of her potential detractors. In a way, it was a remarkable skill. Although, how that affected her personal or emotional life was hard to fathom. Surveying the office once more, she asked, "Where will I be working?"

"Close," she said, jerking her thumb toward the administrative offices next door. "All right?"

She was starting to understand that Georgie would simply ask her when she was unsure of whether she was right or wrong. She stood, following Georgie through the same back corridor Zoe had pulled her along just that morning.

Steps from her office, Georgie turned and pointed out the private kitchen. Opposite and with a spectacular view of the South Erie shoreline were two glass-fronted offices. Each was about half the size of the CIO's. Susan Chan's name was on the far office door while the one closest to Georgie's was empty. A desk and bookshelves lined one wall, a love seat had been pushed against another. This was not what she was expecting. When she first applied for the position, she had imagined being sequestered to a tiny cubicle and having to prepare coffee and photocopy reports. Turning a complete 360 degrees, she took in what looked like brand-new office furniture. Indeed, the sofa still had tags hanging from one arm, as did her office chair. The desk and bookshelves were empty, but looked handsome and inviting. She could actually imagine working here, really working on serious issues affecting this company. Before she could comment, Georgie pointed to the glass office door. It was propped open, so she hadn't noticed a door inscription had already been added.

"I hope...okay. Marnie...will tell this," she said, pointing to the door, adding a warning, "Some know...babysitting too!"

Tyler read the lettering on the class panel. *Dr Tyler Marsh, PhD. Director, Special Projects.*

Still pointing she asked, "...You want that?"

"Are you kidding me? Wait, are we talking about the same type of work, addressing ethical issues, economic impact statements and analysis. The whole works?"

Georgie nodded. "Sorry, I...never explained...

"I understand," Tyler said, squeezing her arm to halt the confused apology. "I have to tell you. This is not what I was expecting. It's good. Actually, it's great. This is something I know how to do. It's the other half, assisting you. I don't want to let you down."

"Dr Marsh," Georgie offered formally. "Marnie...the list?"

"The list?"

"Details...what is managed. Oh, managed...Manager is better?"

Tyler tipped her head toward the office door, "Well, according to that, I'm the Director of something called Special Projects. Manager sounds like it would be a step down."

Georgie smiled, really smiled, for the first time since their introduction. Reading from the door placard she said with pleasure, "Welcome aboard...Dr Tyler Marsh, PhD, Director of Special Projects."

* * *

"I swear that man will be the death of me! One day he will have to learn the difference between a general ledger and General Motors." Tyler's mom stopped short at the sight of her eldest daughter. She was sitting at the kitchen table, stacks of papers, reports and booklets spread out over the entire surface. The only clear spot was occupied by her perpetual coffee cup. She had changed out of her interview suit into a pair of old jeans and a T-shirt that read Carl's Auto Body, with a cartoon depiction of a toothy Corvette. Her mother gave her an appreciative little backrub before turning to the coffeemaker to fix her own cup. "So I take it things went better the second time round?"

"Dad told you?"

"He told me it was complicated," she answered, stirring cream into her coffee.

She noticed that her mom's dark hair was starting to show even more gray, ravages of raising three headstrong girls. Willowy tall, dressed in her work clothes, jeans and a V-neck sweater embroidered with Carl's Autobody across the front, she pulled out a chair and sat down across the table without messing up Tyler's spread. "This reminds me of your undergraduate years. When you were here at State. I hadn't realized how much I missed having you home until right this minute."

"Mom!"

"Don't mom me! I can't help if I like having you here. I hated it when you were down in the Big Apple. Almost as much as I hated having you away at graduate school. I know honey. I see your look. It can't be that bad, living with your mom and dad, is it?"

"Of course not. Although I will admit, it does wreak havoc with my love life."

"Oh honey, you could always bring your girlfriends home." This she added with the same spark of mischief Tyler recognized in her dad.

She groaned. It wasn't that she didn't want to introduce anyone to her parents, it was that she had no one to introduce.

As if she could read her thoughts, her mother offered gently, "Maybe you'll meet someone at this new company. There's got to be some lovely ladies you might be interested in."

"Lovely ladies? Mom, when are you from?"

With blue eyes darker than Lake Erie, Debbie Marsh laughed, age lines adding a certain air to her affection. Sipping her coffee appreciatively, she was obviously unwilling to comment on her generational slang. "So what's all this?"

Tyler set her pen down, frustrated by the interruption but in need of fresh coffee anyway. Grabbing her cup, she returned to the coffeemaker, deciding just how to explain what she had learned. Padding back to the table, her bare feet appreciated the heated tile floor. She was wondering how often they had done just this. Sit together and discuss her work, her research, even as far back as public school. She loved doing her homework at the kitchen table if for no other reason than to share the ritual with her mom. "This was a surprise. Turns out my new boss wants to put my skills to work. And, it turns out, the only way she could convince her company to hire an Ethicist was to accept that she needed an assistant too."

"Your dad says this DiNamico woman is a vet, that she needs a little help. How bad is it?"

"It's actually not what you'd imagine. Her head injury only affects certain aspects of her right brain function."

"The right brain, that's the analytical or the creative side?"

That surprised Tyler. "You know about brain hemispheres?"

Her mother nodded, enjoying another sip of her brew, slouched in her chair, something she only did after work. And cradling her cup in both hands, something Tyler had seen her do for ages. How she managed to keep her long hair so neat and her long nails so perfectly manicured while working in a body shop never ceased to amaze her. She'd worked in her parents' shop every summer for as long as she remembered and never made it home looking so good. If she didn't know better she would have been shocked to learn the casual beauty across from her ran the busiest body shop in town. "Your dad and I watched some program on the Discovery channel, or maybe it was PBS."

Tyler nodded appreciatively. "Well, you basically know as much as I do. But of course it's more complicated than that. According to this letter written to her sister from her neurologist, Georgie has suffered permanent damage to some key areas. The amygdala is the first."

"What does that part do?" She sat up straighter, all business again. Tyler had always admired that in her mom. The articulate and sincere interest she displayed instilled confidence and had the added effect of renewing her own curiosity in a subject.

"According to this," she said, holding up her iPad, "it's the fear center. Which accounts for her lack of common sense."

"Oh? What's that about?" A *mom* tone creeping back into the conversation.

Tyler opened a video link before passing the tablet to her mom. "This was taken last year. I think it was early December."

Clearing a place on the table for her coffee cup, her mother tapped on the play arrow, then watched the footage of Georgie DiNamico jumping overboard into the icy lake, and the steps her crew took to find her and haul her back aboard. "Holy crap! Tyler Ann Marsh! If you ever pull a stunt like this, I will kill you myself!"

There was no doubting her words. In this house Debbie Marsh was the boss and what she said was law. As kids Tyler and her twin Kira had never gotten away with anything. Oh they could run to their dad for sympathy but even he bowed to Debbie's rule. It had become the family's running joke. The biggest linebacker in town was afraid of his skinny raven-haired bride! Laughing, Tyler retrieved the iPad while assuring her mother, "Don't worry. You raised me to be smarter than that. Thank God!"

"So I guess this is the part where the babysitting comes into play?"

"You got it."

Debbie, uncharacteristically quiet, seemed to be carefully considering her daughter's new job.

"Don't worry, Mom. I see that look. She's been diagnosed with PTSD."

"That seems to be a common thread for veterans these days. Are you surprised?"

"Not at all. I guess my concerns are more about managing her emotional states, if I can put it that way."

"It's not like you to back away from a challenge."

"Oh, the challenge part I'm up for. I'm just concerned that my lack of knowledge could make things worse. Georgie's already been through so much. The last thing I want to do is be the one who screws her up any more."

Her mother gave her a knowing smile. "How about we go out for dinner to celebrate. Just you and me?"

"Now you're talking."

Debbie Marsh had been battling her daughter for the last sweet potato fry when she asked innocently, "So? I'm getting the impression you really like this Zoe person. Is she family?"

"How do you know that expression?"

"What? I get around!"

Tyler giggled, enjoying her local brew. "Don't let Dad hear you say that."

Her mother's face was bright, she was clearly enjoying their time together. "I can't tell you how much I love having you girls home." She held up her hand, halting any protests. "I see your look and I know you're an adult with your own life, still…It's lovely to have you and Kira home. Megan, on the other hand, is proving to be far more of a challenge than you two ever were. Your dad's been trying to convince her to go back to school in January. I don't know what he's finding more frightening, another semester of Megan sitting around doing nothing and hating the world for it, or two o'clock feedings when your sister's baby comes."

"I'm a little nervous about the whole baby thing too."

"You'll be fine," her mother assured her. "Why don't you tell me some more about this Zoe? You only mentioned her like a hundred times. So you do like her? Are you going to ask her out? She is gay, right? Not like it matters but it's probably easier?"

Tyler just shook her head. "I don't know where you come up with these things."

"I'm just trying to be gender-neutral. It's a new world and my girls are part of it. I'm so proud of you two. You found the kind of work that inspires you, and Kira's decided to go ahead and make her own family all on her own. I really raised some great girls!"

"Not exactly sure who you're complimenting, but if I'm included, I'll take it."

"And ask Zoe out?" her mother pushed.

Tyler groaned and rolled her eyes. It was hard to believe this was a conversation taking place between two grown women, one of them her mother. "Yes Mom. I promise, I'll ask her out."

* * *

Marnie found her sister, head down at her worktable, soldering iron in hand. "I thought we agreed you'd let Skip handle all the sharp objects."

Looking up from the oversized magnifying work lamp, Georgie managed to burn her hand the moment she took her eyes from her task. She dropped the soldering iron.

"What did I just say?" Marnie pulled a chair over, taking hold of her sister's arm and examining the new burn.

"No sharp objects?"

Marnie just groaned. Fetching the always ready first aid kit, she sat back down and carefully dressed the wound. "This isn't as bad as the last one." Dressed much like her sister, her custom-made suit was much more fashionably cut in contrast to the more traditional look Georgie preferred. Together with her long hair, she was a softer, curvier version of her older sister. "I do wish you would be more careful. What if I wasn't here?"

"No interruptions!"

"Speaking of which, did you make any plans for the weekend?"

Georgie shrugged. "Ask Friday."

"Today is Thursday. Georgie! You should be out having fun, meeting people, visiting with friends, that sort of thing."

At her sister's blank face she asked gently, "Are we still on for tomorrow night?"

Georgie groaned, but didn't say no.

"Don't let Lori hear you complaining. She's been hyped all week about taking you to that infernal bar."

Finally beginning to relax, Georgie grinned like a schoolgirl. "Hyped…you in lesbian bar…Mr. Charming at home!"

Marnie laughed. "Yeah, smiling Jack's none too happy about it either. Men! I swear they imagine a bar full of women as some sort of sexual playground for them, even when they're completely superfluous!" She laughed at her own joke. "I swear, one day I may have to pound some sense into that big swinging dick of mine!"

"Jack is…loyal."

Marnie harrumphed as she taped the gauze over the treated burn. "Just keep that covered until you're done branding yourself. After you shower, put some more of this cream on." She reached across Georgie, tucking the tube into her shirt pocket. "How did things go with Tyler Marsh the second time around?"

Georgie seemed confused. "Good questions?"

"That's not what I'm getting at. Tell me if you still want her as your assistant."

"She is smart."

"And…" Marnie coached her.

"And…not afraid."

"And…"

"I like her."

"Good. Then it's settled. She starts Monday."

"What?" Georgie looked panicked. "Not ready!"

"Will you relax? It's not a military inspection. It's just when your assistant will start helping you, and besides, I've got her scheduled for most of next week with orientation and the standard products course." When Georgie finally acknowledged this with a nod, Marnie gave her a hug. "I love you, you pain in my backside! Now remember, I'm out of the office tomorrow and Henry will be up at the Big House on the weekend. That means you're on your own for meals. Will you remember to eat or should I call you?"

Georgie just shook her head, trying to turn her attention back to her work.

"Oh no you don't. Look at me and tell me if you still want to stay here. If you don't, we can go pack a bag and you can come home with me."

Time spent with family at the Big House was an emotional trigger for Georgie's PTSD. She and the counselors all agreed that spending time in her grandfather's home, now Henry's, or more accurately Lou's, was a painful reminder of all she had lost. Marnie secretly believed that Georgie's own desire for family, or at least someone to share her life with, was now a long shot. Believing she was too broken to share anything, much less a normal life with anyone, Georgie had been steadily working to isolate herself all the more. It wasn't a solution and Marnie had no intention of letting her only sister, the most vibrant woman she had ever known, become some sort of techno-hermit. Maybe she wasn't up for the whole trophy wife scenario, house, kids, little league and peewee hockey, but she was still a very lovable woman and that had to count for something.

"I am...okay Marnie. Go have...enjoy your family. Good to go!"

"Okay, that's perfect." Marnie gave Georgie another hug then headed out, calling over her shoulder, "Wear something hot tomorrow night, and when I say hot, I am not referring to winter weight clothing! Got that Georgie Porgie?"

"One day...I will remember your kidname...nickname!"

"Yeah, yeah," she offered from the door, "and one day I'm going to be the Queen of Sheba and wear a funny hat!"

CHAPTER THREE

Georgie opened her eyes carefully. Maggie's big head was inches from her own wet face. "Slobbering?" she asked, while using both hands to wipe the moisture from her face. Maggie, as ever, sat patiently waiting, leash in mouth. Pulling up the hem of her T-shirt, Georgie wiped away the last of her errant tears. "Cannot blame you."

"I think you're on her bed."

She looked up from her place on the floor next to the dog. Henry was dressed as he was every night, in his signature blue pajamas and a pair of old moccasins he preferred to slippers. While she was sleeping better, it was still rare for her to sleep all night. The early mornings, usually between three and four a.m., were always the most difficult. Tonight she had crawled out of her own bed in her sleep, dragging herself into the far corner of her room where Maggie usually slept. Well-versed in the stages of her nightmares, Maggie had begun patiently nudging her awake. Henry too, hearing over the baby monitor the telltale signs of a person falling from bed, had made his way to her room to check on her.

Georgie sat up, propping herself against the bedroom wall. Henry had already made his way to the room's only chair to rest his ancient bones. Wiping the rest of the sweat from her face, she patted her lap, signaling for the dog to lie down and rest her head. That was all the signal Maggie needed. Dropping her leash, she immediately hunkered down beside Georgie, resting her big brown head across her lap. "Henry? You have knobby knees."

"You and my dear departed Glory Bee are the only women who ever noticed."

"Why do you call…her, Aunt Gloria…that?"

Henry smiled. He had told her the story a million times but for some reason, after the nightmares, it was always the first thing she would ask. "Well, it was a routine training flight. I tell you, it was a perfect day. Me and your daddy, we took off in our separate Super Sabres, heading up to Placentia Bay, then over to Goose Bay to refuel before heading for home. About halfway back to base, I started having engine trouble. Old Danny boy was having some problems too, so we figured we got bad fuel. Now, it's not like there's a whole bunch of places to put down on the Rock. So, here we were, pushing for home but with no luck. I tip my hat to your daddy. He managed to put his bird down on a little skinny road. All I could find was damned torn-up fields. Sure enough, I plowed that bird in nose first and rolled her kettle over teacup. I remember thinking, I sure hope Dan finds me before some big moose decides to make me his mamma!"

"That never happened."

He chuckled. "Don't you know it! Well, I remember waking up and wondering if I was dead. Here I was, a big black man with my very black skin, in a big white bed. The walls were all white with these pretty hand-painted roses all around the trim. I remember everything about that moment. The window was open, with the sea breeze causing the curtains to flutter. The linens smelled like lavender, clean soap and fresh air, and oh it reminded me of the way my momma would hang the sheets out to dry. Then there were all these white women bustling around me and speaking in hushed tones, like they were in church.

Well, I thought if I'm dead, this must be heaven. Then I heard the voice of an angel. 'He's waking up! Dear God, my sweet poor Yank's waking up!' Oh, that was some sweet words. I tried to sit up, look around a bit, but out a nowhere comes my angel, and glory be to God! This freckly faced whiff of a white girl sits on down beside me. Dear baby Jesus, I thought her hair was on fire and it was all frizzy crazy like I remember my little sister's hair always being. And the tears in her eyes! I'll be the first to admit the white women up in Newfoundland never treated me like white women did here at home. Not the way they did back then. But here was this white girl, with the greenest eyes and all that fiery orange hair, and she was hanging on to my hand like I was the president of these United States. And just like that, I just knew I could love that girl forever."

"Just like that?"

"Just like that, child. Just like that!"

"What...how, Uncle Henry?" she asked, always returning to the moniker she had preferred since childhood. "How do you know...when...in love?"

"Now that's the easiest and hardest question in the world. Why do you ask?"

Georgie shrugged in response. "I guess...I do not know. I guess...maybe I want that...too."

Henry nodded solemnly. "Me too little Georgie, me too!" With that said and his work done, he dragged his aching bones from her room and back down the hall to his own.

Georgie sat on the floor, slowly brushing Maggie's neck and rubbing her ears. *What do you think, girl? Do you think there's actually a woman out there who would put up with me crawling into your bed every night?* She rested her head against the wall, contemplating her situation. When she couldn't find an answer or even a temporary solution, she did what she always did. Getting up from the floor, she grabbed her clothes from the arm of the chair and hurriedly dressed. "Time!"

Retrieving her leash, Maggie padded to her side.

This would be another long night.

* * *

It wasn't until the following Thursday when Tyler finally sat down at her desk. She had arrived bright and early on Monday, prepared to wade into the deep end. She hadn't expected to spend most of the day completing forms and being shuffled from office to office. Instead of the obligatory welcome greetings and introductions she had endured at other jobs, Tyler had been presented as the chosen problem solver. For whom everyone had questions. Lucky for her, most were well intended and demonstrated a common concern for Georgie DiNamico's welfare. There were also a few unkind words about work policies and other topics far removed from their job titles. Tyler decided to make a mental note of their opinions and ideas. She knew she would have to call on some, if not all of these people in the coming months, and had a feeling she might not be as welcome then.

She spent day two and three in the training room, along with three other new hires, completing employee orientation. It was really just a crash course on the marine industry and everything DME. Everything except for Georgie and her bio-tech plan.

This morning, Tyler had met with Lou Phipps, the company CFO and Zoe's dad, in a staff meeting. He had delivered the most detailed and painfully boring report on DME's income from the international licensing program.

If Tyler thought Georgie's sister Marnie was tightly wound, Lou Phipps was a whole other thing. He had begun his briefing, as he called it, at exactly nine a.m. At ten thirty, he accompanied her to the cafeteria, having invited her to take coffee with him. There he spoke amiably of the Phipps and DiNamico families but never shared anything but the vaguest generalities. At precisely ten forty-five, she followed him back to his seventh-floor office where he immediately resumed his monologue. During the long morning she had asked him to call her Tyler more than once. The fact that he never outwardly responded to her invitation didn't bother her nearly as much as his own missing invitation to address him by his given name. He was the only person who hadn't.

She was so put off by his behavior, she opened her notebook and Googled him. The company website listed him as CFO and VP of Finance. It wasn't until she clicked through several secure pages on the company intranet that she found something interesting. The next meeting of the Board of Directors was scheduled for late February. A list of invited attendees was attached to the schedule. Beside each name was an annotation differentiating board members from those presenting reports. Her name was listed with the annotation: (GD support). *Georgie DiNamico support? No wonder Lou Phipps was acting as if my interest was superfluous.* Then she noticed something even more interesting. Lou Phipps wasn't listed as a board member either. The (MP support) annotation, she was sure, referred to Marnie Pulaski.

Tyler was hunched over her desk, reading the company organization chart, trying to comprehend Lou Phipps's relationship and his attitude, when she sensed more than heard someone waiting at her door. When she looked up, Georgie was standing there. She had the strangest look on her face and her head was tilted as if in deep concentration. Before Tyler could think of what to say, Georgie walked into her office and around her desk. Without a word she dropped to her knees.

"This is wrong...do not move," she ordered, immediately getting back on her feet in an efficient, almost military manner, before disappearing out the door.

Tyler sat all but frozen at the order. Then, feeling silly for her reaction, she was about to head to Georgie's office when the woman walked back in with a small canvas satchel in hand. Without a word of explanation, she dropped to her knees again and began fussing around the base of Tyler's new office chair. *What a day to wear a skirt and heels.* Again she was all but frozen in anxiety. Her new boss was on the floor beside her and evidently so deeply involved in whatever it was she was doing, she was unaware of the hand she had placed on Tyler's knee.

"Please…" Georgie began to ask, before seeming unable to explain. Resorting to hand signals, she gestured for Tyler to stand. Georgie flipped the chair over and disassembled the base.

Tyler watched with interest as in seconds the woman stripped the complicated swing and tilt mechanism down to its base components. She unscrewed and pried apart the piece that looked remarkably like a fat shock absorber. With the grease-streaked innards in her hand, she corrected the orientation of the shock in its sleeve before reassembling the entire base. Still on her knees, Georgie flipped the chair back on its rollers and turned it to face her, and pointed. Now understanding, Tyler resumed her place. The chair was four or five inches taller, too high now but better.

Georgie stood without a word, removing a cotton hanky from her pocket and wiping grease from her hands. She gestured for Tyler to move toward her work surface. She stepped back, studying Tyler with intent. She had the look of an artist surveying a large canvas as she continued wiping her hands in the cotton hankie. Again she dropped to her knees, this time concentrating on the chair back and arms. Gently, almost cautiously, Georgie took her hand and was leading her through the range of the various adjustable levers when the sound of someone clearing his throat startled them both.

"Georgina!" Lou Phipps was standing in the office door. He shook his head and without further comment, stormed down the corridor.

Shocked by the reaction, Tyler took in the scene from his perspective. She was sitting quite straight in her chair, with Georgie on one knee and holding her hand. She would have laughed if Georgie didn't look so horrified. She was still on one knee and still holding her hand. Wanting to make things better, she gave Georgie's hand a light squeeze before helping her to her feet.

Georgie apologized, "I am so…sorry."

"For what? You were just helping me."

Georgie hung her head, ashamed. "Now he is…telling Marnie I…recruited you!"

"You already recruited me, hence the fact that I now work here!"

"Not that kind," she offered, clearly uncomfortable. "Toaster oven recruit. I am…so sorry…will explain."

"You most certainly will not!" Tyler wasn't sure which offended her more, the thought that Lou Phipps would run to Marnie because he believed Georgie had acted inappropriately or that Georgie was worried people would think poorly of her if they believed she was lesbian. She had assumed that a company with two open and out lesbians, Georgie and Zoe, would be more progressive. She also realized, almost belatedly, that this would be a good time to come out to her boss. She was about to do just that when Maggie padded in, leash in mouth. Just like that the woman and her dog were gone and for a moment all the air in the room seemed to rush out with them. Half bewildered and half in shock, she sat motionless.

Zoe walked in. Slipping into the seat across from Tyler, she sported a serious look. "My dad can be a real arse at times. You all right?"

Still in shock, Tyler nodded. "What the hell was that?"

"I'm afraid my dear old dad just outed you. He's in Marnie's office demanding to know why Georgie did not notify him that you and she are *involved*!"

"What?"

Zoe offered a weak smile. "He jumps to conclusions all the time. I've come to believe it's just the way his mind works. If it's any consolation, having a queer daughter has been lovely payback." Smiling for the first time since walking in, Zoe tilted her head in question, "You all right?"

Was she? "Georgie was just fixing my chair." As if to prove her point, Tyler swung around and retrieving the still open tool bag, pushed it across her desk. "The dog came for her! I am so sorry."

"Not to worry. That's why we have the big mutt," Zoe explained. "She'll take a short walk then head down to the machine shop. I'll take you down there later. Whenever something's bothering her, they take a walk then head down to spend time with Henry. Let's give her a few minutes to settle down. Okay?"

Tyler nodded. What else could she do?

Zoe accompanied her to the basement of the DiNamico building and down a long drab corridor to a steel door marked Machine Shop. Tyler was expecting to find an assortment of greasy old stationary tools like the drill press and band saw in her parents' auto body shop. The spacious and bright electronics lab they entered was a complete surprise. The long narrow room had to run the length of the building. A comfortable couch and recliner were grouped in one corner. An elderly African American man was fast asleep in the recliner while Maggie, Georgie's service dog, watched them without much interest from her cozy dog bed right next to his chair. Beside the lounge area, there were several workstations with high worktables and shelves loaded with electronic gadgets and gizmos. Beyond the workstations was a large central work surface which looked a lot like a light table. Tyler watched as Georgie and two others discussed something they were jointly reviewing.

"That's Henry," Zoe said, tipping her head back toward the lounge area.

"Henry Phipps?" Tyler asked, looking back at the sleeping man. He was dressed in blue work pants with a plain shirt and old cable-knit sweater.

"Let's not wake him. Come on, I'll introduce you to some of Georgie's boys."

Before they had passed the first test bench, a young man came crashing through the shop entrance, a super large Slurpee in one hand and a milk crate crammed with electronic junk under his other arm. Before he could make it more than a few feet, Zoe challenged him, "Have you lost your mind?"

"What?" he asked, clearly confused by her remark.

"Your T-shirt you nob! Georgie will freak if she sees you're not up to code!"

Tyler watched as the young man's attention waffled between her, Georgie in the back of the room and Zoe. "What code are we discussing?" Tyler asked, as if sensing the young man needed a moment to frame a suitable reply.

"Dress code," Zoe explained, adding, "the engineers are not required to wear suits or dress slacks but that T-shirt is definitely a no-no!"

"Zoe, please," he whined. "I'm working my ass off. Christ, I was lucky to find a clean T-shirt to wear!"

"Report!" They all turned at Georgie DiNamico's order. Standing tall at the head of the light table, she had the air of a general in the middle of a briefing from her commanders. She directed them with hand signals to join her at the light table. When they did, Tyler realized they were standing around a display terminal: a table-sized monitor with touch input for a work surface. Georgie and her engineers had several technical drawings open and were making changes to one. "Report," she repeated, no nonsense.

Zoe stepped up first. "I was just reminding Skippy here that employees, even engineers, have to adhere to the dress code."

Georgie seemed to examine the young man Zoe had called Skippy. He was wearing a plain gray T-shirt and black jeans. Both looked clean and presentable.

"Sorry boss." Skippy seemed to wilt under Georgie's examination. "It's just, well, I've been concentrating on this…" He raised the milk crate containing a jumble of unidentifiable electronic components.

"Understood." Turning to Zoe, Georgie began tentatively, "Was it today? Shirt order…suits?"

"Yes, I thought Tyler and I could take care of that this aft?"

"Very well." She took her time, seeming to need a moment to decide on a course of action. Retrieving her ever-present smartphone from her suit pocket, she tabbed feverishly for a half minute before turning her attention back to Zoe.

Looking up from her own phone where she was reading Georgie's message, Zoe was skeptical. "You want me to pick up a half dozen new shirts for my brother? And ties too?" She frowned her disapproval, while Skippy beamed at the offer. "You know Dad will never go for that."

Georgie's attention returned to her phone, sending another text message.

Zoe, reading it, crossed her arms and shook her head. Clearly she wasn't going to follow orders.

Tyler watched the exchange with interest while the engineers gathered around the table stood motionless.

"Fine," Georgie acquiesced. "Charge my…personal, account."

Zoe huffed at that. Still shaking her head, she exclaimed, "Georgie, you can't favor him like that!"

Looking up from the diagrams, Georgie was plainly frustrated. "Fine," she said, before turning to the young man. "Skip, new deadline," she offered, before texting the requirements to him and his sister.

"You want me to buy him six shirts and two ties now, as a reward for making some deadline that hasn't happened yet?"

Skippy beamed. "Thanks boss."

"Challenge!" Georgie growled her correction. She was visibly angry.

"Noooooo!" Zoe exclaimed. "It's still favoritism! You must see it's just the kind of thing Dad's always complaining about. What you should be doing is sending him home for the day without pay. If it was any of these other blokes, you would have!"

Instead of sending another text message, Georgie opened a text document window right on the worktable. A keyboard diagram popped up, allowing her to quickly type a memo. One Tyler could see would be sent to all the engineers before Zoe could mount another protest. The minute she finished typing, email notifications went off on every phone and tablet in the room. Instead of responding to her own, Tyler decided to observe the reactions of the group gathered around the table.

As she expected, Zoe was the first one to comment. "Have you lost your mind?"

A red-faced Georgie turned from Zoe to Tyler. "Please…" Instead of trying to explain, she simply grabbed her cell, sending Tyler her suggestion on how to manage the challenge she had just issued to her entire department. Looking up to get her reaction, Georgie asked simply, "Understood?"

Tyler nodded. It would now be her job to survey the entire engineering department. Zoe had not managed to stop Georgie's offer to buy Skippy shirts and ties. Georgie had simply made the same offer to the entire department. In the memo, she set a new delivery date for a product only identified by number. She would buy six shirts and two ties or scarves for everyone now, in the assumption they would all make their deadline. For those who didn't, they would be responsible for paying her back. Anyone in the department who didn't particularly want the new duds could opt out of a voluntary challenge that was open to everyone in engineering. Tyler could only admire the way she had handled the situation. Although her head swam with the thought of how much it was about to cost her new boss—dozens of shirts would be involved. She read through the text message asking her to find the shirt sizes for every member of Georgie's engineering team, then, when she and Zoe were shopping, to order six shirts and two ties or whatever for each team member, and charge them to her personal account. Tyler nodded her understanding. "Do you have a color preference?"

"Dr Marsh…I trust you."

Georgie turned back to her engineers. "Responder notification?"

"What if we used a subscription formula?" was one suggestion.

"What if they fail to subscribe? Who gets the notification?" another argued.

Georgie agreed. It was interesting to note that once she did, the other engineers followed suit. Tyler watched while she drew on one of the large diagrams. "Virtual PBX?" she suggested to the team. Smiles and nods were universal as she encouraged them to keep voicing solutions.

"What about the voluntary priority…"

"…we certainly can't perform a data dump. What about…"

Tyler tuned out the engineers. Following Zoe, she headed back through the lab to the main door. Maggie, halting their progress, padded over to Tyler and nuzzled her head against her thighs before returning to her dog bed.

Tyler silently considered the experience. It was hard to decide what had surprised her more, the dog's interest in her, Georgie's temper or Zoe's insistence that the rules be adhered to. Rules she herself had attributed to Marnie Pulaski's need to control everything DME. From what Tyler had just witnessed, it was Zoe who had jumped on the young engineer…The light dawned. "Wait, Skippy—he's your brother?"

"Yeah," Zoe admitted as they boarded the elevator. She swiped her hand over the ring of blue sensors before announcing the floor, "Six. Georgie's always been soft with his wimpyness!" She sighed. "Sorry there, Tyler. It's the whole prodigal son thing. I swear my dad thinks he's a frigging genius!"

The elevator doors opened and Zoe charged out heading directly for Marnie's office. She was barely through the double doors to HR when she began her angry narrative of the encounter down in the so-called machine shop. Marnie stood up and with a simple wave of her hand, indicated her current meeting was over, forcing the co-workers gathered around her desk to leave. Tyler didn't like the gesture and judging by the look of those filing out, they weren't happy either. No wonder co-workers were suspicious of the perceived effort to accommodate Georgie. Most of the staff, except for the engineers, might only know her by incidents like this.

While Zoe rattled on about Georgie's supposed breach of company policy, Marnie stood listening to the report without interrupting. As was her habit, she had her ballpoint in hand and clicked furiously in time to Zoe's protest. Once Zoe had exhausted her point, Marnie gave her a list of more immediate concerns and dismissed her.

With the door closed after Zoe, Marnie turned to Tyler. Laying her pen on her desk, she said bluntly, "Tyler, I don't have time for this today." Sinking back into her executive chair, she added, "The twins, my twins, are in some sort of trouble at school. I have to meet the principal in less than an hour."

"I can handle this and make it fair for everyone in engineering, I promise. At least I think that was Zoe's issue. I'm sure there's a lot more involved."

Marnie snorted. Picking up her pen again, she began clicking out her frustration then slammed it back on the desk. "Please sit down," she said, letting out a long labored breath. "I love Zoe but she can be a real pain in my backside. Here's the deal. The twins, Zoe and Skip…"

"They're twins?"

Marnie just nodded. "They're obviously not identical twins, but twins they are. When they were little, they were both crazy about Georgie. They followed her everywhere, would try anything she did and she was great with them. I have to give her credit, she never favored either of them even when they competed for her attention. Of course, they were teenagers when she deployed the last time. So…neither really noticed when she left. Then when she came home, well, you know kids. Their world is very small and it's easy for them to convince themselves of stupid things. Zoe became very judgmental, wanting to blame Georgie for being over there, for getting hit. Sometimes I think she was just angry that Georgie survived. Skippy was the exact opposite. He blamed himself. You know how it goes. *'If only I had spent more time with her before she left, she would have been looking out for missiles, instead of thinking about me!'*" She held up her hand. "Honest to God, that kid came up with more crazy reasons to explain his misplaced guilt than I can shake a stick at. It was a tough time. Thank God my kids were too young to really be affected."

"You know, I didn't really pick up on any bad blood between Georgie and Zoe until this, whatever this was."

"What this was and is about, is the dynamics of this family. I think I mentioned we all assumed Georgie would take over one day?" At Tyler's nod, she pushed on. "How do I explain this…Before my grandfather died, he divided the company shares between his three children. Daniel, Georgina, and Henry each received a third. Henry, as you may have guessed from his ethnicity was not really his son but old Luigi loved him as much and made sure Henry was rewarded for his hard work and loyalty. Of course, when their children grew up, they too entered the family business. I'm sure you know Danny, my dad, died two years ago? Okay, so it's when we get to the kids that things get messed up. All the grandkids grew up together. Georgie's the oldest, then me and Lori Phipps. By the way, Lori runs the boatyard, officially DynaCraft, just so you know. Anyway, Lori and I are only four months apart. Then there was Leslie. She's a chef. She owns the Fleet Street Grill down on the ground level and manages the cafeteria for us."

"That explains why the food is so good."

Smiling, Marnie nodded. "I'll tell her you said that. Lou came almost nine months to the day after Leslie was born. I'll tell you, Henry's taken some razzing for that. Anyway, we were all inseparable as kids. Georgie was our leader and protector. Lori and I were the troublemakers, Stella was the quiet one, Leslie was the tagalong but Lou was, well Lou was Lou! He was always the painful glass-half-empty, sky-is-falling, no-good-will-come-of-this kind of guy but Georgie just had this way with him. It was amazing and it got us out of hot water on many occasions. I miss that about Georgie, the way she could soothe anyone with just a look or a few kind words. When I see her struggle now just to communicate the simplest thing…well, it breaks my heart."

Marnie picked up her pen again then set it down gingerly. "I have to tell you, when Lou came storming in here this morning, it was all I could do not to laugh in his face. Christ, when Zoe explained what happened I nearly pissed my pants. I tell you, I laughed that hard. Of course it pisses me off to no end that Lou keeps going after Georgie. He wants her out and he'll use any excuse he can. You should have seen his face when I explained the requirement to declare the existence of a personal relationship does indeed extend to Georgie but it was the responsibility of the lower-ranking employee to file the declaration with me. If he was determined to file a misconduct report, I explained, I would be happy to fire you once you finished your initial two-year contract!" Winking, Marnie added a wicked smile. "It's the first thing that popped into my head! Anyway, your salary comes partly from the employee health and welfare fund and the rest from Georgie's discretionary budget."

"How does that work?" Tyler asked. "If I may?"

Marnie nodded. "At the completion of each fiscal year we review the departmental budgets. When a department spends less than allotted, the manager of that department gets a bonus. They have several options on how they can split that money. Georgie has always rolled her entire bonus into a separate account to be used for her department. Hence the title discretionary fund!"

"Do the other managers do the same?"

"My husband Jack—have you met him yet?"

Tyler knew Jack Pulaski was the VP of Sales and Marketing, and at Tyler's nod she continued. "Anyway, Jack and Lori use what little they save to sponsor a charity golf tournament every summer. It's turned into a real rivalry between the sales staff and the boat builders. As for operations, my bonus has been going into the health and welfare fund. Of course, the year the state finally started kicking in toward healthcare is the year I'm so over budget it didn't help at all."

Tyler gave her a dutiful smile. "Is that all of the departments that have budgets outside of what...operations, engineering, sales, and boat building?"

"You forgot finance, Lou's department, and before you ask, yes he very cleverly comes in under budget every year and yes he takes his bonus. He's the only one to do it."

Tyler could tell there was a story there but her head was already swimming with new facts she needed to assimilate. About to take her leave, she stopped. "I was surprised when Zoe challenged Georgie so sharply and didn't let up but I was more surprised by Georgie. I half expected the dog to break it up, but Georgie held her ground. Does that happen often?"

"I wish," Marnie admitted as she stood to walk Tyler to the door. Dressed in an expensive suit, her high heels and long wavy hair were the only real contrast to her much more conservative sister. "The machine shop is her safe place. Only her guys and Henry spend any time down there, and the dog. Other than them, only you, me and Zoe have access. Now I'm starting to wonder if Zoe should be on that list. What do you think?"

"She did really hold her own! I was startled by the contrast between the run-in with Lou and this latest incident."

Marnie nodded. "Georgie has an appointment next Tuesday with the occupational therapist. It's mostly speech therapy. I usually go with her but I think you should start taking her. It will give you a better insight into how she's struggling and where she's making progress." She retrieved her pen and began clicking. "I'll be honest with you. There is a lot of pressure to push Georgie out of the company. Not that we would, it's just that…well, the annual general meeting is only a few months away. It would really make a difference if Georgie could stand up and explain her vision herself. She can do it with the engineers, but…"

"But not so much with everyone else, or perhaps everyone not so enamored by the new Georgina DiNamico?"

Marnie nodded, and walked her out of HR.

Returning to her office, Tyler sat quietly before considering the directive Georgie had given her. Grabbing her tablet, she opened her email client list but before she sent out a flash text to everyone in engineering, she set up the survey app Georgie used to share ideas with her team. It was simple. She entered the fields she wanted to capture, posted the survey then sent an urgent email to the department. She gave them each thirty minutes to take up Georgie's challenge.

With that done she turned her attention to the next task. Just that morning, a dozen banker's boxes had been unceremoniously dumped in her office. They contained items from annual reports to technical bulletins and everything in between. Tyler had begun to catalog the lot before shelving them in order. It only took her a moment to find what she was looking for. A hardcover book that had been published in the seventies: *The Dynamic Marine Machines.*

Pulling the glossy volume off the shelf, she made herself comfortable on the new leather love seat. The couch, she learned, was one of the furnishings Georgie had ordered specifically for her. Chapter one had everything she needed to know. It told the story of how old Luigi DiNamico had come to America just after the First World War. A trained Fiat mechanic, Luigi had served in the Italian Red Cross driving an ambulance, right alongside an American writer he referred to as "Hemi." Tyler doubted that it was actually Hemingway, but had to admire the old man's gumption. The introductory chapter went on to describe the early days of DynaCraft boats and some of their famous buyers. Looking over a series of photos taken of various cedar strip runabouts, she had to admit that maybe old Luigi wasn't as full of it as she suspected. A double page colorized picture from the thirties revealed a long sleek dual cockpit speedboat. Two Hollywood beauties waved from the rear bench. Up front, a ruggedly handsome Luigi DiNamico stood waving next to the operator, who did indeed look suspiciously like a young Ernest Hemingway. Flipping to the next page, she read the caption. "Lou DiNamico and *Toronto Star* reporter Ernest Hemingway take the first DynaCraft Lake Master for a spin! Circa 1920, Buffalo, New York." *Interesting!* Tyler thumbed through the rest of the book, only stopping at the last chapter: "The Dynamic -Future." Among the horsepower charts and engine diagrams were several more pictures of boats, motors and personnel. The second to last picture was a family shot. The now elderly and frail-looking Luigi DiNamico stood in front of a sailing yacht in dry dock. The caption listed the people beside him as his three children. Sure enough, beside the old guy stood Danny and Henry and Georgie. She had to take a closer look to realize the Georgina in the picture was not her Georgie but Georgie's aunt.

Examining the photo carefully, she admitted their looks were similar but not identical. She had to wonder about the woman who had once held the reins, ever so briefly, at DME. Flipping to the front page, she checked the Library of Congress catalog info. The book was a first edition; she doubted there were any others. It had been printed in 1979.

A notice sounded from her tablet. Putting the book aside, Tyler returned to her desk to review the results of the challenge she had posted. Surprisingly, all the engineers had taken the survey. Scrolling through the results she smiled, wondering what Zoe would make of her response to Georgie's directive to use her own judgment. It would certainly make their planned afternoon shopping venture interesting.

As if reading her mind, Zoe breezed into her office asking breathlessly, "You ready?"

"It's a little early for lunch, don't you think?"

Zoe just grinned her most mischievous grin. She was wearing a multicolored print dress that screamed nightclub not office. She had already donned her winter boots, tall leather things with heels even Tyler wouldn't risk. "Marnie wants us to give Georgie's wardrobe the once-over. Boat season is just around the corner. If we don't get her squared away now, we may not get a chance again for months and months."

"The boat season? It's only December!"

"Boat Show season, sorry about that. Everything kicks off right away, once the New Year rolls in. As for the rest of this month...well, I did warn you this is a family company."

"Every day!"

Zoe laughed off the retort, waving at Tyler to follow. "Come on. How often do you get to rummage through someone else's wardrobe?"

Tyler had to admit this would be a first.

* * *

At precisely eleven thirty a.m., Georgie DiNamico turned on her cell phone and opened her email. It had long been her habit to work without disruption until eleven thirty, and while Marnie had made that rule the law at work, she could only control so much of the outside world. In response, she had insisted that Georgie make a habit of blocking out all distractions for as long as she could. Together they had set aside the entire morning, or at least until half-past eleven, as her dedicated research time. While Georgie always started long before eight, protecting her attention as she worked her way into her day was paramount in making sure she herself judged the time well spent. They could hold her calls and email, even turn off notifications, but she couldn't prevent interruptions from certain family members. Whenever something interrupted her process, Georgie would head down to the machine shop and help her team with their roadblocks. It had proven to be the best way to put her back on track. That and a long walk with Maggie.

Georgie slid into her desk chair, grumbling to herself as she tried to put the events of the morning into perspective. She couldn't decide what bothered her more, the fact that Lou had assumed she would act inappropriately with an employee or Marnie laughing at the idea of Georgie proposing.

"It could happen!" Openly sulking, even she had to admit it was a long shot. Marnie was always introducing her to women she would call good wife prospects and to be honest they were all very nice but...but who was she kidding. She couldn't talk and chew gum at the same time. Hell, there were days when she couldn't remember how to tie her shoes, although she never forgot certain basics: her name, who she was and where she was from. She could clearly recall the details of her life before the accident with surprising clarity. Even after that fateful period, her memory was highly functional. Her problems stemmed from an inability to understand why she remembered the way she did, as if those things she did recall were simply stories that had been told to her, not her own experiences. How could she explain that to someone or even communicate how much she cared when she wasn't always certain of her own knowledge?

As for Marnie's prospect list, they were all very nice women but she knew them from the Yacht Club and in most cases that was the be-all and end-all to their world. She understood why Marnie considered them good candidates. They were all wifely types. The type of woman who can make a career of being the perfect spouse. Georgie even understood how attractive that could be, having someone to care for you, and it was exactly what turned her off to Marnie's prospects. Care versus share. Having someone to take care of you sounded nice and all but it didn't sound like much of a partnership. Having a wife would solve many things for Marnie but was that really a reason to get involved with someone? As lonely as she was, it didn't sound right or fair.

Removing a leather-bound journal from the locked top drawer of her desk, she flipped it open. She wanted to get her thoughts down on paper. Moments of such clarity, whether personal or technical, where always more easily recorded on paper. It was a technique one of the doctors had introduced, explaining that she would be using a completely different set of neural pathways when writing about a thought as opposed to talking about it or even entering the exact same words on a keyboard. Finding a new page, she recorded the date, adding:

I have been telling myself I don't want a relationship because it wouldn't be fair to my partner to assume the extra care I may one day need. Maybe that's an excuse. I'm lucky to be alive. I'm lucky to have a great family. No matter what the future may bring, I'm financially sound and in a position to hire any assistance I need. So what's really scaring me? Am I too old? Too broken? What if no one wants someone like me, no one but those Yacht Club social climbers?

She could admit that helping Tyler with her chair had been an excuse to drop in and see how she was adjusting. Of course, she chided herself, a normal person would just ask how she was doing. Before she could berate herself more, an email popped up from Tyler. Putting the journal away and relocking the drawer, she clicked it open.

Georgie had to admit her relief that Tyler hadn't sent her notice that she quit. After Lou's temper tantrum, she had been beside herself with anxiety over Tyler's reaction. She couldn't help but feel she had let her down. If only she was as fast with her mouth as she was with her hands. She had felt like she should have defended her from Lou, although the idea was ridiculous. Tyler was a grown woman who could stand up for herself. Still, it irked her to have failed to come to her defense. Of course, she would have, given enough time or if Lou were actually determined to carry his prejudicial assumptions forward. Then there was Marnie's reaction over the entire thing.

After Georgie and Maggie had spent some time in the machine shop working through some new ideas with the guys, she had presented herself to Marnie, prepared to explain herself and remove any blame Lou may have pressed on Tyler. What she didn't expect was Marnie's jovial attitude. Yes, stomping on their cousin Lou was always good for Marnie's mood but the real joke had been squarely aimed at her. Which hurt more, the fact that her sister thought it was hilarious that her gaydar hadn't pinged on Tyler? Or that Marnie believed someone like Tyler would never go out with the likes of her?

She read through Tyler's email, noting that all the engineers had taken up the shirt and tie challenge. Georgie ran the numbers through her head, quickly checking the order listed.

Shirts – Men's: 252
Shirts – Women's: 42
Ties – Bow Ties: 4
Ties – Neckties: 84
Ties – Neck Scarves: 10

The numbers looked good, even though the total ties was heavy two orders. Thinking about it, she realized that two of her female engineers had probably asked for neckties instead of those scarffy things. She couldn't blame them. She could never figure out how to wear one of those and had to admire those women who could. Trying to concentrate on the email, Georgie was overwhelmed by the temptation to calculate the length of material needed to drape around Tyler's shoulders one, two...

Rereading the email, she stumbled at Tyler's request. She would be placing orders for several items she and Zoe judged necessary to augment her wardrobe for the winter. Now was her one opportunity to voice her preferences. Georgie wasn't upset that Tyler had asked or that she had demanded her immediate feedback. She was caught by simply being asked. How long had it been since someone asked for her opinion that didn't involve a line of code or schematic drawing?

She rested her fingers on the keyboard. This felt like a special occasion or maybe a test. Georgie loved tests. If Tyler wanted her input, she would give it to her but what exactly could she say. *I like blue?* No wonder Marnie and Zoe never asked about such things. Not willing to give up, she began tentatively before accelerating into a furious pace, needing to get everything down while she could. Once she did, she hit Send without rereading her entry. If she didn't reread it, she reasoned with herself, she couldn't change her mind.

* * *

Tyler read Georgie's email while Zoe maneuvered through the downtown core. She was not a great driver, making it all the more difficult for Tyler to concentrate. Finally giving up, at least until they came to a full and complete stop, she turned her attention to Zoe. "By the way, nice wheels."

Zoe all but snorted as she impatiently maneuvered around a car waiting to turn. "This unwieldy bitch belongs to Georgie. Good thing you like it. It's what you'll be driving."

"What—wait! This is a Land Rover! A new Land Rover! You don't actually expect me to drive this thing do you?"

"If I can handle her, so can you."

"I'm not worried about handling *her*! What if someone hits me or…"

"Relax," Zoe soothed. "Georgie doesn't care. 'We're insured' is all she ever says. Here we are," she announced, switched off the ignition and threw the driver's door open. The immediate blare of a car horn made her pull the door back until the threatening vehicle passed. "See!" She offered her carelessness as proof positive of the SUV's perceived ungainliness. "Let's see Georgie's tailor first, then we can grab some lunch. We'll need the time to decide how to tackle this stupid shirt and tie business. Georgie and her bloody ideas!" she moaned as she yanked the shop door open.

They were greeted with the sights of a high-class men's haberdashery although it was obvious this particular outfitter had long adapted to female clients too. While one side of the shop was lined with men's suits and mahogany shelves stocked with a rainbow of shirts, the opposite side mirrored the layout but was stocked with suits and shirts for female clientele. A set of three headless mannequins graced each side and delineated the proprietor's idea of upscale casual, serious business attire and formal wear. Tyler was immediately drawn to the woman's tuxedo on display. She knew she had the height and physique to pull it off, but wearing a tux did nothing for her. Tracing her fingers along the traditional rounded silk collar of the jacket, she could imagine Georgie looking very noble in the getup.

"I don't see the attraction," Zoe scoffed from beside her. "Although you would look rather dashing!"

"Not my thing either," Tyler admitted, "but it would look gorgeous on Georgie." That comment drove up Zoe's eyebrows. "You're the one who said she needed something formal to wear other than her dress uniform. You have to admit the emerald waistcoat is a perfect match to her eyes."

"You noticed her eyes? Should I be jealous?"

"What—"

A swarthy gentleman of indeterminate years shuffled into the showroom, arms stretched in greeting and with a genuine smile to match. "Zoe! My sweet girl. Is it that time of year already?"

"You know it is, you wily old coot!"

"This is how you talk to your dearest uncle?" The old tailor pulled her into a gentle hug before holding her out for examination. "You're more beautiful every year and what's this I hear, you're working for my little Marnie?"

"I am." Zoe took the old man by the arm and steered him toward Tyler. "Uncle John, this is Tyler Marsh. She's Georgie's new right-hand man, er, woman, so to speak."

"Ah, the doctor who will be caring for the little namesake of my beloved Georgina!" he said, turning his eyes toward the ceiling and adding solemnly, "May she rest in peace."

Before Tyler could explain that she wasn't that kind of doctor or ask what he was referring to, Zoe jumped in, challenging him, "Marnie's been on the horn, hasn't she?"

He patted his chest pocket. "I already have the list. Would you like to see what I have chosen for our girl?"

"Hardly." Zoe waved him off. "Well, if that's all set..."

"Wait a sec," Tyler interrupted, surprising the other two. Turning to the old tailor, she stuck out her hand. "Hello John, I'm Tyler and I have my own list from Georgie and I would very much like to see what you have already chosen. I also have something else to discuss. A rather large shirt order?"

"Oh please! Tyler, you're not taking Georgie seriously. Are you?"

Shocked to learn that Zoe had no intention of following up on her boss's directive, Tyler made a mental note about the refusal. "Georgie gave me detailed instructions. Instructions of which Marnie approved."

Zoe appeared momentarily stymied by that statement, while John, first hesitant—then pleased—offered his most gracious smile. "How about this. I'll show you everything and then we'll talk shirts?"

Tyler smiled at the old man. "Sounds like a plan."

It took a little over two hours to completely update and augment Georgie's annual clothing order, along with several additions, including the ladies' tux complete with emerald green waistcoat. The shirt order that Zoe had been so negative about ended up being the easiest part. The app Tyler had used to gather the relevant details from the engineers had created a purchase list of sizes and numbers. Style and color were up to Tyler to decide. With old John's help and surprising insights from Zoe, they chose two white shirts, two colored, and two denim as the gift set. The denim shirts would include custom embroidery above the left pocket, one with the DME emblem and one with the retro DynaCraft logo. For the ties and scarves, they chose one that looked suspiciously like a boarding school tie. The colors were a good match to the DME emblem and would work well with pretty much any clothing choice. As a bonus, it was available in all three styles: necktie, bow tie and neck scarf. That took care of one of the two ties Georgie had offered up in her impromptu milestone challenge.

For the second tie, John suggested, "Perhaps something fun? Maybe a novelty pattern. I have one with little anchors or this one," he offered, holding out a navy tie with white and powder blue sailboats.

Zoe pulled another navy tie from the display. This one featured a discreet pattern of tiny gold specks. On closer examination, it was easy to identify them as three-bladed boat propellers and very close in design to the DME logo. "I think this will work and I think the engineers will get it. Although they're a hardheaded lot."

"It's perfect," Tyler agreed. "It'll go with anything and I think they'll get a kick out of it. Can you order them in all three styles as well?"

"Of course!"

By the time Zoe and Tyler sat down in the restaurant, they were famished.

"I think I'll order a bevy," Zoe stated. "If you're ready to drive the beast, that is?"

Tyler, seated across from her in the sequestered booth, nodded while reading through the menu. "Go ahead. Actually," she added, "maybe I'll have one too."

"Sorry gorgeous, but old Georgie Porgie has two rules about her stupid truck. No drinking and driving, and no pulling the dean's car out of Lake Erie with a mooring line hooked to the back bumper."

The way she said it, so matter-of-factly, Tyler had to replay the comment in her brain. "Okay—that sounds like a story."

Zoe's infectious grin was back. "How 'bout we order?" she asked, tipping her head toward the approaching waitress.

Once Zoe was happily sipping on her imported beer, Tyler pulled out her tablet. "I was surprised to hear the company doesn't do anything for Christmas. I would've thought it would be a big deal in a company that's basically all family."

"That's actually one of the reasons—well, both reasons. The old boys, my granddad and Georgie's dad, both thought the money and effort should be better spent at home. The other is the first Georgina. You know about Georgina senior?"

"I've had a cursory read through the company history."

"The way I understand it, Winnie, Georgie and Marnie's mom, and my grandma Gloria used to give out Christmas baskets to all the employees. You know, turkeys and the like during their big Christmas party the day before Christmas.

They had it out at the boatyard every year. It was a huge deal with gifts, toys and prizes for the kids, all sorts of bonuses and awards and food galore. Anyway, this one particular year they were out at the boatyard for the party. On the drive back there was a fatal accident on the I-95."

"Oh my God!"

Zoe nodded solemnly. "Great-granddad Luigi was driving the grandmums home, and Georgina senior hitched a ride with them. They were hit by a drunk driver. It's still almost impossible to get Henry to talk about it and Georgie, well she was just seven at the time. Marnie, Lori, and Leslie were all just little tots. They were still back at the party with Danny and Henry when it happened."

"Where was your father?"

"Back at the big house with Georgie's grandmom. He was just a newborn. I think he was all of three months. Henry said he was lucky not to be with my grandmom. Evidently he had a little fever, so Sophia had stayed home with him so my grandmother could enjoy the party."

Tyler was silent for a long time. The weight of such a family tragedy was hard to comprehend.

"I can't imagine what things were like back then but Georgie, our Georgie, refused to be separated from old Danny and Henry. Someone said it was like all three had lost their soul mates. I guess in a way it explains the bond she shares with my granddad."

"Of course," Tyler agreed, not really knowing what else to say. The burden of the tragedy was almost unfathomable.

"You want to know the kicker? They said Luigi and the old girls went instantly, thank God, but old Georgina, well she fought like the dickens. The drunk didn't, couldn't kill her. It was the bloody post-surgical complications and infections that did her in!" Zoe smacked her beer glass down with such force that most of the restaurant's patrons turned to look. When curious eyes met Zoe's stern glare, they returned their attention to their own companions.

"I'm so sorry—what a horrible tragedy. It certainly explains why Christmas is such a sore point."

"I think it's why New Year's has become so important for everyone. You know, put the tragedy of the past behind and all that."

On her phone, Tyler opened Georgie's calendar. "New Year's Eve is in two and a half weeks. John promised to have everything delivered in time. Can we count on that?"

"Absolutely! John may be a big poofter who tries to convince everyone he lost the love of his life when Georgina senior died but the man has never missed a deadline. On the other hand, my beloved brother Skippy has never met a deadline he couldn't miss."

"Weren't you just mentioning something about pulling the dean's car from Lake Erie?"

Zoe tried to suppress her amusement as the waitress delivered their lunch and refilled Tyler's coffee cup.

While they launched wholeheartedly into their meal, Tyler had to consider all that she had learned. It was only her first week at DME and it had already included an impromptu inspection of her boss's home. What an eye-opener. When they'd stepped off the elevator on the penthouse level, the first thing Tyler had noticed were the three separate, ornately framed oak panel doors. While beautifully detailed, there were no door numbers or placards to indicate which door belonged to which unit. "How do visitors know which door to knock at?"

Zoe waved a hand at the marble floor. A compass rose was inlaid in fine detail. "Henry's in the northeast unit, here," she pointed before swiping her hand over some unseen sensor. As the lock released, she pushed the door open for Tyler to take a peek. "My aunt Leslie owns the southeast unit, there," she explained, indicating the door opposite Henry's. "Back in the seventies, long before our time, old Luigi converted the top two floors into condominiums. He had planned to convert others. Of course the economy collapsed, changing his mind for him. These suites were already done but never sold. Years later, Henry took one and Uncle Danny—Georgie and Marnie's dad—took the other. We used to call them the old bachelor pads."

"I take it Georgie is now living in her father's unit?"

"No actually. My Aunt Leslie got Uncle Dan's flat. Georgie took one of the empty ones. She wanted to design the layout herself. It's this one: west. Luigi named this one the Bow Suite. Let's try your pass card to make sure it works."

Tyler removed her employee badge from her suit jacket, swiping it along the oak molding where Zoe pointed. Hearing the lock release, she pushed the heavy door open and held it for her to lead the way. Following her along the darkened foyer, Tyler was forced to a stop, suddenly overwhelmed by sunlight, needing a moment for her eyes to adjust. Like Georgie's office downstairs, sunlight pouring through the uncovered windows was temporarily blinding. Once her eyes became accustomed to the brightness of the room, she took a long moment to scan the generous living space.

Georgie's flat, as Zoe kept calling it, turned out to be very nearly identical to the executive lobby and her office. While the apartment lacked the custom two-story windows that the executive level featured, the prowshape of the building's west end featured just as prominently. Zoe pointed out that the bedrooms were actually up on the mezzanine level while the living room, library and the open concept kitchen and dining room were down the circular staircase. Following her down, Tyler couldn't help but admire the highly polished antique brass. "What's with the space around the center pole? I've never seen a circular staircase quite like this. Did they have it custom-made?"

Zoe all but snorted her amusement. "Actually old Luigi found this one. That man was a bargain hunter of the extreme sort. Have you noticed the carved brickwork and all the big brass fixtures on the outside of the building?"

"Of course I have. The DiNamico building has always been Buffalo's best example of art deco."

"Completely by accident," she asserted. "Way back during the Depression, old Luigi and the family fared better than most.

His way of giving back was to go about buying up building materials and such before creditors could grab assets and send them to auction. It made him quite a local hero at the time. Henry says it was a bloody good thing. It made a reputation for the old boy that protected him and the company during the Second World War."

"Protected?"

"Italy was our enemy. Remember? And DiNamico is definitely Italian!"

"Yes of course but…Sorry, finish your story."

"Well from what I understand everyone loved the old boy. This, well," she said, patting the railing of the circular staircase, "there used to be an old fire station out on Route 5. When they tore it down, old Luigi scored it and more, all for a few hundred bucks."

"Oh my God!" Tyler got it now, looking back over the circular staircase from the bottom step. "It's a fireman's pole in the middle! That's too funny."

"Except when Georgie decides to go down that pole; makes the dog crazy!"

"Oh God…" Tyler was still laughing, "That's something I can see! I love it!"

Zoe just shook her head. "You and old Luigi would've got on fine."

Before heading back up to survey Georgie's wardrobe, Zoe took her for a complete tour of the apartment. The open concept living area was about the same size and setup as the executive office downstairs but featured a very traditional finish. Built-in bookshelves and cabinets lined the walls, but there was relatively little in the way of furniture. A single well-worn leather couch sat facing the stone fireplace and was draped with an old wool blanket and mismatched pillows. The bookshelves, in contrast to the empty room, were chock-a-block with books and mementos, making the space warmer and much more personal. Tyler couldn't help but admire the overwhelming number of books. In between the volumes, several personal keepsakes were displayed or used as bookends. The end tables too were loaded with stacks of books neatly piled beside yellow pads of paper and assorted cups full of pens and pencils. "Wow, she really loves books!"

"I know," Zoe grumbled, as if being a bibliophile was a bad thing. Tyler was about to challenge her assumption when she added, "You haven't seen the rest—it gets worse!" Leading them past the fireplace and the only furniture in the room, Zoe headed for the double doors behind them. She waved a hand for Tyler to take a look. "This is the library. Although the whole flat looks like a library to me!"

Inside the medium-sized room was more wall-to-wall custom cabinetry. Only about half of the shelves were stocked and all with binders and manuals. While there was plenty of shelving for more, the entire floor was littered with stacks of books and several boxes overflowing with documents and reports. The only furniture, a folding table, was stacked with reports and an inch thick layer of technical drawings, plus more cups of writing utensils and more yellow notepads. A pair of mismatched folding chairs bracketed the isolated worktable and made the space seem confusingly attractive, forcing Tyler to scold her own academic inclinations. They made her feel sympathetic to the creative desire for organized chaos. It was easy to imagine getting an amazing amount of work done in a room like this. In her parents' home, the kitchen had always served as her study hall. She understood this room. "Why no furniture?"

"I guess she hasn't gotten around to it. It's not like it's a priority for her. Anyway, it works for us."

"How's that?"

"Oh, I guess I forgot to mention, we're in charge of the New Year's Eve party."

"What?"

"Relax," Zoe said, offering her most charming smile. "My Aunt Leslie takes care of the catering. So that's done. And, we have it up here and open up the empty unit. Actually, we open all of the units but the party will be here and next door. So that takes care of the location." She checked off points on her fingers. "Marnie handles the invites, so that's done. We're well on our way to getting Georgie squared away as far as clothing and such. Now all that's left," she added, pointing to her baby finger, "is to get this place squared away and order the tables and chairs, linens and that sort of thing. If you help me with the numbers, I'll make all the calls. How's that sound?"

Tyler nodded her agreement. Taking another look around the room, she had to ask, "What will we do with all this? I mean, if I were working on something this involved, the last thing I would appreciate is having it all put away on me."

"My gorgeous Tyler—you wound me," Zoe said, dramatically placing her hand over her heart. "I am not a beast. I know this all means something to Georgie. We'll just lock this room and the other. No one needs to see Georgie's safe place."

"Safe place? Do you mean a safe room?"

"Sort of. Come on, let me show you the rest." Leading her back up the circular staircase and down the hall, Zoe waved Tyler into a large bedroom. Like the other rooms, this one too featured built-in cabinetry that had been designed to complement the room's furnishings. The antique sleigh bed and matching dressing tables, desk and end tables were darkly stained burled oak finished with a French polish. "This was great-aunt Georgina's bedroom suite," Zoe explained quietly. "Back when the whole family was living out at the big house and Georgina senior passed, they moved our Georgie into her auntie's room."

"Whose idea was that?"

"Georgie's!" Zoe answered. "Granddad and Uncle Danny must have thought it fine or it never would have happened. It's funny, when everything went tits-up with Margaret, this old set was the only thing she fought for. In a way, it really helped her. Sort of put the wind back in her sails. You know, just when we all thought she'd given up."

Tyler nodded, acknowledging the logic. Not completely comfortable discussing her boss's mental health history, she took one last look around the room. "Ah, where's this closet you promised me?"

Smiling, Zoe led her through the master bath to the walk-in, or in this case walk-through closet. Like the rest of the condo, the room was fitted out with custom cabinetry. Spacewise, she guessed it was probably as large as her entire bedroom at home. "All the custom moldings and cabinets must have cost a fortune!"

"You'd think," Zoe huffed disapprovingly. At Tyler's raised eyebrows she added. "'Bout three years ago my dad realized the millwork was losing a lot of money."

"You have a millwork too? What for?"

"We did. It was for the boatyard. They used to turn out all that fancy wood trim stuff they use on the sailboats. Before that it turned out all the shiplaps and such for the original DynaCraft line. You know about those? The old wood runabouts?"

Tyler nodded, then pushed Zoe gently back on point. "So Lou shut down the mill. And?"

"And, Georgie hired back the men who had been laid off until they could get their retirements all sorted. And...she bought all this oak at cost, before the millwork stock auction."

Tyler ran her hand across the closest cabinet. The dark stain was rich in deep chocolates and crimson reds and like the cherished bedroom furniture was finished with a deep French polish. "Still...I can't imagine."

"I guess it helps that Georgie's filthy rich. Well," Zoe said with a grin, "not Oprah filthy rich but at least she doesn't have to worry. Not like the rest of us. Come on, I'll show you the safe space then we can get the inventory out of the way and be off on our adventure!"

"Sounds good to me." Tyler was unwilling to be drawn into a conversation about family and money, two topics she knew from experience could get quite explosive. Following Zoe, she entered a virtually empty room. Unlike the rest of the condo, there were no cabinets or shelving of any kind. The only woodwork was the painted builder-grade baseboards. The sky-blue walls did nothing to alleviate the clinical feel of the room. The one prominent furnishing was a standard hospital bed. Close by, on the floor, lay a large dog bed. Across the room, next to another door, sat an antique upholstered dining chair that looked remarkably out of place.

Zoe pointed to the two other doors leading from the room. "That one's the laundry room, and that one," pointing to the one by the chair, "leads to Henry's. They keep it open at night, just in case."

"Just in case?"

"Just in case Georgie has one of her nightmares."

"Does she sleep in here every night?"

Making her way back to the walk-through closet, Zoe shrugged. "Damned if I know. Come on. Let's get this done then we can head over to the tailor's shop."

Tyler had followed without comment. Switching on her ever-present tablet, she had opened the document Marnie had given her listing her sister's clothing needs. "Okay, where do we begin?"

CHAPTER FOUR

Georgie sat in the backseat of her sister's Navigator, arms crossed and head down, protesting, "No—I am not, no!"

Standing by the open back door of the Navigator and shivering in the freezing night, Lori Phipps begged her cousin with zeal and an exaggerated grin. "Oh come on Georgie Porgie, let's go kiss the girls!"

"Make them cry…" Georgie finished the last words of the well-worn stanza.

"Goddammit Georgie!" Marnie, still in the driver's seat, softened her tone as she said, "Okay, okay, it's not like we expect you to go in there and get laid like Jack suggested. It's just time to do a little socializing. Lori and I will be with you the whole time. Just like always. We'll go in, have a beer, and if you feel like it, you can even drag my old bones onto the dance floor. How about that?" she bargained.

Hesitating a few moments more, Georgie finally pushed herself from the safety of the SUV.

Looping her arm through hers, Lori reminded her, "Relax Bender, tonight's just about reconnaissance, and beer. Recon and beer! And, maybe we can find some big butch broad to drag Marnie out onto the dance floor! Whadya say?"

"Butch...Broads? Really? Oh Aunt Glory Bee..."

"Don't worry, I would never call any butch a broad to her face. My mamma didn't raise no fool!"

"No," Marnie said. "Your father raised you to be a lady. Now act like it. I'll pay the cover while you two cover my back. Every time we do this, Jack worries I'll come home with my own lez-be-friend."

Lori huffed at that. "More like he wishes you'd bring a friend home to share."

"Don't get me started on that," Marnie replied casually. After paying the cover charge, she led them through the familiar local lesbian hangout. The Friday night crowd was packed a little tighter than Marnie liked but this regular exercise was about getting Georgie to socialize, not her own comfort.

They managed to find a table near the back and farthest from the dance floor and the pounding rhythm pouring from the massive speakers. Trying to think and converse with loud distracting noises was very difficult for Georgie. Part of tonight's exercise was to get her talking and keep her talking. Luckily, getting women to their table was Lori's job. She was a regular and well-liked by the staff and patrons. The women who had socialized with them in the past were not what Marnie would categorize as optimal partner material, at least not for her sister. They were mostly young, around Zoe's age, or very working class. Not that class would preclude anyone from Marnie's secret list of perspective wives. She had a very clear picture in mind for Georgie's happily ever after. She wanted someone a little younger, but mature enough to enjoy a quiet life. Someone she could trust with Georgie's well-being, not to mention her money.

As much as she loved her sister, she had, she reminded herself, a family and job of her own. It wasn't as if Georgie took advantage of her time or energy. She was just incapable of a balance. Her entire existence was wrapped around work. That wasn't such a bad thing, at least not as profits went, but as a life—not so much. Georgie worked seven days a week, and often around the clock. If she didn't have to walk that dog, she would never even know if it was day or night. Marnie wanted someone for her who could provide a more balanced life. Someone of similar intellect but not some woman married to her own career. Or after her money. Marnie had her sights set on finding Georgie a real wife. Someone who could go toe-to-toe with her sister, and be strong enough to assume her care, and trustworthy enough to manage her estate. She also thought it paramount that any perspective partner be educated, or at least well read. Georgie had a voracious appetite for everything remotely literary. Her monthly personal reading purchases rarely came in below five hundred bucks, and that was just her Kindle downloads. Looking around, she knew they'd never meet the kind of woman Georgie needed in a place like this. But here at least, she would get a chance to converse with other women.

That's when she noticed Zoe across the room. She was on the edge of the dance floor, longneck bottle in hand and gorgeous in a red dress Marnie would have killed to be able to pull off for herself. She reached out to tell Georgie who she had spotted when she recognized someone else. Tyler Marsh was standing next to Zoe. She cut an attractive figure in her little black dress. Before she could let her sister know their niece and her new assistant were both there, Lori slammed four bottles down.

"Guess who's here?"

Marnie watched as Georgie turned an anxious eye to her cousin. Before Lori could drop the bomb, a soft-looking blonde in too-tight jeans and a too-loose blouse threw her arms around Lori, planting on her a long showy kiss. When the woman pulled back, she leaned around Lori and stuck out her hand. "You must be Lori's cousin. I've always wanted to meet you," she said, slapping Lori on the arm. "Why didn't you introduce us, you oaf! She's cute! Now get out of my way so I can get acquainted."

"Back off, Jersey!"

"What's the problem? I thought you wanted me to meet her?"

"Not that one, you dumb ass!"

Confused, the blonde turned back to the table, seeing Georgie for the first time. "Oh—well…Is that beer for me?"

Before Lori could say more, the blonde circled around her, pulling a chair up beside Marnie. It was at times like these when Marnie actually felt bad for her husband. Jack was roguishly handsome, fit and fun, and the women flocked to him wherever they went. Most would back off when they learned he was married but there were always a few who considered it a challenge. She had accused him of enjoying the attention a little too much but after being hit on by more than a few women, she had come to sympathize with her husband's plight.

Across the table Lori slid into her seat and putting an arm around Georgie, pointed to the dance floor. "Looks like our Zoe's found herself a new babe. Wonder how long this one will last." While Georgie's eyes searched the dance floor for her young cousin, Lori took the chance to guzzle a third of her beer. "I wish I had her stamina," she added. "Christ, if I could get my hands on a hot skinny piece like that, I'd nail her ass against…"

Georgie had been combing the dance floor for a glimpse of Zoe. As Lori began graphically describing her interest in Zoe's date, she spotted her and Tyler.

Before Marnie could intervene, she grabbed Lori by the scruff of her neck and held on as she knocked them both to the floor. "STOP!" Marnie ordered. She had her hands on Georgie's arm, pulling her back. "Georgie, let her go for Christ's sake!"

Georgie began to loosen her hold, but wouldn't unhand Lori completely.

When the bouncer pushed in to break it up, Marnie admitted defeat. Chalk up one more social disaster for her family. As the bouncer manhandled Lori and Georgie out the door, Marnie followed, after gathering coats and bags.

Once they were clear of the entrance and the line of women still waiting to enter, Marnie scolded them both. "What the hell was that? You two embarrassed the shit out of me!"

"You? What about me?" Lori challenged. "Old Bender here just got me heaved from my local!"

Both women turned to Georgie for an explanation. Her face was pale and she looked cold.

"In the truck!" Marnie ordered, wrapping Georgie's coat around her shoulders. Once they were in the Navigator and welcome heat blasted from the vents, she turned to her cousin. "Lori, the young woman you were so graphically...graphic about, works for us. Actually, she's Georgie's new assistant."

Wide-eyed, Lori turned from the passenger seat to Georgie in the back. "Hey dude, I am so sorry! Way out of line there!"

"She's nice...smart. Educated..." Georgie trailed off.

"And going out with Zoe? How does that work? No offense Georgie Porgie, but Zoe doesn't do nice!"

"Okay that's enough!" Marnie warned them both. "What goes on between two consenting adults outside of work is none of our business. Is that understood?"

"Hey, I'm cool," Lori offered, raising her hands in surrender. "I was just pointing out the obvious. No hard feelings. Okay Bender?"

"Yeah, cool," she said quietly, before cheerily admitting, "Cannot remember...last time, kicked out of—a—bar?"

CHAPTER FIVE

Still shivering from the early morning cold, Tyler hung her winter coat on the back of her office door and retrieved her inside footwear from under her desk. She had been prepared to adjust her working style to suit her boss's schedule but after three weeks at DME, she realized it was Georgie DiNamico who seemed to need time to adapt to her presence. Both women would get their best work done early in the day, and Tyler, now better acquainted with her boss's trouble with keeping focus, knew Georgie preferred to not be disturbed unless needed. Tyler would wait until exactly eleven thirty each morning before sitting down with Georgie to review her afternoon appointment schedule. Georgie never took morning appointments, not even with Marnie. If Marnie needed something, she would wait like everyone else. Only one person continuously broke that rule. Well, two actually: Henry, who seemed to have some sort of sixth sense about Georgie's vulnerability, and the chief financial officer, who didn't appear to care if he was interrupting her or how his interruption might affect her work or her mood.

While she was tucking away her insulated winter boots, Zoe wandered in with two coffee cups. Tyler smelled the happy aroma of the custom coffee blend long before hearing her workmate's standard greeting, "Hey gorgeous! Ready for another kick at the can?"

"Good morning Zoe!" Smiling, she accepted the coffee, breathing in the aromatic steam, letting the hot mug warm her hands. Tyler did appreciate Zoe's compliment; she just wondered why she continued flirting with her at work. For someone who was such a stickler for the rules, she seemed more than willing to bend them when it came to her own agenda.

"You left early?"

"One a.m. is not early. Maybe I'm getting too old to keep up. You're not mad are you?"

Zoe's smile was more than salacious. "I was a tad disappointed. Don't worry though, you can make it up to me. Next time."

Tyler nodded, sipping her coffee without comment. They had gotten together twice now and Tyler wasn't sure she wanted a repeat. Zoe had been fun to party with but she was young and on the aggressive side when drunk. Their last date had taken them to the local lesbian bar where they had spent most of the night dancing. She was having a blast and couldn't remember the last time she spent so much time on the dance floor. It was the reason she hadn't noticed how much Zoe had drunk. Not until she cornered Tyler in the washroom.

Grabbing Tyler possessively, Zoe had forced her roughly against the wall, kissing Tyler hard and forcing her tongue into her mouth. Pushing Zoe back, she was stunned by the fiery look that greeted her and Zoe's undaunted aggression. Zoe pinned her hands behind her head and holding them in a painful grip, used her free hand to rake her fingers down Tyler's neck and over her breast. It was exciting and upsetting at the same time and took all of Tyler's strength to push her off. "Zoe, what the fuck?" Before she could stop her, the woman leaned back in again and painfully nipped at Tyler's neck.

"Next time," she offered casually, turning for the door.

Tyler followed her back to the bar. Not exactly sure what to do or say. The decision was made when Zoe ordered another drink.

"Listen Zoe, it's getting late. I'm going to head home."

Only half turning to acknowledge her, Zoe waved her off. "Whatever."

Tyler had been stunned by her attitude and pissed off by her behavior and intended to discuss it today over lunch. That plan had been shelved when Zoe called her Sunday afternoon to say she was sorry for being such an ass. While Tyler was more than happy to accept the apology, she wasn't ready to consider another date. Pushing her feelings aside, she took a careful look at Zoe's usually radiant features, only now realizing how tired she appeared. "You okay? You look beat."

Zoe seemed to study her over the rim of her cup. Like Tyler, she held it in two hands, showing off elegant, long fingers and perfectly manicured nails. "I was disappointed when you cut out early. I was hoping to make a night of it."

There was no denying it. Zoe was a beautiful woman. Tyler apologized again. She hadn't been to the bar in some time but the mood, music and women were pretty much the same. She had danced and Zoe had flirted, both with her and with others, but it was something else that set off her warning bells. Zoe's approach had felt like an assumption. As if she just assumed they would spend the night or perhaps the weekend together. Not that Tyler was adverse to a little romance but it hadn't been romantic at all. There was a certain honesty about Zoe—well, about all the DiNamico/Phipps women she had met, but with Zoe there was a sexual current too. Tyler had felt it the day they met. She remembered the excitement of considering the woman's advances. Until she finally accepted the Friday night invitation. It wasn't until they were at the bar and both had a number of drinks in them that the truth of the situation came flooding in. Zoe was a player, and she, Tyler Marsh, PhD, was just the latest conquest. "I'm sure you managed without me," she offered genially.

With a wry smile, Zoe tipped her head, admitting, "After you left, I ran into my old mates from school. We ended up getting together again last night. I'm afraid we got into the tequila." Stretching, moving to the edge of her chair, Zoe looked thoughtful. "I hope you're well rested. I'm afraid we've a mess to deal with."

Before Tyler could even ask, Zoe gestured for her to follow, and led her through the private corridor to Georgie's office. Ready to stop Zoe before she trespassed on her boss's quiet time, she was caught off guard when Zoe suggested, "Better grab your tablet."

Tyler returned to her desk, checking the device for Georgie's schedule to be sure of what they would be interrupting. The morning schedule had been blanked out with an unavailable tag beside the time block. Back in the hall, she showed Zoe the change. "This was not how I left things Friday."

"I know," Zoe acknowledged, waving her hand over the security lock sensor.

Tyler followed her in to the executive suite. With the office lights out the sunshine streaming through the windows lit the room well enough to see the space was devoid of its usual occupant. Since starting at DME, Tyler couldn't remember ever being in this office without Georgie being present. Even when she took no interest in the comings and goings around her, Georgie was always there. Tyler had tried coming earlier and earlier in an effort to beat her boss into the office with no luck. She was beginning to think Georgie was always there. Not up in the condo she owned on the penthouse level but right there in that corner office, day and night. Only the daily change of clothing and the dog's need for outings ever changed the routine. The woman had to be lonely. Could a walking computer be lonely? Even with the head injury there had to be more to life than work.

Everyone, it seemed, wanted to see Georgie comfortable or simply gone from sight. For most of them, that translated into keeping her compartmentalized from everyone else. Georgie didn't actually need quiet or privacy to do her best work. It was only the constant emotional jousts that would derail her concentration. Once she was interrupted, it would take her hours and sometimes a day before she could concentrate on a task, any task at all. It was the reason she kept her morning schedule blocked out. Tyler had learned that it was also the reason Marnie Pulaski had insisted Georgie be moved into Luigi's old office. There were only two entrances. The first was the private corridor from Human Resources they had just used, and the other was the main entrance from the upper lobby which was guarded by the receptionist. No one, employee or visitor, made it past either gatekeeper without Marnie Pulaski knowing and there was usually hell to pay when it happened. Other than Marnie and now Tyler, only Susan Chan and Zoe were authorized to drop in on Georgie without an appointment. And everyone, from what Tyler had seen, respected that request. Everyone, except Lou Phipps. For some reason, Lou seemed to go out of his way to challenge Georgie over even the smallest financial details. He would bypass reception, ignoring any protests and launch into whatever had him so upset before Tyler, Zoe or even Marnie could intervene.

Tyler looked around the empty office for signs of occupation since Friday afternoon. Before she could ask where Georgie was or what had happened, Lou Phipps charged into the office, demanding, "Where is she?"

"Dad, please..."

"Don't you 'Dad please' me, young lady. I am at my wits end trying to deal with this outbreak of unprofessionalism! How on earth do you people expect me to run a company with, with this?" He waved his arm around the room as if proof of his claim were written on the walls.

Tyler was stunned by his outburst but not enough to prevent her from defending her boss. "Mr. Phipps. If you have a need to meet with Ms. DiNamico, I will schedule an appointment. Perhaps later this week?"

Turning to Tyler, he seemed almost surprised by her presence. Giving her an arrogant snort, he turned and left.

Tyler watched him through the perimeter glass wall only noticing then that the glass appeared to be heavily smudged. That was new. Usually the cleaning staff kept the glass walls and doors pristine. Before she could take a closer look, Zoe picked up the remote from the coffee table and began changing the room setting. As the transparent glass switched to fully opaque, and the lights came on, Tyler turned from the door to reception to take in the entire glass perimeter. Every inch, top to bottom, for the entire length was covered in writing. Most were diagrams, some looked like formulas or application coding. She wasn't sure which. "What the…"

"That's what I said the first time it happened."

"So…" Tyler took a long sweeping glance at her boss's creation, "this has happened before?"

"Oh yeah."

"Does it happen a lot?"

"What…no, no not a lot. But, I will warn you, when it does it usually spells a new project or patent. At least it has so far."

"That's good, right?"

"Good for the company. Good for profits. For you and me, not so much!" She pointed to the tablet pinned under Tyler's arm. "Best you start snapping pics while I find the Windex."

Tyler did just that, carefully working from one side of the room to the other. She took her time, cautiously overlapping each picture and adding a description of the order and place each shot was captured. By the time she was done, Zoe had cleaned her way across one wall. "Why don't you let me finish that?" Tyler offered.

"I've got this. You can check and make sure everything's been put back in its proper place. I don't expect we'll see Georgie much before noon but just in case…"

"Got it." Tyler opened the room setup chart Marnie had given her the first week on the job. Marnie was absolutely sure keeping things in exactly the same place every day would help her sister, ensuring she wasn't wasting her time trying to remember basic things. From everything Tyler had been reading on head injuries, she wasn't sure that was the best strategy but she wasn't ready to challenge the misconceptions of the big boss. "I hate to ask, but what's up with your dad?"

"Oh, nothing really," Zoe offered casually. "He has his ways. Georgie doesn't take much notice but I guess that could change. I do wish she would try not to rile him so much."

"Rile him?" That caught Tyler by surprise.

"Yeah, he thinks she should be setting an example, not giving in to all this craziness." At the mention of craziness, Zoe waved her hand at the glass wall.

"Has he always been this upset with her?" Tyler asked, trying to understand.

"What?" Zoe looked up from wiping the last of the glass wall panels clean. "I guess, but it's really just been the last two years. Since Marnie moved her in here, he's been worried about how the public will view the company, you know, when they see a crazy woman occupies the corner office."

Unsure if it was Zoe's tone or the repeated use of crazy to describe her boss, a woman who had been nothing but forthright and intelligent, struck Tyler deeply. "What about you Zoe? Do you think she's hurting the company?"

"Me?" She seemed genuinely surprised to be asked. "I guess. Still, it's up to my dad and Marnie to work it out. Once Dad's named president, we'll have to deal with his decisions. I think he just wants to move her back down to the machine shop or perhaps the boatyard. She's always liked it there."

Speechless, Tyler wasn't sure which shocked her most, Zoe's willingness to hide Georgie away or her belief that her dad, Lou Phipps, would be the next president of DME. Georgie had been groomed for the job and the only thing holding her back was the deficits caused from her head injury. Deficits Tyler believed were more than manageable. Even if Georgie DiNamico was crazy, she was good crazy, in a way that had been immensely profitable for the company. Surely as chief financial officer, even a hardheaded Lou Phipps would be forced to admit that fact. And hiding her in the basement electronics lab made no sense when she had everything she needed in her workspace here. Yes, she was in the corner office, but Tyler had come to realize it was also the least accessible office in the building. No one dropped in on Georgie. She met with each and every engineer almost daily, reviewed all design work, and consulted on all proposals. Georgie was carrying one of the heaviest workloads in the company, if not the heaviest. Learning that the woman also lived upstairs in the penthouse, and basically had no life other than her work, had upset her. Marnie, for all of her protection and concern, just wanted to know her sister was safe and cared for, while Lou Phipps, her cousin and fellow officer of the corporation, wanted her out, hidden away, or gone completely. And Zoe…Zoe seemed to second her dad's position. "I thought you liked Georgie?"

"What?" This time she turned to face Tyler. "Don't get me wrong, she's brilliant and all that, but…Hey! I'm not saying anything that hasn't already been said."

Tyler nodded. Hiding what she knew was not her first disappointment with her new friend.

Back in her office she set aside her own research to sort out all the materials she'd copied. There was no way to know what had happened between leaving the office Friday and returning Monday morning. Well, the option of going to Marnie and asking for details did exist, but not at the top of her list. She didn't dislike the woman, and she wasn't intimidated the way many of her co-workers were. Marnie was driven but sensible. This was just her third week on the job and she already felt a real loyalty to Georgie. She knew she wasn't the only one. The woman was a natural leader and even with her limited ability to communicate verbally, she always found a way to make herself understood. More than that, the people on her team felt exactly the same way Tyler did. Everyone in engineering got face time with Georgie no matter how big or small his or her contribution to a given project.

Carefully combing through each of the pictures, Tyler transcribed everything exactly as Georgie had written it on her office wall, including pasting in the drawings, schematics and gobbledygook she couldn't translate. It took her the better part of an hour but when she was done, she felt good adding it to her daily briefing file. Then she did what she'd been itching to do all weekend. Opening the last of the file boxes that had been littering her office, she began sorting through volumes of financial statements. These were all from the engineering department but Tyler had been given a master password that allowed her access to all the accounting companywide.

After two hours of going through online statements and ledgers, Tyler was absolutely sure something was wrong. She just had no idea what. A master's degree in economics had given her an insight into the accounting process but not much more. Reading through the general ledger she had been overwhelmed by the number of accounts that existed. What was worse was the number of transfers between accounts. Then there were the foreign currency accounts. Several holding accounts both domestic and offshore and the retirement fund.

Logging out of the accounting programs, Tyler stood at her desk and stretched. It was almost eleven thirty. Right about now, she was usually preparing a cup of tea for Georgie and gathering up any mail or messages, and her own tablet for the morning briefing. Only problem, Georgie wasn't in her office and she hadn't been seen or heard from. Not exactly knowing what to do, and not wanting to be caught doing nothing, she grabbed a tablet and headed to Marnie's office. *Sometimes the mountain must go to Mohammed.* She tapped on the doorframe and waited.

Marnie, the phone in one ear, covered the mouthpiece, ordering, "Just go upstairs and get her. I don't know what shape she's in but you can figure it out." When Tyler didn't immediately make haste for the penthouse apartment, Marnie growled something into the receiver and set it down on her desk. "She's had a rough weekend. It happens. Anyway, just go upstairs and get her back on track. Can you do that for me?"

"Of course," Tyler replied, not really knowing what she could do and not knowing what to expect.

She headed upstairs. This would be her third visit to Georgie's apartment. The first had been with Zoe to review Georgie's wardrobe. The second had been to meet the woman who cleaned Georgie's flat every week and saw to the groceries, laundry and dry cleaning. That had been interesting. Georgie's cleaning lady had turned out to be another cousin, Stella, a sweet woman who was quick to laugh and had a smile that traveled from her mouth all the way to her eyes. It was reminiscent of the way Georgie would sometimes light up. Like when she was desperate to explain something. When Tyler caught on she would run with it, often making Georgie animated. Her satisfaction was easy to read.

Zoe had complained bitterly when it came to compensating for Georgie's limitations. Tyler on the other hand was starting to realize there was no compensation required. A little patience and imagination were all that was needed and went a long way toward improving the situation. Actually, she was finding it far easier to work with Georgie than she had imagined. Maybe she simply understood the way her mind worked. At first she had found herself silently finishing Georgie's thoughts. Frustrated to find Georgie so far behind her. Once she'd reminded herself several times that it was Georgie who couldn't communicate, not her, she began speaking her mind, throwing things out, the words and the ideas she imagined Georgie was trying to explain and by luck or fluke she seemed to be almost always right. Standing at Georgie's front door it was hard to imagine why anybody else had such a hard time with her.

Tyler knocked, then knocked a second time. When there was still no reply, she ran her employee badge over the hidden sensor. Standing just inside the door and hesitating, she listened. Music was coming from somewhere on the main floor below. That was a relief. The last thing she wanted was to invade Georgie's private space. Much less risk embarrassing her by walking into her safe room. She headed down the circular stairs, hearing the music more clearly, and knew it was coming from the library. At the door she tapped lightly. The double doors were wide open and Georgie was inside, bent over the worktable. Poring over some sort of technical drawing. Music emanated from unseen speakers, just loud enough to prevent Georgie from hearing her. Tyler didn't want to frighten the woman; she was clearly engrossed in whatever she was reading. She had to admit the view wasn't bad either. She grinned at the admission, realizing she was staring at her boss's ass. She'd noticed Georgie's athletic build before but had never seen her without her suit jacket and certainly not from this viewpoint. There was no ignoring the muscles in her back and shoulders, the way her plain gray cotton shirt stressed every curve. And her butt in those pants..."Good morning, Georgie," she called over the music.

Georgie stiffened, then straightened up and turned around. It wasn't until she actually took Tyler in that her face lightened. "Good morning."

Tyler smiled. "I see you've already been hard at work. I have everything on file for you," she said, holding out her tablet as proof. "Would you like to have our morning briefing up here? I can slip into the kitchen and make us a cup of tea."

Georgie shook her head and pointed to the empty chair on the other side of the table. "Need to talk."

"Absolutely." Tyler sat down clicking on her tablet and tabbing to her agenda.

"No." Georgie waved her hand over the tablet to get her attention. "Talk about you."

"What? No. I mean, yes of course. What would you like to know?"

Nodding, Georgie pulled out the other folding chair and sat down. Quiet. Thinking.

Tyler was suddenly uncomfortable. Something was wrong. Something she couldn't quite name. She waited patiently for Georgie to ask her questions before she realized this was one of those times when Georgie might appreciate her taking the lead. It also felt a bit like a test. "Did something happen on the weekend? Something that spurred your hyper-creativity?"

"I like that." Georgie admitted. "Hyper-creativity," she repeated but still seemed reserved.

Clearly whatever had happened had been a good thing judging by the amount of work completed. "Can you tell me what you're working on? It seems like you made great progress."

"Rescue app."

She started to ask more, when her boss raised her hand. It wasn't unusual for Georgie to use hand signals. Maybe it was her Italian heritage. Something about her talking with her hands made sense.

"About Zoe."

Tyler sat frozen not knowing what to do or say.

"Your privacy…I respect." She shuffled a few papers on the table, as if looking for something of importance.

While Georgie's focus was on her papers, Tyler fought to maintain her composure. If she lost this job because of something…"I can explain. Georgie, I don't want to lose this job. Please," she begged.

Looking up, Georgie took in Tyler's expression with confusion and something more, something like relief. "You… Nothing wrong. No worries. Understood?" she asked, genuinely concerned.

It was hard for Tyler to look at those green eyes. They were more than concerned; her eyes betrayed a deep level of caring. So much so that all at once the situation was overwhelming and before she realized, tears of hot relief streamed down her cheeks. "I'm so sorry," she mumbled now thoroughly embarrassed.

Surprising her, Georgie reached across the table and took her two hands in her own. "You…do great. Too smart to lose." She gave Tyler's hands another squeeze, before standing. She dragged a folding chair to the same side of the table as Tyler and sat down beside her. She handed her a stack of papers. "Read these…Later."

Tyler scooped them up, reading the title from the first page. It was the company policy on employee privacy and fraternization and included several forms required when declaring a relationship, or a conflict of interest.

"See this?" Georgie asked, pulling her attention back to the large blueprints and technical drawings spread across the table. "Aunt Georgina…hers. All these. Many…apply, still. What do you think?"

Emotionally spent, Tyler tried to focus on the drawing closest but without luck.

Georgie patted her shoulder patiently before handing her one of her ever-present pocket hankies. "I will make tea…You read," Georgie suggested, giving Tyler's shoulder one more consoling squeeze and heading from the room.

Tyler wiped her eyes and blew her nose in the cotton handkerchief. She felt like a fool. Yet there was nothing Georgie had done or said that made her feel bad. Picking up the policy documents again she began reading the summary. It was quite simple. If two people worked in the same department they were required to declare the relationship. If they did not work together it was nobody's business unless one or the other was in a position to influence any portion of the partner's job. That made sense, and the resolution was straightforward. A simple form was required from the member of the couple holding a more junior position.

It was easy for Tyler to recognize that the document had been written by Georgie. The voice on paper was distinctive. The language of the directive wasn't flamboyant or overtly noticeable. It was simply stated and complete and always explained the reasons. Including the possible outcomes of policy violations and how they would affect not just the company but other employees and the people directly involved. She liked the policy. There were a few areas she thought could use a tweak but as Georgie had already told her several times, she could... *Rewrite it. Fix the mistakes. Help me understand what I got wrong.*

Sorting the policy documents back in order, Tyler tidied them with a paper clip and set them under her tablet. She ran her hands over her face making sure her cheeks were dry, and hoped beyond hope that her nose wasn't too red. By the time Georgie returned, she had read through the first two large sheets of drawings and had been combing through a third trying to piece the ideas together in her mind. "This is fascinating," she told her. "I don't think I understand all of it but I do get this part about linking all these different frequencies together. Could you use something like this now?"

"Not in that way." Georgie replied, setting a cup down in front of Tyler and slipping back into the seat beside her. "You are right...smart. Instead...Bluetooth not VHF. Cell phones not radios."

When Georgie looked at her she knew she was waiting for her to make a connection. It suddenly occurred to her that Georgie not only lit up when she was mentally engaged but the earlier misunderstanding was washed completely away. "Oh I think I see. In this schematic she was trying to filter emergency radio traffic to one responder frequency. I don't know if that's possible even now but you're right, the idea of linking cell phones, that's easy to do. Isn't it?"

Georgie smiled, "Crowd sourcing," she explained, now really smiling for the first time since Tyler walked in the door. "Thank King Harold Blue Tooth...Nice smile...too!"

CHAPTER SIX

Tyler had taken to Georgie's Land Rover like a duck to water, but driving her boss around in the expensive SUV made her nervous, really nervous. "I'm so sorry," she said after cutting the corner too close and jumping another curb. When she finally pulled into the clinic lot, it was all she could do not to cry. "I'm so sorry," she offered again before shutting off the engine.

"Why?" Georgie asked without rancor or sarcasm.

"For abusing your truck. I don't know what's wrong with me. I'm usually a better driver than this."

Georgie, sitting in the passenger seat, made no comment.

Pulling her phone from her winter jacket Tyler checked the time. "We're really early."

"Good shortcut. Nothing changes...Lackawanna!"

"It wasn't complicated. Just a quick shot down Route Five."

There was no further response or any comment about her driving. Tyler, with key fob in hand, had her gloves on but Georgie didn't seem to be in any hurry to get out of the car. Not sure what to do or say, Tyler sat quietly, surreptitiously watching her boss tab away on her cell. When she heard a muffled ringtone, she immediately looked to Georgie before she realized it was coming from her own phone. Pulling it from her jacket, she answered it as quickly as she could. She didn't need to read the display to know who it was. She had set *Darth Vader's March* as the ringtone to alert her to calls from Marnie Pulaski. If she had learned anything in her weeks at DME, Marnie would not be trifled with. When she called, she expected you to answer and answer immediately. "Tyler Marsh."

"Where are you?"

"The VA clinic."

"In the clinic?"

"Uh no. We're in the parking lot. Is there a problem?"

"Put her on the horn. Now!"

Tyler reached across the console, touching Georgie's arm to get her attention. "Marnie's on the phone. She wants to talk."

Head down, with eyes glued to her own phone, Georgie simply shook her head.

Not exactly sure what to do, Tyler tried again, nudging gently, "Georgie. It's your sister. She needs to talk to you."

When she shook her head again, Tyler put the phone to her ear, more than a little intimidated at having to tell Marnie no. "Ah Marnie. She's a little busy at the moment. Can I get her to call you back?"

"Goddammit! You listen to me. She is not squirming out of her session. Do you hear me?"

"Okay…" Tyler was at a complete loss, until a thought occurred to her. "Georgie, did you just text Marnie?"

Georgie halted her furious tabbing. Without raising her head, she nodded, then stuffed her phone in her pocket and crossed her arms.

"Let me call you back," she said to Marnie, hitting End before the big boss could argue. Turning to the sullen woman beside her, she commiserated, "I do this at the dentist's office. I don't know why. We've had the same dentist since Kira and I were four." She reached over again, giving Georgie's arm an encouraging rub. Dressed in her standard business suit and wearing what Tyler's grandmother would have called a car coat, a thigh length wool winter jacket, it was hard to tell if Georgie was even aware of her touch. "When we were kids my mom was always up on the latest and greatest child-rearing techniques. I guess she read somewhere that introducing children to the dentist before they actually needed dental work would build confidence and prevent us from forming anxieties." Tyler watched carefully. Her head was down and her still too-long bangs had fallen to partially cover her eyes. She knew Georgie was listening, she just wasn't sure she was getting through. "So, Kira and I were barely four but off we go. We're so excited, we love new adventures, and we trot into Dr Kopel's office, happy as can be. I have to admit, I was so mad when Kira got to go in first. She loves to remind me that she popped out of our mother ahead of me. Anyway, she goes in and comes out five minutes later with a huge smile and a stupid little doll. Well in I go, interested to learn what all the hubbub is about but before I know it, I'm in the big chair, with the big light and all the instruments and scary stuff, and all I can think is, no way is this going to be worth it, if all I get is a stupid doll!"

"What…you do?" Georgie asked quietly, head still down.

"Screamed my head off! I just wailed like it was the end of the world. I think my father came running from the parking lot; that's how bad it was. The best part was Dr Kopel's reaction. The man pulled up a chair and started screaming with me!" Chuckling at the memory, she rubbed Georgie's arm again. "In time, I learned to handle the dental thing, but I will give the man credit. He very effectively halted my tirade. And like a good clinician, he took the time to explain things to me in a way a child would understand. And the best part? He offered me a doll too, but I just shook my head no. So, he opens a drawer and pulls out a teeny little fire truck! Can you believe that?"

Finally Georgie began to smile, lifting her head but still not willing to make eye contact. She asked quietly, "Still got it?"

"Actually I do. It now resides in my jewelry box, but after admiring some of those small display boxes you have, I think I'll get one and put it on display."

"*Aide-mémoire*! First…successful negotiation!"

Tyler let out a genuine laugh. "You're right. I've never thought of it that way."

"I could study…technique, yours. Maybe use…next board meeting?"

"You know that's a great idea. As a matter of fact I could patent the idea and teach it all over the country."

"Oooh, DVD course…infomercial. Every insomniac… clamoring, order the Marsh Method!"

"Oh that's good, the Marsh Method! Should we head inside and give it a try?"

"Try…trying to coax me?"

"Yes, yes I am. And you're stalling. Please tell me why?"

Georgie was silent again but she hadn't retreated, not completely. Reaching over, Tyler rubbed soothing circles on her arm, explaining gently, "The anxiety is normal. Feeling scared is normal. It might be new for a big bad rescue pilot but it is normal for the rest of us. I myself have been the queen of screaming scared all my life."

"Not me."

"I know," Tyler said, admitting it as much to herself as Georgie. "But it's a natural state everyone has to face at some point in their lives. Everyone grows up differently, which explains why a pair of twins can grow up in the same house with the same family and friends and still turn out such opposites." Tyler was about to add the fact that Georgie had grown up instantly, the day her aunt and mother died, but stopped herself, not knowing how Zoe's indiscretion at revealing this would be met. Instead, she offered encouragement. "Will it help if I go with you? Maybe the speech therapist can teach me some techniques that could be helpful."

"More than…Marsh Method?"

Tyler laughed again. "I'm not sure my brand of negotiation would be appreciated here!"

Finally, Georgie smiled. "Okay," she said, pulling on her gloves and climbing from the Land Rover.

Tyler fetched Maggie from the rear cargo area. Finding Georgie standing motionless by the passenger door, she offered her hand. Hesitantly Georgie accepted, allowing Tyler to lead her and Maggie into the VA Clinic.

"You're more stubborn than the marines I get in here and they invented stubborn!"

Georgie crossed her arms over her chest.

"Let me try," Tyler volunteered, hoping to defuse the tension building between the very frustrated therapist and her boss. Tyler moved closer to the whiteboard where Georgie had been tasked to explain a basic idea. In this case the theory of flight. With marker in hand, Georgie had begun the basic lesson she had delivered umpteen times before her injury. The only problem, every time she turned from her audience of two, Tyler and Katherine her therapist, she would forget what she was saying. She had just started to make progress when Katherine started throwing curveballs, like questions or off-topic comments to push her harder. Georgie began shutting down. As both the neurologist and Marnie had explained, Georgie's ultimate safe reaction was to shut herself off. And now that she had, she was behaving like a spoiled child, unwilling to take her medicine.

"Georgie, we're not picking on you," Tyler explained gently. "Please listen carefully. No matter how vigilant we are, there will always be people who will interrupt you or ask questions at the wrong time. You don't have to answer those questions or even acknowledge anyone. I promise!" she added, finally making eye contact. When Georgie nodded, she gave her arm an encouraging squeeze before resuming her seat.

"Okay, Major," said Katherine. Georgie's longtime therapist cut an athletic build in her air force uniform. A thin woman, she looked to be in her sixties, with premature gray that could very well be the result of working with difficult clients. "Please begin."

It took more than a minute before Georgie could actually lift her head and start her lecture again. "Let's begin by introducing the four forces at work in creating flight." Turning to the board, she drew a basic profile of an aircraft wing. Then four arrows. "Forward propulsion, or thrust…"

"Which one is a drag?" Katherine asked jokingly.

Georgie, still facing the whiteboard, stood frozen.

Tyler watched as her hands repeatedly balled and relaxed in a habitual manner she recognized from Marnie's anxious pen clicking OCD. She was about to stand and join Georgie again when the therapist gave her a silent hold signal.

Georgie finally returned to her diagram. "In opposition to thrust," she added, turning to face her audience and making eye contact, "we have drag. In order to…" Suddenly unsure of the word she made a hand motion of taking off.

"Fly?" Katherine offered.

"Yes!" she answered enthusiastically, as if her student had just made an intricate connection. "Yes, thrust must overcome drag. But we do that every time we get in our automobiles. Yet we never get off the ground."

"At least not when you're doing it right!" Tyler gave her an encouraging smile, which she noted almost derailed Georgie's attention. She made a mental note that too much encouragement was almost as bad as none at all.

"All right, class," Georgie said, calling for their attention. It was easy to imagine a time when she had delivered this lecture without a second thought. "If we can overcome drag and achieve momentum with thrust, why aren't we in—the—air?" When neither of her acting students answered, Georgie faltered for a moment before adding the up arrow. "Lift! We need lift but just as thrust must overcome drag, lift has her own…nemesis. Her name is weight! And just like thrust overcoming drag, we need lift to overcome weight in order to…" She made the hand signal again before connecting with the word and finally adding, "… fly."

Tyler and Katherine clapped furiously, jumping to their feet. Tyler had to admit she was overwhelmed with pride. It had been a long session with challenge after challenge. She now had a much better understanding of how difficult complex exchanges could be for her boss. Every time she was forced to change her focus, such as addressing Tyler and the therapist, to writing on the board, she'd lose her thread. The resulting frustration had been building and building, and Tyler had half expected her to lose her temper. She had actually hoped it would happen, if only so Katherine could witness the cognitive transformation. Fascinated by the interplay of injury and brain chemistry, she was hopeful for Georgie's continued improvement.

As she was gathering up their coats and bags, Maggie nuzzled up against her leg. Tyler looked up to see several young people also in air force athletic gear stroll in. One, spotting Georgie, stood formally, barking, "ATTENTION!" Immediately all the others followed suit, lining up in formation. "Morning Major!"

"At ease!" Georgie ordered, offering her hand to the speaker. "Staff Sergeant Feynman, Axelrod. How is the new leg working out?"

While Tyler watched the exchange with the dog at her side, Katherine slipped up beside her. "Watch this," she suggested quietly, tipping her head toward Georgie and the airmen.

"So, tell us Staff Sergeant, is it the chick magnet I keep hearing about?"

The young airman laughed so hard he couldn't answer but his buddy, standing beside him, slapped him on the back.

"The Major's on to you!"

"And what about you Mr. Winowski, come up with a good pickup line to go with that limp?"

While the young man she was chastising looked forlorn, his buddies howled, agreeing that the Major had nailed it!

"Ah come on ma'am! A guy's gotta try!"

"Yes you do, mister, and do not stop. Women in the greater Buffalo area would weep, bereft of your charm!"

"Yeah what she said!" Winowski said with pride, as if Georgie had just defended his honor in some indescribable way.

"Good morning Corporal Gianni," she offered pleasantly, as she made her way down the line, "how is your mother? Are you two all set for your trip to Italy over the Christmas break?"

As Georgie made her way through the group, she took her time to greet each and every one by name, referencing their injuries without embarrassment, instinctively knowing if and how each person would react.

Tyler wasn't sure which shocked her more, Georgie's detailed knowledge of these young people, the jovial response she received, or just how much they respected her. These were the very people, the young veterans, she and her family cared most about helping and here was her new boss, clearly a hero in their eyes. Speaking quietly to the therapist, she noted, "You would never know it was the same woman who was having a temper tantrum two minutes ago."

"It's quite remarkable how she can push herself with this group. Loyalty is a stressor that pushes her into this mode. It won't last long and it exhausts her mentally and emotionally but she does it whenever her men are here."

"Her men? I thought they all died?"

"Men and women from her unit," Katherine explained. Tipping her head to Maggie, who was sitting pressed against Tyler's leg, she added, "That dog has taught me more about therapy than most doctors. See how laid-back she is right now? She gets like that whenever Georgie's in command mode. Totally calm and unconcerned, like she hasn't a care in the world, but watch as you leave. Georgie will start to deflate and the dog will move in to take up the slack."

Sure enough, as they left the center and headed to the SUV, Maggie moved close to Georgie's side. When Tyler opened the rear door for the dog, she refused to move until Georgie took a deep, relaxing breath and nodded. Maggie leaped in without further fuss while Georgie climbed into the passenger seat.

Tyler started the Land Rover. Stopping her, Georgie placed her hand over hers. "Lunch?"

"Okay..." Tyler hadn't planned for lunch, nor had she been briefed on the when, where and what usually attached to everything in Georgie's well-orchestrated life.

"Down Route Five...On the lake. We can sit...outside."

"Okay..." she began tentatively, before remembering that she had better results when she was up front with her boss. "You do remember it's December. In Buffalo? I'm not sure I can sit out in the cold and wind for five minutes much less for an entire meal."

"Oh…" She pointed her thumb toward the backseat.

"You're right, it's too cold to leave her in the truck. I'm sure we can bring her inside."

Georgie's look ranged between wide-eyed to skeptical but she nodded, then tabbed through the SUV's navigation unit and set the destination for an already-stored address. Tyler decided that was a good sign. Wherever they were going, Georgie had been there before and in her truck, which meant someone had driven her there.

It took just a short ten minutes on Route Five before Tyler pulled up to The Dock at the Bay. The historic wayside hotel had long been converted to a restaurant. Tyler knew the place and had driven past it a thousand times but had never bothered to stop and check it out. "I've always wanted to try this place. Let me grab Maggie."

At the front door, Georgie hesitated again.

"It's all right. I have her registration and she has her Buffalo Service Dog tag on her collar. I checked!" she added at the skeptical look.

They weren't two steps in the door when someone stopped them but not with the challenge Georgie was so worried about. "Ms. DiNamico! Oh how lovely to see you, and you've brought someone new with you," the older woman gushed, turning her attention to Tyler. "Welcome to The Dock at the Bay. Let me show you to your table. Somewhere near the window?" she asked, looking to Georgie. At her nonverbal approval, they were led to a table farthest from the main door and with a view of the patio and the beach.

Outside the December day looked frigid and ice gray. Tyler shivered at the sight. Surprising her, Georgie began rubbing brisk circles on her back.

When Georgie stopped her impromptu back-warming session, it was to take off her own winter coat. Slipping into her seat, she gave the dog a hand signal, then pointed under the table. Tyler was surprised again when Maggie settled down on the floor between them. Tyler knew Maggie would have her head on Georgie's feet just like she did in every meeting. Slumping her rear end on Tyler's feet was new but somehow heartwarming. Looking down, she realized the dog's legs and massive paws were in the aisle.

"They know," Georgie offered as if that was explanation enough.

Tyler was about to ask what she was referring to when the proverbial light went on. Georgie would share only the information she was sure you needed to hear. Which meant the staff already knew enough to watch their step around the dog. She would still warn whoever approached but she was beginning to connect with Georgie's communication style. "You did really well with the men and women from your unit. Have you known them for a long time?"

Georgie, who had been reading the menu, placed her index finger on the place she had left off. Tyler had seen her do it in a report whenever a question came up. "No. Marnie gives…the list. I memorize it," she answered, before returning her attention to the menu.

Determined to get a full explanation, Tyler pressed again, "Please tell me how that works?"

Again Georgie put her finger on the menu and before looking up, read off, "Dock burger with sautéed mushroom and cheddar cheese." She then closed the menu and turned her entire attention to Tyler. "I remember some…no details. Details are important…to them."

"So?"

"So…Marnie gets…personnel…overlapping appointments. I memorize it…before going. I have one…Boatyard too."

"Why?" Tyler asked. The effort involved for someone with a head injury had to be significant. She watched as her boss's attention seemed to drift out the window. Tyler now knew better and waited patiently.

"Do not see…missing leg. You see a man…missing leg. Do not know…young woman…limps…"

"But you notice she does," Tyler said, finishing the sentiment.

Georgie nodded, and tapping her index finger against her temple, said, "Nothing to see. No aha moment. For most, this," she tapped again, "synonymous with…mental health issue." She let out a little exasperated huff. "Tired…people call me crazy. My men do not…need me, but need to know…they matter."

Making a mental note to ask Marnie for this list, she turned her attention to the other issue raised. "So you're aware of the accusation. The crazy accusation, I mean."

She nodded, again taking time to consider her answer. "Lou thinks can…" She shook her head. "Bean counter…no leader. No imagination."

"What about you? Have you thought about taking over?"

"Assumed I would. In my…since…fuck!" she swore in frustration. Staring out the window again, she finally turned back to Tyler, explaining, "Marnie needs to lead. Lou in charge? A fire sale: the boatyard, my patents, everything, just to…days on a Florida beach…drinking…little umbrellas. Our employees… unemployed!"

Tyler wanted to argue but what could she say to defend Lou Phipps? Oh no, he wouldn't? Of course he would. Lou was the type of man who wanted the most expedient path to the fastest profits. She had read every proposal Georgie had written and all the feedback and meeting minutes that followed until a new product was introduced or scrapped. She had been shocked to see how many of those ideas did not make it past inception. Whenever the question of seed money or capital purchases had come up, Lou had waded in hot and heavy, determined to stop whatever Georgie proposed. Even when there had been no capital outlay, Lou would challenge the man hours or the design time estimates, or any other aspect he could bite into. And he won more often than Tyler thought was right. From what she had read, DME was sitting on over a dozen stalled and very viable projects because Lou Phipps had worked nonstop to make them go away. No wonder Georgie wanted to divide the company into three new entities.

"In the new company organization chart you showed me. The bio company would be yours. The boatyard would operate as its own entity, and I assume with Lori Phipps at the helm?" When Georgie nodded, she continued, "That leaves DME and the new parent corporation. Let me guess, you want Marnie to head that new parent company and give the old DME to Lou."

"Very good, Dr Marsh...Please tell...why?"

"One, it would make him president, which he dearly wants. Two, it would take him out of your face, which I'm sure would please you as much as me. You would literally be working for different companies which also means he would be out of the loop both with new business and as company finances go. Wouldn't it put him in a position to control the existing patents? Aren't you worried about that?"

"Those contracts...written in stone! He would...sales of old tech, control of. A risk, but, no blaming me...mistakes, losses."

"And you want Marnie to wear the big hat?"

Again she nodded. "Earned it. Good at it...and something else. I want...my division out...to move to the boatyard. Commercial real estate," she said, and pointed up to indicate the increased demand in the market. "Will make Lou happy... Bonus!"

"You're certainly right about the real estate market. Even my parents have had offers for their commercial lot."

Georgie smiled her reply as the waitress reappeared, carefully stepping over the sleeping dog's legs. "What can I get you ladies today?"

Georgie tapped her index finger, much as she had when her menu was open, and recited the entrée exactly as written.

"Medium, right?" At her confirmation she asked, "To drink, will that be hot or iced?"

"Hot tea...please."

"Perfect, I'll have the chef cut up some lemon for you. And for you?" she asked Tyler.

Tyler gave her order but when the server asked if she wanted coffee, she immediately said no.

"Okay here," Georgie explained. "Big room...lots of smells."

"Are you sure?" she asked, not wanting to push her luck.

"I will never...say yes...when I mean no."

Tyler ordered coffee and handed the menus back to the departing waitress. "You know, I really have to see this boatyard someday. Especially if you're thinking of moving the division out there."

"Just south of…old Ford plant. Marina…dry-dock, finishing shed. Room to build."

"A new building? No wonder you want to divide up the company. There isn't a hope in hell Lou Phipps would allow you money for that!" It was out before she even realized what she was saying.

Georgie never took her eyes off the lake, but she did smile. "Dr Marsh, how warm…your boots?" At Tyler's wide-eyed expression she asked, "Warm enough for…boatyard?"

"Yes!" Tyler answered with enthusiasm. She had been looking forward to the outing since hearing stories from Zoe about the boat building line and the wild aunt who ran things.

"Good," Georgie offered with a smile. "Good to go!"

* * *

As they made their way down Route Five, Georgie read her cheat notes on the boatyard personnel to Tyler. "Okay, I knew Susan's husband worked out here but I had no idea he was one of the carpenters Lou laid off." Georgie, her head down, concentrated on her cell phone and the file she had opened. Tyler had watched her do it a million times but now understood it was her way of maintaining focus. Signaling her exit, Tyler reached over, touching Georgie's shoulder. "We're slowing…"

Forced to raise her head, Georgie stuck her cell phone back in her pocket as she watched the traffic. Clear of the highway, she thanked Tyler before continuing with her story. "I didn't know. When I found out…Lou had sold…millwork, I flipped. Could not…undo. Too late. I bought…surplus stock. Put boys to work. Gave Marnie time…some early retirement? Then Lori convince them…hire back two, for custom installations. That's how Anthony…got back."

One of the disgruntled comments she had heard while getting to know her co-workers was a warning that those not in the family circle were mere fodder for the DiNamico/Phipps war of the cousins. It had troubled her deeply and not just the implications. How could this caring woman be so misrepresented? She was sure Georgie only ever acted in the best interests of everyone concerned but it never hurt to keep tabs. "How did you decide who would be hired back and who lost their jobs permanently?"

"Lori's...her bailiwick. She let them...carpenters decide."

Not sure what to say, she filed that fact away and changing the subject, asked, "So this is Derby, New York?" She said it with a near perfect English accent.

Georgie, eyes still on the road, followed her lead with a smile. "Welcome to Derbyshire."

"Derbyshire?"

"Technically...Irving, New York. Named for...illustrious family but none...here."

"I bet they still own the land."

Georgie practically snorted at that comment. "Nuh-huh!" she added before ordering Tyler to stop the car. "I own all north and...this side." she indicated the street they were stopped on, Allegheny Road.

"Wait, what?" Tyler took a moment to look up and down the two streets. Both were dotted with modest homes on well cared for lots. Turning right, she cruised down Exchange Street, "Who owns the homes?"

"I do. Most are rented...long lease. Tenants...company, retired."

The street ended at the Cattaraugus Creek. She pulled into the marina lot to turn the Land Rover around. Zoe had been all wrong about the SUV, except for one point: it had the turning radius of a semi-truck. The two-story marina building in its vibrant blue looked almost new. "How do you manage all of this?" she asked. Having read what she believed was Georgie's entire portfolio, she was sure she would have remembered any rental income or the mention of a marina.

"Elaine, Henry's sister. She runs...the marina, tack shop. Stella manages properties...rental properties...for me, Lori too."

"Lori owns something out here?"

Georgie pointed back the way they had come. "Other half. Across Allegheny. Stella warned...how we learned Lou...trying to sell property."

Tyler stopped the Land Rover facing the river. "If it's your property, why would Lou try to sell it?"

"Did not...does not know. I lease boatyard to DME... one dollar a year. In exchange...DME must...maintain public access...environmental stewardship."

Tyler was battling with a thousand questions but lost all train of thought as Georgie placed her hand over hers.

"Want to see...place, new house?"

Still teetering over the fact that Georgie owned half the Cattaraugus peninsula and that Lou Phipps had no idea she did, she simply accepted her boss's hand direction. Back on Erie, she followed the skinny road back to Allegheny and up to the boatyard.

Like the marina, the boatyard buildings were the same vibrant blue with low pitched white roofs. A small building looking very much like a cottage stood proudly in front of the compound. There were no fences and no gate, but a young man in a security uniform trotted out, welcoming them, walking directly to the passenger side of the vehicle. Tyler was sure he recognized Georgie's truck. Sure enough, the minute Georgie lowered the window his face broke into a huge grin.

"Hey Georgie! Welcome back to the action."

"Hey Ethan! Marine?"

Tyler watched the lanky young man as he draped himself on the window ledge. "Not yet—not yet!"

"So?"

His smile lit up his face. "It's official—I report to Quantico the eighth of January. I've got OCC then the Basic School."

"Basic flight?" Georgie asked cryptically.

"Pensacola. I'm hoping to make the fall course."

"Florida in winter…no better! So happy…Ethan. You will be exceptional, marine aviator!"

Tyler watched the young man's reaction. Even with his dark complexion, it was obvious he was embarrassed and proud. Proud to make Georgie proud!

"Dr Tyler Marsh…my favorite nephew…Ethan Henry Phipps, graduate of U Buf…soon United States Marine Corps aviator!"

Tyler reached across the console and offered her hand to Ethan. He wasn't the first cousin once removed she had met, nor the first Georgie had referred to as her favorite. "It's nice to meet you, Ethan. Will I see you at the New Year's Eve party?"

The young man flushed with the attention. "Yes ma'am! I look forward to learning your opinion on the current administration's military policies!"

"Okay…Well, I'll look forward to that too," she offered, not exactly knowing what to say or expect.

"Lori?" Georgie asked, pointing to the small cottage.

"Nah, sorry. No ma'am!" he corrected, "She's over in the paint shed supervising the twins." At Georgie's raised eyebrow he added, "I don't know what they did but they're suspended from school until the New Year and Aunt Marnie dragged them out here and told Lori to put them to work."

"Prepping the mold?"

He smiled a most playful smile before stepping back from the truck, snapping to attention and delivering a parade perfect salute. "Welcome to DynaCraft, Major DiNamico, Dr Marsh. Ms. Phipps can be found in the paint shed," he said, directing them to their destination with arm signals that looked to be styled for waving in aircraft, not directing traffic.

Tyler pulled ahead following the driveway around the two large production buildings. Separate from the long blue building were two older looking units. While both looked very much like average New England-style barns, one featured new blue siding that matched all the others. One was slightly larger and had what appeared to be a new roof but the siding was a mix of heavily rusted corrugated metal and old sun bleached barn boards. Following the gravel drive, Tyler continued to the blue barn. She was sure it was the place they were aiming for when she pulled up in front and read the sign outside: Paint Shed Access: Open. "What does that mean?" Tyler asked, shutting off the ignition.

"Important...keep clean. When a mold is prepped... especially when painting, it is important...no contaminants inside. Oh...health and welfare too."

"Can we still go in?"

"Now yes. Assembly plant next time." Georgie stepped out of the SUV, moving to the rear door to stop Tyler from opening it. "She stays. Dog hair," she said as explanation.

"Okay that makes sense."

Following Georgie into the blue barn, she had to admit it was not what she had imagined. Sunshine poured in from huge skylights. Overhead was a massive gantry crane, at that moment suspended over the third and largest of four bays. In the first two, what looked like large inside-out boat hulls lay unattended. The third bay was brightly lit with a combination of natural light and huge work lamps. As they moved closer, Tyler realized the mold they were working on was like the first two, but split apart along the keel line and lay like an open book. Several people were standing around while two teens worked on their hands and knees on the mold surface. "That has to hurt. Working on your knees, all bent over like that?"

Georgie agreed, "Worst job...ever!"

"Are those Marnie's boys? The twins?"

Stepping up to join the others watching the boys suffer through their punishment, Tyler whispered to Georgie, "I think Marnie called them Satan's spawn the other day!"

Georgie looked at her, laughing openly. "Two weeks... worked for me!"

"You? Oh my God, you spent time on the punishment line? Were you as young as these guys?"

Georgie nodded. "Younger, but these two...more experience needed. I learn fast!" she said with pride and the silly grin.

Giggling, Tyler agreed. "I remember when we were fourteen, my father made my sister clean out all the grease traps, right after she told them she was far too pretty to be working part-time in an auto body!"

Before Tyler could inquire into her boss's adolescent misdeeds, a tall statuesque woman of color strode with purpose toward them. Even in heavy work clothes, the woman was clearly the handsome butch Zoe had described. Stepping up to Tyler first, she removed her hard hat, offering her hand in a gallant show of chivalry.

"You must be the lovely and talented woman I've heard so much about. Allow me to introduce you to everyone." Holding Tyler's hand captive, she tipped her head toward the twins. "Those two miscreants are our nephews and are currently learning the art of don't piss off Marnie! The rest of these lazy buggers are my guys. Say hi guys!"

"Hi guys!" they returned with laughter.

"Ignore them, pretty lady, for it is I whom you seek." Finally relinquishing her hand, she placed her own over her heart. "Lori Phipps, delighted to make your acquaintance, Doctor."

"The Phipps family does have its fair share of charming women." Lori's bomber jacket was unzipped, hinting at a tight T-shirt stretched across high firm breasts and taut abs. Her hair was long, held back in a loose braid, and showed the consequences of hours under a hard hat.

"Please call me Tyler," she said, then waved her arm to include Georgie in the conversation. "We thought we'd stop in for a tour."

Lori stepped back, giving Tyler an appreciative once-over, offering a grin that could only be described as rakish. "Sorry little lady but not in those boots! Let me treat you to a coffee, while old Bender here works her way up to telling me what she's really here for."

"Bender?"

Lori howled with laughter, taking Tyler by the arm and leading her from the paint shed back into the crisp winter afternoon. Strolling casually to Georgie's Land Rover, Lori hauled the back gate open, letting Maggie out. She closed the gate and leaned against the rear ladder, lighting a cigarette.

Without a breath of preamble she launched into her story. "You see, me and Georgie Porgie here were out partying with some of the guys in her advance flight class. We were all talking about how the female pilots always got nailed with these secretly sexist call signs, like 'guns.'" To demonstrate the actual meaning, Lori cupped her own breasts and gave them a squeeze, then took another long drag on her smoke. "So the guys tell us they think old Georgie here's going to get nailed with Breaker." At Tyler's blank look she explained, "That one secretly means 'Break-her' as in break her in. I know, I know," she said, holding up her hand. "So I hear them tell her this and I'm half in the bag…"

"Half?" Georgie questioned, just now catching up.

"Okay, a little more than half. Anyway, I say to old Georgie here, 'I never pegged you for the kind of girl who'd want to Break-Her!' and Georgie, who by the way was a little more than intoxicated too says, 'Breaker? Why would I break her, when I can bend her all she likes!'" Well the guys laughed their asses off and the next day Georgie graduated and learned her call sign was Bender. Those stupid asses were so drunk, when they retold the story they fucked it all up and thought she was talking about a character from some sci-fi cartoon!"

Tyler chuckled with some effort, only then realizing Maggie was pressed against her leg. "What is it, girl?"

"I think you're on the verge of losing your charge."

"What?" Tyler asked in confusion, looking around she caught on to the fact that Georgie was nowhere to be seen. "Shit…"

"Don't sweat it. If I know Georgie, she's gone to look at her house."

"She has a house out here?"

Tyler and Maggie fell in step with Lori. Lori's strides were long and powerful, forcing Tyler to keep up. That was unusual. She was always conscious of her height and often, even without thinking, would shorten her stride or even stand slightly stooped. With the Phipps family she had discovered a band of Amazon women. Tall, fit and proud. And evidently all lesbian!

"So Doc, how are things going? You handling things with Georgie?"

"Things are going fine, and Georgie's great."

"No problems with our short-ass 'Head-smashed-in-Buffalo' gal?"

"Short-ass?" That caught Tyler by surprise. She had never stopped to consider Georgie's height. Even with the deficits the woman seemed a giant in person. "Georgie's not short."

Lori laughed. "That's good to hear! 'Cause I can see why she hired you. Our Georgie loves her a tall girl!" At Tyler's distressed look, she added, "Oh now Doc, you're not gonna let this old dyke upset you when I have so much to share?" When Tyler didn't reply, she took that as permission to continue. "Why, back in the day, Georgie would have climbed up one side of you and right back down the other." Lori stopped in her tracks, grabbing Tyler by the elbow. "I'm sorry I'm being such an ass. Please forgive me. When it comes to Georgie I get all messed up. I miss the old Bender so much. I guess when I saw you were with Zoe and how much it upset her, well…I would just hate to see her hurt again."

"Okay, first of all, Ms. Phipps, you are not the first woman to speak to me in such a direct manner. I'm a big girl and I'll tell you when it's time to fuck off! Next, I am not dating Zoe. I don't know where anyone got…"

"We were at the club Friday night." It wasn't a fact, it was a challenge. "We got quite a show with you two on the dance floor." All Lori's bravado and warmth were gone. "I'm going to share three facts with you, Dr Marsh. One, if our Georgie hand-selected you for this job, it's because you're the very best and she believes in you. Two, you're just her type, tall, slender and smart. And three, I will not let another tall, smart, doctor of something or other come in here and take advantage of her. Is that understood?"

Tyler stood frozen. No one, not even her parents or an angry ex had ever come at her like this. "Look, not that it's any of your business, but yes I did go out with Zoe a few times. That's it. End of story. As for Georgie, I have no intention of getting involved much less hurting her. And as far as being her type, Georgie has zero interest in me. Understood?"

"Zero interest? Really! Tell me Dr Marsh, how would you tell if she was interested?"

"Don't be ridiculous!" Tyler hurled at the infuriating woman. Spinning around, she spotted the dog, then Georgie out by the breakwater.

"Excuse me," she tossed over her shoulder, quick-marching her way to Georgie's side. She had to force herself to calm down. Whatever was going on had nothing to do with Georgie. Maggie immediately picked up on her mood and bared her teeth. "What the…"

"What happened?" Georgie asked earnestly, using hand signals to bring her in closer. The wind off the lake had picked up and while the afternoon was clearing nicely the improved conditions came with a much colder air mass.

Shivering, Tyler wrapped her arms around herself. She looked first to the dog who seemed to now understand her tension and had pressed herself against her thigh, then Georgie herself. The woman remained open, but didn't approach her. Tyler imagined how she must look in Georgie's eyes. She was like a wounded bird, cornered and afraid, and it helped her see Georgie in a different light. She was unafraid, not vacuous by any means, just fearless. She was concerned and clearly cared but she was treading lightly, perhaps not wanting to invade Tyler's private space. Not sure what to say, Tyler obfuscated by simply switching the subject. "So, where is this house of yours?"

"You are standing…living room." At Tyler's confused look, she added, "I want to build…here."

Tyler made a slow 360 degree turn to take in the strip of land. "You own all this?"

"All east side…peninsula. Lori…west. Funny shape plot." Crouching down, the light dusting of snow just thick enough to carve out her illustration, she drew out the shape of the peninsula and divided it with a large T.

Bending down beside her, Tyler joked, "That looks a little like a T-bone steak." She was immediately rewarded with a smile that helped soothe her worry. Watching as Georgie added a billowing rib steak to the left side before depicting a skinny tenderloin on the right. "This side," she tapped on the left side of the snow steak, "inherited by Lori. I took this side," she explained by pointing to the boatyard. "This bit...the sirloin tip. Is mine too. Maybe one day...build here...live here."

"What about your work? The condo seems so convenient for you."

"I guess, but...you know better. You grew up...house, family business. Some days perfect..."

"And some days you can't get far enough away."

Georgie just nodded. "See one more? The millwork shed?" she asked, starting back toward the boatyard. When she realized Tyler wasn't following, she casually offered her gloved hand.

Without conscious thought, Tyler accepted it and fell in step. Only then considering how it would look if anyone spotted her and Georgie walking across the yard hand in hand. *Fuck you, Lori Phipps! If Georgie wants to hold my hand and stroll around her property, so be it! Bitch!* Maggie, who was off leash and obviously believing neither of them to be in immediate peril, spotted a rabbit making its way through the tall frozen reeds lining the riverbank and made a mad dash. "HALT!" Georgie ordered with crisp command.

Tyler, who stood paralyzed by the impending horror, was shocked to see Maggie skid to a stop. While she growled and continued to make her displeasure known, she held her place. Georgie walked to where she sat and clipped on her leash without scolding the dog in any way. Together they watched the rabbit disappear from sight before turning to resume the hike to the millwork shed. Falling back in beside the pair, Tyler immediately missed the comfort of holding hands. *Was it just the comfort of holding hands or was it holding hands with Georgie?* Shrugging off her query, she accompanied Georgie as they traversed the entire length of the boatyard, even passing the paint shed before heading for the only building not finished in the vibrant blue of all the others.

"We should take...pictures...notes...for the proposal."

"Will we need contractor bids or estimates?"

Georgie watched as she snapped pics with her smartphone. "Depends. What you decide."

That caught her by surprise. Of course, everything about Georgie DiNamico was surprising. Tyler mentally pinched herself. She had put herself in Georgie's corner and had to admit it was starting to shape up into something she had never expected.

* * *

It was only half past five when Marnie pulled her Navigator into the boatyard parking lot. Bypassing security, she was heading for the paint shed when Lori scooted out of the office waving for her to stop.

Lori barely had her foot in the door of the passenger side when she announced, "Houston, we have a problem!"

Groaning, Marnie continued down the gravel driveway. "Please, please, please don't tell me they're in more trouble. One more misstep by those two little bastards and it's military school for them! I can't believe those two ever shared a womb or that it was mine!"

"Hey relax dude. Frick and Frack are in good hands. Another couple of weeks on their hands and knees and those two will be begging to kiss your ass."

"Really Lori? I swear you get more graphic every year. And people say I have a potty mouth!"

"It's not like I have to be the kiss-ass face of DME. I just have to make sure our boats are as pretty as you are."

"Oh no," Marnie said seriously, parking her big SUV directly in front of the entrance to the paint shed. "What the hell's gone so wrong that you're sucking up to me? Jesus, you haven't done that since…"

"Marnie! Eye on the prize girl. I said we have a problem and it's big!" At her cousin's wide eyes and frightened stare, she explained. "I think Georgie's got it bad for the new girl. And I don't like it, and I don't like her. Not one bit."

"You don't like anybody. Why should this one be any different?"

"What? Because it's Georgie, you snot. We have to protect her now."

She carefully studied Lori's worried face. "Okay, I think she's got a thing for the girl too. What do we do?"

"She's got to go. There's no other way; we can't risk it."

Marnie was uncharacteristically silent. It took a long moment before she could formulate a reply or even decide if she and Lori had a right to intervene in Georgie's work and life. As she considered the situation, the twins came ripping out of the paint shed. They looked tired and filthy, crawling into the back of the Navigator, heads down grumbling their greetings. Quietly she asked Lori, "Is Ethan still here?"

"In the office."

Backing out of the parking spot, she drove them back the short distance to the little cottage that was utilized as both Lori's office and security.

When she pulled up out front, Lori trotted in, promising to send her young cousin back out to supervise the student drivers for their trip home.

Marnie turned to the twins and announced, "Change of plans, guys." Removing the key fob from the ignition, she tossed it into the backseat for the boys to fight over. "I want you guys to head home and start dinner for your father. Ethan will go with you. And no fighting! I want you taking turns driving. If Ethan tells me you two didn't behave, it'll be the last time you get to drive this truck. Is that understood?" In the rearview mirror she could see they were still jostling for the key.

While they both grumbled their agreement, one objected with a piercing whine, "Do we have to drive Ethan home?"

"Of course you have to drive him home."

"Then how are we supposed to get home?" the other complained.

Marnie groaned internally. This is just the sort of thing that made her want to smack their heads together.

She thought with affection about Ethan and his mother Stella, who lived in the big house that Luigi had built fifty years ago to house his extended family. The one-hundred-and-twenty-acre plot had been purchased by him in the early fifties. The large gray stone Georgian Manor house had been his one big extravagance but like everything he did, there was always room for opportunity. Sure enough, a new home developer had gone broke in Syracuse, trying to upscale the newest craze for tract homes. Old Luigi had bought out all the unused materials from the failed subdivision, and instead of using them to build a dozen stone bungalows, he also bought architectural plans from a discount supplier he had found in the back of a magazine, and built the imposing grand house on the shores of Lake Erie. In a place with eleven bedrooms, two kitchens and enough common spaces to accommodate an entire regiment, Stella and her son were not the only ones in residence. As expected, Lou Phipps and his brood had assumed the post of primary residents. While Henry still spent his weekends in the big house by the lake, Marnie and Jack had their own home. Shortly after they were married, Danny and Henry had sat down with them and asked if they would prefer their own residence. They'd jumped at the chance to build their own home on the property, and with the blessing of the old boys, they designed a very modern glass and steel showcase to suit their lifestyle. While most of the family referred to it as the Glasshouse, Lou openly called it the hideous monstrosity impinging on his home.

Marnie said to her sons, "You will drive Ethan to the big house. If, and this is a big if, he says he trusts you two, you may drive the truck back down the driveway to our house. Nowhere else," she ordered, emphasizing the point with a shaking fist. "Get your butts back to the house and get dinner started. Understood?"

They grumbled their agreement but piled out happily waiting for their mother to vacate the driver's seat. Once Ethan was buckled into the passenger seat and waved his farewell, Marnie turned for the office and headed inside.

The little building really wasn't much more than a shack. Actually it was a beautiful little replica of Lori's own house. She'd built it as practice for the real thing, and Marnie had agreed to pay for the materials, knowing a little cottage would look better in front of the assembly building than another stupid shed. Other than the washroom, there were only two rooms in the security cottage, the main room and a tiny kitchen. Passing under the security counter, Marnie dumped her purse on one of the two desks, asking point blank, "What the hell happened when they were out here?"

Lori just smiled at her. "Marnie, chill a minute, will you?"

For a moment it looked like Marnie's head would blow, then she began laughing. "Holy hell girl, what a friggin day!" she said, dragging a chair out and sitting down. "Please tell me the sun's over the yardarm somewhere?"

Lori pulled a bottle of Canadian Club from a desk drawer. She grabbed two clean glasses and some ice from the kitchen, calling out, "You want Seven or Coke?"

"You have to ask?"

"All right," Lori conceded. She poured two fingers of CC in each glass, then topped them up with Coke. "So who pissed in your porridge today?"

Marnie almost choked on her drink. "Shit!" she said, wiping her drink from her chin. "I swear you are the worst influence on me."

"Me? You're the one who always comes up with great ideas. One of which may be just about to blow up in our faces."

After slugging a third of her drink down, Marnie smiled with her most mischievous grin.

"Oh no," Lori said, arms held up in surrender and practically backing into the wall. "I know that look and I smell trouble!"

"Really? What does the smell of trouble look like?" Marnie huffed at her, taking another generous swallow. "When I saw you waving your arms like a madwoman, I assumed it was about my evil offspring, not this…this shit!" Finally relinquishing her hold on the half-gone beverage, she said amiably, "Tell me everything."

Lori filled her in on the boatyard visit and the sight of Georgie and Tyler strolling along the breakwater hand in hand.

"That doesn't mean anything. Hell, I've had to take her by the hand on more than a dozen occasions."

"Take her hand, not wander around in the afternoon sunshine, hand in hand!"

"I take your point," she huffed again. Examining Lori's expression, she had to ask, "That's not all, is it?"

Lori shook her head, a little more than embarrassed to admit she had challenged Tyler. "We kinda had a disagreement."

"You and Georgie?"

"No, no! She and Maggie went out for a walk on the spit. I was talking about Tyler. Well, I kind of cornered her and asked what she was up to."

"Jesus Christ Lori! Are you trying to get us sued?"

"Sued! Really Marnie? That's where you're going with this? That bitch is playing our Georgie and I will not stand by and let another gold digger have a go at her!" Lori was back on her feet and pacing to control her anger. "That woman you're so worried might sue us, has just invited our Georgie for Christmas dinner. Christmas! Can you believe that?"

Marnie looked like someone had just slapped her face. Picking up her drink, she set it back down without comment. It was obvious she was stunned. "Georgie told you this?"

"She sent me a text. She wants to know if I would take her shopping and tell her what to buy for Tyler's family." Sliding back into her chair, Lori looked broken. "What do we do?"

Opening her Day-Timer, Marnie flipped to the page she sought. "Here," she offered, writing an address down on a Post-it note. "Take her to this gift shop. They sell collector memorabilia crap, including car stuff. I've been meaning to take Georgie over there." Handing over the list, she looked like a general ordering her men into battle. "Let's divide and conquer! You take Georgie to lunch and then shopping. Tread lightly, Lori. I want you to find out what's happening, not start a bar brawl in a gift store. Can you handle that?"

"Yeah, no problem." Lori got to her feet, grabbing the bomber jacket she had slung across the other chair. You gonna take on the gold digger?"

"Don't call her that, at least not until we know what she's up to. Set a date with Georgie, soon, like tomorrow. While you're out with her, I will have a conversation with little Miss Tyler." Checking her watch, Marnie explained, "Family dinner night. I can't be late. You mind running me out to the house?"

Lori retrieved the keys to her Jeep from a hook on the back wall. "Only if I'm invited for dinner."

Marnie just laughed, pulling on her winter coat. "Don't complain if Satan's spawn tries to poison us with their culinary efforts."

Following Marnie out, Lori set the alarm and locked up the security cottage. "You really have to stop calling them that!" she said, but couldn't keep a straight face. "Good God, you should've seen them today. It was hilarious listening to them grumble on their knees. The best part was lunchtime. All the guys were talking about how they spent their time doing penance in the paint shed. I swear those boys really thought this was just for today, then Anthony goes and tells them how Henry had banished him to the paint shed for an entire summer. You should've seen their faces! God I love my job."

Marnie harrumphed, never forgetting her own experience with Lori at her side, learning to clean and prep the sixty foot mold for a classic DynaCraft fiberglass hull. She had learned her lesson and so had Lori.

CHAPTER SEVEN

At home, sprawled on the couch, Tyler watched her very pregnant sister waddle into the family room. While they weren't identical twins they shared many features. Raven-haired and with unusually vivid blue eyes, they had turned heads in high school even after Tyler came out. Having a straight twin to watch her back had made all the difference in their world. Now in their thirties, both women stood tall and slender, perhaps even caffeine thin by some standards. With Kira's pregnancy, her chiseled face had softened with what she was proud to call baby fat. Tyler was glad to see her put the baby's health before any concerns for her own appearance. Somewhere in the deep recesses of her mind she worried for their connected intuition. Something their dad call the spooky twin thing. Would having a baby change that? Certainly all the boyfriends that had come and gone had had no effect on their connection but a child was different. At least Kira was home with them all and letting her share in her concerns and excitement. "Sounds like Megan's in trouble again," Kira offered with a grin.

Ensconced in her corner of the sofa, Tyler had been staring at the blank screen of her notebook for several minutes. Resigning herself to the interruption, she closed the lid and moved the computer to the side table, along with several reports.

Kira, carefully maneuvering herself, sat down beside Tyler. "Want one?" she asked, holding out a jar of dill pickles and a fork.

"Really?" Tyler asked. "I thought that was a cliché, eating pickles when you're pregnant."

"Nope! After this I'm going to have some of that strawberry pie Dad brought home."

Before Tyler could remind her sister that the strawberry pie was meant to be served with Sunday night supper, an upstairs door slammed and their younger sister's scream carried throughout the house, "YOU DEFEND THEM ALL THE TIME! WHY IS IT OKAY FOR THE SLUT AND THE DYKE, BUT NOT ME?"

While their mother's voice was not raised, it was definitive and crisply authoritarian. "Your sisters are grown women. I support the choices they've made. Both your father and I are proud to have them home with us. The difference between you and your sisters, Megan, is twelve years of adult life experience and a lot of common sense. Something you have yet to demonstrate."

While the older sisters knew better than to interrupt the raging debate, both were sympathetic. Putting her legs up on the couch, Kira unceremoniously dumped her feet in Tyler's lap.

"Holy smokes, Turtle, have you seen the size of your ankles?"

Crunching on a dill, Kira whined, "Rub my feet?"

Tyler covered one foot with the blanket on her lap, and began her ministrations on the second. "How long have they been this bad?"

"A few days now," their mother answered for Kira, entering the room from the staircase. She bypassed her twin daughters, heading for the kitchen and the ever-brewing coffee. She returned a few minutes later with coffee for her and Tyler, and a tall glass of milk for Kira. "If I ever complained about you two, please forgive me. I knew not what I spoke of. Good God! You two were hell on wheels but to be fair, you were always respectful, even when you were breaking the rules."

"I don't understand why Megan's so mad about us moving home," Kira remarked. "She was the first one to complain when we left. Now all she does is bitch that we're back!"

"Don't worry about it. She's just striking out. She's at that age. She's angry and upset and doesn't know who to blame. So she's blaming you two. When you're not here, she blames your father, or me, or the milkman or God knows whoever pops into her head." Debbie Marsh shook it off. "Let it go. Once she cools down a bit and has a chance to think about what she said, I'm sure she'll apologize."

"Where's Dad?" Tyler asked.

"He's meeting a couple of the guys from the car club. They're trying to find a workspace so they can put some of their members back to work. They came up with this idea to restore cars on speculation, like your dad did during college."

"How would that work?"

"I think the plan is pretty simple. They have at least a dozen guys in the club who are out of work. So they want to find a couple of cars to restore and a workspace. I guess he figured the guys are sitting around anyway, so they can work on donor cars, then sell what they finish and split the profits when all is said and done."

Tyler covered the foot she'd been massaging with the blanket, before moving on to massage Kira's right foot. "Doesn't Dad have room in the shop?"

"For bodywork! Plus, I really don't like the idea of half a dozen guys just hanging out all day. Even if they're working on a project, I have enough trouble keeping your dad's guys on point without adding his buddies to the mix."

"Are they really serious about this?" At her mother's nod, and her sister's insistent foot prod, Tyler explained, "I might have a space they can use and maybe even a project."

"Really? That would help your father so much. Let me call him and see where he's at."

While her mother made her phone call, she finished the foot rub then placed an ice bag across her sister's ankles. "I think you should keep your feet raised."

Kira sank her fork into the jar of pickles, spearing another dill. "I don't think I can wait till dinner. Can we have the strawberry pie now?"

Tyler rolled her eyes, turning to her mother for guidance.

"Finish off last night's apple pie first."

Kira groaned. "Actually, I think I want a grilled cheese instead."

"You just had steak and eggs with Dad!" Tyler commented. "Are you really that hungry?"

"If I say yes will you stop bugging me?"

"Girls!" Debbie groaned at her twin daughters. "Your dad's next door at the shop, Tyler. Why don't you head over while I make your sister a sandwich?"

Tyler strolled through the back entrance of the shop, making her way to the lunch room. It was her dad's preferred workspace and where he and his buddies would gather to drink coffee, talk about restoring old cars and, lately, commiserate about the economy. As expected, Carl Marsh was seated at the large round lunch table. The surface, covered with a plastic tablecloth, was strewn with auto magazines and used car buying guides. Her father, hunched over his laptop, peered at her over his reading glasses. "Hey pumpkin."

"Hey Dad," she offered, heading past him for the coffee machine. Picking up the half-full carafe, she swirled the black brew before taking a whiff. "How old is this?"

"Better make a new one."

While he worked away at whatever had his focus, she emptied the old pot and rinsed it carefully. Replacing the coffee filter and scooping in the fine grind Maxwell House from the giant Costco tin, she surreptitiously watched her dad. She couldn't help but notice he was getting older. Oh, he was still a good-looking man but the years of hard work and the stress of the business, not to mention raising three strong-willed daughters, was beginning to show. "Is it worth it?"

Carl looked up at his daughter, eyebrows raised high above his reading glasses. "Uh-oh! My pumpkin's awfully reflective for a Sunday."

Tyler leaned back against the lunch counter, arms crossed and head back. listening to the coffeemaker hiss and spit. "Isn't that what Sundays are for?"

"I don't know. Used to be you girls thought Sundays were for shopping! Nowadays not so much."

Before her dad could comment on her mood, or worse, ask the kind of soul-searching questions that always forced her to focus on the things truly bothering her, she changed the subject. "Mom says you and the guys have a plan and just need some space."

"Space and a project. I think I've found one," he revealed, tipping his head to the computer.

With her coffee in hand and a fresh cup for him, Tyler slid into the chair beside him. "Can I see?"

"Sure." He adjusted the laptop so they could both see the screen. "We found three cars in our price range. This Dodge is probably the best of the lot."

She read the stats carefully. "A four-door? I would have assumed a coupe or convertible would be a better choice?"

"They would. If we could find one."

He reached past her to open another tab on the browser. "I've been going over the sales stats for some of the big auction houses. These are some of last year's sales at Barrett-Jackson. Have a look," he offered, turning over the laptop to her. While she scrolled down the list he asked casually, "See the pattern?"

Tyler shook her head while she continued to read through the list of cars, features and the final sales amounts. "Wait, I would expect to see some commonality around price with similar models, but these numbers are all over the place. What's the defining difference? Quality of restoration?"

"You would think," he said. "Actually the range between a good DIY frame-up restoration and a Concours car is not that big. The two factors I found are horsepower and custom versus stock."

Now it was Tyler's turn to sport the Marsh raised eyebrow. "Custom versus stock I get, but horsepower?"

He nodded. "Okay compare these two Corvettes. Here's a '63 split window. Really nice, all original stock car with a small block 350 under the hood. It sold for 84K. Now look at this '64."

Doing just that, she read through the sales summary. "Holy smokes…240 grand! For a '64? A Concours '63, or even a '67 with a big block maybe but…"

"Read the vehicle stats," he suggested, clearly interested to see her reaction.

"Oh my God, they gutted her! They completely replaced everything. 'L88 engine, six-speed tranny, Dana rear end.' What the hell—why waste a vintage 'Vette body on what's basically a new Camaro? And who the hell pays two hundred and forty thousand for what's basically just a factory stock car?"

"I think these guys are buying them to race. Vintage racing is all the rage these days. Especially on the west coast. So only the car body need be vintage to qualify."

"I get that but this," she pointed to the fact sheet displayed. "It just seems wrong. Not that the 1964 Corvette was anything to shake a stick at, but this seems sacrilegious to me."

"You and me both pumpkin. You and me!"

"So…" she reflected. "If you're not going to drop more horsepower into a car than anyone could ever use, how do you get top dollar?"

"Total custom," he explained, adding, "and it has to be top dog—total showroom quality."

"Can your guys do that?"

"I think so. We'll need some help designing the reinforcements for the convertible top and we'll probably need to pay someone else to sew the custom upholstery."

"What's your budget?"

"We pooled together a little over twelve grand. It's tight but I think we can do it, if we can find a reasonable work space."

Grinning, she offered, "How about a free workspace and a second project, a paying project?"

Carl smiled, enjoying her enthusiasm. "I like the sound of that. Tell me what you've got in mind already."

"May I?" she asked, tipping her head to his computer. At his nod, she pulled it closer, typing in a URL from memory. "I drove Georgie out to the boatyard the other day. We took these pictures of the old millwork shed. I think it might have started life as a barn. It's a large timber frame building. The tin siding outside looks like hell but inside the place is immaculate. They still store wood moldings up in the loft but the ground level is empty except for Georgie's cars."

"Cars?" he asked, eyebrows raised, "as in plural?"

"Don't get so excited. It's not a collection or anything." She scrolled to the pictures they had taken of the cars stored in the mill. "This Packard was her grandfather's."

"Nice! All original?"

"And pristine," she added, clicking on the next image. "This Town and Country is a '61 I think, and all original. It was Georgie's aunt's car. Not my cup of tea but nice."

"Nice but not in need of much attention," he commented.

Agreeing with him, she scrolled through several shots of the timber framing to find the image she wanted. Clicking on it, she angled the laptop to give him a better look. "You may find this interesting…All the DiNamico grandkids got new cars for their sixteenth birthdays, all but Georgie."

He studied the photo carefully before scrolling to the next in the series. "Boy you don't see many of these little Jeeps anymore. Is it a Kaiser or a Willy's?"

"I'm not sure. Evidently, it was the plow truck for the boatyard. When Georgie was turning sixteen, her dad offered her a new Subaru Brat. Instead, she asked for flying lessons and he agreed, offering her the old Jeep if she was willing to spend the time and effort needed to keep it running. She was telling me about a short in the electrical system she just couldn't find. No matter what she did, it just chewed through batteries. Evidently, she got really good at parking on hills and push-starting it herself."

"Been there!" he said, chuckling. "She sounds like good people. It's been close to a month now, how are you two getting along?"

Tyler considered his question carefully. "It's complicated. I mean it's not what I thought at all. Georgie's very accommodating and respectful, but she's surprisingly protective."

"It makes sense. If you've suffered such a serious trauma, wouldn't your self-preservation kick in?"

"Actually, I meant protective of me. Last week she took a chunk out of Lou Phipps for referring to me as 'her girl.' That woman may have many challenges communicating, but getting her point across when she's very, very angry is not one of them."

"Lou Phipps, that's Zoe's dad, isn't it?" At her nod, he quipped, "I always assume men with daughters would naturally be more respectful."

Rolling her eyes, she said, "You would think, but no! When that man looks at me, all he sees is the help."

"Does he know you're dating his daughter?" he asked. "Maybe he has a problem with that."

"Then he has nothing to worry about. I told Zoe I wasn't interested in pursuing anything."

"Oh?" He gave her a look of parental concern.

"Let's just leave it there, Dad. Now what about restoring this little Jeep and the millwork shed. Think your guys could make it work?"

"It will depend on overhead costs, but as far as the space and the project, they're perfect. Do you really think she'd consider renting it to us?"

"No Dad. She won't rent it. I know that." At his crestfallen look, she added, "She will want you to use it for free. Maybe what you could do is cut her a deal on the restoration cost. She's really into fair trade projects."

"And you really think she'll go for that?"

"Dad, a few weeks ago, when she offered to buy her nephew some new shirts and ties, Zoe accused her of favoritism. In response she put out ten grand of her own money to make the same offer to all of her staff."

"Okay then! When do I get to pitch the idea?"

"How about Christmas?"

"Christmas?" he asked with surprise. "Won't she be with her family?"

"No, and before you ask," she said, "it's a long story and it's part of the reason I want to invite her for dinner."

"Okay…and the other part?"

Tyler sucked in a deep breath. "I get the sense she's really lonely. In a way, she's very much an outsider in her own family. Don't get me wrong. Since the accident, each of them has taken responsibility for some portion of her life but they don't really involve her. They just do what they think is best and leave it at that."

He considered her worries carefully, finally asking, "Are they doing what's best for her?"

Tyler sighed. "I'm sure there was a time when they were, but things change. She's by no means back to her old self but she's not helpless either. Just, well…isolated, might be the best way to describe things."

"Families are complicated," he offered without judgment. "Why don't you clear the invite with your mom, then we can hammer out a proposal for Ms. DiNamico."

"We?" Tyler asked with a grin. "When did I get roped into this?"

"When you started driving your boss's Land Rover!" At her baffled look, he added, "Now we have to worry about your baby sister driving your mom's car again. Good God, that girl does not possess an ounce of the common sense my pumpkin and my little turtle had at half her age!"

Tyler laughed, pulling the laptop closer. "I guess we should add a project plan to your budget. What about the little Jeep? Any idea what would be involved there?"

"Actually I do. Let me go pull out the shop manual and I know I've got a bunch of parts catalogs around here somewhere. Why don't you have a look over my budget for restoring that Dodge while I find everything?"

"Add another cup of coffee to that list and I'll turn 'our' proposal into a masterpiece!"

Carl smiled, reaching over to give his daughter a hug. "Boy, I missed having you home pumpkin. I really did!"

* * *

"Get your ass in here!"

"Really Marnie?" Zoe said, poking her head in the office door. "Some days you're as crass as Aunt Lori!"

Caught off guard by the challenge to her behavior, Marnie smiled, deciding in that second to take a different tack. "Let's sit down and chat before you take off for the break."

Zoe blanched. "Are you firing me?"

"What? No! I just want to talk. Family stuff. Grab a coffee with me?"

"I'll get it."

"I'll come with you—'tis the season and all that."

"Straight from the mouth of Scrooge Pulaski! Really Marnie? Since when did you give a rat's ass about Christmas?"

"Now look who's being crass." Stepping into the private kitchen, Marnie watched as Zoe prepared two cups. From where she was standing, she could see into the side-by-side offices of Susan Chan and Tyler Marsh. She watched as Tyler worked steadily, head down and focused on her task. As Marnie followed Zoe back to her office, she stuck her head first in Susan's door, offering Susan and her napping husband a happy holiday, before stopping at Tyler's door. "Hi Tyler. Happy holiday. Almost ready for the break?" At her nod and returned well wishes, she ordered, "Drop by my office before you go. Say about one o'clock?"

Back in her own suite, Marnie closed the door, offering Zoe a seat in the corner sitting area. Marnie rarely made use of the space, preferring to have her staff gather around her desk. To say Zoe looked suspicious would be an understatement. Recognizing the jig was up, Marnie put her coffee on the table and asked plainly, "What the hell is going on with you and Dr Marsh?"

"Oh Christ, Marnie! I really thought you were going to fire me!" She put her hand on her chest, taking a big calming breath before wiping an errant tear from her eye.

"I'm sorry kiddo; I really am. It's just that I need to know if we have a problem with Tyler."

"Tyler? I did not see that one coming. Has Georgie complained?" she asked, visibly surprised by the situation. "They seem to be getting on well. What's the problem?"

"There's no problem. I was just interested to hear how things were with you two. You looked pretty cozy last week in the bar."

"The bar—how would you—you were in a lesbian bar?"

"Don't be so shocked. Back in the day, I used to go to Toronto with Lori and Georgie. We'd hit all the bars on Temple Street."

"Church Street," she corrected.

"Whatever." Marnie waved off the correction. "Now stop stalling and tell me how things are going. I want details, girl!"

Zoe laughed at her. "You want details? Well that's a first. Sorry to disappoint but I've got bad news. Seems the uppity Dr Marsh isn't interested in a little fun with me. Although, I must say, she was quite kind about the whole thing. I guess that's her education at work."

Marnie seemed to chew on that. "When did this happen?"

"To be honest it's been off and on from the start. But she dropped the bomb the other night; we were out having drinks."

"Oh."

"Oh?" Zoe asked.

"So, did you like her? I mean was this someone you, you know. Someone you envisioned a future with?"

"A future, hell no! Are you cracked?"

Now it was Marnie's turn to raise her eyebrows. "Some of us like the cracked future thing!"

Zoe practically snorted her laughter. "Really Marnie, the only future I was interested in pretty much ended that night. Nothing personal, but our Miss Tyler is a bit of a prude and far too vanilla for my taste."

Marnie wasn't exactly sure what that meant but decided in favor of Tyler. "So, in the language of my husband and sons, she wouldn't put out! Is that what you're telling me?"

Zoe grinned. "What an education you've been getting. I'm sure Aunt Lori's been rubbing off on you too. I can't imagine Georgie talking like that. At least I can't remember her ever doing so."

"You're too young and to be honest, I think she was always on the formal side. She always went for that officer and gentlewoman crap!"

Laughing outright, Zoe shook her head. "What's got into you? The last time you let loose and had some fun was the twins' sixteenth birthday."

"I know, I know! I got a little tipsy that night. Can you blame me? My babies were turning sixteen! Christ, they already had Jack talked into taking them straight to the DMV the next morning. I was scared shitless!"

"Now you see why my idea of a long-term relationship is three days in bed then *arrivederci!*"

"Don't ever say that in front of Jack! My idea of three days in bed sounds like a reading marathon. I almost have him convinced that women need longer recuperative time between sexual interludes."

Zoe had to cover her mouth to keep from spewing coffee all over. "Sexual interludes? No bloody wonder he's such a frustrated man! Really Marnie, you should consider putting out a bit."

Marnie laughed that off, standing and heading back to her desk. "Believe me, Jack Pulaski gets all he needs." She put down her coffee cup and turned to Zoe. "Thanks for yakking with me, kiddo. You're right, I sometimes forget to have fun."

Zoe beamed her gratitude. "Not a problem. Let me get you a fresh cup."

Checking her watch for the time, Marnie asked, "Would you please bring one for Tyler too? I have to go over Georgie's schedule for the break. Speaking of which, do you two have everything under control for New Year's Eve?"

"We do. Want me to sit in with Tyler?"

"No, you can take off and tell Susan and Anthony to get out of here too."

Once Zoe delivered the fresh coffee, Marnie found herself staring at Tyler's unclaimed mug. For a sliver of a moment, it was easy to sympathize with those women in historical novels who would resort to poisoning to get their way. *Oh, for a little arsenic!* She was still fantasizing about murdering one Tyler Marsh when the woman knocked at her door.

Staring at her, Marnie admitted grudgingly that she was a consummate professional. She wore conservative suits daily, showed up early, left late and always made sure Georgie was cared for, focused and capable of continuing safely without her company. She respected that. And the woman was working hard. Sifting through reams and reams of crap Georgie believed had some future application. She knew whatever they were working on wouldn't see the light of day until the annual board meeting and she was fine with that, and glad the days of Georgie painstakingly trying to explain new ideas to her were over. So why was she so pissed? "Let's sit on the couch. I hope you're good for another coffee?" she asked, carrying both mugs to the sitting area.

She watched as Tyler took her seat. She was poised and polite, which Marnie appreciated. For a sister-in-law, she could do worse. "So Tyler, I wanted to catch up before you take off for Christmas. I'm interested to hear how things are shaping up." Marnie watched as Tyler seemed to weigh her options.

"It's very kind of you to take time out of your schedule for me. Let me cover my secondary duties first. I'm proceeding with two reports for the annual board meeting. One dovetails with a proposal Georgie will make. The other is a white paper on ethical issues facing the marine industry along with an accompanying report on any outlying areas of liability those issues may raise."

Marnie nodded, sipping her coffee. "And your primary duties?"

"Georgie you mean."

"Yes. How are things going with her?"

Tyler locked eyes with her. "Marnie, if there's a problem, I would respectfully suggest you be direct."

"I see." She took more time to sip her coffee. Finally putting her cup down, Marnie blurted, "Christ, this was so much easier when I thought you and Zoe were dating!"

"Not you too?"

"I'll admit my respect for you has grown dramatically since learning you're not interested in my lovely little heart-breaking niece!" Missing her ballpoint pen, Marnie tapped her frustration on the arm of the couch. "Dr Marsh, you're an educated woman and very observant, so I'm not going to waste time explaining why I'm not a touchy-feely person. Just suffice it to say I'm not. Another fact you don't need reminding of is this is a family company. Even so, we have some rules about dating and relationships."

"I've read the company policy manual."

Marnie growled, "Let me finish." It was not a suggestion. "Do you know why our policy requires the junior ranking employee to declare a relationship to HR, when the employees in question work in the same department?"

Tyler looked ready for a fight but clearly hadn't expected that. "No actually."

"Georgie! After her first deployment, she came back with concerns about a new issue they were having over there. The military calls it Command Rape." At Tyler's shocked look she explained, softening slightly, "They had all these young women coming home saying they had been forced into sexual relationships with their superiors, superiors who had filed the requisite paperwork declaring the relationship so they wouldn't be violating their code of justice. Starting to see what her concern was?"

"Yes I do. Although from an ethical standpoint and liability, requiring disclosure from both employees and oversight would be a better policy."

Marnie wanted to gouge out Tyler's eyes. Surely the woman knew she was talking about her and Georgie. "The point," she explained, trying dearly to keep any contempt from her voice, "the point is...oh crap!" Marnie got to her feet, pacing. "Tyler, what the fuck? Last week I see you out with Zoe. I wouldn't have believed it if I wasn't there. Now Lori tells me you're taking Georgie home for Christmas. You do know the effect you have on her. Don't you?"

Tyler gaped at her. "I don't know what you're talking about."

"Really?" she asked sarcastically. "So the fact that she saw you dancing with Zoe on Friday night, started a fistfight with Lori, and by Monday morning had finished her fifty-thousand word thesis on God knows what—think all of that was just a coincidence?"

Tyler was on her feet, but the panic in her eyes betrayed her blamelessness.

"You didn't know?" demanded Marnie.

Collapsing back down, Tyler shook her head. "I'm sorry. I'll resign immediately."

"Oh no you don't, young lady," Marnie all but spat, she was so mad. Realizing this was not one of her children, she softened, sitting down beside her. "Tyler, you're not in trouble. I had a feeling you didn't know but I needed to be sure. Now before you panic about Georgie, I can assure you she will never make a pass at you. I know how that shake-and-bake brain of hers works. If you treat her professionally, she will do nothing but the same. Treat her as a friend and she will take only those liberties one would expect from a friend but if you're interested in more, you'll have to let her know and in no uncertain terms. I do mean that literally."

"Okay Marnie, I'm a little behind the curve on this one. So let me see if I've got this right. You saw me dancing with Zoe, in a lesbian bar, on my personal time, and somehow you think that's related to Georgie's latest breakthrough? I'm sorry but the cause and effect are a bit too convenient for me."

"Really?" Marnie's voice was tinged in anger but she supposed Tyler deserved the whole story. "Lori and I have been taking Georgie out every other Friday night for months now. Most nights we end up going to that damn bar and yes, we were there last weekend and yes Georgie saw you with Zoe and took it badly. How do I know this? Here's how the evening usually goes. We find a table and settle in while Lori goes to the bar for the first round. When she returns with our drinks, she always manages to bring a friend to introduce to Georgie. A friend she just happened to bump into while ordering drinks. Of course, she invites these women out long beforehand and coaches them on Georgie's peculiarities."

"A setup?"

"Yes it's a setup goddammit! And it's consistently failed to draw even the least bit of interest from Georgie. Until last week. And do you know what happened last week?"

"She met someone?" Tyler actually looked upset.

Marnie would have cheered if she wasn't so fired up. "Really? No Tyler, she didn't meet anyone! She watched you dancing with Zoe. Then Lori, not knowing who you were to Georgie, made an inappropriate crack about what she would do with and to you, given half the chance. Well Georgie did not like that. Not one bit. She went straight over the table after Lori. The bouncer and two very masculine women carried them bodily out the door! Now, can you see how I've connected cause and effect?"

Silent and embarrassed, Tyler finally admitted, "I don't know what to say."

Feeling as if she'd finally connected, she sighed, conceding, "You don't have to say anything. I just want you to know the rules or at least the way Georgie makes up rules in her head. Look, I don't know if you're interested in my sister and frankly I don't want to know. My point in sharing all of this is to let you know you're making headway with Georgie. It may not be in the direction you had planned but you are. I was dead serious when I said she would never cross a line with you. If the effort you've been making is about being a friend to her then don't worry. She'll never ask for more and I can't thank you enough. Now, before you leave for the break, I think we need to talk about one more little concern."

"Let me guess," Tyler asked without humor, "Christmas?"

"Ah yes indeed. Christmas! The famous DiNamico black holiday." Marnie picked up her cold coffee. "Some days it's a wonder I don't drink at work."

Tyler held her mug up in salute. "I'm with you there sister!"

Marnie laughed so hard, she snorted. Using her coffee mug, she offered a toast. "God help fools, small children and Georgie DiNamico!"

"Hear, hear!"

CHAPTER EIGHT

"Is it okay? Maggie will not…offend anyone?"

"How could this sweet girl offend anyone?" Tyler asked, walking Georgie and the dog to the truck.

After hauling the rear gate wide open, Georgie unclipped the dog's lead and carefully stored it in the door pocket. Once she was in the Land Rover, she immediately double-checked that Maggie was in the rear of the truck. Tyler watched her do it every time they loaded up. She wanted to assure Georgie that she wouldn't leave the dog behind but knew instinctively that Georgie needed to check.

"Tell me about…them?" Georgie asked.

"Did you get the list I sent?" Knowing how important it was for her to feel prepared when meeting with people, Tyler had created the same style cheat sheet Georgie used before visiting the boatyard and the VA Clinic.

"Father: Carl Marsh, ex-professional football player, co-owner Carl's Autobody. Mother: Debbie Marsh, nee Becker, CPA designate, co-owner Carl's Autobody. Twin sister: Kira

Marsh, Attorney, am I allowed…her pregnancy? I mean, some families are…old wives' tale?"

"Superstitious?"

"Yes. Sup-er-sti-tious," she said, as if tasting the word for the first time.

Tyler had come to understand that this process was a lifesaver for Georgie. Without feedback she would often stall, stuck trying to sort her way through her own linguistic nightmare. "Are you…are they superstitious about…"

"About the pregnancy? I would say yes and no. For the average family the yes comes at the beginning, when you don't know what to expect. As the mother and baby progress normally, the old superstitions fade away, replaced with insight, education and experience."

"How pregnant is your…Kira?"

Tyler smiled to hear Georgie describe her twin as *her* Kira. "Eight months, and before you ask, she hasn't experienced any complications to date."

"Are there…I should not ask?"

"I can't imagine but there's always a first. Why don't you try your questions out on me?" She knew Georgie had made a list ahead of time, going as far as to memorize the questions so she could deliver them in normal sentences without having to stop and think her way around the words.

"Kira, I'm curious, who knew you were pregnant first, you or your mother?"

Taking a quick glance at her boss in the seat next to her, Tyler had to smile. One thing she knew after a month at DME, Georgie could always be counted on to ask the least expected questions. "You know, most people would want to know who the father is or the sex of the baby."

"Too personal. Besides, they will volunteer…when comfortable. Better to wait…listen."

"And asking who clued in first. What's that about?"

Georgie angled herself in her seat to better converse with Tyler. "I find the…connection…empathy between familial women…fascinating. When Cory got pregnant…"

"Sorry, who's Cory?"

"Oh, ah Lou's wife...first wife. Zoe and Skippy's mom."

"Okay, 'when Cory got pregnant,'" she coaxed.

"When Cory got pregnant," Georgie continued, "they tried to hide it. Cory's grandmother knew...called Henry."

"To congratulate them?"

Georgie laughed. "Uh no. Seventeen-year-old Mister... Uptight...got his girlfriend in ...family way."

"Busted!" Tyler chortled, pleased by the revelation. "Oh I shouldn't be enjoying this so much, but it's a blast to learn Mr. Perfect isn't so perfect after all. So, what happened? Did they have the baby?"

"Two babies." Georgie corrected. "Zoe Angelica...Henry Junior!"

"Another Henry?"

"When baby Lou...born, Henry did not want...name little Henry. Lou is named after...grandad...Luigi Henry. In time... just called him Lou. When Cory had twins...they named Zoe and Henry but...we call him Skip...skip-a-generation."

Tyler smiled. She loved this most about working with Georgie. The woman could tell a story, even when she lost complete track of what she was talking about. And she enjoyed sharing. She was enjoying how casual Georgie could be with her. She would sit turned in the passenger seat, sharing fact, information and funny stories. She especially loved the radiance she projected whenever she became animated. While she spoke with her hands and her words, her green eyes were as telling as anything she shared.

"How did we get...this subject?" Georgie asked.

"Pregnancy."

"She eat weird things?"

"Weird, like what?"

"Like...pickled sweet and sour turkey balls?"

Laughing so hard, Tyler had to force herself to drive the truck. "Really? Is that even a thing?"

"I do not know...Never pregnant."

"God you make me laugh sometimes. 'Pickled turkey balls!' Dad will love that one, but we better not tell Kira. I wouldn't want to give her ideas."

Now it was Georgie's turn to laugh. "I like this...Dr Marsh! What is next?"

"Well we haven't discussed my own family's version of Satan's spawn."

Georgie looked at her, wide-eyed. "Megan?"

Tyler nodded, still grinning from ear to ear.

"Little sister...bad as Marnie's twins?"

"Oh brother, if you think little Danny and Luc are a handful, you haven't seen anything. And I'll warn you now, if she gets rude with you, you're more than welcome to take her down a notch."

"Tyler...Parents are protective...of their children, even... completely out of line. Want to see protective instincts...mother bear? Insult Marnie's kids. You see...fast!"

"Oh no. Not going there. I wouldn't take on your sister, not for all the tea in China!"

"Still make tea in China?"

"I think they make tea in China every day. Do they still grow tea might be a better question."

"Very well...Doctor smarty-pants! Still *grow* tea in China?"

Tyler laughed. "As Zoe would say, 'I have no bloody idea now, do I'?"

Georgie chuckled too. "You pegged her. You could pick us up...same time. Do not need...special trip for me."

"What are you talking about?"

"Driving me...and Zoe to your house for..."

"Christmas," Tyler finished for her, suddenly irritated. "Who told you Zoe was coming?"

"I, uh...guessed. No worry, not...her idea to invite me. I know. Zoe would never...include me, in personal life."

Gripping the wheel tightly, Tyler fought to control her temper. It wasn't Georgie's fault that everyone had assumed a few social outings with the office gossip had escalated into a relationship. Surely even Georgie, as isolated as she was, would know Zoe was a player and not the girlfriend type. "Okay Georgie. Riddle me this. Do you really think I would get involved with someone like Zoe Phipps?" She knew it was a provocative question. With the 'someone like' description open to all sorts of discriminatory allegations. She could feel Georgie's eyes on her and knew by experience the woman was taking her time to consider the question in all its connotations.

"I hit Lori," she admitted quietly, as if that fact explained her own disbelief.

"She had it coming Georgie. Please don't be upset with yourself." Reaching across the console, Tyler took her hand. "Lori jumps to conclusions. God love her. Her heart's in the right place, but she's spent so much time trying to protect you, I'm not sure she sees who you really are anymore."

She nodded. "Broken."

"Not broken," Tyler urged, squeezing her hand. "Look at me. You are not broken, just reorganized!"

That made Georgie smile as they pulled into the driveway next to Carl's Autobody and followed the laneway marked private. Behind the shop and on a well treed lot sat the Marsh residence. Georgie took in the building, seeing immediately, as Tyler had known she would, that it had begun life as a war-time bungalow, but had been expanded into an impressively sized home. "Wow, your parents...do this?"

"Pretty much. They've expanded the shop and the house over the years. I can't remember a time in my childhood when we weren't renovating or building some addition. Which for a kid is always interesting and a hell of a lot easier than moving to a different school every time you grow out of your house."

Georgie agreed. "Why old Luigi bought...at Eighteenmile Creek and built...big house."

"He wanted to provide a safe haven. It makes sense, after losing his family back in Italy."

At Georgie's astonished look, Tyler added, "I read the book!"

* * *

Hours later Georgie stood in the foyer of her penthouse apartment, rubbing her hands vigorously together while she waited for her eyes to adjust to the dark. It was well after midnight when Tyler finally had driven her home. She'd enjoyed the visit immensely but both she and Maggie were due for a good long walk, so she'd asked that they be dropped at the waterfront. Tyler had been skeptical, even worried, preferring to take them straight home. Instead she gave in to the request, dropping them where asked. Fifteen minutes later as Maggie and Georgie made their way back to the main entrance of the DiNamico building, she spotted what looked like her own Land Rover parked a few blocks down Fleet Street and suspected Tyler had lingered to make sure they made it home in one piece. Not wanting to embarrass her, she ducked into the building and headed upstairs. Georgie's hands were so cold she had difficulty getting the security sensor to read her embedded chip.

Finally home and in the door, she berated herself for not remembering to leave a light on. Letting Maggie off her leash, and giving her the off-duty command, which was actually a hand signal, Georgie found the light switch and made her way down the antique staircase. Other than her Friday night outings with Lori and Marnie, this was the first time she had been out on her own and she felt a little disoriented coming in so late. Falling back on the routines Marnie had put in place, she opened her late evening checklists. Her email notification flashed. She dismissed the notification happy to see it was the promised proposal from Tyler. Wanting to concentrate on her checklist first, she followed the routine religiously. Once the doors were double-checked, the alarm set and fresh water set out for the dog, she made a cup of tea, retrieved her tablet and headed for the only furniture in the room, the old nail head Chesterfield sofa that had once graced her grandfather's office. Her hands were still cold when she grabbed the remote, selecting music and turning on the fireplace at the same time.

What an incredible evening. It was easy to admit now that she had been nervous when Tyler picked her up. Meeting new people was always difficult. And she had good reason to be concerned. In Buffalo society the DiNamico/Phipps family was considered neither cornerstone nor superstar, but they were the new elite and a long-term business success. That came with a lot of expectation. Georgie DiNamico was one of those people everyone thought they knew or wanted to know. Often people were excited to be introduced. Georgie was tired of watching their enthusiasm dim, along with their opinion, every time they realized she couldn't string more than three or four words together at a time. It was funny though, Tyler never got hung up. She seemed to get where she was going most of the time and had no problem filling in the blanks. Talking with her sometimes felt...well normal again.

Finally starting to feel warm, she pulled the old four-point blanket over her legs, patting the cushion beside her for Maggie. "Come." The giant dog, now off duty, checked her bed to make sure everything was good, grabbed her squeaky toy and joined Georgie on the couch. She rubbed the dog's head, feeling a kind of satisfaction. She always enjoyed her late-night reading time sprawled on the couch with the dog, fireplace on, music...but it was always missing something. Tonight she knew what that was. It was nice to finally have someone other than her sister and her cousin Lori to share things with. Even better to feel someone understood her beyond the people who cared for her. People needed more in life. Something more, she admitted.

Opening the email from Tyler, she was not surprised by the length of the proposal. A good proposal would include a detailed financial projection along with crosschecks and milestones. And for proposals like this Tyler knew she would want to see details of the work breakdown, assignment strategies and how members could opt in or out during the project. Reading the table of contents she was pleased to see all of those issues had been addressed along with several others. Tyler was smart that way.

Judging by the evening she would say her parents were too. She had thoroughly enjoyed their company. Her first impression of Debbie Marsh: strong, smart and analytic in nature. Definitely an alpha female. Carl Marsh, on the other hand, was the joker and a jock. It turned out the man had actually played professional football up in Canada, and he and Georgie had spent a good half hour debating the pros and cons of the differing rules of the game between CFL and the NFL. It had been a fun discussion but the real eye-opener came when he took Georgie for a tour of the shop.

While there was definitely an automotive feel to the place, it wasn't much different from the paint shed out at the boatyard. Of course scale and techniques were different but the smells were the same. It was when they finally reached Carl's office that Georgie got a true glimpse of the man. First off, he shared the place with his wife. In fact, she had most of the space. On the wall behind her desk were the certificates and professional seals expected of a CPA, and a few family shots. In contrast, Carl's wall was covered frame to frame with photographs. For a man who had played college and professional football and had won several awards for his restored vehicles, she was surprised to see nothing but family photographs. Although usually with cars in them. Still, every single one had one, two or all three of the girls. When he noticed she was looking over the pictures, he was quick to grab his prized possession off his desk. Handing it over with pride, he explained it was taken recently, on their thirty-fifth wedding anniversary. Georgie had taken the framed photograph in her hands and examined it solemnly. In a studio shot of his family he and Debbie stood side-by-side, with the three girls around them. It made her smile to think a big tough guy like Carl Marsh would cherish his family above all else. After the tour, she had chatted with Tyler's sisters, teasing Kira and commiserating with Megan. She spent time asking Kira the baby questions she had memorized and let Megan argue with her knowing it was just her age. It'd been a perfect evening. More than that, it'd been an evening with Tyler.

She put her tablet aside, setting a reminder to add the proposal to tomorrow's reading, "This first" she annotated.

Part of her reason for taking a long walk in the frigid cold was more about sorting out her feelings about Tyler than Maggie needing a long walk. Of course, Maggie never complained although she was starting to lift her paws the last few yards before the main door. Georgie usually found a good walk beneficial when she was trying to sort something out. It hadn't helped this time and she could only assume it was because this time something was completely different. If Tyler was a thing, she realized, like a project or an idea, she would map it out or create a pseudo code. But Tyler wasn't a thing. She was a friend. A kind of friend. A caring friend. Friend. She hated that word. It was a ridiculous idea to even think that there could be more between them. Even without mapping it out, she knew there were too many outliers. Tyler was clearly smart. Smarter than her and capable of so much. The last thing Tyler needed was to be saddled with someone like her. And then there was the age difference. All right, eight years wasn't that big a deal this day and age. It wasn't like she was an old woman. Hell, her father had been fourteen years older than her mom, and Henry a full two decades older than Aunt Gloria! Still, there was more to it than age.

She sat deep in thought for a long time. It was as if some key piece of the puzzle was missing. The one little piece that once in place would pull everything into focus. She actually laughed to herself to realize it was an ideal puzzle to take to Tyler. She shook her head and woke up Maggie. "Come," she said, giving her the 'time to head upstairs' signal. She watched as the dog rolled off the couch, retrieving the squeaky she had dropped in her sleep, and headed up the staircase.

As she followed her she realized she only had two options. If she couldn't share her feelings with the person they were about, then she could turn to Marnie or Lori. They had always been there for her and she knew she could count on them. She just wasn't sure she was ready to 'fess up to what was churning around in her head, not to mention other places. Georgie smiled about that. It'd been a long time since she felt that longing for someone. Still this wasn't the same. Oh, the longing was there but there was something more. When she didn't keep her feelings in check, all the fluttery things would let loose inside her. That was completely new and something she definitely needed help with.

In the bedroom Georgie stopped in front of her dresser, unloaded her pockets and plugged in her phone. *What the hell, sink or swim!* She tabbed to Lori's number and sent a quick text message. *Can't remember how to 'bend-her,' don't want to 'break-her,' can you explain?*

Moments later Lori's reply flashed back: *LMAO! I know you still got it baby! I'll pick you up for brunch. OK?*

Georgie responded with a quick affirmative and smiled when Lori sent a silly emoticon in reply.

CHAPTER NINE

Tyler laughed at herself when she realized she'd been singing along with the music. Zoe had shown her how to use the app Georgie had designed to control all the electronics in her apartment including the sound system. She had three playlists programmed. She felt a little uncomfortable the first time Zoe suggested she feel free to put on the music whenever she was in the apartment attending to her personal assistant duties. With names like Get Up, Work and Get Down, it was easy to feel like she was invading her boss's privacy. Although it didn't stop her from browsing through each playlist.

The Work music was almost a disappointment. Mostly all classical, with some jazz and more modern instrumental numbers. The Get Down list was interesting. She had to admit she would've named it Relax and Chill. It was the Get Up list she usually played when she was in the apartment. She didn't really know any of the tunes. They were a mix of rock and pop from the 70s and 80s. She had to wonder if it was really Georgie's favorite music or an auditory anchor to her early childhood.

She had been singing along to "Wild, Wild Horses" when she recognized the song but not this version. Grabbing her tablet, she opened the playlist. She laughed realizing the song she believed an old English ballad had actually been written and recorded by the Rolling Stones in 1971. Though not a fan of Mick Jagger's vocals, she couldn't deny the longing the song invoked.

"There you are!" Zoe said as she pushed through the service door behind the kitchen. She propped the big steel door open and began pushing a large box-cart inside. "How's the shirt stuffing going?"

"Not too bad."

Old John, the family tailor, had been good as his word. On December 29th, as promised, all the shirts, ties and scarves had arrived. John had provided two other services that she truly appreciated. The new shirts were cleaned and pressed, and properly folded to fit in the gift boxes he had supplied. These weren't the average fold it yourself white boxes with the store name on top but true gift boxes in paisley patterns in a variety of colors and were large enough to fit the six shirts, along with the scarves or ties that Georgie had promised each engineer. Tyler had already printed out the gift labels, and now had each box set out in rows along the kitchen counter. While the big island counter was huge there still wasn't enough room for sixty-two boxes. With four dozen laid out, she planned to stuff the boxes in stages and was halfway through the first set. "I've got it all organized so it's really just stuffing everything in now."

"Brilliant," Zoe noted. "I'll take care of the rest of this lot if you like. Skippy is helping Aunt Stella bring up Georgie's new togs. She wants you to see how she organizes everything. I swear that woman thinks you're Georgie's nursemaid."

"Your aunt is a singular woman. She likes things done a certain way and I appreciate that. You know," Tyler teased, "your father and Aunt Stella are very much alike."

Zoe groaned. "Ugh, don't remind me."

"Besides, I'm starting to enjoy taking care of the basic things."

"I guess," Zoe conceded. "You must be a bit relieved after having your head stuck in the quagmire of economics, ethics and whatever it is that Georgie always goes on about."

"You know, I put the denim shirts in first but now I'm thinking maybe we should go with the stripes first then the denim. I thought we'd put the white one on top so the ties would really stand out folded above them. What do you think?"

Shaking her head, Zoe stood with her hands on her hips. "I can't believe how much care you put into all these silly things she comes up with!" At Tyler's impish grin, she smiled. "Of course you're absolutely right." With that she began handing Tyler the shirts in pairs, and matching the sizes Tyler called out. Once that was done it only took a few more minutes to add the white shirts to each box, top them with the tie sets, and finish boxing them up.

Tyler and Zoe were stacking the last of the gift boxes when Skippy came ambling down the circular staircase. Long and lanky like his twin, he lacked her grace and style. He was already wearing one of the new shirts Georgie had purchased for him, and Tyler had to remind him not to wear one of the denim shirts or the ties yet, at least not until all the other engineers had received their gift too. That wouldn't happen until tomorrow night, for New Year's Eve, when the DiNamico and Phipps clan would host their annual gala.

Tyler and Zoe had already reviewed the guest list several times. Even though it was considered a company event, all the invitations were plus one. Every employee past and present was on the list. All of the DiNamico family and the extensive Phipps clan were included along with business associates, plus several guests Zoe had described as gold diggers and social climbers. The type of people more interested in the accumulated wealth of the two families and their influence within the community. Tyler knew those people existed everywhere. Even within her beloved academic community, one couldn't attend a single event without tripping over some sort of ass-kisser or brown-nose. She figured it just came with the territory.

Leaving Skippy to help Zoe get all the boxes next door and into the empty suite, she headed upstairs to lend Aunt Stella a hand. Stella was Henry's niece but clearly the Italian influence of the DiNamico family had been at work when Stella and her mother had come to live at the big house just months after the tragic Christmas accident. At twelve years old she was already a powerhouse, stepping in and taking on the moniker of aunt to a boatload of motherless children. It wasn't the first time Tyler had wondered what that first year must've been like. As Stella had said herself, she'd been nothing but a bored careless tween when her mama packed them up and shuffled them off to Buffalo. She had also learned it was the catalyst Georgie had used to claim her right to move into her aunt's bedroom. She wasn't little Georgie anymore, she had claimed way back then, and Tyler could imagine the bold seven-year-old, hands on hips, and claiming she had grown up. She was big Georgie, and would live in big Georgie's room, while Aunt Stella, a girl of twelve, had become her protector and confidant.

A clothing rack had been rolled in to hold the half-dozen garment bags containing the new clothing order. She knew the rack usually found its home in the empty condo on the eighth floor. Once Tyler was finished with the new delivery, Skippy had orders to station it in the lobby to accept the outerwear of tomorrow night's guests. "I'm not sure where to start." She was relieved to feel Aunt Stella's hand on her back. "I bet you have a plan?"

Stella laughed. "No worries girl, we'll go at this one at a time."

Agreeing, but still overwhelmed, Tyler began unzipping the garment bags and removing the new duds.

"Just set those aside for now," Stella suggested, pointing to the zipper covers protecting the new suits. "Once we have everything sorted and put away we can use them for the clothing going to the VA."

That caught Tyler by surprise. "The VA?"

"Uh-huh, they have a program for young airman and airwomen. It's an exchange of sorts. You know, nice clothes for interviews and the like. Helps those folks trying to get back on their feet in civilian life."

"Wow, I had no clue. That's a great idea!"

"I have a system I've been using for years now. And if you don't object…"

"Object? Oh Stella, I bow to your superior knowledge," Tyler said with a smile, admitting how out of depth she felt. It was strange to be standing in her boss's closet. Yet like everything about Georgie, the place was organized and functional. What's more, it felt just like Georgie. Trailing her hand along the shoulders of a dozen suit jackets, each one two inches apart, she had to ask, "How do you keep everything lined up so precisely? I'm so amazed every time I walk in here."

Stella grinned at her. "That would be Anthony's doing," she explained, removing four suit jackets and the heavy wooden hangers. "Slide your fingers along the pole, sweetie."

"Oh my God! There are special grooves. They must make the hangers slide into place."

"From what I hear, Georgie originally asked him if he could paint lines on the poles so she could line up her hangers. You know, sort of like a measuring tape. Well, since Anthony and the boys had nothing but time on this job, they carved the back of each pole by hand. Quite ingenious I'd say!"

"Absolutely." It was one thing she truly understood about Georgie. The woman appreciated organization, although she wasn't quite as organized as the world would believe. Just the other day, she'd been working quietly at her desk when Maggie padded in and stared at her. This was something new and not knowing what else to do, she had stood and followed the dog back into the executive suite. Sure enough, Georgie was in trouble but not the kind the dog could help with. Strewn across every inch of her desk and work surface was every type of financial report, spreadsheets of expenses, R&D requests, engineering change notifications and who knew what else. Georgie stood in the middle of the organized chaos with another ream of paper spread between her two hands and had still another report in between her teeth. Tyler couldn't imagine finding a more forlorn and overwhelmed figure anywhere.

It'd taken an hour altogether, but with her help, she had managed to put Georgie back on track. By the time they were done, Tyler knew two things for sure. She could trust the dog to come to her before there was trouble, and from what she had gleaned from the reports, something was not kosher when it came to the DME books.

To swap out the oldest of Georgie's wardrobe, demote her middle-aged clothing and put all the new items away hadn't taken as long as Tyler had planned. When they were done, she surveyed the room to be sure it was exactly as Marnie wanted it. It was Stella though, who had maintained Georgie's living quarters these past five years, so it was her approval that mattered most. "I think that's everything," she told her. "Does it pass inspection?"

Stella snickered, giving Tyler an affectionate shove. "Ah now girl, the top sergeant himself would get down on his knees and weep to have a closet like this! Well done!"

"I take it that's a good thing," she said with a smile, asking the question that had been bothering her since first touring the place. "Does it strike you odd that everything is gray, blue or black? I mean there's not a lot of color anywhere in her wardrobe. When we were placing the order I kept thinking we should find a couple of striking pieces, something a little brighter. I mean," she added, a little uncomfortable now that she had mentioned anything, "she's a very attractive woman, and she dresses well, but a little on the drab side."

Unfazed by the comment, Stella pointed to the tall cubbyhole shelves that held Georgie's shoes and boots. "Tell me what you see."

Not wanting to miss whatever she was being shown, she studied the shoe rack for a long time. "Well, they're all black except for the cross trainers and the Top-Siders." Stella encouraged her to keep going and she started looking for commonalities. "Okay, let's see…well first we have these ones. They look military, so I'm going to guess they go with her uniforms…I'm sorry Stella. I know you're trying to help me connect the dots but I'm not getting it."

"Pick up a pair and put your hand inside."

That confused her, but she did as directed, selecting a pair of white Top-Siders suitable for use on a sailing yacht. They looked new, like everything else, but in her hand she realized the soles had been worn smooth with steady wear. A little reluctant to stick her hands in her boss's shoe, she reached in gingerly and was surprised to find an index card folded inside. "I don't understand. What is this?"

Stella took it from her, unfolding it. "Back in the day our Georgie was one snappy dresser and you're right, that girl can wear any color and make it look good. Sadly, those days are gone," she lamented. "Nowadays, she can't remember what things go together. Before we got this organized, we couldn't trust her to figure out what to wear from one day to the next. I swear she used to walk in here and put on the first thing she found. It used to send Lou through the roof! Anyway, now I've got it all organized and she's got her little cheat sheet here and everything."

Taking the little index card back Tyler read it. "Oh I think I've got it. Tell me if I'm right? So the top line identifies the item which in this case is Footwear: Top-Siders. Beside the UOD it says Civ-Casual. Civilian casual?" At Stella's nod, she read the next line. "'Worn with pants: socks are optional. Worn with shorts: do not wear socks!' I had no idea."

"That's all right. I'm not sure anybody really understands how difficult the touchy-feely side of life is for her. Sometimes the kids call her a walking computer. Marnie's boys are the worst. God I love those two dearly, but it's really not fair to our girl, and I know it hurts her deeply. She might not know how to match up her shoes with her clothes anymore or figure out what colors go together but she's still a person, she's got feelings, and it makes me mad as all get out when the kids forget that."

Tyler folded the card, putting it back where she found it, returning the shoes to their place on the rack. Overwhelmed by what she'd just heard, and more than a little curious, she reached into the breast pocket of one of the older suit jackets. She found another folded index card. "UOD. What does that mean?"

"Uniform of the Day. And before you ask she didn't make it up, it's just air force jargon. Military acronyms came back to her first, before anything, and we found it was the easiest way to communicate with her. In the morning before she dresses, she reads that personal schedule you maintain for her. The items you enter create the codes that go on these cards. Marnie had Skippy add a widget to her schedule program. From the moment she steps out of bed until the end of the day, she relies on that schedule. Uniform of the Day is simply the way she understands how to dress for her scheduled activities."

"So…if it's a business day she comes in here and picks out…" Checking the card in her hand she read from the UOD line: "Business-Standard. Are there other classes of business wear?"

"Of course," she said, smiling. "The military is much like old Uncle John, the family tailor. You met him. Anyway, according to those two experts, there are always three levels of dress, with three forms of that dress. To begin with we have casual, standard and formal." Stella led her down the row to where Georgie's military uniforms were organized. "Here we go. Think of these combat uniforms—what do they call them, battle uniforms—as casual clothing. You know, something to wear when you don't want to worry about getting dirty. I'm not a fan of the potato sack look but our Georgie pulls it off. Although to be fair, as a pilot, most of her days were spent in these flight suits. The tan is for desert duty and the sage is everything else. Now, this here jacket and skirt would be considered standard dress. She has slacks to go with it too. Her suits from old John are almost cut exactly like this uniform. And let me tell you, when that girl wears her blues, it never fails to bring a tear to Uncle Henry's eyes."

"Wow, I see the similarity now. It's a bit on the plain side, at least compared to some of the other services, don't you think?"

Stella smiled at her assumption. Pressed and hanging, Georgie's uniforms were void of any of the military accoutrements she had earned. Pulling a nearby drawer open, she carefully removed several items, setting them out for Tyler to see.

"Oh my God! Are all those hers?"

"Yes indeed. Our girl's a bona fide hero!"

Tyler examined the four and a half rows of ribbons, the command and unit badges along with her Master Aviator wings. "I had no idea. I think I may cry if I ever see her wearing this."

"Oh you'll see her wear it! And yes my dear, you will cry. Our girl's a giant in uniform even if air force blues *are* a little on the plain side," she offered with a wink. Removing one more item from the drawer, she unwrapped the mounted set of medals. They matched the same order as the ribbon set but included the actual medals. Stella handed them over. "Go on, take a good look now. You recognize any of these?"

Tyler took her time, cradling the set as if they were most precious. "I think I've seen the one on the top."

"That's the Purple Heart, sweetie."

"And the rest?"

"Hmm, I only know a few. Oh this one here is the Air Force Commendation. And these ones with the stars means she's received more than one of that type."

"What about this blue striped one, it has a V on it?" Tyler asked.

"Oh that's for Air Force Achievement and the V is for Valor, but don't be looking to me for the story. That's Georgie's department."

"I can see her marching around in this, being all formal and in charge."

"That girl's always carried herself well. It's probably the only reason she can pull off her mess kit. It's the air force's idea of formal. I think it's a horrendous sack to put on a beautiful woman but the military hasn't come by my door to ask my opinion," she added with a grin. She pulled out the waist length blue jacket with silk lapels, holding it up for Tyler. "Now this is worn with a white shirt, silk neck tab and a blue satin cummerbund over an ankle-length skirt."

Tyler recognized the style of a military tuxedo but had to agree with Stella on the adaptation to the female form. "I'm curious, Stella. What do you think of the tux?"

Judging by the wicked grin she received, it was a good bet Stella approved. "Now I'll be honest with you, a tuxedo for a woman is not my first choice but for Georgie, I think you did terrific. Oh, and that green vest! Girl, you nailed it! I can't wait till tomorrow night to finally see our Georgie out of those air force blues. And you," Stella said. "I assume you picked up an appropriately lovely dress for tomorrow night?"

"Me? Oh no. I'm on duty, so I'll just be in a regular dress; it's not like anyone will notice me."

"What?"

What Tyler didn't say was that after a year unemployed she couldn't afford something new and had decided to make do with her standard little black dress. But flippant as she was, the truth of it was written on her face. Thankfully, Stella was both kind and perceptive.

Retrieving her cell phone from her back pocket, she sent a quick text message before looking to her young friend. "First of all honey, a girl like you will always be noticed! Second, you're not just Georgie's right-hand man. Because of her…limited social graces, you are the de facto host for these events and that means you gotta get all dolled up!"

"But…" Before Tyler could formulate a protest, her own cell phone went off. The sound of *Darth Vader's March* was partially swallowed up by the room. Still she kicked herself when she realized Stella knew exactly who that notification was from.

"Better read it. One should not keep Darth Marnie waiting… Dark Side and all that," she said with a grin.

Embarrassed, Tyler checked her phone.

Joanne's Boutique in Williamsville. GO NOW!

"Okay…"

Stella simply laughed, giving her back an affectionate rub. "Don't you worry, I'll keep an eye on our fearless leader. Head on over there and get yourself a pretty dress. Joanne will put it on the company account for you. After all, this goes to your expenses. You're not to be out-of-pocket for these things. You remember that, sweetie."

Tyler was stunned. "You know?"

"Of course I do girl. Oh, I may not have a fancy title like those other buggers, but when it comes to taking care of our

Georgie, I've been the chairman of the board since day one. Well," she amended, "day one was the military. Day two was that tramp, Margaret. Day three we got our girl back, and I've been on duty ever since. It's a real relief to have you on the team, Tyler. You can't know how much of a difference you have made for Georgie. You truly have!" She all but dragged Tyler from the room and all the way to the elevator. "Now, I will see you tomorrow night and not one minute earlier. Is that understood, young lady?"

Tyler laughed, pressing the call button. "Thank you Stella. Thank you so much."

In the dressing room at Joanne's Boutique, Tyler's head snapped around at the sound of her sister slurping the last of her chocolate shake. "Kira! Stop behaving like a brat. I can't believe you brought that in here."

"What? I'm pregnant," she said as explanation while patting her belly. "Everyone knows I'm eating for two."

Shaking her head, she sat down beside her on the dressing room bench. "This is kind of weird. Just waiting for someone to bring you dresses. Don't you think that's weird?"

"Will you relax? This is just how these classy places work. I don't understand what you're so strung out about. You were just complaining the other night that you didn't have something nice to wear tomorrow."

"I have nice things to wear." But she was right. Tyler had complained about her limited wardrobe. She had several dresses but they seemed to come in two varieties, the ladylike, wear-to-faculty-dinner-parties-type dresses and what her sister had described as the slightly slutty, party girl dresses. The only thing in her closet remotely formal was the fuchsia-colored bridesmaid's gowns both she and Kira had endured for their cousin's wedding.

Moments later the shop owner herself carried in several gowns and hung them on the display rack. Tyler judged her to be about the same age as her, Marnie and Lori. Italian-looking and with a wicked sense of humor. She secretly wondered if Joanne was another of the DiNamico cousins.

"Why don't you two look these over while I go grab one more?" She retrieved Kira's empty shake and headed out without comment.

Standing and stretching, Kira began rifling through the small selection. "You must admit the woman pegged your size, but most of these are on the plain side."

"What do you think?" Tyler held out a simple black dress. Well, it was long, so that satisfied the formal aspect but frilly details had been added to the back of the dress and all down the arms. "I'm not sure this works for me."

"It's ugly as sin. Besides, the last thing you want to do is decorate your backside and your arms. They're your best features. You shouldn't hide them."

"Better than my face you mean?"

"Noooooooooo," she dragged out like a dramatic tween, then, almost whispering, she hissed, "I meant over your boobs, you pumpkin head!"

"Hey, just because the baby business is suddenly giving you big boobs doesn't mean you can pick on mine."

Kira laughed at that. "Well, Mom says after she finished nursing you and me she pretty much went back to being flat as a board."

"Hardly! Our mother is not flat-chested."

"Not now." She added, "She blames Megan for making her a C cup."

Holding a dress in front of her, Tyler asked, "What about this one?"

"Oh my God!" Kira snorted. "That one's worse than the other."

"That's what I thought." She hung it up, feeling pretty miserable with their prospects. "I shouldn't have left this so late. I just really thought I could get away with something simple."

"And you can't? Why is that?" she asked, shuffling back over to the upholstered bench. "I mean, it wouldn't be a crime or anything."

"Well, according to Aunt Stella, I'm supposed to act as the evening's hostess on Georgie's behalf."

"Hostess?" she giggled. "That sounds funny. Speaking of which…"

Joanne was back in the private viewing/dressing room. This time she had only one dress, still wrapped in tissue paper. Hanging it on the end of the rack, she tore the paper away to reveal a shimmering slender evening gown.

From where Tyler was standing, the gown seemed to be black but as she moved closer the light reflected back with highlights of vivid greens, blues, and shimmering black. "Wow!"

"I know," Joanne answered. "This was actually a custom order. It didn't come in until this morning. Lucky for you it came in late, or someone would have snapped it up by now."

Even Kira struggled back to her feet to take a closer look. Examining the fabric closely, she asked, "What are these, some sort of sequins?"

"Tiny glass beads. They're actually black. It's the dress that's made up of several colors, but with the beads over top of it you don't notice until the light catches it in just a certain way."

"It's beautiful," Kira said. "Try it on pumpkin head. I have to see what it looks like on you."

Taking a deep breath, Tyler began stripping out of her work gear. Unceremoniously dumping her dress boots, she grumbled about her socks and not having on the right underwear.

"Yeah, yeah." Kira clumsily sat her heavily pregnant body back down on the bench. Retrieving her oversized purse, she sorted through the quagmire, finally tossing a pair of three-inch heels on the floor. "There you go, whiner, I knew you'd need these. Got you covered…as usual!"

Tyler slid on the designer shoes, and concentrated on the collar of the dress while Joanne zipped up the side. There was no back zipper because there was no back. She stood transfixed at her own image. If she hadn't known better she would've sworn the dress had been made for her. Every cut and curve followed her long form, softening her looks and adding an air of elegance and something else.

"Holy smokes pumpkin! Check out your booty in that thing. If Zoe doesn't throw herself at you tomorrow night, I'm sure all the guys will!"

Tyler had panic in her eyes as she turned her head to get a better look at her backside, "Oh no no no no," she stammered, stepping away from the full-length mirror. "This is too…too…"

"Too what?" Joanne asked politely and with a grin.

When she didn't answer, Kira stood again, turning her sister so they were facing one another, communicating silently in their spooky way. Finally she said, "You look beautiful. I know you're feeling a little shy, sweetie, but you've got it, so flaunt it!"

Tyler was still wide-eyed.

"Yes your ass looks great in this thing and so does the rest of you. Go on, take another look." Coaxing her in front of the mirror, Kira prompted Joanne for her opinion, asking, "Do you know what any of the other women might be wearing?"

"Of course, including myself."

"You're cousins, aren't you?" Tyler asked.

Joanne grinned at the pair. "Guilty. And yes I'll be there tomorrow night. And no you will not be the only woman wearing something this hot. I think it's perfect." Just then the doorbell rang in the front showroom. "I'll leave you two to talk. If you like it, don't change yet. I'd like to take the hem up just a bit. Unless you're planning to wear a different pair of shoes?"

"Those are perfect, if you'd like to borrow them?" Kira asked, pointing to the heels. "Not like I'll need them. The fanciest I plan to get tomorrow night is my pink bunny slippers."

Tyler just nodded, waiting patiently until Joanne was clear of the room and hopefully out of hearing range. "I can't do this. No Kira, I'm serious. I can't pull this off…can I?"

"You can and you will." Kira gave her arm a squeeze. "Hey. I know you've been in a slump lately. Hell, it's been a hard year for everyone. But I know my other half better than anyone else and you got this. You look fantastic and you know it. So why don't you tell me what this is really about?"

Sitting together on the bench, Tyler removed her sister's Jimmy Choo's, pretending to be giving them a once-over. "These are nice."

"So are pickles when you're pregnant. That's not what I asked."

Tyler let out a long frustrated breath. "There's nothing going on between me and Zoe. I mean, we've been out a few times but she's just too...young. Anyway I told her that last week and she was cool. Then I had this weird conversation with the big boss. Turns out everybody in the place thinks Zoe and I are hot and heavy. Oh and I didn't tell you the best part. When Zoe and I hit the bar, we weren't the only ones there. Turns out Georgie was there along with Marnie, and Lori, their cousin from the boatyard."

"Oh-oh!"

"Oh-oh is right," she said, pushing her hair back.

It was her stress *tell* and Kira had seen her do it a thousand times. "I can't believe there would be fallout! Your boss seemed so cool when she was over on Christmas. I know you said she had to work really hard to keep up the conversation but we all understood her. She seemed so nice. I can't believe she would be upset with you."

"I guess that's the part I'm a little bit mixed up about."

"Why don't you just tell me what the big boss said, as close as you can to her exact words and let my lawyerly brain sort it out for you?"

Tyler nodded. "Okay. Evidently, Zoe and I were on the dance floor when they arrived. Georgie hadn't noticed we were there until Lori, wait, I told you about Lori?"

"Hot sexy bitch?"

Smiling she corrected, "Hot sexy *butch*! Anyway, Lori had spotted us and in the most graphic nature, described for the world what she would do with Zoe's date, given half the chance."

"God, it warms my heart to know that women can be as bad as men!"

"I know!"

"Okay, so what happened then?"

"Georgie started a fight!"

"What?" Kira seemed confused. "With who, Zoe?"

Tyler shook her head. "No with Lori. They even got kicked out!"

"Kicked out of that dump! Holy crap, pumpkin. That must've been some fight!"

"I know. When Marnie told me, I convinced myself Georgie was just protecting my honor or some such bullshit, then Marnie drops the bomb. She says, 'Don't worry, my sister will never make a pass at you no matter what she feels.'"

They were both silent for a minute contemplating that bit of news. "Does it bother you? I mean, I know she's a few years older and she's a bit whacked, but she'd have to be to fit in our family." When Tyler didn't answer, Kira wrapped her arm around her shoulders. "Is that why you're so scared of looking hot? Thinking the boss may corner you and put you in a bad position?"

"Georgie? No not for a minute. I've been going over everything Marnie said. I think what she was really trying to tell me was that regardless of her feelings, Georgie would never say a word. After that I had to face Georgie. That was weird. Evidently, she was so upset all weekend, she worked from the time she walked out of the bar to a few hours before I walked in on Monday morning. So I get called up to her apartment, she's in the library and she's got all these forms for me and a copy of the employee policy on fraternization. And the worst part was, seeing how hurt she was to think that I was involved with Zoe."

"Did you straighten her out?"

"Of course." Leaning into her sister, Tyler rested her head on Kira shoulder, "The worst part was realizing how much I hurt, knowing I hurt her."

"Oh boy pumpkin. What are you going to do?"

"Not a clue sis. Not a clue."

* * *

Stella stuck her head in Marnie's office. "Is the coast clear?"

Marnie waved her in, motioning for her to take a seat on the couch where Lori was already waiting. "We're good. I have Zoe driving Henry and Georgie home."

"Good call. And you're right about the dress thing. It never occurred to her to take up Georgie's offer for clothing expenses."

"Did you send her over to Jo-Jo's?" Lori asked, referring to their cousin's dress shop.

"She did," Stella answered, adding, "she was texting her sister when she was leaving. So I think she'll have help making a selection."

Marnie got up from her desk, grabbing her ever-present coffee cup and making her way to the sitting area. She slapped Lori's feet off the coffee table and sat down with a thud. "I can't believe it's already New Year's. Boat season is next and we hardly have any time to get Georgie ready."

"Marns…are you sure about this one?" Lori asked Marnie but it was Stella who answered.

"Marnie is the absolute best judge of character I have ever met. It's why she's so good at her job and why I have every confidence that she's found the right girl for our Georgie."

"Thank you."

"Oh I have every confidence," Lori explained. "I'm just not sure the girl has the same…How shall I say this, *interest*, everyone else has?"

"Don't worry," Marnie said, "Tyler may not know how bad she's got it for my sister yet, but I have a secret weapon. I wasn't planning on pulling it out quite yet, but I've got a good idea now might just be the perfect time."

"And Zoe?" Lori asked.

"You said it yourself. Zoe doesn't do nice. And Tyler Marsh is way too nice to sacrifice to Zoe's antics."

"For your sake and ours, I sure hope Zoe understands."

Marnie groaned. "Me too. Seriously, I worry about her too but it's too late to undo what we've started. Best we can do now is let things play out and pick up the pieces when we're done."

"Don't worry girls," Stella reassured them, "I've a good feeling about this."

CHAPTER TEN

Tyler wasn't surprised when Marnie called her at home to update her. But her long apology did seem a little out of character.

"I hadn't planned for all of this to fall on your shoulders. At least not this year. I was hoping Zoe could handle everything, but I'm afraid I simply dropped it in her lap. I should've checked in sooner with both of you. Lucky for us Stella's on the ball."

"I understand. I'm not upset. Actually, if I'm anything, I'd say I'm just a little overwhelmed."

Marnie sounded unexpectedly patient when she suggested, "Why don't you grab something to take notes on, and let me go through the agenda in detail? I'm sure you'll feel a lot better once you have a good lay of the land."

Tyler grabbed a notepad and sat down at the kitchen table, setting her phone to speaker. For the next forty minutes they went over all the particulars she should've been apprised of weeks ago. Some she knew in detail, like the names on the guest list, and the protocols appropriate for the dignitaries that would be in attendance. Some were a complete surprise. Such as the fact that she was expected to arrive early enough to attend a family supper. Then see to all the pre-party details, before addressing and greeting the arriving guests.

Finally Marnie hit her with one last curveball. "I need someone to accompany Georgie on New Year's Day. She'll be attending the afternoon reception with the Air National Guard. Usually she goes with Henry, but he's asked to bow out this year. He says he's too old to stand around, drink in hand, posturing with the other old boys. If you're not up for it, Tyler, I understand. It's not like I put it on your schedule."

"No. No it's okay. I might be a little tired but if Georgie can do it then so can I. What time does the company New Year's Eve party usually break up? Just so I have an idea how fast I need to get back to the house, get cleaned up, and back to get Georgie there in time."

"Actually if it's not too much of an imposition, why don't you stay at Georgie's? She has a lovely guest room and you'll need to use it anyway to get ready before the party. So you might as well stay the night. Unless that makes you uncomfortable."

"Georgie won't mind? Wouldn't it bother her if I was there?"

"Georgie wouldn't notice a herd of buffalo traipsing through the place. Besides, I can't remember a single year where there wasn't somebody sleeping in Georgie's guest room. You're lucky you weren't around for Thanksgiving. She drew the short straw and got saddled with my kids. I swear those three played Halo all Saturday night straight through Thanksgiving Sunday." Marnie went on to explain the schedule for the evening, including people Georgie might need to be screened from, filling her in on several situations that had come up in the past.

When Tyler finally got off the phone, all she could say for sure was that the next forty-eight hours would be busy.

When she arrived at the DiNamico building the next day, she was startled to see both the catering staff and security had already arrived. While she was waiting for the elevator, Skip sauntered out of the Fleet Street Grill and trotted up to join her.

"Hey Tyler, how's it going?"

"Good Skip, you?"

He took the garment bag from her arms, leaving her free to manage her overnight bag and purse. "Are you staying at Georgie's? It's okay if you are. I understand. Aunt Leslie said I can stay at her place if you were."

For some reason the question made her panicky. Before she could think of what to say, he picked up where he'd left off, in his unassuming and rambling way. "I mean, I could stay up at Granddad's but I do that every year and well, it would be kind of cool not to have to share a room with Zoe. I mean like I'm gonna be twenty-one soon. I shouldn't have to share with my sister. What do you think? Do you still have to share with your sister? Zoe said you're a twin too. That's so cool…"

Stepping off the elevator on the ninth floor, she noticed the doors to each suite were all propped open and several of the catering staff seemed to be congregated in Leslie's apartment. Zoe had already explained that the empty suite on the eighth floor would serve as the ballroom while Georgie's main floor living space, directly across the hall, would be the reception area. Henry's apartment, in his absence, would be used as a VIP lounge to entertain dignitaries and the like, while Leslie's apartment was completely taken over by the catering staff.

Skippy, ever the gentleman, gave her completely unnecessary directions to Georgie's guest bedroom. The guest room, like literally every other room throughout the apartment, was fitted with the same style security locks found throughout the office building. Tyler had to search through her purse to find her employee badge. Trying to help, Skip swiped his hand over the sensor several times without luck. Finally pulling her badge out of the bottom of her purse, she swiped it, worried it too would be rejected. When the door unlocked on the first pass, she was both elated and confused. Had someone taken the time to program her access to the room and bar everyone else? Had it been done when she was hired, or set up specifically for this night? In a way she hoped it was the latter. If it was, at least she would not have to worry about who else had access. She chided herself on that one—she knew the answer. She had a master password to the security program. It would take all of thirty seconds to find out when the access had been changed, who changed it, and who, if, anyone still had access. Setting that aside for now, she hung up her evening gown, retrieved her tablet and followed Skippy downstairs. It was time to find out where she could best help—or, at least, where Georgie was.

As Marnie had explained it, tonight was the night they would let go of the past for another year and look forward to the future. From what she had gathered, DME was in for another great year. Even in a flagging economy, they had made smart decisions. Decisions like building sailboats instead of cabin cruisers, building for quality instead of quantity, and new cutting-edge engineering technologies had made the company bulletproof. Such long-term success from such a small company would normally have made them a takeover target, if they weren't privately held. Indeed they had received several offers to take them public. Offers Danny DiNamico and Henry Phipps had rejected outright. As far as they were concerned and as far as she could tell among the key players now, that sentiment hadn't changed a bit.

"There you are, gorgeous," Zoe called, entering from the lower corridor that was opened only for the party.

The heavy steel door that separated the eighth floor corridor from Georgie's main floor had been unlocked and pushed open. The empty suite across from Georgie's was completely open as well. Marnie had explained that the ninth floor elevators would not open for guests this evening. Guests would disembark on the eighth floor, giving them access to the reception in Georgie's living room and the ballroom. The catering would be managed out of Leslie's apartment on the ninth floor, with them stuck using the service stairs to move up and down. Guests could access the ninth floor but only by the circular staircase in Georgie's apartment. And with all the upstairs rooms locked off to guests, there wasn't much point in going there except maybe for the view.

"Hey you," she said to Zoe. "I was looking for Marnie or Georgie. I'm not sure where to start."

"No worries love, the old girls will be here soon enough. Let's you and me take a walk-through just to make sure everything's up to snuff before they arrive."

Tyler headed up the circular staircase again, ruminating over Zoe's description of Georgie and Marnie as old. Something else occurred to her. Skippy had said he was turning twenty-one. It had never occurred to her to ask Zoe how old she was. The fact that her twin brother had just outed them as minors almost stalled her in her tracks. She had to wonder what Zoe thought of her. At thirty-three she was a hell of a lot closer in age to her aunts and father than she was to the young woman. It wasn't the only difference she'd been chewing on. While she still enjoyed hitting the bars and dancing all night, partying for the sake of partying no longer held any appeal and hadn't for years.

"Let's start at the top shall we?" Zoe suggested from the landing at the top of the circular staircase.

Back in the hall, their first stop was Henry's apartment. It was decorated traditionally in masculine shades and appeared to be the work of a decorator. Still, much like her own father's office, one wall had been plastered with photographs of his entire family, both Phipps and DiNamico. It made her smile to see so many happy faces. Spotting a baby grand piano in one corner of the living room, and remembering Marnie's briefing, she knew someone had been laid on to play and now she knew where.

"That was my gran's," Zoe explained. "Georgie made a big fuss about bringing it out here for him but," she conceded, "it did make him happy." Then, with a wicked smile, she added, "But wait until you get a look at the lovely thing we've hired to play for the VIPs. Not sure if she's family yet. Guess we'll have to find out!"

She ignored Zoe's wolfish comment about the musician in favor of viewing the photographs assembled on top of the piano. Picking up the first of two book-hinged framesets, she considered the three jointly framed photographs. The first she recognized right away. It was the same picture used in the company biography. Old Luigi stood proudly in front of the first of the Dynamic Marine sailing yachts with his three children by his side: Danny, Henry, and Georgina Senior. The second photograph was much newer but also taken at the boatyard, with a sleek DynaCraft '59 in the background and Henry and his entire extended family gathered around him. The last, and the one that truly caught her interest, appeared to have been taken at the same time. In it, Danny and Henry stood much as they had in the photograph taken forty years earlier. The only difference, this time their companion and cohort was little Georgie. "When was this taken?"

Looking over her shoulder, Zoe remarked, "The things you notice! Let's see, I think that was the summer before Uncle Danny passed. That," she said. pointing to the sailboat in the background, "was our first fifty-niner. It was quite a day, I must say. We had one right royal blast. My hat's off to Aunt Lori for that. She may be old but she can still throw a party."

Again with the old! "What's with you today? You make it sound like your aunts are a million years old. How old do you think I am?"

"Oh age doesn't matter." Zoe fluffed off the question. "I just think the older they get, the more complicated they make this night!" Dragging Tyler back into the upper level of Georgie's apartment, she explained, "Once the caterer's set up, you'll see how having the buffet up here sort of creates a dividing line. This way the VIP guests can slip out of Henry's without being accosted by the great unwashed."

"I would hardly describe tonight's guests as the great unwashed!"

Back to her upbeat self, Zoe playfully trailed fingernails down her arm. "You haven't seen Lori's bunch at their best yet! Just wait," she promised.

"Well, that's something to look forward to. What about Georgie?" At Zoe's raised eyebrow, she explained, "Marnie was quite firm in her command that I not let Georgie out of my sight."

"Of course!" The sarcasm was clear. "Another night where we all must cater to Georgie's peculiarities," she added, leading them back down the stairs.

That remark caught Tyler by surprise.

"Expect her to spend most of her time in here. It's not like she can be trusted to chat with VIPs. She might slip into the ballroom for a wee bit but usually that's at Marnie or Lori's insistence. They like to trot her round the dance floor every year. I guess the effort is to let everyone know she's still got it."

"Okay, I'm starting to get the impression that you're not happy about something."

"What's not to be happy about?" Zoe said with a grin before moving close, running both hands down Tyler's arms. In an ardent tone, and just above a whisper, she added, "I just think it's a shame to waste good music, fine champagne and the company of a beautiful woman."

Tyler wasn't sure which confused her more, Zoe's tender gesture, or her overt flirtation.

Behind them, someone cleared her throat. Swiveling around and out of Zoe's loose embrace, she stood face-to-face with Lori Phipps. Admitting she was intimidated was easy. Knowing what to do about it was another thing, and judging by the look on Lori's face, any chance she had to earn this woman's respect was pretty much blown. There was no point reiterating that she and Zoe were just friends. Zoe had seen to that with her quasi embrace. Or was it her fault? She thought she had been clear with Zoe but now she wasn't so sure.

"Everyone's downstairs waiting. Let's go! Leslie's set a place for both of you," she said grimly, indicating Tyler should lead the way.

Tyler headed straight for the elevator. When she turned to press the button for the lobby level, she noted that Lori had Zoe's elbow pinned in her strong grip. Her much younger than she imagined friend was in a bit of trouble.

Reaching the lobby level, Lori stepped in front of the doors blocking their exit, growling a low warning, "I expect you two to be on your best behavior." Then she turned and marched directly across the lobby for the doors to the Fleet Street Grill.

Following along, Tyler could feel her face flush with embarrassment. Trying to remain calm, she made a note to herself to confront Zoe. Finding a suitable time and place to do it would be another question.

Inside the restaurant, waitstaff bustled about setting up tables and preparing for the biggest evening of the year. Tonight Leslie would run a restaurant, cater the party upstairs, and see to the VIP guests. Marnie had often quipped that Leslie was the hardest worker in the entire family. Considering the night ahead would involve two sittings of a hundred here in the restaurant, plus fifty or so VIP guests and more than three hundred others, the claim was certainly true.

With the dining room occupying the entire west half of the building, the distinctive prow shape and bullnose window featured prominently. Marnie had explained that the extra early supper had become a tradition since the passing of old Luigi and the ladies. Danny and Henry had halted all Christmas celebrations but after a year of mourning they had decided to host a New Year's Eve party for employees and customers alike. As this was one of the few occasions when children would not be on hand, the two men had made a point of sharing an early supper with them and ringing in the New Year eight hours early.

So, at exactly four p.m., Henry Phipps stood at the head of the large table set in the bullnose of the restaurant. Tyler stood with everyone else, and raised her glass with him.

"Tonight is the night we remember those we've lost. Tomorrow we will stand together as a family and fight the good fight!"

"Hear, hear!" Lou cheered.

Tyler wasn't surprised to see he had planted himself at the other end of the long table. It was so typical of him, needing to be seen as in charge or at least the heir to the kingdom. His behavior bothered her on so many levels. She'd tried to shake it off but there was just something about the man that irked her.

She was sitting in the seat she was assigned next to Zoe, who kept making a point of touching her or including her in her conversation with others. It was all she could do to keep from slapping her hand. Lori, sitting across from her between her father and Georgie, seemed to be watching her very carefully.

"Danny! Luc! Bring them here, both of you," Henry ordered sternly.

Dead center along the long table, both boys, Marnie and Jack's twins, looked up from their laps and their not well hidden cell phones.

"Unless you two would rather spend all of next year in the paint shed?"

Embarrassed for being called out and looking for an escape, Danny complained, "Aunt Leslie has hers!"

"Yeah Uncle Henry, it's not fair!" Luc chimed in.

After the two of them had spent most of the month on their hands and knees working prep in the paint shed, Tyler was shocked to see how little they had learned. Of course, she wouldn't have expected any better from her own sister, Megan. She had to hide her smile when their mother retrieved their phones, and Henry explained that they would now be on dishwashing duty in the restaurant for the remainder of the night. When they started to moan and complain, Henry warned them again. The timber in his voice must have resonated with them from his years in the military. It always did with her.

At his orders they stood and began the family tradition of sharing a story from the past year. When finished, they bowed repeatedly, accepting a round of applause, any lingering resentment gone when they realized their Aunt Leslie had *accidentally* poured them each a glass of wine.

When Zoe suddenly grabbed Tyler and pulled her to her feet, she felt as embarrassed and called out as Marnie's twins had ten minutes earlier. Of all the stories or memories Zoe and Skip could have chosen to share as part of the dinner tradition, it was the stupid shirt challenge they described. The story they retold seemed slightly out of sync with the reality she remembered. Still, it was nice to hear a kind word from Zoe's mouth about Georgie. With prompting, Tyler told her part, about meeting old John and placing the surprise order for close to three hundred shirts without batting an eye. As everybody clapped, she sat and slid down in her seat like her legs had turned to Jell-O. She could feel the heat crawling up her neck and face and imagined her cheeks were fire engine red.

Leslie was next, and had her siblings and cousins on the verge of tears when she told of finding one of her mother's old cookbooks. The binding rotted and many of the pages falling out, but stuffed in the back were hundreds of discolored note sheets, handwritten recipes, most in pencil and in the most beautiful hand. On the back of a cake recipe were the birthdates of all their mother's siblings, along with a note describing the favorite birthday cake for each. It was a sweet discovery which sparked a fun debate about birthday cakes and dessert choices among the family.

As they joked and made good fun of one another, Tyler felt calm enough to look at the one person she'd been avoiding since sitting down. It wasn't that she didn't want to see Georgie, or that she had nothing to say, it was just that every time she began to stray in that direction, Zoe would do something inappropriate again. Tyler had already extricated her roaming hand from her lap and asked her quietly to remove her arm from around her shoulders. Sure enough, when she looked across the table, Georgie was watching her. There was confusion in her eyes and something else, something less tangible. Was it hurt? Interest? Considering everything that was going on, she was leaning toward confusion.

People were clapping again, as Georgie got up. She went old school, removing several sheets of paper from her pocket and unfolding them and straightening them out carefully. Tyler could almost feel Lou bristling from the other end of the table. If she'd ever felt angry before, it didn't compare to her physical need to hurt Luigi *Lou* Henry Phipps in this moment. But, knowing he was underestimating Georgie, she sat back smiling, waiting for Georgie to deliver.

"Tonight…my challenge, to share a memory. Not just any memory but the oldest memory I have of Winnie and Gloria."

Tyler was both impressed by her pacing and her ability to make eye contact as she spoke. She knew immediately that Georgie must have completely memorized everything she was about to say. The folded pocket notes were probably a memory prompt, or simply a red herring for a certain hostile cousin. Tyler listened, enthralled like everyone else.

"Most of you may not know this, but once upon a time you could park on the roof of the Transit Road Mall. On this particular occasion, and being the person I am, I begged Mom to park there. Always obliging, she was halfway up the parking ramp when this big Cadillac starts down and blocks us. Now, that ramp was always tricky, which probably accounts for why it's now gone. It was barely a single lane wide and curved like a half-moon. I remember Mom and Aunt Gloria in the front seat looking at each other. Their station wagon was the size of Granddad's big runabout and about as easy to maneuver! It would have been difficult for anyone to back down that ramp. Well, when we didn't immediately get out of his way, the big giant man in the Cadillac sat on his horn. At the same time this guy is trying to intimidate us, Marnie and Lori were in the far back of the wagon testing the springs. Mom tried everything, backing this way then inching forward again and backing that way, but it was soon obvious there was no way she was getting back down that ramp. It was at that point that Mr. Cadillac, who by the way was only a few feet from the top, got out of his car and began marching toward us. Well Mom was every ounce of upset a woman could be, but Aunt Glory Bee was an imperial pound of mad!

"While I sat in the middle row of the wagon, wide-eyed and watching the scene unfold, Lori and Marnie in the far back jumped steadily, bouncing the car up and down, up and down, up and down. Leslie, strapped into her car seat beside me, was singing her own special baby mashup of her two favorite streets, *Coronation* and *Sesame*!" Looking down the table she quipped, "She was always singing! Meanwhile, Mr. Cadillac, who to me looked a little like the Pillsbury doughboy in a blue seersucker suit, was storming his way toward us with a large cigar in one hand and a ham-sized fist swinging in the air. If you've ever really known a redhead, you would know to never…ever…go there! I can only assume the Pillsbury Cadillac man had never had the pleasure. Aunt Gloria flew out of the car first, and was halfway up the ramp in less time than it usually took Lori to toss Leslie's bottle out the window."

Sitting next to Georgie's empty seat, Lori groaned, dumping her head in her hands. "Oh say it isn't so."

"As Gloria charged up the ramp, Mom jumped out of the station wagon to join her. From the perspective of my little self, I watched as Winnie and Gloria surged forward like a line of fire racing to and surrounding their prey. With red hair flaming and faces like tomatoes, I swear that man must have thought their heads were on fire! *Flame on!* For me, it was an up-close lesson on how mothers protect their young. In front of me a pair of female red wolves, with nothing more than a few well-said words, scared the living daylights out of one round pompous arse. I can't tell you how proud I was to watch my mommy and my aunty make a grown man cry! When we got home, I had to run to my room. Along with Wonder Woman and the Bionic Woman, I now had two more names to add to my growing pantheon of women superheroes or s'heroes as I used to say! Mr. Cadillac had run back to his car like a whiney little brat, reversed his way off the ramp and probably as far from them as he could get. Good old Winnie and Gloria climbed back in, high-fiving each other, proud for standing their ground. Mom put the car back in drive and edged the rest of the way up the ramp. It was only once we were on the roof and they began unloading all us kids that they noticed a sign clearly identifying the ramp we'd come up as being one-way and you guessed it. It was the down ramp! I have never heard my mother or my aunt laugh so hard in my life. So, while Lori and Marnie ran in circles like perpetual jumping beans, and Leslie sang her *Coronation* slash *Sesame Street* mashup, I spent the day watching our moms. I remain in awe of their spirit, their humor and their fight! Bless them both!"

Tyler was so proud, she almost cried when Henry stood to give Georgie a huge bear hug.

Before dinner was over there were more stories, more moments of elation and heartache, but more than anything it was Georgie's night and Tyler was determined to make it last. By the time the final course was cleared away, the restaurant staff had already begun seating customers for dinner. Everyone took their time thanking Leslie for a magnificent meal. The twins, with a little pressure from Henry, offered their services in the kitchen and headed off in that direction. As everyone else drifted toward the elevators, Tyler found herself in step with Lori Phipps.

"I take it Zoe didn't warn you about the storytelling?"

Seeing the woman in question ahead of the group, walking arm in arm with her father, Tyler said plainly, "Lori, I don't know why Zoe's behaving the way she is but I swear to you, there's nothing going on between us."

"Whoa there, tiger. I just wanted to tell you that you did great."

Confused by the compliment, she was suddenly unsure what to say. Lori wrapped an arm around her shoulders. "Come on kiddo, I want to show you something."

They took the elevator to nine. When the doors opened she followed Lori across the foyer to the fire stairs. "This will be open for the staff to go up and down between eight and nine. The security guys will block everyone but VIPs from using the stairs but certain people, a certain person we know who doesn't always enjoy a crowd, sometimes slips out here for a little quiet time." Lori stopped in front of the door marked Roof Access Only and pushed it open. They both shivered as a brisk wind blew in off the lake. Letting the door bang closed, they stood under the eerie glow of the exit light.

Tyler had to ask, "Why are you being nice to me?"

Lori shrugged. "You seem like a nice person, Tyler. I don't know what my nasty little niece is trying to do, but I have a good feeling it has nothing to do with you." She stopped on the landing, taking a quick look down the half flight of stairs to be sure they were alone. "Something hit me tonight, something that never occurred to me before. Everybody in this family has someone to lean on. Like you having a twin and me and Marnie being born just months apart and growing up to do everything together. Lou and Leslie had that. My mom and Aunt Winnie had that. Even Granddad had Uncle Danny. Now there's the kids but even they have siblings, but in all the stories and all those years Georgie has always been alone. I guess…"

"You just want to know someone's there for her too." She filled in the blank for Lori, much as she would have with Georgie herself.

Lori sat down on the edge of a stair and motioned for Tyler to join her.

"I'm sorry."

The admission wasn't what Tyler was expecting. "I'm sorry?"

"No, I'm sorry," she said with a wink. "I know exactly what Zoe is and I should've warned you about her bullshit before. It's just that, well, when we saw you in the bar, I just assumed…I won't tell you what I assumed, suffice it to say I'm sorry about that. I'm not like Marnie. She can tell you all about a person by just reading their résumé. Georgie and me, well we're just not built that way. Especially when it comes to women! Anyway, I think you're a good person and I see how you look at Georgie. I might not be good with people like Marnie is, but I think you get her, Georgie I mean."

Not sure what to say, Tyler asked the one thing that had been bothering her for days. "What's the deal with your brother? I mean, I just get the feeling he's out for blood when it comes to her. I just don't get it."

Lori groaned, standing and offering her hand to help Tyler up. "Fucked if I know. But if that little bastard doesn't stop soon, I may have to take him out to the boatyard and put him to work in the paint shed!"

It was a toothless threat. Still, it did make her smile. "I bet it's been a long time since that happened."

"Nuh-huh! That's one job little Luigi Henry Phipps has always managed to avoid. Now that you mention it, he's the only one in the family who's never spent time on his hands and knees on the punishment line! Little slime-ball, kiss-ass," she grumbled.

As Tyler followed her down the stairs, they could hear music coming from the ballroom. Heading in the opposite direction, she followed Lori through the back entrance to Georgie's living room. As expected, Marnie, stylus in one hand and her tablet in the other, was going over last-minute details with family members and the security team. Leslie, after checking on the catering staff, had returned to the restaurant. Henry too was gone. Jack, tasked with driving Henry home, had already left. She was a little surprised to realize Lou hadn't bothered to offer his father a drive out to the big house, nor was he anywhere to be seen.

"Tyler, I need you to take over for the next hour," Marnie ordered. "We'll get ready in two shifts. Me, Lori and Georgie will go first. Tyler, Skip and Zoe—where the hell is Zoe? Skippy go find your sister!" As he skated out, Marnie handed Tyler her tablet and the electronic pen. "Everything's there, just keep people moving in the right direction. Expect guests to start arriving around eight thirty to nine. It won't take me more than forty-five minutes to get ready. Once I do, you can head upstairs and get all dolled up. Understood?"

"Absolutely. What about these guys?" she asked, pointing to the rest of the security staff milling around.

"Oh damn I forgot. Check their badges and give them access to the meeting room on the first floor. Leslie can arrange for food and pop to be brought in for them. That's where they need to hang when they're not doing, securing, whatever…Tyler?"

"I've got it," she said, and began asking the security staff to hand over their badges for her to update. By the time she had added each number to the security protocol for the first-floor boardroom, Marnie and family were gone. With the temporary security people squared away, she sent them out to take up their duties, then remembered to check the settings for the guest room. She wasn't at all surprised to find that Georgie had changed the settings and just that morning. She had also restricted her own master access from the guest room. It was a sweet gesture. She knew Georgie could change it back at any time. The fact that she had provided Tyler with complete privacy was a first-class gesture and definitely all Georgie.

* * *

It had taken Georgie less than twenty minutes to shower, primp and coif. She began dressing in the new tuxedo. When she finished buttoning her shirt and tucking it in, she realized she didn't know how to tie a bowtie. Checking the time on the tablet mounted on her dressing table, she saw it was early yet. So she slipped on her shoes and went in search of help. Surely Jack knew how to tie a bowtie if Marnie could not. Halfway down the circular staircase she heard catcalls from somewhere but with head down and her mind concentrating on the task of fitting her cufflinks, she had no idea who was the focus of attention. Stopping on the bottom stair, she searched the expectant and welcoming faces of the people gathered around the kitchen island. "Where is Marnie? I can't…my tie?"

"Stop the music! We've a new baby butch in the house!" Zoe cried.

"Zoe knock it off already. Besides, I'd say more like Sporty Spice!" At Zoe's blank stare Lori added, "Spice Girls?" With no response she turned her attention back to Georgie. "Come here Bender; let a real woman show you how to do that."

Towering over Georgie, Lori made several attempts to get the bowtie just right but without luck. Admitting she couldn't do it on someone else, she said, "Sorry." Turning to Tyler in frustration, she asked, "How 'bout you, tiger?"

Stepping up beside them, Tyler took the cufflinks out of Georgie's fidgety hands and fitted them to her shirt cuffs. Once both were properly secured, she reassured her, "There you go, that's one thing done. I'm really not sure about the tie," she said, then had an idea. "Hold tight." Retrieving Marnie's tablet from the counter, she explained, "I'm sure I can look it up. There has to be a million How-To-Tie-A-Bowtie pages!" Before she could type in the first word in the search box, Zoe pushed past her and Lori.

"Let a real woman show you how to do that!" she repeated in mockery of Lori, but before she could do anything, she managed to spill her glass of wine down the front of Georgie's shirt.

"That's it!" Lori grabbed Zoe by the arm and dragged her out of the apartment.

Skippy made a mad dash for the kitchen drawer that held the dishtowels, while Tyler stood helpless. Georgie raised her hand, signaling for everyone to stop. Without a word of complaint, she made her way back up the stairs.

Heading straight into the master bath, stripping off her shirt on the way, she ran cold water slipping the stained shirt into the sink before thinking club soda might've been a better choice. Not sure if the shirt could be saved, she left it to soak before washing away the wine that had penetrated the starched cotton to soak her skin. In the walk-in closet, standing in front of the long stack of folded shirts, she had to admit she had no idea what to wear. Tyler had chosen the tuxedo and probably the shirt that went with it. She owned several white shirts but after examining the index card for each, she was sure none would do. Unwilling to admit to Tyler or even Lori that she didn't know how to match anything herself, her only option was her Mess Dress uniform. It was clean and pressed and good to go, although the idea didn't make her happy. The tuxedo had been chosen by Tyler and for some reason, not wearing it felt like she was letting her down. She also had a pretty good idea that what had just happened was no accident. Both Lori and Marnie had warned her that their niece was up to something.

Georgie began laying out all the intricate pieces required to assemble a military uniform. Rank insignia, command badges, miniature medals, and her wings. She had just brought up her uniform checklist when something occurred to her. Stepping in front of the full-length mirror she checked her tux trousers carefully. By luck or by fluke they were free of wine as were her shoes. She smiled at her image, challenging an unseen nemesis. She might seem old and broken to some, but she'd be damned before she let Zoe make her look like a fool!

It hadn't taken Tyler very long at all to get cleaned up and changed. Now, standing in the bathroom of the guest bedroom, she checked her hair and makeup one more time. She hadn't planned on going to the extra fuss of putting her hair up but Zoe's little stunt had spurred her on. She couldn't figure out for the life of her what the woman's problem was.

Flicking off the light switch, she headed for the door. It was almost eight thirty. She wanted to be at Georgie's side, and not just because of Marnie's order. Tonight she felt an overwhelming need to shield her and the thought of her standing alone spurred her to move faster.

CHAPTER ELEVEN

By the time Georgie marched back down the antique staircase, Lori was back, along with Marnie, Stella and Leslie. Jack Pulaski, just back from driving Henry home, stood with most of the family men. Skip, Anthony and Ethan were all decked out and looking dashing. She thought the women of her family looked lovely tonight too, especially her sister and Lori. It was almost eight thirty, time for Marnie's last-minute talk or what she often thought of as her Go Briefing. "Where is Lou?"

Marnie glanced up from her tablet, taking a long hard look at her sister. "What happened to your shirt?"

Before Georgie could try to explain, Lori skated in, wrapping her leather clad arm around her. "I love it. I think you look fantastic!" Turning to Marnie she explained, "Our helpful little niece managed to spill a glass of wine down Georgie's new shirt."

Marnie finally nodded. "You're right Lori, very nice. You look great sis! Okay, let's get on with this…"

Georgie interrupted, counting off the names of those missing. "Lou, Bonnie, Zoe, Tyler…"

"Let's not worry about the first three for now," Marnie said, before pointing to the stairs, "and Tyler's here."

Everyone turned their attention to the circular staircase. Of course, it wouldn't have mattered if they were to suddenly self-combust or jump out the windows, Georgie wouldn't have noticed. For her, in that moment, the only existing thing was Tyler Marsh.

When Tyler stepped from the bottom stair, Georgie was there, silently offering her hand. She'd always considered Tyler attractive but in the sleek sleeveless dress she was absolutely stunning. Feeling breathless, standing only feet apart, the desire she felt was overwhelming. It was hard to take in all of the woman. Her subtle curves, her delicate neck, slender soft arms and her hair. Georgie had always loved that color; the dark natural shades that contrasted so beautifully with her piercing blue eyes. Her hair was up, but a few tendrils had been allowed to escape and it was all Georgie could you not to reach out...

"All right you two, let's get on with it!" Marnie ordered, shattering the moment and reminding her that the room was full of family.

Georgie listened along with everyone else as Marnie delivered orders for the evening. Tonight wasn't just New Year's Eve, it was business. Getting drunk or acting like an ass in front of employees and customers was unacceptable and she drummed that in before going over the list of VIPs and her expectations for the evening. Finally she reminded everyone to have fun, sending them to man their posts.

Georgie had been assigned three objectives: listen to a pitch by a local charity, and another from the Coast Guard. The third was clearly Georgie's crucible. She was to be seen by everyone as having fun. Usually a mandate of that type would have driven her to abandon ship. This year though, she had Maggie at her side, and the real confidence came from knowing she could count on Tyler. She believed it was a combination of her competence and confidence that she found so reassuring.

As everyone scurried off to their duty stations, Marnie looked to her and then Maggie. "You dog! Come here," she ordered. It was probably just as incredible to Marnie as it was to everyone else when the dog complied with her order. Retrieving what the dog was carrying in her mouth, she examined it carefully. Holding it up, she asked, "Georgie, is this your tie? Your bowtie?"

Realizing the dog must have picked it up, somehow knowing it was important, Georgie praised Maggie, "Good girl."

Shaking her head, Marnie stretched it out in her hand, inspecting it for dog goober. Satisfied that it was still presentable, she looked to her sister then shook her head. "Too 'Chippendales' for me!" With surprising swiftness, she wrapped it around the dog's neck and had it tied in seconds flat. "Now you match your mommy," she said, awkwardly patting the dog's head before dismissing it outright. Handing Tyler her tablet, she warned, "You're my backup tonight, kiddo. Seems as how I've lost my assistant somewhere."

"What about…" Tyler started to ask.

Georgie took the tablet from her hand, and opening the same kitchen drawer Skippy had accessed earlier, shoved it in. "Ready!" she announced with a smile.

While Marnie shook her head, Lori wrapped an arm around her. "She's back, baby!"

"Mrs. Pulaski," one of the security people interrupted, "I was told to tell you when the Coast Guard people got here."

Marnie thanked him, pushing past Lori and Georgie to retrieve her tablet. Handing it to Tyler again, she said with a smile, "You're on kiddo. Get her upstairs. I'll join you shortly."

As ordered, Georgie headed up the back stairwell with Maggie leading the way and Tyler beside her. Halfway up she stopped, and turning to Tyler said quietly, almost shyly, "I…You look…Wow!"

"Thank you," she offered sincerely. "So do you. The vest without the shirt…" She shook her head, pleased. "I love it; it's so you," she said, continuing her climb up the stairs.

If Georgie had been overwhelmed by the sight of Tyler coming down the stairs, the sight of her going back up took her breath away. Forcing her eyes away from that most amazing view, she pushed herself to concentrate on the meeting ahead. Lucky for her it was the Coast Guard who would be doing most of the talking today. The local commander had an idea for a new safety product but lacked the technical expertise or the funding to get it done. Tonight was the night that had been set aside for situations just like this. While there were only two pitch sessions specifically scheduled for her, she knew there would be more. There always were. It was something her father and Henry had started long ago. They believed, as did she, that using their expertise and resources to help their community was just as valuable as their generous cash donations, and in some cases, more.

Walking into Henry's apartment, turned VIP suite, Georgie immediately noted that things were not as they should be. The mystery of her missing family members was immediately solved. Zoe, who should have been at Marnie's side welcoming new guests and generally being helpful, was seated on the piano bench beside the woman musician Marnie had hired. They were flirting and kibitzing outrageously and were distractingly loud. Bonnie, Lou's wife, was schmoozing with a young Coast Guard officer while her husband had cornered the commander. To make things worse, Lou was smoking a honking big cigar, which was definitely a no-no. Not just tonight but anytime. After all, this was Henry's home. And if there was anything Henry hated, it was stale cigar smoke. Before Georgie could even consider what to do, Tyler gave her arm a squeeze. "I've got this. Why don't you grab us something to drink? I believe the bar is in the dining room."

"You...something. What will you...have?"

Grinning, she set Georgie at ease. "Wine, please. Something red but not too sweet. You pick." And with that she headed first for Zoe and the musician.

Georgie couldn't tell what was being said from where she was standing, but she noticed Zoe's quick change of attitude. While her niece stood and left the room, the musician, now suitably chastised, began her first set. It was some nondescript light jazz piece and surprisingly unobtrusive. At the bar, she was tempted to order a stiff drink but heeding Marnie's warning, took two glasses of wine, and turned in time to watch Tyler take on Bonnie and Lou. She was smart. There was no denying that. She intrinsically understood the advantage of divide and conquer. First she interrupted what Georgie could only describe as a full-blown flirting session between a young Coasty and Lou's wife. Whatever Bonnie had been told by Tyler, it was enough to spur her into action. She immediately clamped onto Lou and steered him out the door. "Nice!" she acknowledged under her breath.

A moment later Tyler was there, retrieving her wineglass, and making the introductions to the Coast Guard Commander and his young communications officer. She was amazing, managing the interaction from start to finish.

Some minutes later, when Georgie realized the proposal the commander was discussing was the very thing she'd been working on, she became quite excited. Here was one of her secret projects. One of many. They were ideas and technologies that intrigued her, but more than that, they were projects she instinctively knew Lou would shut down simply because they were ideas beyond his grasp. Now she had proof positive that she was on the right track with her Rescue App, and could take the Coast Guard's needs directly to the board for approval.

When they finally wrapped up, Tyler left her on her own while she escorted the Coast Guard officers out. Checking her watch, Georgie was shocked to learn it was after ten. The room was busier now with several more guests. Some had gathered around the piano. She admired the way the young musician could carry on a conversation without missing a note.

The bar, a natural gathering space, was crowded too. Seeing everything in order and not wanting to be dragged into a conversation, she signaled Maggie and slipped out of the apartment intending to check on the rest of the party.

The foyer was jammed with a combination of caterers attending to the buffet next door. Slipping into the service stairs, she was about to head down when something caught Maggie's attention. She took a few steps up the stairs before turning back to Georgie. "Stand down." It was her release command, and meant the dog was free to pursue her interest. Following the dog, she headed up the stairs to the roof level. The door was propped open, and snow was tracking in.

For several years now the roof had been used as a smoking lounge for the VIP guests. Though lights and propane patio heaters illuminated and warmed the area, it was easy to see how the raging snow had driven even the hardiest smoker inside. She didn't mind and neither did Maggie who was busy rolling and playing in the new swelling powder. It was spectacular. Blowing in from the lake, the wind was fierce yet the snow was soft somehow, almost sweet. She stood there enjoying the fierceness from inside a bubble of artificial light and warmth. The snow pelted the bare skin of her face and hands, covering her with silver dollar-sized snowflakes that would melt before she could wipe them away. It was invigorating and freeing, and made her feel alive.

She sensed before she heard Tyler. Turning, she could only wonder if the woman thought she was absolutely mad to be out in this. Instead, she recognized the very thing she felt. Alive! She also looked…cold? Whipping her jacket off, she wrapped it around Tyler's bare shoulders, pulling the lapels closed tight. In the dreamlike glow, fierce winds whipped around them, cocooning them while soft heavy snow fell all around. It was ethereal and magic all at once and for the life of her, she couldn't let go. Since the day she'd come home from Afghanistan, she had been living day-to-day. Days had become weeks, the weeks months, and she had accepted that she had found a way to live. But here, now, with this woman standing in front of her, living wouldn't be enough. She felt alive; more alive than she'd ever felt.

Tyler held her gaze, and instead of taking hold of the jacket, she placed her hands over Georgie's. "It's amazing. The storm's energy," she qualified. "I've never felt anything like it."

There was so much she wanted to say. So much she wanted to ask. Yet, standing here, so close together while the snowstorm raged on, she understood there was absolutely no need. In a way, Tyler understood her better than she understood herself. If she'd thought differently, the last few hours had certainly proven that wrong. The woman just seemed to get her. And it wasn't just her ability to figure out what she was trying to say and say it for her. Tyler was her own person and had no problem raising her own concerns, offering solutions and even lobbying, as she had this evening, on the Coast Guard's behalf. Georgie loved that.

"You were wonderful tonight," Tyler told her. "When you showed the Commander the logic diagram for the rescue app, I thought he was going to cry. He really thought he was about to revolutionize marine communications. At least he felt better when you told him his networking solution was superior. That was very nice of you."

Georgie practically blushed at the praise. No matter how much snow came down or how much wind whipped up, standing here in this moment, holding Tyler's hands, all she could think about was how much she wished she could kiss her. Perhaps they could find time to talk. She wanted to, no, *needed* to explain some things, make sure of some things. She didn't want to make a mistake with Tyler. She needed to explain. It was just that standing here, in this moment, all she wanted was to kiss her. It would be so easy to overlook policy, forget caution, let go of who she was for what she wanted, but that wasn't Georgie DiNamico.

Deciding to explain, she took a deep breath and closed her eyes for the tenth of a second she needed to see the words she wanted to share. Suddenly Maggie was beside her, pressed hard against her leg. She opened her eyes to the last face she ever wanted to see.

"There you are! We couldn't figure where you got to," Zoe said, with a mischievous smile. "Look who I found. Just in time too. I think Dad was going to bore her to death."

Georgie just stood there angered and offended. Tyler had dropped her hands when Maggie had warned of the intrusion. "Tyler Marsh," she said, now offering her hand to the newcomer.

"Dr Margaret O'Shea."

If Tyler recognized the name of Georgie's former partner, she did not indicate it, just coolly shook her hand.

Zoe implored them, "Now that all the formalities are done with, can we move back into the blessed heat?" It sounded like a question, but she was already through the door.

Tyler and Margaret, however, were waiting for her. Feeling trapped, she placed one hand on the dog's head, signaling with the other for the two women to lead them back inside. What the hell else could she do? Nothing, until someone explained to her why Margaret was there and why she'd been allowed to get as far as the ninth floor, much less up to the roof. It was easy to imagine that Zoe was part and parcel of whatever was going on. She was leading the group back down the stairs and directly into Henry's apartment. The place was even busier now and if there was one rule Marnie had, above all else, it was no family fights in front of the guests. That might keep her from wringing her niece's scrawny little neck, but it wouldn't stop her from demanding answers from her ex. "Why…are—you—here?"

"Georgie!" Zoe admonished. "Margaret's our guest. She's here with her father."

"It's all right Zoe; you know Georgie doesn't like surprises." Margaret said it with such aplomb one could almost ignore Georgie's glacial expression. "You must be the doctor helping my Georgie," Margaret said to Tyler. "I'm Dr O'Shea. It's a pleasure to meet you. I'm sorry I missed your name when Zoe introduced us. Whatever were you two doing out in that storm? It's just crazy out there! Talk about a night not fit for man nor beast!"

As Tyler introduced herself again, Georgie stood passively listening to the surreal conversation flow around her. *What the hell! Who had invited Margaret and her bloody father, of all people?* If she ever created a list of the people she never wanted to see again, Margaret would be on top, with her grasping social climbing father a close runner-up. Picking up on the gist of the conversation, she knew they had wrangled their way into an invitation with the intention of pitching her on their latest charitable endeavor. Bristling, it took everything she had not to blindly punch somebody out. *Charitable endeavor, my ass!* As far as she was concerned, the only charity the O'Sheas were interested in, were the O'Sheas. Sure enough, the O'Sheas *were* the charity pitch she was scheduled to hear. Remaining calm, she sat listening to father and daughter drone on about the need to add a veterans wing to their clinic. For over forty minutes they pressed her on the needs of the community, Georgie's needs and how the two dovetailed perfectly with their plans to expand. Georgie wanted to throw up. These two had been angling for ways to expand an already upscale O'Shea Medical Clinic built with DiNamico money. Trying to tempt her by offering to name a new wing after her father had been the last of many mistakes.

Georgie stood, straightening her vest. She had forgotten to retrieve her jacket from Tyler, who now held it out for her to slip on. Nodding thanks, she hoped that Tyler would realize how much she was both grateful and relieved to have her there. Knowing she was understood by Tyler was immeasurable. Not for the first time she was more than aware of the fact that her ex, who was casting meaningful glances at her, even after all this time didn't understand a damn thing about her. The DiNamico and Phipps families were not about self-gratification. They didn't do things to get their names on buildings! They did what they could when and where they could because they believed in giving back.

"Dr O'Shea," she murmured, offering her hand to Margaret's father, "my pleasure." Then she nodded to Margaret and walked out.

She regretted having to leave Tyler to clean up her mess. What else could she do? She would find Marnie and let her know just who the big corporate guest was and ask how that had happened. She had been warned that Zoe was up to no good but this was beyond her doing. She was sure Lou was behind this. He was the one who had added the second pitch session for a "veterans' charity" to her list. *Charity my ass!*

* * *

Tyler escorted the O'Sheas through the foyer and into the upper level of Georgie's apartment. She had wanted to escort them completely out of the building, but they quite pretentiously explained they were guests of the company president, Lou Phipps, and were staying for the party. Changing directions, she took them around the buffet tables and down the circular staircase to the reception area, leading them directly to Marnie Pulaski. She was at the center of a small group and in the middle of a conversation. When she finally turned to be introduced, she faltered for a moment, before accepting Margaret's outstretched hand.

"Margaret. How nice of you to make it. And I see you brought your father," she said, offering her hand to the senior O'Shea.

Tyler observed the interaction between the three with keen interest. While Marnie schooled her emotions well, anyone with half a brain could see she did not like the pair. In fact, Tyler was pretty sure the woman had a big hate on for Margaret's father. Not normally a troublemaker by nature, she wasn't sure what had gotten into her when she explained to Marnie, "The O'Sheas are a guest of Mr. Phipps, the company president! As a matter of fact, Georgie and I were lucky enough to hear about their expansion plans for the O'Shea Medical Center, and how they hope to cater to veterans in need."

That caught Marnie by surprise. Both facts did, but just like finding the O'Sheas standing in Georgie's living room, she took those body blows like a prizefighter. Taking the senior O'Shea by the arm, she led him toward the bar. "It's so nice to see you, James. I'm glad to hear you're doing so well. I know you've wanted to expand the clinic for some time…"

As they trailed off, Tyler turned away intending to find Georgie. Instead, Margaret O'Shea hooked her arm, halting her on the spot.

"Don't run off! I wanted to ask you how my Georgie's doing. Poor thing!"

"I'm sorry Margaret. I'm not at liberty to discuss Ms. DiNamico." Still, she was unable to extract herself from the woman.

"Oh," she said, patting Tyler's arm with such sincerity she was temporarily taken aback. "I'm sorry, I should've explained who I am! I'm not a stranger. Georgie and I were, well let's just say very close. If it hadn't been for Afghanistan…" she lamented, almost seeming sincere. "So, tell me how she's doing?" She placed a dramatic hand on her chest. "I had no idea it had gotten so bad she needed full-time help!"

"You misunderstand. I'm Georgie's executive assistant, not her medical aide."

"But Zoe said you're a doctor. What's your specialty?"

"Ethics! I'm a PhD, not a medical doctor."

"I see," Margret said, although clearly she didn't, or didn't care.

She couldn't tell which and considered herself lucky when the woman simply turned without further comment and walked away.

Tyler paced the length of the guest room. Where was Georgie? Had she misunderstood or gotten it all wrong? She racked her brain, replaying everything that had taken place. After the run-in with Margaret, Georgie's ex, Georgie had taken the dog for a long walk. Tyler was thankful she had created a contingency just for this. Before the party she had taken Georgie's heavy winter coat, gathered up her best mitts, a hat and her winter boots, and stored them in the machine shop. She even remembered the dog's winter coat and spare leash. When she learned that Georgie and Maggie, dressed like the abominable snowman and her sled dog, had snuck out the back door, she arranged for security to alert her the moment they returned. At one a.m. Georgie had successfully snuck back in as quietly as she had slipped out and Tyler guessed she was hiding in her room. She knew she could call up the security program and pinpoint Georgie's exact position in the building but she wanted to respect her privacy. She also didn't want to impinge on Marnie, who was busy putting out all the fires Lou Phipps kept setting every time he opened his big mouth. Instead she nabbed Lori, asking her to help.

It was the right move. Lori had Georgie on the dance floor within minutes and it was pretty much where she'd spent the remainder of the night. She danced with her cousins, her sister, and even Tyler a few times. Always fast songs, and always quite innocent. At least compared to their moment on the roof.

Dammit, she wanted to kill Margaret O'Shea! In truly despicable fashion, the woman had shown up asking for money, and she'd spent the night trying to play nice and acting as if she were still family. One consolation was her complete lack of interest in Tyler. If only she'd been uninterested before destroying their moment on the roof.

It had been sublime. The snow, the wind and the wildness and Georgie's eyes. She'd had a good idea Georgie had escaped to the roof but nothing could have prepared her for the emotions the wind and weather evoked. Standing alone on the prow, staring into the blizzard, she seemed a titan, fearless and alone. Wind and snow seemed to sail around her, as if she herself were the eye of the storm. And as Tyler watched, she questioned whether she should disturb her until Lori's comments replayed in her mind. Georgie had always been alone. Not by choice but forced by the circumstances of her life.

She had gone to Georgie, drawn in a way she could barely comprehend. And for a brief moment it was just them. Alone together in the eye of the storm and she knew Georgie wanted to kiss her, hold her and she ached to be taken into her arms. They had been so close yet she had stalled, as if needing to explain something, and then the moment was gone.

When Lori finally dragged Georgie downstairs and out onto the dance floor, Tyler had secretly rejoiced. She wanted to see her have fun but more than that she just wanted to see her. She cheered with everyone else when all the DiNamico/Phipps women took to the dance floor together. It was already after three a.m. and almost all of the guests were gone. She watched as Georgie and her family danced and joked and finally got to let loose. She was disappointed when the music stopped but lucky for her Marnie had yet to dance with her husband and asked the DJ for one more song. Georgie had come to her then with an unassuming smile and an open hand. Still it made her knees weak. She had shed the tuxedo jacket. She had the arms and the shoulders of an athlete, accentuating the striking emerald-green waistcoat which was a perfect match to her eyes and complemented her light olive skin. Leading her to the dance floor, she took Tyler in her arms in a manner that seemed almost shy. There was a sweetness about Georgie. A kindness that she'd come to count on but it was always her eyes that betrayed her emotions. Tyler was sure Georgie was feeling everything she was and more. *God, the woman had control!* When the music ended they stood inches apart but still holding hands. Georgie's eyes said everything she wanted to hear. Everything! So why was she still alone?

Grabbing Marnie's tablet from the dresser she did the one thing she promised herself she would never do. Bringing up the security program she entered the master password. It was easy to convince herself she was just checking that everyone had made it home, or at least out of the building. Forcing herself to go through the motions, she began with the first floor, before tabbing through each consecutive number until reaching nine. On the plan diagram, six little triangles were displayed. Not good with maps, she had to orient the drawing to understand it. It was easy to see that three of the triangles were in Henry's apartment. She didn't have to tap them to know it would be Lou, Bonnie and Skip. There was one triangle in Leslie's apartment, which made sense, and in Georgie's there were two. Hers in the guest room, the other was Georgie. So she was in her bedroom. The realization almost crushed Tyler.

Tossing the device on her bed she stood and began pacing again. Why hadn't Georgie come to her? Had she changed her mind? Had she misunderstood? She racked her brain trying to decide what she'd done wrong. She had seen the way Georgie looked at her. She felt the way she had held her, touched her. Even her halting condensed speech intimated her interest. So why was she still alone?

Then it occurred to her. Why was Georgie in her bedroom? At night she always slept two rooms over. She hit the reload button for the program data and watched as the triangles were re-populated on their floor. Georgie was definitely in her bedroom and not the safe room she slept in. It took Tyler a long minute to compile the pieces. Georgie had been trying to tell her something on the roof. Something important. She knew, because she'd spent so much time learning to interpret her interactions. She truly understood now that Georgie could do or say but not at the same time. To communicate complex ideas she needed to see the words before she could speak them. Tyler had watched her do so it many times, yet standing there in the center of the storm, she'd held her breath. She could see the importance of what Georgie wanted to share written across her face. More than that, she could feel it in herself and in every essence of the woman who had wrapped her jacket tightly around her and stood there arms bared to the tempest. That was just like Georgie. Needing to make sure she was understood, to share and to acknowledge…And that's when it occurred to her.

"No, no, no, no, no, no, no!" Georgie and her rules! Georgie and her fairness! Georgie…"You can't come to me."

She understood immediately and knew that regardless of their feelings, ethically Georgie was in the place where she couldn't make the first move. Why had she not thought of that! She wasn't sure whether she should scream or cheer. Now the question was, could she go to her?

She paced back and forth a few times trying to work up her courage. *Is that why Georgie is in her bedroom and not her sleep room? Is she waiting for me?* Retrieving the tablet she tabbed to a different page. Tyler wasn't the only one with the master password. She'd used it that afternoon to check the security settings for the guest room and was delighted to see Georgie had taken the time to bar everyone including herself. Searching down the list of electronic locks associated with Georgie's penthouse apartment it only took a moment to find the serial number for the master bedroom. When she clicked on the number only two employee names were listed under access: Georgina DiNamico and Tyler Marsh. For a moment Tyler thought she might faint.

She hadn't been wrong. Georgie wanted her and Georgie was waiting for her.

She was out the bedroom door and around the long balcony to the south side master suite. At the door she suddenly halted. Before she could even think to back away or change her mind the bedroom door opened quietly and she was there.

There was a way about Georgie. A way that was sexy, and exciting, and gentle all at the same time. Accepting her outstretched hand, she followed her into the room. She was still wearing the tuxedo pants and vest but like Tyler, she had shed her footwear. Her gaze devoured Tyler in her gown. Standing toe to toe, she could see the questions in Georgie's eyes and realized she needed to be sure. "Yes," Tyler whispered, "I want to be here." She watched as her words made their way to Georgie's eyes. Georgie's hands were on her face, holding her, touching her, then sweetly, sweetly kissing her. Her lips glided over Tyler's and telegraphed desire throughout her body as she deepened their exploration. She felt overwhelmed with desire and almost light-headed and giddy from expectation. "I'm going to fall down, if I don't sit down…"

Georgie leaned back slightly, looking in her eyes, recognizing the arousal on Tyler's face. Taking her hands, she took several steps back toward the bed. With a smile she was starting to recognize was just for her, Georgie unzipped the side zipper on her evening gown and let it slide off her shoulders onto the floor.

If Tyler's legs had been weak before, they were now reduced to slush. She stood, frozen in place as Georgie began removing her vest and the tuxedo trousers. She pushed them down her thighs, revealing smooth athletic legs and the sexiest underthings. The way her tanned body fit the black lace bra and panties was enough to make Tyler weep. When she tossed the trousers away, she offered her hand, just as she had when the night began, and continued moving back and onto the bed. Any shyness Tyler had felt earlier was now completely gone. As she followed Georgie on top of the bed and on top of her, a long involuntary moan escaped her, "Oh God!"

The sensation of full contact was so overwhelming she thought she would come on the spot. As if sensing the height of her arousal, Georgie slowed her with her hands before rolling her into her arms. Side-by-side, her arm wrapped firmly around Tyler's back made Tyler feel connected and safe. Georgie's other hand was on her face, stroking her hair gently from her eyes and teasing away the long wisps. Her lips followed everywhere her fingers touched. Cheek, brow, eyes, then, oh yes, and then her mouth.

Tyler tried desperately to govern her breathing under the kiss but when Georgie trailed soft fingertips down her neck and over her small sensitive breasts, all thoughts of self-control evaporated. Pushing her onto her back, Georgie stripped off Tyler's panties with skillful speed before sliding a strong thigh between her legs. Easily matching her rhythm, she continued to encourage her with her hands and lips.

"Don't stop, please don't stop!" Tyler begged. Looking in Georgie's eyes told her everything she needed to know. Her, Tyler, she. She was all that existed in those gorgeous green eyes. Suddenly knowing she was the only thing holding Georgie back, she begged her, "Yes, inside baby, please…"

Georgie was inside her and she couldn't control the scream. Involuntarily digging her nails into her strong back, she rode out spasm after spasm in Georgie's strong arms. Somewhere in the back of her brain she was aware that she was saying things, calling things, words and sounds she'd never imagined could come from her and all the while Georgie was there, holding her, coaxing her, pushing her to feel more. The orgasm had come with such intensity that when she was once again aware, she found herself hanging on to Georgie for dear life. Her head was nestled in Georgie's neck, one arm tightly wrapped around Georgie, the other fixed in a death grip on a length of bed sheet wound tightly in her fist. Forcing herself to breathe, she wrapped her arms around Georgie's neck. It was at that moment she realized she had been in such need, Georgie was still in her underwear. As pretty as the bra and panties were, they definitely had to go. It only took a moment to search for and unhook her bra clasp. Without even looking, she could feel Georgie smile. Face to face, Tyler admitted with embarrassment, "I'm so sorry—I feel like a teenage boy, going off like that, it's just that…"

Georgie halted the apology with a deep smoldering kiss. When her lips moved on to her neck, Tyler struggled to gulp in air.

Exploring her collarbone, her mouth trailed lavish caresses all the way to her breast. "Again? Wait, I…Oh God!" A greedy mouth assaulted her breast with a laving tongue, while her hands continued to explore and discover Tyler inch by inch.

Involuntarily arching, she dug her nails mercilessly into Georgie's back, knowing she couldn't stop if she tried. Those hands were everywhere. On her breasts, her legs, and combing fingers up her thighs…Struggling with the onslaught of sensation, Tyler wasn't actually sure of anything anymore. As Georgie parted her thighs wide, she continued her downward progress. "Where, what, oh no you're not…" At Georgie's abrupt halt, she had to replay her words in her mind. Overwhelmed and excited beyond imagination she opened her eyes. There was concern in Georgie's eyes and something more, something beyond feral. *Damn those green eyes!* At that moment she knew she would never be able to say no to that look.

"Yes!" It was her new magic word. Dropping her head back, delighting in letting Georgie have her way, "Yes, oh yes you are…"

When she woke Georgie was still holding her and had pulled part of the duvet up to keep her warm. Judging by the gentle caresses along the length of her side, she knew Georgie was awake. Opening her eyes she was rewarded with a smile and something more. Tyler could see it but in her stupor was slow to understand. "What is it baby? I know you're trying to tell me something."

Georgie's hands stilled and as she had done so many times before, she closed her eyes for a brief moment to frame her reply. "You are so beautiful."

Caught off guard by her sincerity, Tyler wrapped her arms around her shoulders, squeezing tight. "Oh Georgie, baby. I can't begin to tell you how you make me feel. How I want to touch you so bad!" She accentuated her statement with a crushing kiss before lifting her head back just far enough to see those eyes. The pain was clearer than any statement could be. Suddenly she understood. "Oh my God! That bitch!"

Georgie's eyebrow raised barely a millimeter.

It was all the invitation Tyler needed. Instead of explaining, she left the conversation for another time, focusing instead on the woman in her arms. She'd been so aroused by the time she made it to Georgie's room it was no wonder she'd come within seconds of falling into her arms. The second time, well technically the second, then the third and fourth, were just greedy. Although she wasn't about to apologize for that. Pushing Georgie onto her back, she held a firm hand to the center of her chest. "I'm not surprised to learn Margaret was a pillow princess. Just tell me one thing? Is that the way you want it now?"

Georgie's breathing was shallow and her face flushed. She shook her head.

Proffering a playfully wicked smile, Tyler trailed a single finger down Georgie's abdomen, before hooking it on the upper band of the lacy shorts. "Well then, the first thing we need to do is get rid of these." More than eager, Georgie pulled them off for her. "You're enjoying this aren't you?"

Georgie tapped her lips and stilling her hands, asked innocently, "Start?"

"Umm, good idea." Leaning in, Tyler savored the moment and the way it felt each time their lips met. Georgie's mouth was hungry and exploring but with an appetite that perfectly matched her own. The only thing she liked better than having Georgie's mouth on hers was having that marvelous mouth everywhere else. Moving down her neck, she took her time wanting to worship her every curve.

Georgie was so different from most of the women she had been with. In her suits and even the tux, she cut an athletic figure but here, stripped of her official façade, the woman was a study in the divine female form. Feminine curves softened hard lines of taut muscle while a startling warmth radiated from her sensuous skin. Cupping her full breast, she stroked her thumb back and forth across Georgie's nipple. It was amusing to realize that she, not Georgie, was the one groaning at the sensation. *God!* If she wasn't careful she'd come again and just from touching her! Lowering her mouth, taking in the hardened nipple, she couldn't help but moan again. Under her, every inch of Georgie was alive. Even the simplest caress was enough to invoke pleasure and Tyler didn't want to stop. Still, she wouldn't risk doing anything without asking. And with Georgie, asking was the easiest thing. She lifted her head just high enough to see Georgie's face and waited for those expressive eyes to open. When they did she was rewarded with that smile that made her melt. The one she knew was just for her. "Baby," she practically moaned the word. "Baby, I want to be inside you." And there it was again. That smile, that look that said anything, everything.

Holding Tyler's face in her hands, she seemed to be interpreting her expression, hearing her meaning. She nodded before forcing the words out, "Please...yes."

Tyler took her time, teasing more sensation with every new caress. Trailing her hand along Georgie's side, she circled her hip before running down the length of her leg. Sliding it slowly around her knee, she traced her nails up the inside of her thigh. She began slowly, with just one finger. When Georgie stilled, she looked to find so much longing on her face and in her eyes.

"More," she begged.

Her breathing was so shallow Tyler worried she would pass out before her orgasm. "Baby. Breathe, please baby breathe!"

Even as she complied, the energy of her arousal radiated from her.

Withdrawing her finger, Tyler took her time gliding up and down, enjoying every detail. Georgie arched hard into her when her fingers found and circled her clit. Half expecting to feel nails in her back, Tyler braced for the response, only realizing when it didn't come how much Georgie was holding back. "Oh no you don't. Don't you dare hold back on me!" Her expressive eyes betrayed her fear. "Baby, I promise you, I can handle anything you throw at me. Please, don't hold back."

There was still an uneasy look in those deep green eyes but there was something else too. Trust. As Georgie's trepidation dissolved so did her hesitation. Tyler plunged two fingers deep inside, curling them back again and again. The response was immediate and she all but had to brace herself. She placed a hand in the center of Georgie's chest, pushing her down, to keep her on her back and on the bed.

Georgie clamped onto the headboard while her hips pulsed hard with every thrust from Tyler's hand. Her breathing was rapid and erratic as she tossed her head from side to side.

"Easy baby, that's it," Tyler encouraged her, pushing harder to curl her fingers. This time as Georgie's hips came up to meet her thrusts, she was able to slide her thumb in beside her clit. The action almost catapulted Georgie from the bed. Georgie's arms sliced down like blades, pounding the bed. Each hand dug deep into the sheets, clamping on before pulling hard. She ground herself up and into Tyler with more strength than seemed possible.

"That's it baby. Oh God that's it!" As she said it, she couldn't hold back her own crushing orgasm in time with Georgie's. The sensation was excruciatingly beautiful. Interwoven sensations flooded every inch of her. So this is what it felt like when two women could orgasm together. With her eyes closed she could feel herself drifting. Not wanting to lose a single conscious moment, she opened her eyes to watch the woman in her arms. She was still fighting to catch her breath as another aftershock took them both.

She had no idea it could be like this. Though she had thought about it, even tried to imagine what it might be like... "Georgie?" she asked, just above a whisper. "Baby, I need to talk. There are so many things rolling around in my head that I need to get out. I know it's probably just my pheromones causing me to blabber, and I don't want to be a pain..." She could feel Georgie still and knew by the sight of her closed eyes that she was seeing the words she wanted to say.

Finally, soft unfocused eyes opened and she tried to explain, "Always talk…don't ask. I…love to hear. Feels…" As explanation, she laid Tyler's hand on her chest. "Always good. You…always."

"How is it you can say so much in so few words?" When Georgie shook her head with doubt in her eyes, Tyler didn't know if she should laugh or cry. "It doesn't matter if no one else gets you, baby. I do. I don't know why that is, but…well, you just make it so easy." For a moment she wondered if she had said too much or worse, assumed too much. Feeling Georgie's eyes on her, she knew it was better to ask than to wonder. "We…I…"

Georgie pulled her in closer, as close as they could be and still look each other in the eye.

The sensation of being wrapped in each other's arms, legs intertwined, was all the strength she needed. "I feel things for you. I feel…" She closed her eyes for a moment. Maybe if she used Georgie's technique she could find the words she wanted to share. A single night of lovemaking did not make a relationship but if this night was any indication…"This is a thing, right? You and me? I'm not just making it up in my mind, am I? It's just that…"

Georgie laid a hand gently on her cheek, then stilled. "Yes."

Feeling breathless, and at a loss for words, Tyler tunneled in closer, hanging on tight. Georgie's responsive embrace was strong and unyielding, erasing all her concerns. Finally beginning to relax, she loosened her grip, laying her head on Georgie's shoulder as she let her feelings play out across her face. It didn't matter if Georgie saw how happy she was.

This is a thing! This really was. She smiled. Close in her arms, she was happier than she remembered being in a very long time. There was still so much to learn, to know, to understand. Still, even though she hadn't known Georgie for that long, she was sure she understood her. Maybe not completely but better than most. Certainly better than her ex ever did. Even here, now, intertwined in Georgie's arms and legs, the thought of that woman could sour her mood. How Georgie ever put up with… Before she could finish the thought, she realized Georgie had picked up on her change of mood.

"Baby, I will never treat you the way she did. I know you know that. I just wanted you to hear the words. Some things just need to be said!"

Georgie stretched to reach for the duvet, pulling it back over the two of them. Now properly settled in, her fingers trailed featherlight over Tyler, checking to be sure she was comfortable and tucked in tight.

Finally closing her eyes, Tyler felt herself drifting off. On the verge of sleep, Georgie's soft caresses stilled. Knowing it was important and never wanting to miss a single word she could share, she lifted her head off Georgie's shoulder to look at her. She saw both her unassuming expression and something more.

Right from the start, it had been like this. Georgie held things in. She had too but not with her. Not anymore. Tyler had made that clear from day one. It had taken a few tries for them to get it right but now she knew for certain that Georgie trusted her. And she knew something else. Lowering her head again, she snuggled in tight. "I'm here, baby."

She heard Georgie's breathing catch, and then she said simply, "Don't let go."

CHAPTER TWELVE

Tyler woke in Georgie's arms. She could almost call the moment sublime if it weren't for that incessant noise. That's when she actually heard it. Not the first two or three times but on the fourth or fifth repetition. Panicking at the sound of *Darth Vader's March*, she was instantly embarrassed to have Georgie learn she had set it for Marnie's ringtone. She also had no idea where it was coming from and was temporarily confused when Georgie reached to the bedside table and retrieved her own phone.

"Go!" she growled.

Tyler knew "Go" was her standard greeting for family and friends. Well not really. It was mostly just for her and Marnie. Everyone else always opted for the easier route of a text message. That's when it hit her. She and Georgie used the same ring tone to warn when a call was from the big boss. Suddenly the thought that Marnie was on the phone while she was here, in bed like this, almost made her hide under the covers.

"No," Georgie repeated.

She wasn't sure what that was about but knew there was some sort of argument going on. Worried that maybe they had overslept and missed the afternoon reception, she sat up to check the bedside clock. It was just after ten a.m. They still had plenty of time so that couldn't be Marnie's issue.

"No!" Georgie said, sitting up beside Tyler.

Leaning back against the headboard, Tyler adjusted the heavy duvet against the cool morning air. She could hear Marnie's voice and half expected Maggie to appear with leash in mouth. *Where is Maggie?* Before she could ask, Georgie's eyes were on her. Without a word she simply handed the phone over then sat back, arms crossed and visibly frustrated. Not sure how she would explain why she was with Georgie when the phone call had woken her up, her voice was on the timid side when she said, "Good morning, it's Tyler."

"Get her up and dressed right now. Goddammit! I don't have time for this!"

"I beg your pardon?"

She could hear Marnie huffing and puffing and could imagine her corresponding pen clicking or finger tapping. Finally, she said, "Tyler, I don't even know where to start with you. Right now, let's just put this aside, whatever this is. We—"

"I'm sorry Marnie, I can't do that. I need to explain and you need to hear me. Georgie has done nothing wrong. She hasn't broken any rules or protocols or policies. I came to her. I initiated this. And I promise you, you will have the appropriate paperwork before the end of the day, because 'whatever this is,' I have no intention of letting anyone set it aside."

There was a long silence on the phone. So long, Tyler checked the screen in case she had lost the connection. When the reply came it was nothing like she expected.

It was a good hearty laugh. When Marnie settled down enough to talk, she admitted, "Ah, Lori warned me! She said you're the best thing that could ever happen to Georgie and that you'd kick ass. I wasn't sure if you had it in yah, girl. Good for you!"

A little confused and feeling sheepish for her brash response, she ventured, "I take it the reason you called this morning has nothing to do with me being here?"

"Oh, it has something to do with you being there, just not the part you were thinking. Here's the thing," she started to explain, then thought better of it. "Put me on speakerphone. If I have to regurgitate all this crap, I only want to do it once."

"Go ahead. We're listening," Tyler assured her.

They could hear Marnie take a deep breath. "We have a problem. I think you both know Lou was a little out of control last night. I thought it was just the booze talking, then I got a call from Lori. She was out walking the dogs bright and early and guess who she spots out at the boatyard? Lou and Bonnie, and that idiot Frank Hann!" When neither Tyler nor Georgie commented, she sang, "'*Frank Hann, the real estate man!*' Please tell me you at least recognize the man's stupid jingle?"

Georgie nodded to Tyler, who explained, "Sorry Marnie. I guess we had to hear the tune to put it together. Why was he out there? If I recall correctly, Lou has already been told the company doesn't actually own the boatyard, at least not the land or the buildings."

"Well that's something we're all going to have to talk about because of several other factors Lori and I have just put together. When will you two be ready?"

"How soon will you be here?" When Marnie didn't immediately answer, Tyler pushed for more information. "Is there a problem?"

"I don't think we should meet at the office or upstairs."

Marnie was silent for so long that Tyler asked, "Marnie what's going on?"

"We need to talk. I need all the cousins, but we can't meet there. I have a sneaking suspicion Lou has spies everywhere. The same goes for Lori's house and the boatyard. I would ask you to come out here but he'll recognize Georgie's truck and if Lori's here too, he'll know something's up. I can't put Henry through that. Not yet. Not until we have a plan in place. That means we need to sit down now."

"I might have a place, if you're not offended to meet in my parents' kitchen?"

"Offended?" Marnie scoffed, "Good God girl! The way Georgie tells it, visiting with your family is better than hitting a five-star resort! Go ahead, make your call. I'll be here."

Tyler turned her attention to Georgie. Once the debate between the sisters had ebbed, Georgie had curled up around her. Needing both hands to make the call, Tyler apologized, "Sorry baby," before pulling both arms loose and dialing her father's cell. She explained the situation.

"And you're thinking here will work. Of course. You don't have to ask but since you did, how soon can we expect you and the ladies? Have I got time to throw on some lunch?"

"Dad, you don't have to go to any fuss."

"No fuss," he promised. "Ask Georgie if she likes chili?"

Before she realized what she was doing, Tyler lowered the phone and did exactly that. It was only on seeing Georgie's amused grin that she realized what she'd just done. "Uhm…"

"You are so busted!" her dad said, highly amused. "This is so great! I can't wait to tell your mother. See you when you get here." And with that he was gone.

"Oh my God!" she squealed, then thought of something else. "He did that on purpose! Oh my God! Did everyone figure it out before we did?"

Georgie was laughing as she rolled Tyler on her back. Retrieving the phone, she started texting the details to Marnie, including Tyler's address when she pointed to her bare wrist, asking for a time.

"I can be ready in a half hour and it won't take us more than fifteen minutes to make the drive today. That just leaves whatever amount of time you need for Maggie. Wait, where is Maggie?"

Coloring slightly, Georgie admitted the dog had gone home with Lori.

"Oh my God! Even you thought we were a foregone conclusion!" She yanked the pillow out from under Georgie's head and thumped it on top of her. Georgie just laughed as she thumped it down again, "You! Do you know how long I waited?" she demanded with a huge grin etched across her face. "Oh baby you are in so much trouble!"

Georgie waved the phone and the text message up for her to see.

Still poised with the pillow over her head, she read the message again. Georgie had added the time needed before they could meet. "Ninety minutes? Tell you what—make it two hours. You have an extra thirty minutes to make up to me!"

* * *

"Leslie said she's voting with me. That little bastard had someone in there last week to appraise the value of the restaurant!" Lori exclaimed.

Georgie banged her teacup down a little too forcefully, while Marnie demanded more information. As it turned out, Lou Phipps had been a busy boy. He'd had appraisers out looking at every piece of the family holdings. As explanation, he had told both Lori and Leslie it was a requirement for the new insurance company. It was easy to see no one believed him but Georgie also knew it to be impossible. For the three years preceding her last deployment, she had been sitting where Marnie was now. As chief operating officer, she not only managed the day-to-day tasks, she had written most of the policies and quality standards in use. It was how she knew Lou was lying. Before any change of suppliers could be made, quotes were required from at least three companies, and required signoffs from several departments but especially from the COO. That COO was now Marnie, and Georgie looked to her for what she knew.

"Honest to God, Georgie, he hasn't said a word and nothing's come across my desk. I really don't think this is about insurance. If it was he wouldn't be dragging real estate agents around."

Sitting in the kitchen, parsing through the evidence available, they had been unable to understand what Lou was up to. The whole situation was like a forest fire. No matter how hard they tried, they couldn't quite pinpoint the source smoldering under the surface with so much smoke obscuring their way.

When Tyler suggested showing the financial reports to her mom, Marnie was quick to bring her in along with Tyler's sister. Kira was a real estate lawyer and had never done any corporate work, but still, her interest was piqued and she offered to join their group.

After an hour of poring through reports, sharing their observations and compiling a list of issues, Carl managed to convince them all to have some lunch. He'd been puttering around with his homemade chili and served it up with fresh garlic bread. Everyone dug in, even Marnie who, among the cousins, was considered a notoriously picky eater. After lunch Carl had managed to move them, *en masse*, to the spacious family room.

They had been back at it for over an hour when Debbie Marsh broke in, apologizing, "I'm sorry ladies, but these foreign currency accounts just don't add up."

Tyler retrieved several printouts from her mother and handing them to Marnie, added, "Georgie and I found the same thing. Although it doesn't look like money's actually missing."

"How's that?" Marnie asked.

"From what we could figure out it looks like he's been moving operational funds into holding accounts and vice versa."

Lori, who was seated beside Marnie, let out a long loud whistle. Pointing to one of the spreadsheets, she said, "Where the hell did we get this kind of money? Every time I go to that bastard to upgrade something, he cries poor, and now I'm seeing we have an account with *sixty million dollars* in it?"

Marnie looked over the figures then handed the sheets to Georgie. She took a moment to compare the totals to her own notes. "Pension fund," Georgie explained. "Not ours."

"Fuck me!" It was out so fast, Marnie actually clamped both her hands over her mouth, as if doing so would take it back.

"If she's right," Debbie warned, "a few choice words will be the least of your problems. Employee contributed pension plans are protected by law. You could be looking at jail time."

"We," Marnie corrected her. Before Marnie had given Debbie Marsh access to the company's records, she had asked her to sign a nondisclosure agreement and had given her a retainer right on the spot. When she learned Kira was a lawyer, she had immediately done the same with her too.

"Guys," Kira interrupted. She had been reading through a stack of legacy documents related to the estate and how it was to be divided. "Your father's will makes reference to the original proclamation in Luigi DiNamico's last will and testament." Holding up the document in question, she said, "This is a copy. Do you have the original?"

Georgie nodded. "Everything."

Kira had managed to get her uncomfortably pregnant self into her father's recliner. Now, lowering the footrest, she sat forward as earnestly as she would with any client when delivering complicated information. "Your grandfather had a unique vision of family for a man of his generation. He, or his lawyer, spelled out his values in detail. It's not only unique, it addresses those things he considered discriminatory but allowable by our legal system at that time."

All three of them, Georgie, Lori and Marnie, nodded; they were more than aware of the security old Luigi had put in place to ensure fairness between his three children.

"According to this, he describes his three heirs as his children, two biological and one by choice, and each by the Grace of God. He then goes on to specifically say that no preference will be made between them based on race, sex, age or marital status. The family company must be evenly divided between all three but here's where it gets interesting. Once the estate passes into the hands of his children, your dad and your aunt, the future of the company and its division is strictly up to them. There is no requirement for them to pass their share to all of their children, or even any of them. He simply asks them to consider his example."

When no one understood, she looked to her mother and Tyler. Seeing their helpless faces too, she tried it from a different angle. "Without getting into Georgina Senior's estate, let's just consider what happened when Luigi died. The company was divided into three equal shares, with only three voting board members. Technically Lou doesn't even have a vote. Actually Lori, neither do you."

Lori waved her off. "Yeah, yeah. Henry's explained all of this. In his will, he divides his share of the estate evenly. Although I don't know how Lou plans to divide the big house!"

"Going back to the will, you need to know it only applies to DME and the legacy DynaCraft Companies." Still seeing their confusion, she was blunt, telling them, "Guys, you only inherited the company."

"What?" They all were confused, peppering her with questions. Tyler listened while Kira explained the provisions in detail. She hadn't expected Georgie to raise any questions but her sudden withdrawal signaled that she knew more than her sister or cousin did. Quietly giving her a nudge, she said under her breath, "You knew."

Georgie nodded, looking embarrassed, but said nothing.

"So?" Marnie asked, unable to put the pieces together.

"Maybe it would be better if Georgie explained," Tyler suggested.

Grabbing one of the spare financial reports they had printed out and flipping it to the blank side, Georgie said, "Complicated." Scribbling *Companies* across the top, "DME!" she said, adding it on the page with a large '33% EACH' written below. She added DynaCraft boats, with Danny's and Henry's names, and a 50/50 notation, then finally wrote DynaCraft Engines with the notation G. "Georgina."

"Holy crap!" Lori took the page from her trying to figure out the split. "So my dad, Henry," she qualified, "owns half of DynaCraft?"

"Boats...only."

Tyler was way ahead of them and had already created a diagram on her tablet. She passed it over to Lori and Marnie.

Lori stared transfixed at the set of pie charts. "Okay I'll bite. Who inherited the engine division from Aunt Georgina?"

Georgie groaned, head still down, and allowed Kira to explain. Referencing the copy of Georgina Senior's will, she flipped to the first page she had indexed with sticky notes. "This is another interesting one. Let's cover the real estate first, shall we?" She didn't wait for consensus. "Georgina divided her estate into three separate parts. Her personal real estate holdings. Her share of the family real estate and of course the company—sorry, companies." Feeling their anticipation, she offered consolingly, "Your aunt had an impressive real estate portfolio. The majority is in the Cattaraugus Creek property. The division of which is not detailed here. There is a reference to a special letter and a document requiring a signature from each of the heirs on or about their thirtieth birthday. Guys, this is significant." Flipping to a copy of the surveyor's diagram, she explained before handing it to Marnie, "According to that, she owned some three hundred sixty acres of prime waterfront property. I have no idea how many miles of shoreline that translates to…"

"Five," Lori contributed, now just as embarrassed as Georgie.

"…And I have no idea from this, who the land actually passed to?"

Tyler wasn't the only one who could tell when Georgie was holding something back. Marnie, studying the map carefully, said, "I had no idea she owned all this. Georgie and Lori inherited everything out there, but I'm not sure how that happened?" she asked, looking to her sister and cousin for an explanation.

Lori took the photocopy from her hand and picking up a highlighter, divided the property into three sections. "Okay," she began showing the map to the others. "Aunt Georgina had bought up everything north of the train tracks from Silver Creek to Cattaraugus Creek, including the island here. When I turned thirty, I was given a letter to read—"

"Wait," Marnie interrupted. "I never got a letter when I turned thirty!"

"Would you shut up and let me explain?" Lori gave her an affectionate nudge. "Anyway…I'm sitting in the lawyer's office and he's all embarrassed trying to prepare me for some big shock but keeps stalling, so Georgie grabs the letter from him and tells him to get over it. Well I was shocked. I had no goddamn idea!"

"Still not getting it!" Marnie warned. "What the hell was this letter about?"

Silently, Lori looked to Georgie for permission to share the confidential details of their aunt's personal message. At her nod, she explained with great glee, "Aunt Georgina was lesbian! I know! I couldn't believe it either, but it was all there in black and white!"

"What?" Marnie was shocked. "How come I'm hearing this for the first time?"

"The letter," Georgie began tentatively. "Different time… she worried for…us," she said, indicating herself and Lori.

"Wait!" Tyler interjected. "I spent half an hour last night listening to John lament the loss of his beloved Georgina!"

Lori laughed. "That old poofter!"

"Her…beard," Georgie explained, reminding them again, "Different time."

Continuing with the explanation, Lori filled in the gaps. "The letter was really, really personal. Can I tell the story?" At Georgie's nod, she continued, "When Aunt Georgina was in college, I think she said it was her last year, she met someone. Remember this was back in the seventies. Anyway, according to the letter, she fell madly in love with this woman Helen but kept the relationship on the sly, worried how her parents would take it. At some point she sat down with Uncle Danny and Dad, who said they'd stand by her no matter what. I guess it was just a little after the big wedding, you know when Mom and Dad and Uncle Danny and your mom got married. I guess that's when she came out to her parents. I can only guess things did not go as well for her as they did for me or Georgie."

Lori stood suddenly, still as affected by the story as she had been eight years earlier. Finally settling on the arm of the couch, she clamped her hands above her knees, her long arms locked straight to support her heavy shoulders. "Evidently old Luigi was heartbroken, but I guess having lost so many relatives back in the old country, he wouldn't throw her out but he made it clear he wanted nothing to do with that part of her life."

Debbie Marsh, sitting in the chair beside her, reached over, giving her leg a gentle rub. On the opposite couch, Tyler had discreetly done the exact same thing with Georgie before getting up to retrieve a box of tissues from the other room.

Always the tough guy, Lori was trying desperately to keep her emotions in check. Finally giving in, she accepted the tissues. Wiping her eyes and giving her nose a quick blow, she began haltingly, "See the thing is, I really loved Sophia. Marnie, I know you say you don't remember her, but I really do."

"Wait. Who is Sophia?" Tyler asked.

Clearing her throat, Marnie answered for her. "Our grandmother. She…died a few years after the accident."

"Oh my God!" Debbie was shocked.

"Oh it gets worse," Lori reassured them. "See, when Georgina came out, her mother freaked. Total complete meltdown. You know, saying things like 'drop-dead,' 'never want to see you again as long as you live,' and my all-time favorite, 'I will pray for God to strike you down.' After that Georgina said they never spoke again. Even at things like family functions, Sophia wouldn't even acknowledge her. She went around telling all her friends that Georgina was dead. No wonder Georgie Senior's life became nothing but her work."

"I'm sorry," Debbie interrupted, asking, "What about her lover? What happened to her?"

Surprised by the question, apparently never having considered it before, Lori turned to Georgie hoping she might know but it was Kira who had the information. "There was a provision for, let me see…" She read through several of her sticky note tabs, finally flipping to a different page. "Here it is. 'And with great affection I leave the beach house on Moran Lane, Cattaraugus Creek, to Helen Jensen of Tonawanda.' Wow, she must've really loved her to leave her a house! Oh, there were some bonds too."

"Bitch!" Lori threw her hands up. "Yeah well, I can tell you she and Mister Jensen have been very happy in that house! Oh, man…that bitch!"

"Lori!" Georgie growled for her to calm down, finally signaling her to finish the story.

Suitably admonished, she apologized to Debbie and Kira for her language while suggesting Tyler get used to it. "Georgina's letter was so…kind. Or maybe forgiving would be a better description. Eh, Bender?" At her cousin's nod, she pushed on.

"Georgina was very forgiving not to mention generous. She wrote that letter at a time when she had lost all connection with her parents, so what does she do? She fell madly in love with old Bender here. Seems our little Georgie Porgie was the only one out at the big house who would spend quality time with her. She was at that age, you know, when little kids don't understand boundaries. She was so infatuated with our aunt. The letter included a sweet story about old Bender here starting school. Seems our Georgie got school and work mixed up, and howled like a banshee when she realized our aunt wouldn't be going with her. Aunt Georgina's solution was to drive her to school every day. She even went so far as to pick her up once a week and take her back to the office or the boatyard so Georgie could… *help out.*" She made quotation signs in the air, shaking her head with amusement. "Can't you see it? Our six-year-old Georgie marching around the office in her little school uniform!"

"That year…" Georgie began haltingly, "her gift, Christmas…was, little suit…like hers."

Marnie snorted. "Oh God, I remember that! Wait, wasn't there a little matching briefcase too?"

"Oh yeah," Lori confirmed, chuckling. "And don't forget that erector set we were never allowed to touch! If it'd been Georgina's, Georgie didn't just covet it, she protected it with her life. What a pain you were! Anyway, back to the letter. She spoke highly of our moms but said she barely knew them, you know, since she worked so much. She loved Danny and Dad. That was clear in her letter. She wrote it just a few months after I was born. She said she saw all these babies coming and worried about what would happen if any of them turned out to be gay. She was sure that as long as old Luigi was alive, us kids would always have a home. Sophia though…not so much," she said, shaking her head. "That's when she decided that her estate should be divided between any of the kids who turned out to be gay or lesbian. That's why the thirty years of age thing. When you turn thirty the lawyer has to ask you if you're a homosexual. If you self-identify as LGBT and sign an affidavit to that effect, then a portion of the estate goes to you."

"No one asked me," Marnie said.

Lori plopped down on the couch beside her, wrapping a strong arm around her shoulders, pulling her in for a hug. "Marns, you were married with two children. That pretty much self-identified you as a good old het!"

"Evidently marriage is an automatic disqualifier," Kira explained, still reading from the will.

"That takes care of me and Lou," Marnie said. "What about Leslie? She wasn't married when she turned thirty."

"Asked," Georgie said, adding, "we," indicating her and Lori, "explained."

"Yeah, good old Les! We couldn't even convince her to lie for a third of the loot. Can you believe that?"

Tyler nodded. "She's very nice and strikes me as a real straight arrow."

"I'm sorry," Debbie interjected. "There's been so much tragedy in your family, I hate to ask but I have to know, what happened to Sophia after the accident? I mean, losing your husband like that would be crushing. Plus the boys must've been shattered to lose their wives and have all you kids running around, all so little and needing love and attention. I can't imagine what that was like and then the guilt..."

"You never mention her," Tyler said quietly to Georgie. "Do you remember her?"

She nodded but left the explanations for Lori.

"Sophia was good with us. I mean, she really tried but you're right, her heart was broken and there was guilt in everything she did. I swear she practically built a shrine to Georgina. She hung pictures of her everywhere, and then she was gone."

Georgie cleared her throat, saying the one thing Lori never could: "Suicide."

After a long silence Marnie, still sitting with Lori's arm around her shoulders, turned the conversation back to their business concerns. "Okay, I guess that explains why you two got the property. That's cool by me. And I knew the boat division was split between Dad and Henry. The engine division though, who got it?"

Kira answered, her tone a little sheepish, "According to this, Georgina DiNamico Junior."

"And who else?" Marnie asked.

"Just Georgie Junior," she said, tipping her head to her.

When Georgie nodded her confirmation, Marnie said, "I don't understand. We've all been receiving dividends from the engine division."

Georgie nodded again, trying to explain, "It is…fair."

"I see. So…" Marnie picked up a few pages of the financial report Debbie had been working on. "Tell me if I've got this right. Lori, Leslie, Stella and I, each own about, what, a sixth of the company?" When Debbie gave her a signal that she was close, she added, "Off the top of my head, it's sounding like Georgie here controls almost half of the family holdings."

"Forty-three percent."

"And we each own fifteen percent?" Lori asked, waving a hand between her and Marnie.

"Yes but your actual share, along with your brother and sisters,' is held by your father."

Lori waved off the detail impatiently. "So just how much of everything goes to Doofuss? I mean, the way he's been acting you'd think *he* had inherited half of everything!"

"Is there any way he's acting on Henry's behalf?" Tyler asked.

While Georgie and Lori didn't think so, Marnie believed it was a distinct possibility. Or at least possible that Lou believed he was acting in Henry's best interest.

It was Marnie who stood this time. She was like a general, gathering the last important facts before delivering her battle plan. "Debbie, you said Georgie's share is forty-three percent. What's mine, in hard numbers?"

Debbie flipped through a few pages. "This is just a rough estimate but assuming Henry's portion of the estate is distributed as promised, and God bless him not too soon, then you, Lori, Stella and Leslie will hold fourteen percent of the entire estate each. Lou will inherit eleven percent. The difference can be attributed to your house at Eighteen Mile Creek. For Leslie, it was the condo."

"If you're wondering," Kira offered, reading from the estate documents, "Danny left a provision in his will for Lou. While the family estate is owned by the company, it guarantees him a five-acre building lot too." Flipping to the photocopy of the site plan, she let out a loud low whistle. "So this is where the big family home is?"

Lori moved over beside the recliner and, planting herself on the arm, pointed out the details for her. "Now that rectangle is the big house. That's what we call that big monstrosity old Luigi built for us. Don't get me wrong, I love the place, but I think Marnie and Jack's house is much cooler! It's that big square over here." She pointed to the five-acre plot that had been subdivided for Marnie's use. "We call it the Glasshouse. It even won some awards back when they first built it."

"Sounds nice. I'd love to hear all about it. At the moment though, the baby's standing on my bladder. If you'll excuse me."

Lori helped her up and out of the recliner before turning her attention back to the group. "Tell me Marns, have you got a plan?"

"Actually no," she admitted, collapsing back onto the couch. "Come on guys, let's figure this out. He's moving money around like crazy but we can't actually find anything missing. It's just in the wrong place. He's been cutting jobs and programs and projects all over the place and now he's getting appraisals? If I didn't know better I would assume he's preparing to sell the company and assets. Why would he want to do that?"

"Tyler," Georgie said. "You think he...for Henry? Approval or...anticipation?" she asked, while shaking her head. "Misguided."

"You're right," Tyler acknowledged. "This may very well be a misguided attempt to earn Henry's approval. How, I can't imagine. Policy in publically traded corporations is usually driven by profit. After all, your first responsibility is to your shareholders. There is no such requirement in a privately owned company such as yours. Currently DME policies are driven by a vision of responsibility to family and community. That includes customers, employees, the community within the Greater Buffalo area, and the marine industry."

"Yeah," Lori confirmed. "With us it's always been about quality and responsibility. It's not like we run things at a loss but profit is…"

"No!" Sounding shocked, Georgie looked to have figured something out. She gave Tyler's arm an appreciative squeeze before trying to explain.

Suddenly Marnie stood too. "That S.O.B.!"

"What?" Lori asked, gesturing to Marnie to sit back down.

"All right you guys, add this up for me: a consecutive increase in profits every year for five years; a decrease in labor expenses; a reduction in R&D costs; a reduction in manufacturing costs; increased offshore production, and let's not forget international licensing. Put it all together and what have we got?"

Debbie suggested, "It sounds like he's preparing for an IPO."

"Bingo! Is that what you were thinking?" Marnie asked Georgie.

She nodded while Lori's hand gestures made it clear she had no idea what they were talking about.

"Initial Public Offering," Kira explained, as she waddled back in the room. "Help me back in the chair there, Queen of the Amazons!"

Lori was happy to get her settled, speculating, "So, he wants to take the company onto the stock market. Is that right?"

Debbie nodded, explaining that it wasn't necessarily a bad thing. "IPO's are usually staged to raise cash, usually a lot of cash, and very quickly. A company with a financial record like yours could easily raise fifty million in an IPO."

"Then why don't we do it?" Lori wanted to know.

When Marnie just groaned, Georgie explained, "Double-edged sword."

It didn't take long for Debbie to explain the risks of stock price volatility to her.

"Yikes! I'm running a tight ship now. I'd be screwed if the stock fell below the opening price."

"Which is why it's a strange move for such a well-established company," Tyler noted and Georgie agreed.

"We have our why," Marnie noted. "All we need to do now is figure out what we want to do about it."

"And soon," Lori added. "The annual board meeting is only six weeks away."

"Girls..." Debbie warned them much as she would have with her own daughters. "I don't think you can wait until then. This mess with the employee pension fund could blow up in your faces, and soon!"

"Agreed," Georgie said plainly.

"Okay," Lori said. "So it's down the rabbit hole. Yay!"

Marnie gave her a slap on the leg. "Before we do anything we need to get Lou out of the office."

"I could get him out to the boatyard and keep him busy for a day," Lori offered.

"We're going to need more than one day," Debbie warned. "You need a full audit and you're going to have to have someone sit down with everyone in his department to sort this out. I'd say weeks but probably more like months."

"Damn!" Marnie stood, asking Debbie, "I know you've got your own business to run, but is there any way you can take point on this, at least until Kira's baby comes?"

"Not a problem. It's a slow time of year for us. But I may need more help depending on what we find."

Plainly, Marnie now had a plan in mind and she grinned. "If he wants to play head honcho, I say we let him. If we up our presence on the boat show circuit, you know, really go big, then we'll need someone from senior management on hand."

"I thought Debbie said we couldn't wait, that we had to do something now?" Lori asked, looking more confused than ever.

"No," Georgie offered. "No games. We sit down...Henry, Leslie too."

Groaning, Marnie collapsed back into the couch. "I know you're right. I was just hoping to avoid a confrontation. If we call the Board before Miami, he'll freak. If it turns out he is actually up to something, we'll be giving him time to cover his tracks and...wait," she said, thinking of something else. "Not if he calls the meeting! You two—" Marnie pointed an accusing finger at Georgie and Tyler. "You two have to knock it off, understood? I'm giving you each an employee warning!"

"What, wait, Marnie. I told you on the phone—" Tyler started.

Lori and Kira began tossing in questions too, trying to figure out what Marnie was on about.

"Stop! Listen, all of you. I am not saying you two cannot continue to see each other. I'm just—"

"Whoa there people!" Kira interrupted. "Am I getting this right? You two are a thing?"

"Yes we are," Tyler stated, fiercely proud. "And we are not going to let Lou Phipps or anyone else dictate the terms of our relationship!"

Marnie smiled at her stance while Kira and Lori continued to pepper them with questions.

Debbie Marsh, watching the exchange with interest, offered casually, "I think I get it. You're going to get him all riled up about these two, so riled up, he'll call an emergency board meeting?"

Nodding, Marnie sat back, explaining, "Lou is a reactionary man and he's quite vain. For whatever reason, he has been working hard to capsize any chance of Georgie taking over. If he finds out about these two, he'll want to present his motion immediately."

"You really think this would be catalyst enough?" Tyler asked.

"If he really wants to take the company public, he has to convince Henry, and Henry has always voted with Georgie. Trust me, if he thinks he can use this against her, he will."

Lori had to ask, "How exactly do we execute this plan? I mean, he'll smell a rat if any of us spill the beans."

"Zoe," Georgie said simply.

"Oh right on Bender!" Lori said, "I forgot about our little Mata Hari! Still, we have the same issue. How do we let her know without tipping our hand?"

"Let me take care of that!" Tyler said. Picking up her tablet, she opened a new app and began to edit the profile details, showing the changes to Georgie.

Her face colored a little but the smile made it clear how happy those few words had made her. Nodding, she gave her agreement for Tyler to update her Facebook status.

A second later the notification sounded on Kira's cell phone. Just as curious as everyone else, she opened it up to read Tyler's Facebook status change. "Oh my God! My sister's in a relationship! This is so cool, but you didn't say with who?"

"She doesn't need to," Lori explained for everyone. "If I know Zoe, she'll be on the phone the second she sees that, and digging for all the juicy details."

"Well that's it. Let the games begin, or as Georgie would say, we're good to go." Satisfied that the plan was in motion, Marnie stood, offering, "Debbie I want to thank you and your family for your hospitality. I'll see you bright and early Monday morning in my office. You too kiddo," she said to Kira. "I know you're ready to pop that baby out any day now. You've got a sharp eye. I'd like you in on this. More than that, I'd like to talk to you about something more permanent. That is, after your maternity leave."

Turning back to Lori she urged, "Come on, Wonder Woman, I'd like to get home before the football game is over and the boys and their father descend on my kitchen."

CHAPTER THIRTEEN

Georgie rattled around the empty condo. She hadn't realized until now how little she had in the place. Her books were here—some of them. She had filled an entire wall in the machine shop with her engineering texts. It made more sense to store them down there where her team could have access. Sitting down on the old leather couch that had once graced her grandfather's office, she patted the cushion beside her. Maggie retrieved her squeaky toy from her bed before climbing onto the couch beside her, and curling up for a nap. This was their routine but for some reason Georgie was out of sorts. She was still bothered to learn of Lou's misguided direction but that wasn't the real problem. She was missing Tyler.

Unable to sit, she paced to the window but it was too dark to really see anything. Instead she sat on the wide windowsill. With arms crossed, she surveyed the empty space. The New Year's decorations still hung in place while two large panel carts, heavily laden with folding tables and chairs, had been pushed into a corner. Monday morning Stella would have her maintenance staff focus their efforts on getting the condos, hers, Henry's, Leslie's, and even the empty unit, back in shape. Still, the caterers had done a pretty good job cleaning up. She should really thank them. Whenever her apartment was set up for a party, the place took on a functional look. Here, now, with everything gone or folded up, it just looked vacant. How had she lived like this for so long? The room, like her life, was completely empty except for a few mementos from before Afghanistan. Actually, all were either from the military or from her life before she met Margaret.

Margaret! How the hell had she fallen for a woman like that? It was a question she had asked herself a million times. Suddenly the answer was as clear as day. She recognized in Margaret a facet of her own singularity. Margaret was an only child of a man who had lost his wife early on. It was easy to see in her that lone part of herself. Wanting to fill that void, she imagined Margaret would do the same for her. Of course it had been the exact opposite. Margaret's only interest in her had been about what Georgie and her family could do for Margaret and her father. Georgie had never really put it all together until this moment. How long had she wanted what she had seen so readily within her whole family? Lou always had Leslie, just a year older, to lean on; Marnie and Lori were inseparable and had been since sharing a crib. The fact that both women had remained such steadfast friends, when both had grown up to be such different people, was a testament to the strength of their bond. Georgie hadn't realized until that moment just how much she craved that type of friendship. Intimacy too, had to be part and parcel of the package for her. If that was all she was after, Tyler would be the hands-down winner! But the woman was so much more than that. Who was she kidding? Tyler was amazing! Beautiful and brilliant, she understood family, but more importantly and quite unfathomably, Tyler understood *her*.

Frustrated with her thoughts and feeling terribly alone, she pushed off the window ledge, unsure what to do with herself. Tyler was meeting Zoe for a drink, and to confess to her affair with Georgie. She bristled at the term *affair*. It wasn't an affair.

It was a "*thing*." Tyler said so! She groaned at her own assertion. *What the hell is a thing?* Georgie had taken that to mean they both had serious feelings for one another. She groaned again wishing she'd asked more questions. Of course, the last thing she wanted was for Tyler to have to define everything for her.

Plunking herself back down beside the sleeping dog, she picked up her phone, hoping Wiki could explain the stages of a lesbian relationship to her. When that turned out to be a bust, she searched the Internet, stumbling onto the site for the Other Team. Their advice was fun and full of interesting tidbits for getting a girl, but none for keeping her. She closed her browser and speed-dialed Lori. Like her, Lori was no expert on relationships, but she did have a long line of women vying for that coveted spot.

"Hey Georgie Porgie! You're missing your girl, aren't you?"

"No."

"Yes," Lori laughed. "Oh, I knew you had it bad. Well, if it's any consolation, I think she's crazy about you too!"

"Yeah?"

"Yeah! So stop worrying. It's why you called, isn't it? Let me guess: you don't know what to do next, not without a checklist. Am I right?"

"Yes." Georgie's response was full of shame. "I…"

"I know. You don't want to screw it up. Hey, I get that Bender. There's no shame in that. Especially with this one. I gotta hand it to you, I really think she's the one. So, I take it she's still taking libations with Mata Hari?"

"Yeah."

"Okay, that's good. When she gets there, she should be good and hungry. You can start by taking her down to Leslie's for a nice romantic dinner." When Georgie didn't immediately reply, Lori questioned her. "You did invite her to come over, didn't you?" Georgie's groan was all the answer she needed. "Oh buddy, do I have to teach you everything?"

"No…Yes…"

"Don't stress it. I'm here for you. Okay, here's what you're going to do…"

* * *

When Tyler walked in the door she saw Georgie asleep, sprawled on the old leather sofa. Maggie, sensing her presence before she entered the apartment, was at the door to greet her with a wagging tail. She followed Tyler, happily supervising as she quietly set the takeout bags on the large kitchen island. Shucking her coat, she tiptoed over to the couch, pleased to see Georgie out cold. She wasn't surprised. Considering it was well after eleven and it wasn't as if they had gotten any sleep the night before. That thought immediately put a smile on her face. She sat down on the edge of the couch, wanting to be close but not ready to wake her. While she seemed to sleep deeply her face looked troubled. Her hands repeatedly clenched and unclenched. Taking those troubled hands in hers, she kissed each one.

"Tyler...Okay?" Georgie asked quietly.

"Hey, I didn't mean to wake you. Have you eaten? I brought food."

As she sat up she shook her head, then wrapped her arms around Tyler in a welcoming embrace.

It was funny how easy it was to return her affection. She had wondered if it would be awkward between them, even worried about it. Things were so easy with Georgie. What a difference a month could make. She marveled at how open and accepting she was and how quickly that had happened. The truth was, they had achieved a level of intellectual intimacy almost immediately. With that had come trust and she now understood that trust was everything for Georgie. No wonder! Not after everything that had happened. The best part was that she knew she could trust her with anything, maybe everything.

She took a deep breath, savoring the moment. When she felt Georgie's lips on her neck slowly making their way toward her mouth, she leaned back abruptly, questioning with humor, "Does this mean you missed me?" Judging by the look in Georgie's eyes she more than missed her, she wanted her.

Tyler couldn't hold back a smile, silently thanking all the gods in all the heavens. She gave Georgie a quick kiss. One she was sincerely tempted to deepen, but giving in to her logical side, she wanted to deal with their more basic needs first. "I called Leslie to find out if you had eaten, she told me you were waiting for me. Thank you, baby. That was so sweet. I hope you don't mind but I brought everything up here." Standing, offering Georgie a hand up. "Guess we can eat here on the couch?"

Georgie shook her head. Her smile was mischievous as she pointed across the room. She'd set up one of the folding tables with two chairs. Two formal place settings sat on a white linen tablecloth. From somewhere she had managed to find fresh flowers. Beside a vase of blue flag irises, lit candles flickered, inviting them over.

"It's beautiful. Oh baby, you're so sweet. I'll put the food out, if you take care of the wine."

Georgie nodded, accepting the bottle Tyler pulled from one of the takeout bags. "Wine…your pick?"

Setting the food out, Tyler smiled, pleased that she had noticed. "Actually Leslie and I came up with that one together. I think it's a little sweeter than you usually drink, but she was sure it was a better complement for the sirloin tips."

"Nice," she noted, taking an appreciative whiff.

"I thought you'd enjoy something different. Everyone's always worried about upsetting the status quo with you. I swear it's like they're all stuck in the same gear."

"I know," Georgie admitted with a grin. Pulling out Tyler's chair for her, she moved closer for another kiss.

Tyler couldn't stop herself from wrapping her arms around Georgie's neck and savoring the sweet sensation of her mouth. When she finally pulled herself away, she was breathless and a little light-headed, but said nothing. That was hard. She took her seat and waited for Georgie. Picking up her wineglass she asked, "If I were to make a terribly sentimental toast, would it put you off?"

Seeming to consider the question seriously, she shook her head before trying to explain, "Better to be…open? Sure footing…"

"You think it's better to know than to guess?"

She nodded, but her face showed she was bracing for bad news.

Suddenly realizing how the question must have sounded, Tyler put her glass down, reaching across the table for Georgie's hand. "I promise you, I have good things to say. I know it's really, really early for us. We have literally only known each other for a month. Oh God Georgie! I don't want to be one of those pathetic U-Haul lesbians, but when Marnie started telling us we couldn't see each other, I thought my heart would stop!"

Relieved, Georgie, now holding both her hands, squeezed them and smiled. "Marnie approves."

"Oh she does, does she?" It wasn't really a question. "What about the rest of the family?"

Georgie just smiled, giving her two thumbs-up.

Retrieving her wineglass, Tyler raised it to make her toast, then stopped. "You're doing it again."

Georgie raised her hands in surrender, as if not sure what she was referring to.

"Baby, here's to your beautiful green eyes always giving away every single thought in your head!"

Georgie laughed with her but that didn't stop the color from creeping up her neck.

"You are so busted!" They clinked glasses. There was no denying the desire in Georgie's eyes. Tyler wasn't just appreciative, she was relieved.

She had spent the evening listening to Zoe's warnings and condemnations. The worst part was her overpersonalization. While she continued to badmouth Georgie, she flirted outrageously and repeatedly trespassed on Tyler's personal space. What a contrast these two women made, aunt and niece. They were polar opposites in so many ways Tyler could have easily devoted an entire graduate thesis to the comparison. Still, a few things that came up were prickling in the back of her mind. Putting a wineglass down, she said simply, "I think we need to talk."

Georgie placed her fork on her plate, studying her carefully. "You are afraid?"

"No." But the question seemed to set her off. Realizing she was getting upset and unfairly so, she sat back, admitting, "Lori was right to warn me. Zoe had a lot to say about you."

Surprising her, Georgie stood, carrying her chair around the table, and sitting down next to Tyler. She offered her hand but never assumed. That was reassuring. As much as she had teased her the night before about being a foregone conclusion she knew in her heart Georgie had not for one moment made any assumptions. Accepting the outstretched hand, she gave it a weak squeeze. She wasn't sure where to start.

"Now or then?"

"What? I'm sorry, I don't know what you're asking me?"

"Your questions? Before Afghanistan...after?"

Tyler looked down at her lap, surprised to see she was still holding Georgie's hand. She'd meant to keep herself separate, isolated from the woman's gentleness. "She said that there were a lot of women. That you..."

"Yes," Georgie admitted without prodding. "Could. Did... Not proud."

The answer felt like a slap to the face. Removing her hand from Georgie's, she sat with her arms crossed. "I'm sorry. I just never thought of you as the type who would cheat."

"What?" Confused, Georgie offered her hand again. Even when Tyler took no notice, she remained open. "Tyler...please, explain?"

Still withdrawn and ignoring Georgie's outstretched hand, she said, "I don't like Margaret, but even as much as I dislike her, I don't think it's right that you cheated on her and then to admit it so casually..."

Georgie stood so abruptly she knocked her chair over. Stepping away without picking it up, she paced the length of the long bow-shaped room. When she finally turned to face Tyler, she stood completely open to her. "I—never—cheated—on—Margaret...Never. I—would not...ever!"

"But you admitted to being with other women."

"Before!" Georgie hissed, her frustration evident.

Tyler was stuck somewhere between disbelief and relief. She didn't know if she should ask more, argue based on the things

Zoe had said, or just shut up and apologize. Before she could decide, Maggie was at Georgie's side, leash in mouth. Tyler almost cried. She had done the one thing she had promised herself she wouldn't do. She had fallen for one of Zoe's lies and instead of just telling the story and listening to Georgie's side, she had questioned her, accused her. Now here she was, sitting alone at the romantic table Georgie had set for them. She had been looking forward to this all night and instead of just enjoying her time with her, she'd accused her, the most forthright and honorable woman she had ever met, of lying and cheating. What should she do now? Wait while Georgie took the dog for a walk? Follow her and try to explain? Leave and call her tomorrow? Or just leave? Staying felt wrong but leaving felt worse. Suddenly she felt a hand on her shoulder. It was Georgie. She wasn't gone. She hadn't taken the dog out. Instead, she moved around Tyler and kneeling beside her, took both hands in hers.

"I respect you. I—will always—respect you…my Tyler."

As much as she believed her, and as much as she wanted to fling her arms around her and forget the whole thing, there was still one issue that just wouldn't die. "Zoe said…" She closed her eyes, stalling and trying desperately to find a non-combative way to frame the question. "Why did you hire me?"

Georgie hadn't been prepared for that. After a long moment she stood. Retrieved the upended chair and sat back down. Not across the table but not as close as she had been.

Tyler immediately missed the closeness. She missed her hands.

"Ask…details?" She was not unkind but her earlier more ardent mood was gone.

"It's just that she said, well, that you and Marnie had basically been shopping for more than an assistant! If you know what I mean. She called me your paid little piece on the side!"

She hadn't wanted to say it and clearly Georgie didn't want to hear it. She was up again, but this time instead of pacing she left the room. Tyler wanted to go to her. Apologize. Find a way to make it better. Invent a time machine and take it all back! "Dammit!" Maggie barked at her outburst.

As she wiped her tears away, she realized Georgie was back in the room. She hadn't walked out or stormed off, it looked like she'd been retrieving something from the library.

Sitting down again, she sorted through several documents. Finally selecting one, she handed it to Tyler without comment. As Tyler tried to read it, Georgie moved her chair back around the table and resumed her meal. Surreptitiously watching her, Tyler felt like a heel to see Georgie looking even more isolated than ever. Forcing herself, she focused on the document in her hand.

The long memorandum was an argument for the hiring of a management level professional to address issues of ethics in new and legacy products. It spoke eloquently of the issues they were facing now, and those that would come with existing and future technologies. It was the very thing they had talked about during her interview and several times since. And it was the work she had been doing. She flipped back to the first page and read the date. "You wrote this a year ago?"

Georgie nodded. "Lou said no. Marnie offered…assistant. You applied…You…" Frustrated, she was up again. She filled her wineglass and retired to the couch without looking back.

Tyler sat there feeling like a total jerk. It was really just chance and circumstance that had put them together. Grabbing her glass and the wine bottle, she walked over to the couch, setting both on the end table and taking a seat beside her. "Baby, I'm so sorry. The thing about women like Zoe that makes them so dangerous is they always lace their lies in half-truths. I'll be honest, I don't have the confidence you do. I mean, I will with us, in time. It's just that this is so new and I don't exactly have a great track record myself. Actually," she admitted with some shame, "I've pretty much been a train wreck on that front. I guess that's why it's so easy to get me riled up. I am so, so sorry. I didn't mean to ruin our evening, I really didn't."

Even though Georgie accepted her outstretched hand, she couldn't help feeling there was no repairing the damage she had done. Maybe what she needed to do was go home. Maybe giving Georgie some time, both of them some time, would fix this thing. Who was she kidding? She knew full well if she walked away now, there was every chance Georgie would shut down or give up on her completely. Still, what mattered, first and foremost, were her own needs. What did she need? What did she want? The only person who had ever really asked her that was sitting beside her. Plenty of people wanted to see her succeed but this woman had gone out of her way to help her do it. Zoe had warned that everything would come with strings attached. Was that true? "She said you'd probably let me go if I stopped...putting out."

Now Georgie was angry. Repeatedly clenching and unclenching her hands, Georgie explained, eyes closed and repeating from memory, "When a senior employee engages in a relationship with someone in their department or a junior member of the company or its associated holdings, and if the junior member has declared the relationship as required by company policy, said senior employee, regardless of position or board standing, relinquishes—ALL—supervisory privilege."

Feeling sheepish and aching inside, she admitted, "I don't know what that means."

"You work for Marnie...not me. I—have—no—say, now. Since you, since signing...papers."

That caught her off guard. Although it shouldn't have. Marnie had explained in detail how Georgie had rewritten the employee policy with an aim toward protecting juniors from being used in the manner Zoe had so blatantly described. Now what could she say? She absolutely hated herself for letting Zoe get to her like this.

"Jack...too." Georgie tried to explain by example. "Marnie is senior...but..."

"She really has no say when it comes to her husband?" She couldn't imagine Marnie Pulaski being told to butt out where her husband was concerned.

Georgie just nodded. "Me and Henry," she said. "Set goals... wages...bonus scale. Now, Henry and Marnie," she pointed to Tyler, "for you." As if to prove her point, Georgie grabbed her tablet and pulled up the employee files for her department and showed the list to her.

Marnie hadn't wasted any time. Tyler's name was still listed as a department member but when she touched the link, a warning box popped up, advising access was restricted to Marnie Pulaski and Henry Phipps.

Embarrassed and heartsick to think she could have ever doubted her, she set the tablet on the end table. Head down she was actually afraid to look at Georgie, afraid to not see that loving look anymore. Afraid and ashamed. She had never acted like this with anyone. She could honestly admit that it was her habit to cut and run the moment things got complicated but this wasn't the same thing. How could she undo everything she had just done? She couldn't believe that her first worry had been for her job! It wasn't like she wanted things to go back to the way they were. She loved working with Georgie. Enjoyed the way her mind worked. Respected what she believed in and stood up for. She wanted a professional relationship but what about the personal one? She was now certain she could safely walk away and still keep her job. Was it enough? *Not on your life!* Being with Georgie, today with her family, last night on the roof, then later in bed…

"I'm scared!" she admitted. She said it simply, almost surprising herself with the truth.

Georgie moved as close as their knees would allow and taking both her hands, said simply, "Me too."

"Can you forgive me?"

"Nothing to forgive…You," Georgie said with such warmth and honesty, "need to know. Me too! Ask…always ask."

Tyler shook her head. She shouldn't have been surprised. She knew in her heart that Georgie understood the way she needed to work through things, the same as Tyler had learned to interpret and communicate her abbreviated speech. Still, she couldn't bring herself to look at the woman. When she felt her raise her hand and kiss it, she forced herself.

"Oh God baby." And there it was. That look said everything.

Georgie squeezed her hand then placed it high on her chest and holding it, explained everything so clearly, "You are here."

She threw her arms around Georgie's neck and tackled her back onto the couch. "Baby I am so sorry! Oh God, she was such a crass little bitch and the whole time she knew how much everything she was saying hurt. I hate her!"

With her arms wrapped around Tyler, she held her tight, one hand brushing hair out of Tyler's wet eyes. "So...sorry, my Tyler."

Lifting her head, she smiled as she wiped the errant tears away. "My Tyler? I like that. I feel stupid asking, and I know you're going to say never to feel stupid, but...well, this is a thing, right? It's not just me?"

Smiling she finished wiping Tyler's face dry, then shutting her eyes, explained, "A thing is...not sure, but you...me..." She smiled, opening her eyes and said the thing she had memorized. "Feels like love to me."

Tyler squealed in delight. If she wasn't already on Georgie she would have knocked her down to get this close. "I love you too, baby. I was just too scared to say anything. I keep thinking this is crazy—we hardly know each other—but that's not true. In a way I feel like I've known you all my life!"

Georgie was grinning like a rock star. "Waited a long time... my Tyler."

"My Tyler! Oh God, I love that, and I love your eyes you geeky techno savant, and I love you..."

Georgie smothered her soliloquy with a hungry mouth.

And I love the way you kiss me like I'm the most beautiful woman on earth, and how you touch me when...

CHAPTER FOURTEEN

Henry, uninvited, marched past Tyler and into the penthouse suite. Behind him both Skippy and Ethan looked embarrassed, skulking, and apologizing as they dragged themselves inside. She had been alone in the apartment and tidying up after breakfast while Georgie and Maggie were out for a run.

They had slept in together, enjoying a leisurely morning. She was surprised to realize how well they clicked on the domestic side. Working with Georgie was complicated and involved an intricate schedule and hard-and-fast rules. Here, and alone, it had been perfect, as if they had made breakfast together a million times. As far as shelter went, Georgie's apartment was definitely on the sparse side. Still, all the basics were here and more importantly so was the woman. Waking up in her arms had been a beautiful repeat of the previous day. It wasn't just waking up in her arms that had left her feeling so whole, it was knowing Georgie had slept, really slept, and she wanted to ask her about that, wanted so much to hear that she was what had repaired that part of her heart. That, however, and everything else, would have to wait.

"Good morning Henry. Hi guys come in please." While the guys grumbled and generally just stood there looking awkward, Henry marched straight to the old sofa and planted himself firmly and without comment.

"Okay." Turning to Skippy and Ethan, she suggested, "Georgie put the Xbox in the guest room. It's hooked up to the Wi-Fi, if you guys feel like a little FPS action?"

With mumbled thanks, they scrambled up the antique staircase and disappeared. She had been making tea for herself when they barged in, so she continued with that task. Pouring a cup for Henry too, she set it down on the end table and took a seat across from him on the fireplace hearthstone. "I don't know what you've heard…"

"Professor Marsh, I am not as learned as you are, but where I come from we don't bite the hand that feeds us, and we sure as hell don't sh…" He cut his word suddenly. He was clearly upset but unwilling to voice his true concern.

"Henry, I'm going to give you a choice because I don't know what you need to hear first. So here goes. You can tell me what you've heard and I promise you I will listen and I will answer all of your concerns. Or you can sit there and stew, but I promise you I still intend to tell you everything."

He grumbled a little, finally admitting, "You're a forthright woman. I respect that. The truth is, now that I'm sitting here, it's hard for me to believe anything I've been told. Except that you are sitting here too. In my time that would've been more than enough to prove your guilt."

"And what am I guilty of Henry? Being in love with your niece? Because if that's your issue you're not being fair, not to her, and not to me!" She was on her feet. She hadn't meant to get upset but she was mad. "For God's sake Henry, you know Georgie better than anyone! You know she would never take advantage of me. I'm here by choice because I want to be here. I want to be with her. Frankly, it's none of your business but I love her and I will fight for her. And mark my words, I will not let anyone use me against her for any purpose. Do you understand?" She was overwhelmed with frustration and practically shaking with aggression.

Expecting a fight, she stood her ground staring Henry down. What she didn't expect was the humor in his eyes.

"Glory be to God! I think my little Georgie's finally found the one." Struggling to his feet he offered his hand, "Welcome to the family, baby girl. You are a most welcome thing indeed."

Bypassing the outstretched hand and relieved beyond measure, Tyler gave him a warm hug. When she began to step away, he took her gently by the shoulders, and implored her earnestly, "Tell me you need her as much as she needs you."

"I don't know if she needs me at all, but I want her. I want to be here for her, with her. Is that too much to ask?"

He smiled and shook his head. "Not for a moment. Now do you mind if we sit awhile? These old man legs of mine are only happy on my caboose or in my bed."

Tyler helped him back onto the couch and made sure he was comfortable before retrieving her teacup and taking a seat herself. "Would you like to talk about some of the things that have been said about Georgie and me?"

"Naw. I might be an old man but I still have a few active brain cells. I know my granddaughter is a horrible gossip. She's always been a storyteller and happy to twist the truth to suit her means. That child was always a handful. Her mother though, if my son had given her free hand, she could have turned that girl around, but that's just Lou. Always trying to control things, always trying to be in charge. It wasn't always like that. I don't know when that changed. That's my failure as his father. So now I'm sitting here with you and I need someone to tell me what's really going on."

"Henry please," she insisted, "it's not my place and it's unfair of you to ask."

"Baby girl, life is not fair but here we are."

The way he said it evoked such sympathy, she couldn't bring herself to call him on the sexist moniker.

Taking his time to drink the tea she had brought him he set the cup down. "Not ready to lay your cards down? I respect that. So I'll go first." Sitting back and turning slightly to talk comfortably, he said, "There are only three voting shares that count. There are several board members but only three stakeholders. I think you know that, and so does my son. Which means to get anything done, you need at least two of us to agree. Frankly, I've been lucky with Georgie and Marnie. The truth is since their daddy died those two have done a damn fine job. Before that, it was just Danny, me, and little Georgie. Now since our girl came home, things have been tough, but have been improving in some areas. I know you've been around long enough to see the type of work that's coming out of her head. Problem is, not everybody understands us engineers, my boy among them. When Danny was alive, Lou didn't worry so much, but since the girls have taken over he's been obsessed. And I'd say he's a man with a plan. I swear the only reason I've lived so long is so I can keep him from destroying everything we took a lifetime to build. Not saying business is more important than family. I'm just saying family's no reason to destroy a perfectly good business."

"What's his plan?" Tyler asked. "You said it yourself, Georgie and Marnie together control the majority. What's his hold? He doesn't even have a vote on the board yet he acts as if he's in charge. Hell, he's been running around telling everybody he is!" She held up her hand, wanting to amend that statement. "I'm not saying he couldn't be, it's just that—"

"Cut the crap Professor! That boy couldn't lead his way out of a paper bag! Sweet baby Jesus, where did I go wrong with him?"

"Henry!" she insisted, "If Lou has a fault it's his need to control things and his desire to impress you."

"Damned fool!" He shook his head. "It's the old incorporation papers. After Danny died, Lou started going through everything. Having Georgie the way she is, and Marnie taking over, just pushed him over the edge. I never realized how much of a problem my boy has with women in authority. Here's the thing," he said, holding his tea cup in both hands and leaning toward her, "it's the original corporation papers. I didn't know, and I'm sure Danny didn't either."

"What is it?" she encouraged him.

"Competency requirement in which all board members have an equal vote, not just the big three. That's how the board used to refer to me, Danny, and little Georgie. The Big Three! Anyway, he's going to try and make her look incompetent. He can do it," he warned. "That boy has watched her like a hawk since she came home. He knows how to push her buttons and frankly, when he does, as mad as I am at him, it does make me wonder about our girl."

"Henry, that's not fair! She has a disability and frankly I really don't see what the problem is. I have no problem communicating with her and I think most of her engineers would agree. Besides, we're only talking about a problem communicating verbally. She is not incompetent in any way!"

She was again getting mad and stood, pacing in front of the couch, arms crossed. "You said it yourself. Georgie's work has brought in record profits for the company. And you know there's lots more to come. As a matter of fact, looking through the books, we've realized Lou has been trying to squeeze out the most profitable department. Now you tell me he wants her out. That would be like cutting the head off the golden goose! Tell me where that makes sense! And when you're done telling me that, please explain to me why the man would want to take this company public! What on God's green earth does he need fifty or sixty million dollars for?"

"Take the company public?" He looked utterly astonished. "Are you sure?"

It was not her place to tell him but she continued heedlessly. "It's the only thing we could figure out. Georgie went through the financial statements, while Marnie and Lori did the same thing at home last night. He's had appraisers out and real estate people poking into everything and anything, most of which aren't even company property!"

"You mean Cattaraugus Creek and the boatyard?"

"Yes!"

Henry was silent for a long time, drumming his fingers on the arm of the sofa. "In the kitchen, in the center cabinet, you should find the instant coffee. It's not great but it's not bad and Georgie girl doesn't mind." Looking at his watch, he added,

"Why don't we have a cup while she takes her shower and gets herself buttoned up?"

They heard the door, and seconds later Maggie trotted in heading straight for Henry. Once her ears were suitably scratched, she gave Tyler a doggie brush-by hug before trotting to her bed and checking to ensure her squeaky toy was safe. Georgie, in her heavy winter running gear, caked with snow from head to toe, waved a greeting then stopped to say, "Hi Uncle Henry. Everything...okay?"

"Don't you worry little Georgie. Sweet baby girl here's been taking good care of me. You go hit the defroster."

She nodded and stepped over to Tyler offering her hand.

She accepted it, unsure of her intentions.

"Henry," Georgie said, then closed her eyes. "I wish to formally announce that Tyler and I have entered into..." She opened her eyes and grinning, announced, "A thing! Okay?"

He just nodded with a big grin, ordering, "Now go get spic-and-span. I think we better head out to the boatyard. Understood missy?"

Georgie just nodded. She gave Tyler's hand a squeeze before making haste for a hot shower.

Tyler asked Henry, "How much time do we have? I mean how much time do I have to get her ready?"

"Not long," he admitted. "I can put him off for a few days but that's it. Expect him to pull out all the stops. He'll have everyone there. All the senior staff, corporate lawyers and the family attorneys."

"How much does he know about Georgina's estate— Georgina Senior I mean?"

He raised an eyebrow then smiled, impressed. "If he knows anything, it would be what the family lawyers were obliged to share with him. Unless..."

"Unless he's managed to get his hands on those documents too. Is there any way he can hurt her with that information?"

He shook his head. "Only if he's trying to create animosity. I don't really know what the girls have been told but it's not like any of them to get mean about money."

"Well he can't shock them—they all know about it."

"Good for her," he said sincerely. "Now more importantly, what about that coffee? I'm an old man, baby girl. I can't wait forever!"

Grabbing their empty teacups, she headed for the kitchen. "I can see where Lori gets her charm!"

"Oh baby girl." He chuckled. "Lori was our first. That one came out screaming at the top of her lungs! I remember like it was yesterday. I've never seen a baby so long and stretched out like a little sausage! And oh that girl was as purple as eggplant. She had this baby fuzz head but her baby hair was as orange as a little old tangerine! And if that wasn't enough to scare you, that girl had the lungs to make a drill sergeant proud! Still, I was the proudest daddy, still am. God I miss her mama. You would've loved Gloria…"

She made them coffee, listening while he reminisced. It was nice to have an older person around. Someone with long memories and opinions crafted from true first hand experience. She had to admit it was one of the traits she found so attractive in Georgie. Considering most of the people she had worked with in her academic career, she found it ironic that the very people who presented themselves as worldly and knowledgeable were rarely either.

* * *

Driving home in the truck, Georgie was more than aware of just how tired she was. She marveled at Tyler whose energy seemed boundless. After the impromptu afternoon meeting at the boatyard, they had spent most of the evening crafting Georgie's response to the situation in which Lou had placed the company. They had several responses. Each was designed like building blocks which could be used individually or chunked into powerful segments. She intended to control the room but she wanted the flexibility to follow the mood and tailor her language to her audience. Since her father's passing, Henry and Marnie had jointly held the title of acting CEO. She hadn't intended to push her agenda forward and wasn't completely satisfied she was ready but that didn't matter now. Lou may have called the meeting but she intended to govern it. No, govern wasn't the right word. To get them through this and stay on the right course, she would need to reign and reign supreme.

Sunday and all day Monday had been devoted to their final preparations and Georgie's long hours of organizing her plan and memorizing the key components of her speech. By Monday night they knew Lou had scheduled the board meeting for Tuesday morning and, he had warned, they would proceed with or without Henry, who had been stalling for time by citing a holiday hangover. He daren't say he was too sick. There was every chance Lou would try to pull the same competency trick on him.

On Monday night, Tyler and her family hosted Georgie, Marnie, and Lori for supper. Afterward, while Carl, Megan, and Maggie fussed around in the kitchen, the women once again settled into the family room for their last-minute prep and review. They were ready. Georgie and Tyler had worked out an amazing system. Not only had they written out the speech, questions and possible responses she would need to address and deliver, Tyler cut everything into manageable and sortable talking points. Tomorrow when Georgie stood to address the board of directors, she would take the podium with tablet in hand. Tyler had cataloged each point and could call them up at random and they had worked out a series of hand signals so Georgie could change tack at any moment. Tyler had created a series of PowerPoint slides and ordered them into sets that would match Georgie's talking points. She would have everything, word for word in front of her, for the entire time she needed to address the board and the influencers who would be invited to attend.

Fussing in her seat, Georgie managed to turn herself sideways. The Land Rover was an extremely comfortable truck, but the forward seats were designed to sit facing forward. Still, even within the confines of her seat belt, she managed to get herself turned so she could watch Tyler as they drove. "You are…so beautiful."

Tyler gave her a quick appreciative glance before turning her attention back to the road. "What, nothing about my brain, or how smart I am, or what a great job I did tonight?"

Georgie just chuckled, and gave her arm a warm squeeze. Tyler was all those things and more. They had worked nonstop prepping for tomorrow's scheduled confrontation. Henry had been right, Lou was like a runaway tanker rushing into port on a full head of steam. He was a shipwreck waiting to happen. The more they had dug into his actions and everything he had planned, it became more and more clear Lou Phipps intended to succeed or go down with the ship. It was too bad his plan would take all of them with him.

CHAPTER FIFTEEN

Georgie had been pacing back and forth in the machine shop. Determined to make an entrance and avoid small talk, she'd been hiding out waiting for Tyler's signal that the meeting was about to begin. When the notification sounded on her tablet, she pinned the device under her arm, and smoothed out her suit jacket. Prepared, and with a deep breath as fuel, she marched upstairs, ready for battle.

Inside the long spacious first-floor boardroom, all the key players had gathered and while many milled around with cups in hand speculating on the agenda, most had been quietly shuffled into their seats by Marnie or Lori. No one was surprised when they arrived to find the meeting would take place in the boardroom. The large coffee urn, though, was definitely something new. Those who paid attention to such things assumed it meant Georgie would not be in attendance. When she strolled in, and immediately took her place at the podium, more than a few heads turned.

As Lou had called the meeting and imagined himself in charge, he began protesting as he rushed forward from where he'd been chewing the fat with his account manager and one of the family lawyers. Before he was halfway across the room, Lori intercepted him, grabbing his arm in her powerful grip and hissing under her breath, "Sit down and shut up or I will flay the living daylights out of you right here and for everyone to see!" Smiling widely, and with everyone's eyes on them, she gave him a half hug. "I missed you too, buddy." With that she pulled out a chair and waited for him to sit. Taking the seat beside him, she was ready to further invade his personal space, hoping to intimidate him long enough for Georgie to make her case.

"Thank you everyone for coming out on this blustery Tuesday morning. I sincerely hope you all had a wonderful long weekend and enjoyed your New Year celebration." Georgie said this last part with an ironic grin, as everyone in the room had been there for the New Year's Eve party. A few stragglers had yet to take their seats, and noticing, she offered kindly, "Once everyone has their coffee or tea, please take a seat. Before we get started, I would like to acknowledge that it was Lou who called us together this morning. So, the first thing I will do is apologize for hijacking his meeting.

"My first order of business is to thank him and all of you for your indulgence these last five years. The road to recovery has been long and to be honest I have dawdled much of the way. While I've been doing my own thing, our company has grown and changed but one constant has remained: We are family!" Looking carefully around the room she was more than aware not everyone was enamored of her presence or the fact that she had commandeered the show. Zoe, along with the accountants were still standing when she waved and invited them to take a seat.

In protest, Zoe argued loudly, "Georgie, really! You're not—"

Georgie growled, "Sit. Down!" It was an order no one would mistake for a suggestion, and with that revelation, the temperature in the room began to plummet.

"Recently, I was challenged to consider the future of our company and my responsibility to our family." The photograph appearing now on the screen was the well-known picture that had been used in the family book. "This is our grandfather, our grandfather who chose this family. These three people pictured with him were his chosen children. As you may know, in Italian families it is considered good luck for the firstborn child to be female. Supposedly it foretells of a large family to come. Even when the babies didn't arrive by the truckload, our grandfather remained hopeful. When my father returned on leave from his advanced flight training, he brought along his best friend in the world. When they met, our grandfather did not see a man of color, he saw a patriot in uniform, he saw a brother in arms to his only son, and a man with a brilliant mind and impeccable upbringing, and he told my father he was proud, proud of him, reminding him that a man is only as good as the company he keeps. Before that first visit was done our grandfather felt truly honored to have Major Henry Phipps consider himself a son. When Henry and Danny retired from the air force and returned home, our grandfather not only opened the doors to both men but offered them the same opportunities. When our grandfather died, he acknowledged and I quote, "My Three Children, Two by Birth, One by Choice, And ALL BY THE GRACE OF GOD!" The volume of her voice, along with her pacing, had built to this powerful point. She stood carefully gauging the room. Discreetly signaling, it took only seconds for Tyler to push the next segment of her speech to her tablet, and the matching slide to the screen.

"Today we stand at a crossroads. Our family has grown and changed as all families do. Yet throughout all of that change, we have continued under the DiNamico banner. Before our grandfather's untimely death, he envisioned a company built on the trinity of his three children. Today is the day that I will ask you to honor our grandfather's wishes." She waved her hand toward the screen where the DME logo was replaced with three distinct company word marks. "Ladies and gentlemen of the board of Dynamic Marine Engineering, allow me to introduce to you our future and the DME trinity of companies: DynaCraft Yacht Builders, BioDynamic Engineering; and last but most importantly our new investment company, DiNamico,

Phipps, Pulaski, or better DPP Holdings. It is my intention to divide DME into three distinct companies, so that they, like our family, will continue to grow in all the varied facets that have made us unique.

"Before I pass the floor to my cousin, Lori Phipps, Master Boat Builder, who will share her vision for the future of DynaCraft Yachts with us, I want everyone to meet our newest company—DPP Holdings."

She spoke eloquently for another twenty minutes, delivering a high-level business plan. The new company would take responsibility for the family holdings, including the compound at Eighteen Mile Creek and the DiNamico building. DPP would become the family's management firm. And while it would begin small, she waxed eloquent about its potential, even suggesting that with the right leadership there would be opportunities to expand into investment management. It was important that everyone buy into her plan and that the new holding company be presented as the jewel in the crown. After all, if they wanted Lou to bite the forbidden fruit, it would have to be the biggest and the best.

Once she had made her case, at least for DPP and DynaCraft, she introduced Lori and took her seat. Marnie quickly slipped into the seat Lori had vacated. She couldn't physically intimidate Lou the way his sister did, but she could embarrass him and make a scene if she had to. From where she was sitting, Georgie watched him carefully while he frantically sent text messages to someone. While Lori explained the developing opportunities in component yachts and custom builds, Georgie surreptitiously surveyed the room wondering who Lou was communicating with, then she spotted him. *That little baldheaded weasel!* It was one of the family attorneys. The one who had been so embarrassed to let Lori read Aunt Georgina's letter. That was only eight years ago! At least the homophobe wasn't one of the influencers on the board, just his runner-up. And soon to be dismissed as the attorney of record. She sent a quick warning text to Marnie. If Lou still planned to mount his challenge, it would come the moment Lori finished speaking but before she could sit down beside him and shut him up.

Sure enough, the minute Lori concluded with her financial projections, he stood, trying very much to look like the man in charge. Before he could finish straightening his suit jacket, Henry was on his feet and Marnie too.

"Thank you Lori," Henry said, adding, "before we ask questions, and I know we all have many when it comes to the legacy of our oldest brand, it's time to take a break."

With the meeting suddenly broke up, Lou's objections, and his steam, evaporated in an instant. While Zoe made haste to join her father, Marnie intercepted the offending attorney. She asked him and the senior lawyer from their firm to join her in the lobby for a private word. As they made their way from the room, she strolled casually, chatting amiably. Lori, alerted by Marnie's quick text and with Henry in tow, followed Georgie and Tyler as they stepped out of the room to join them.

In the grand foyer of the DiNamico building, Marnie stood with her sister and her uncle, the three people who controlled one hundred percent of the family holdings, and told them without preamble, "As our representatives, we have reason to believe you have breached our confidentiality. Therefore, as of this moment, you will no longer represent this family. If you wish to maintain your relationship with any particular member of our clan, you may do so but be warned, we intend to file a complaint with the Bar Association and we are currently considering filing for damages."

With that said, Marnie turned and taking one of Henry's arms, guided him back in the room. The two blindsided lawyers stood there looking dumbfounded. Tyler had retrieved their jackets and briefcases while Lori made it clear they weren't getting back in the boardroom. After some blustering threats and objections they stormed out.

"That's two down," Lori said, offering Georgie a fist bump.

"Modular building...teardowns?" she asked, quoting two new ideas Lori had shared during the presentation. "Nice!"

"You like it?" When Georgie nodded, she laughed, and exclaimed, "You should. It was your idea!" She gave her another fist bump before wrapping her arm around her protectively. "You're doing it Bender, you got them listening. You do know you could have just come in here and strong-armed everyone with your share?" She shook her head in awe. "That's the thing about you that I love and the part Lou doesn't get. I know it never occurred to you but with your share and Marnie's or even just Leslie's vote, you could've made all the changes you wanted. Hell, you could've fired Lou and no one would've said a word! My baby brother on the other hand has earned himself the smallest piece of the pie, yet that little bastard would get rid of all of us if he could. I don't get it! What the hell is wrong with him?"

Georgie shook her head, as confused as her cousin. "Pride?" she suggested, "maybe...only boy?"

Lori chuckled. "You know, I can still remember Sophia changing his diapers. Every time the cold air hit his junk, he'd go off like a rocket! Gramma used to keep his new diaper ready like a catcher's mitt! Thirty-five years later and the bastard's still going off every chance he gets!"

That made Georgie laugh. She made a hand signal mimicking a rocket blasting off into space. "Bean counters!"

Marnie stormed out of the boardroom with Tyler on her heels. "Lori get inside. Tyler take Georgie upstairs, now!"

Tyler, white-faced, looked close to tears while Marnie was ready to blow a gasket. Georgie reached out silently placing a protective hand on her sister's shoulder. "What?" she asked gently.

Almost under her breath and clearly struggling for control, she blurted, "That little bastard filed a written challenge for a vote of confidence. Under the old incorporation papers he has that right. Now we have to vote and you have to leave."

"When?" she asked calmly, "when did he...file?"

Marnie handed her the petition to read. It was stamped with yesterday's date. "By stalling, we actually gave him the upper hand!"

"No worries," she offered with a smile.

"Yeah," Lori added. "Everyone's seen what our girl can do. Come on Marns. Don't sweat it. You and me are gonna go in there and explain the facts of life. After the preview they just got, how the hell can anyone—"

"Get in here girls!" Lou ordered from the threshold of the meeting room. "Some of us have work to do. Stop wasting time!"

Marnie, with her back to Lou, almost went ballistic.

Georgie and Lori, recognizing she was seconds from going all Incredible Hulk on his ass, grabbed on tight. The moment she had enough control not to implode on the spot, Georgie squeezed her arm. "You got this...boss!"

"How can you smile?" she hissed. "We don't know how he's stacked the deck. What—"

"Big guns!" Georgie said, with the most ironic of grins. Reaching into the pocket of her suit jacket, she removed and unfolded a document and gave it to Marnie. Judging by the deep creases in the paper and its slightly yellowed color, it wasn't something she had just pulled together.

As Marnie read the first page her eyebrows began to rise. Now she had what she needed. Without comment, she and Lori returned to the meeting.

Georgie watched without emotion as Zoe, with a smug look, pulled the big oak doors closed. Reaching for Tyler's hand, she walked Tyler to the elevator in silence. Despite an unexpected and unfortunate turn of events, Georgie wasn't upset. Actually she looked quite pleased with herself.

Tyler waited until the elevator closed before asking, "Please tell me that wasn't your resignation? I swear I will kill that man if he manages to—"

Georgie wrapped her arms around her, delivering a scorching hot kiss before admitting, "Not resigning...no worries."

When the elevator door opened Tyler realized they were on nine and not the executive level. Following Georgie inside her apartment, she said, "Okay, still confused. What did you just do?"

Grinning from ear to ear, Georgie wrapped her arms around her again. "My Tyler...Brilliant mind..."

Now Tyler was smiling. She liked this game. "So it's just my mind you're after? What about my smokin' hot body?"

Georgie's hands were instantly inside her jacket, combing up her sides and back. Pulling her close, she offered a single brief kiss, before explaining, "You said something...made me think!

Before last…deployment," she indicated herself, "worried… what if Dad and Henry…"

"You were worried they would pass while you were away?"

She nodded. "Aunt Georgina's shares…only they knew."

"Oh my God baby! All that time and no one else knew you had already inherited a third of the company. What did you do? I know you must have prepared something but I can't imagine what that could be."

Enjoying the opportunities presented whenever Tyler wrapped her long arms around her neck, Georgie's hands migrated from her back to find her small sensitive breasts.

"Oh God, you're doing it again!" She begged, already aroused, "No, no, no. Bad girl!" She pinned the offending digits in her grasp. "I will not have you getting me…not until I know Marnie and gang aren't about to come barging in. Now tell me. What brilliant thing did I inspire?"

"Simple." She laughed delightedly, squeezing Tyler's hands. "Proxy."

It took her a moment to put it together. Shocked at the simplicity, she asked, "You gave Marnie your legal voting delegate? Oh my God, that's brilliant! Wait, is it still valid? Please tell me it wasn't drawn up by those bastards Marnie just fired?"

She shook her head, explaining instead, "Other guys."

Tyler was so relieved she threw herself into Georgie's arms. At the same time, Maggie padded in, dropping her squeaky toy, her warning of an impending family intrusion.

"Moment of truth!"

As she said it a light went off in Tyler's mind. "Oh my God baby. You wanted this to happen! I think I understand. This was your way of settling the 'crazy' issue once and for all!" Still putting the pieces together, something else occurred to her. "You could have pulled that proxy out at any time. I know you, you don't forget things like this. Do you?" she challenged. "I think I get it. You didn't just push people to take a stand, you pushed them to lead. Marnie and Lori have been holding back. They needed to take a step up and take control! You did this for everyone! Still, I can't believe you took this chance."

Tracing her fingertips across Tyler's cheek, she repeated her own personal maxim, "Better to know."

They could hear the main entrance door on the upper level open, and several bodies triumphantly marching in.

There it was again, the gentleness, the amusement and the knowledge Georgie so readily conveyed in her eyes. Accepting the hand she offered, they walked together to greet their visitors at the foot of the antique staircase old Luigi had installed so many years before. Tyler squeezed her hand warmly. She was smiling now and ready to face the music together. "Baby, no matter what happens," she promised with a grin to match Georgie's, "I won't let go."

EPILOGUE

One Year Later

Tyler stood in the galley of the company's newest boat, the DynaCraft Super 69. While she was technically a seventy-foot long sailing yacht, they had stuck to the naming conventions first created by old Luigi. He would always measure the keel length from transom to bow, excluding the bowsprit. He believed, and in some cases it was true, that shaving a foot off the registered length of the vessel would save on docking fees and insurance. Still there had been more than enough jokes, most of them from Lori, on the irony that four lesbians would be taking the company's first sixty-niner for its inaugural shakedown cruise. This new boat featured all the modular design characteristics and breakdown features Lori and Georgie had been suggesting for years. Because the sixty-niner was actually too big to ship by transport truck, it, or more correctly she, had been sent by rail to Newport Virginia, where they watched as she was unloaded by a huge crane then suspended for her christening. Tyler, more than honored, hadn't expected to be asked.

When Lori handed her the bottle of champagne, she explained the technique. "On TV they always hold the bottle by the neck. That's only good for hitting people over the head! Now, what you really do is take it by the label, and you just want to come down with the neck just hitting the edge of the bowsprit. Don't try to hit it, just make like you want to swing right past. When you connect, it should feel like a surprise." Pointing out the place to aim for, Lori moved to stand with Georgie.

Holding the bottle as if she were about to pour, and with the label protecting her hand as Lori had instructed, she gave the bowsprit a quick pass and was surprised when the neck broke cleanly away and champagne spurted out the top. With that done and cheers rising all the way around, the boat was immediately lowered into the water.

Lori and Georgie began the painstaking prelaunch inspection. This would not be Tyler's first sailing trip. Georgie had been teaching her to sail, but a few weekends on Lake Erie in the summer didn't compare to this. They had shoved off from Newport News in mid-January. While the sky was clear, the air was cold and a harbinger of the days to come. Georgie and Lori hadn't been chosen to take the new boat out based on privilege, or the rights of the designers. They were the only two sailors in all of DME qualified to handle a boat this size, and they were good.

They had pushed hard for the first three days. Clear of the Virginia coast, they surprised Tyler by setting course due south and heading straight into the blue. She had marveled to see how well Georgie and her cousin crewed together. While the sixty-niner had an autopilot and a very advanced navigation and communication system, someone still had to be at the helm and on watch twenty-four hours a day. And on a sailboat, even a big one like this, it meant someone had to be outside in the elements. For that reason, and simply because they could, they had pushed the new boat hard, harnessing every ounce of wind her sails could hold. While the wind held up, they had made good time, easily covering three hundred miles a day. Still, Tyler hadn't started to thaw out from the cold until midafternoon on the third day out when they had just made the imaginary point on their southward journey where they would finally turn west for the Florida coast. By the next evening, the lights of the Jupiter lighthouse were easy to spot. At first light they docked in West Palm Beach for provisions and for a chance for Lori and Georgie to address a few glitches they had uncovered.

Happy to leave them to their tinkering, Tyler had taken the opportunity for a little shopping. Georgie, she had discovered, owned all of one bathing suit. She preferred to spend her sailing time in the boat. When she did feel like a swim, she wouldn't hesitate to jump in wearing whatever she had on. Now in Florida and heading for the Caribbean, Tyler was determined to replace her horrid blue one-piece, which looked suspiciously like military issue, with something more suitable. After all, it would be a shame to hide Georgie's smoking hot curves under that potato sack or worse, board shorts and baggy T's. If they were going to spend three or four weeks sailing the Islands, she would need more than one swimsuit. And if Tyler was choosing, it certainly wouldn't be another nondescript sack.

West Palm Beach turned out to be a gold mine for beachwear. She had nabbed more than a half-dozen suits for each of them, including one extremely sexy black bikini she could hardly wait to get Georgie into. Even after all this time, she could be extremely shy. Still, she had coaxed her into her first tankini without a challenge. The boy shorts bikini took a little more convincing but even that was easier than she expected. Tyler, it seemed, had discovered the key to getting her to take a risk. "Do it for me," she would say, and it worked every time. Learning that something was important to Tyler was all Georgie ever needed to hear.

Now, after two weeks of cruising they were anchored in a wide mouth bay leeward of Buck's Island. There had been two other sailboats in the area. One had pulled up anchor that morning while the other was more than a mile away. Lori and her friend had just left with a picnic basket, and taking the dinghy, they had headed out for a day of exploration. Tyler had a good idea just what kind of exploration Lori was planning but was just as happy for the time alone.

Knowing they would be alone all day, she laid the bikini out for Georgie, hoping she would take the hint. Now, standing in the galley, she was barefoot and wearing a sun wrap with her bikini bottoms. The sun coverup was more about protecting her skin than her modesty. Tyler, like Lori and her friend, had no compunction about bathing topless and did so on days like these. Taking a break from the book she had been enjoying from the built-in daybed on the shaded aft deck, she wasn't prepared when Georgie streaked by, tossing the bikini top at her as she raced up the gangway ladder and out on deck.

Still in shock and holding the top in her hand, she heard a splash and, dropping everything, double-timed up the stairs and onto the long wide swim deck. For all Georgie's athletic abilities, she was not a swimmer. Even worse, her head injury made it very easy for her to become disoriented in the water. To combat this little quirk she had taken to jumping in backward so she would always have the boat in sight. Even that was no guarantee and every time she jumped in the water Tyler panicked. Sure enough, she immediately lost sight of her. Tyler, now at full speed, charged off the end of the open transom and over the swim platform and dove in head first. When she broke the surface she searched the sea frantically.

"My Tyler!"

Turning around, she found Georgie behind her, hanging onto the swim platform and grinning up a storm. Splashing toward her, she warned playfully, "You geek! You scared the…" Through the crystal clear waters, she could see Georgie had changed, electing to wear the bikini bottoms only. "Oh baby. What you do to me!" Every ounce of Georgie was fluid and in motion. "I swear, you keep doing things like this, and I may have a stroke!"

Georgie grinned but was treading water as if she might still sink.

Joining her at the swim platform, Tyler couldn't help but smile. Marnie once told her that Georgie lacked all common sense. She now knew better. Georgie didn't lack common sense, she lacked fear. Or more accurately, her only true fear was never risking enough. "God I love you, you crazy woman!"

Not only did that elicit a huge smile from Georgie, she moved in closer, and grabbing onto the swim platform just above her head with both hands, she wrapped her strong legs around Tyler's waist.

If Tyler considered her energetic in bed, the acrobatics she managed in the water were downright astounding. Floating tethered to Georgie, her hands were free, finding their way to her bottom, and the side ties of the bikini. She had selected the bikini in hope of an opportunity just like this. Triumphantly, she pumped her fist high in the air. She had the bottoms in her hand and held them up for Georgie to see.

"Bad!" she warned, before pulling Tyler in close with her strong legs, and delivering a smoldering kiss.

Tyler squealed with delight. Taking a quick scan of the shoreline in each direction, she assured herself of their privacy. Even with Lori and her friend onboard they'd had plenty of private time to enjoy themselves. But here and now, with the sun, the ocean and the wild, wild look in Georgie's eyes, she couldn't imagine anything more perfect. It was divine. With both of Georgie's hands hanging on to the swim platform for dear life, Tyler was free to enjoy the situation. It wasn't like Georgie would object but she could be a bit of a top. It was so amazing to take her like this. Georgie's arms were so strong she could easily have pulled them both up. Instead, she used her muscles to keep them tethered to the boat and no more.

Adjusting to the fact that Georgie could not verbally communicate, not so much as a wayward sound when they made love, hadn't been hard. She so clearly telegraphed every need and want with her entire body. If that weren't enough to drive Tyler mad for her, one look at those expressive green eyes would do the trick. When she did open her eyes Tyler almost lost all control. "Baby, you're doing it again! Oh God, please baby," she begged.

Suddenly Georgie surprised her. Relinquishing her hold on the platform, she wrapped her arms around Tyler's neck, planting a hungry mouth on hers. This was new and Tyler understood at once. It was trust. Complete and unbridled and she couldn't contain her desire. How could it always be like this? She had never imagined two people could feel so passionately, so perfectly, connected. If she didn't know the woman so intimately, she would imagine it came easily. It didn't for Georgie. Still, she had placed her trust entirely in Tyler almost from the start.

It wasn't until that moment, with Georgie's hands on her, that she understood. Everyone assumed it was Georgie who needed her but they were equals, partners in the truest sense, and Tyler needed her just as much. Grabbing the swim platform and stilling them both, Tyler said the only thing that truly mattered: "Baby, I've got you. Don't you ever let go!"

Bella Books, Inc.

Women. Books. Even Better Together.

P.O. Box 10543
Tallahassee, FL 32302

Phone: 800-729-4992
www.bellabooks.com